Our Man in Washington

Our Man in Washington

Roy Hoopes

A Tom Doherty Associates Book
New York

OUR MAN IN WASHINGTON

Design by Jane Adele Regina

Edited by David G. Hartwell

A Forge Book
Published by Tom Doherty Associates, LLC
175 Fifth Avenue
New York, NY 10010

www.tor.com

Forge® is a registered trademark of Tom Doherty Associates, LLC.

Library of Congress Cataloging-in-Publicaton Data

Hoopes, Roy.
Our man in Washington / Roy Hoopes.—1st ed.
p. cm.
"A Tom Doherty Associates book."
ISBN 0-312-86849-9 (acid-free paper)
1. Cain, James M. (James Mallahan), 1892–1977—Fiction. 2. Mencken, H. L. (Henry Louis), 1880–1956—Fiction. 3. Investigative reporting—Fiction. 4. Political corruption—Fiction. 5. Washington (D.C.)—Fiction. 6. Journalists—Fiction. I. Title.

PS3558.O6323 O97 200
813'.54—dc21

00-031792

First Edition: September 2000

Printed in the United States of America

0 9 8 7 6 5 4 3 2 1

For our three wonderful grandchildren,
Lesley, Sara and Scott Hoopes

Acknowledgments

I wish to thank Averil J. Kadis, with the Enoch Pratt Free Library, and Mrs. Alice Piper, executrix of the James M. Cain estate, for permission to paraphrase some of the writings of H. L. Mencken and James M. Cain in conversation in this work of fiction.

Also, to express appreciation to my editor, David Hartwell, for his continuing support and excellent editing of the manuscript.

Thanks also to Alice and Robert Yoakum for their contributions—including Bob's (as well as John F. Baker's) efforts to help me arouse Hollywood's interest in the project.

And, finally, thanks, as always to my wife, Cora, for her patience, support and editing.

PREFACE

All the characters in this novel were alive and active in 1923. However, most of what takes place here never happened, except in my imagination. Specifically, H. L. Mencken and James M. Cain never went to Washington to investigate the corruption and mysterious deaths in the Harding Administration or the president's adulterous affairs. They never met Roxy Stinson, although Cain said his writing was significantly affected by her testimony before the Senate Hearings on the attorney general in 1924. Most certainly, Mencken and Cain *never* played catch with the Hope Diamond. And James M. Cain never wrote a book about their fictitious adventures in Washington.

But I did.

Of course, neither Mencken nor Cain spoke to each other or any other character appearing in the novel as they do here, although the relationship between the two men in 1923 was pretty much as depicted and set forth in my earlier biography of James M. Cain. The young reporter had met Mencken when he was working on *The Baltimore Sun* and the future editor of the *The American Mercury* did recruit Cain to write for his new magazine.

However, I should stress that, although the conversational statements attributed to Mencken in this work of fiction are my own creation, many of the thoughts he expresses in this novel are based on thoughts set forth by him in his books, magazine articles and columns. To a lesser extent, the same is true for Cain. In fact, I made every effort to depict both men as they are portrayed in their writings and biographical material. And to do so it was necessary to make their conversation adhere closely to thoughts expressed in their writings, especially Mencken's.

The Enoch Pratt Free Library in Baltimore (which responds to requests to reprint or quote from H. L. Mencken's works) and the estate of James M. Cain have both given me permission to paraphrase some of their written material in this manner.

Roy Hoopes
Bethesda, Maryland

Part 1

CHAPTER ONE

They threw me off the streetcar about noon.

Well they didn't actually throw me off, but it seemed like it. I had moved up to the open door in the front of the car as it began to slow for my stop. It was a cold, rainy morning in the spring of 1923 and as I prepared to get off I was trying to hold my folded-up *Baltimore Sun* under my left arm while I started opening an umbrella. But the trolley came to a sudden stop and I was sort of thrown onto the platform. I kept my balance, held onto the *Sun* and put the umbrella over me, although I did knock my favorite—in fact, only—hat to the wet concrete.

After retrieving the hat, which was not seriously damaged, it was just a short walk to Marconi's at 106 West Saratoga Street. The restaurant's gray brick façade and black-and-white striped awning only enhanced the gloom of that drizzly morning, but I was too excited about lunch with Baltimore's most eminent journalist to pay much attention to the weather. We were meeting to talk about me writing articles for a new magazine he was planning. A waiter, who I later learned was named Brookes, met me at Marconi's door and I quickly said: "James M. Cain to meet H. L. Mencken. I believe he has a twelve o'clock reservation."

Most people call me Jim, but on formal occasions, such as announcing my arrival somewhere, I like to use my full name. I inherited that from my father, who was president of Washington College over in Chestertown, Maryland, when I was growing up. He was a great one for proper names—and titles: "Doctor," "Professor," "Chairman." He liked to be called "Mr. President" but he stopped insisting on it because whenever he did my mother just started laughing. His name was James, also.

Brookes led me directly to a table in the corner, which I presumed to be more or less permanently reserved for Mencken. And

I had no trouble, as Mencken had assured me I would not, ordering a pilsner. Marconi's did not show the red crab that several Maryland restaurants displayed to signify the availability of spirits. But it would be hard to imagine it, or any other civilized eating place or bar in Baltimore, not finding a beer for a friend of Mencken's, considering that by now, he was the nation's leading and most vocal wet.

Actually, this was not my first meeting with Mencken. That had been last fall when I decided to take three months off from the *Sun* where I was still a reporter to go out to the coal mines of West Virginia to gather dope for a novel.

All right! I confess it was to be the Great American Novel, or "G.A.N." as Franklin P. Adams in his *World* "Conning Tower" column called the book that every reporter at press club bars across the country was talking about writing. To me, America was embodied in its small rural towns, and after spending some time in Charleston, West Virginia, covering the treason trial of William Blizzard for the *Sun,* I had decided that West Virginia would be the locale of my G.A.N.

Blizzard was president of the United Mine Workers, District 13, and leader of a group of coal miners who staged an armed march against some mine owners near the town of Matawan. The mines were defended by men the mine owners and the state called "deputy sheriffs" but who were actually a bunch of thugs the mine owners hired to keep the union out of the mines. Ten men had been killed at Matawan.

Blizzard and several other miners were indicted for treason against the state of West Virginia, but I simply could not believe that a glorified riot, that was to some extent provoked, could be blown up to an act of war. It seemed like a good idea for a novel. And it occurred to me that it might be smart to talk about it with Mencken, who was one of the country's leading authorities on the American novel. I had heard that he liked my West Virginia reporting for the *Sun* and the articles about the conflict between the miners and the mine owners I had written for *The Nation* and *The Atlantic Monthly.* In fact, it was Mencken who recommended me to *Atlantic* editor Ellery Sedgwick. Frankly, I was in awe of Mencken then, like the little boy who had just gotten his ball autographed by Babe Ruth. But it was the *Atlantic* piece that encouraged me, as a writer, to be a pelagic fish, to swim in deep waters.

So I requested a meeting with him and suddenly one day he appeared at my desk on the rim where I was working as a copy editor. He pulled up a chair across from mine and we chatted for about ten minutes. But on that first meeting, even though I knew I was in the presence of genius, I must admit I was disappointed. I wanted some advice on how to approach a novel and I was surprised to learn that Mencken didn't know a damned thing about it. "Two years out of a man's life, that's a novel," was the gist of his counsel.

I went to West Virginia, spent several weeks digging coal, joined the union, talked to miners and mine owners and then came back to Baltimore and for two months tried to put it all together for the G.A.N. I decided I simply could not write a novel and I had to go slinking back to the *Sun* admitting to anyone who asked that the Great American Novel had still not been written.

The great man had not arrived yet, so I settled down to finish reading in the morning *Baltimore Sun* about the curious death of Charles Cramer, legal counsel to the Veterans' Bureau in Washington. Although the authorities decided it was a suicide, some people were suggesting that Cramer was murdered to silence him about corruption in the Veterans' Bureau. The director of the bureau, Charles Forbes, a slick political operator, had helped Warren Harding carry the state of Washington in the 1920 election. As a reward, Forbes, also a close friend of the president's, was given the Veterans' Bureau job and he quickly became known as "the court jester to the best mind in government," which is a real laugh. Forbes was also a card-playing member of Harding's poker cabinet. But he resigned shortly after Cramer's death amid widespread rumors that the Veterans' Bureau was seething with corruption and scandal. Cramer, as Forbes' legal counsel, would have known—or should have—about the hanky-panky at the bureau and if he was not involved, he would have felt guilty for not having exposed it. Suicide was plausible, but so was murder—although you don't often see it in the federal government.

One thing that caught my eye was the fact that the first person to report the death of Cramer was Mary Roberts Rinehart, the mystery writer. The Rineharts were neighbors and friends of the Cramers who lived on Woodley Road, across the street from the Wardman Park, where the Rineharts have an apartment. Cramer, in fact, had bought his house from President Harding, who lived in it when he was in the Senate. By now the rumors about graft in Washington were so great that it was being said that Cramer had paid Harding much more than market value for the house as a way to "buy" his government job in the Veterans' Bureau. It was a half-pilsner story and just as juicy as the beer was wet.

When I finished it, I looked at my watch: 12:05. Our lunch was for noon, so I knew I could expect to see Mencken come through the door at any moment. I had recently read a sketch of Mencken in *The Smart Set* by George Jean Nathan. Nathan said his co-editor is "never late for an appointment." He also said Mencken had missed but one train in his life—and he took a lot of trains because once or twice a month he went up to New York to get out the magazine.

Nathan also said, "The things he dislikes most are Methodists, college professors, newspaper editorials, Broadway restaurants, reformers, actors, children, magazine fiction, low collars, dining out, the New Freedom, Prohibition, sex hygiene, *The Nation,* soft drinks, women under thirty—especially literary women, socialism, the moral theory of the world and the sort of patriotism that makes a noise. He takes no interest whatsoever in sports. He rejects the whole of Christianity and is a lifelong opponent of Puritanism in all its forms."

The moment after I looked at my watch, Mencken burst through the door and headed immediately for this table. He was about five-foot-nine, stoop-shouldered and somewhat stout. He had on a blue serge suit and high-top, black, well-polished shoes. He wore a dark red-and-blue striped tie, knotted against a high starched collar. His sand-colored, straight hair was slicked down and parted in the middle. His eyes sparkled, he had a firm chin and a surprisingly gentle mouth considering how many outrageous, sometimes vitriolic, thoughts came out of it. He had strong, white but irregular teeth, an impudent button nose and protruding ears. His face had a pinkish, well-scrubbed look and his large pale blue eyes seemed to suggest that the whole human race astonished him. He was smoking one of his Willies, which was mostly tilted upward in his mouth. He was in his early forties, but there would be moments when he looked fifteen.

"Well, Cain, I see you're early," Mencken said as I rose to shake his hand. And then looking at my tall paper cup in which Brookes had brought my pilsner, he added, "And Mr. Brookes has taken care of you. Christ! I'm thirstier than a Pizbyterian minister."

Mencken didn't like Presbyterians any better than Methodists. Then, indicating that we should both be seated, he said: "Mr. Brookes, I'm glad to see you're still not afraid of that corps of undisguised bastards, the revenue agents. I'll have a pilsner. In fact, bring me two, and Mr. Cain here may be ready for another."

I nodded agreement and Brookes departed. "I rarely drink before five and never when I have any writing to do," Mencken said, "but I'm through for the day. I finished my column this morning."

"What's it on?—if you don't mind my asking."

"Not at all. Prohibition. This horror of a government regulation is not civilized and we should not put up with it. We've had it more than two years now and what's it accomplished? All good liquors, beers and wines cost three or four times what they used to, which means the poor can no longer afford them but the rich are drinking more than ever. Dining out in private, except with the rich, is no longer very pleasant. If drinks are served, you hesitate to gulp them down freely; if they're not served, you wish your host were in hell. The manufacturing of home brew has reached colossal proportions and all but about ten percent of it—mine excepted, of course—is swill. And the bootleggers are getting obscenely rich."

I indicated agreement by holding up my cup to toast around the room, where some people near our table seemed to be listening to the bard.

Rising and acknowledging his audience, Mencken excused himself to go upstairs to the men's room—"Got to wash up, Cain, to keep all the goddamn germs from attacking my innards. Nathan says I wash my hands twenty-four times a day. This is number eight." As he headed for the stairs, holding his cigar in one hand, he waved to the other people seated in the restaurant, most of whom seemed to know him.

I had not really paid much attention to Mencken until after I returned from France, where I had served with the A.E.F. during the war. Then one day, I was reading a column by Mencken called "A Carnival of Buncombe" and by the time I reached the place where Mencken called General Leonard Wood "a pompous old dodo with delusions of persecution," I knew I had discovered something new and different.

I rushed out and bought a copy of *The Smart Set* and found the same thing. Then I read every book by Mencken I could find, including quite a bit of his monumental *The American Language,* published in 1919, written while Mencken was exiled from his *Evening Sun* column because of his sympathy for Germany. I also tracked down back issues of *The Smart Set* in barbershops, friends' houses and libraries. After I read as much as I could find, I knew my writing would never be the same.

Brookes arrived with three tall paper cups of pilsner just about the time Mencken returned from the men's room and plunked down in his chair. He quickly picked up one of the two cups in front of him and drank it straight down, almost with one swallow. Looking greatly relieved, he held up his cup for those in the restaurant who were watching us and said: "Another toast to Andrew J. Volstead."

Then he said to me: "You never told me how you did with that novel of yours, Cain. I liked the idea—God's angry man trying to break up a system that was strangling his people. How'd it turn out?"

"Too much reporting," I replied, not wanting to get into my failed attempt at a novel then. "I didn't seem to have the least idea where I was going. I finally said, 'The hell with it!' I guess I'm not a novelist."

"Don't give up," Mencken said, his eyes opening as big as saucers. "I really like your work," and he quickly reached in his coat pocket and pulled out a clipped magazine article which I recognized as my *Nation* piece. " 'West Virginia is still young,' " he said, starting to read from the tag, " 'it may have a touch of industrial indigestion, or its malady may be more grave. Give it a century or so. Then possibly it will shoot the piano player and call for a new score.' "

As Mencken went on, I started thinking that maybe he was confirming what I had already decided, that I was an article writer, not a novelist.

"Good stuff," he continued, "your *Atlantic* article was also a fine piece of work. Jeesus—and I hope He records that He heard it from me first—I'm going out on a goddamn limb and say you write as well as Red Lewis and someday you're going to make a break-through like he has . . ."

I started to mumble a "thanks" for the compliment, but Mencken, as usual, was hard to interrupt.

"Have you read *Babbitt*? Whatta novel! I remember when Nathan and I first met Lewis. He was introduced by a Boni and Liveright editor. Red had already had a couple of pieces in the magazine, but we still didn't know much about him. He's a big, tall, red-headed fellow with a pocked face, almost as good looking as you, Cain, and he put his arms around Nathan and me and said in a mock German dialect: 'So you guys are the critics, are ya? Well, let me tell you something. I'm the best writer in this here gottdam country and if you, Georgie, and you, Hank, don't know it now, you'll know it gottdam soon!'

"Jeesus! Nathan and I couldn't wait to get out of that apartment, and when we were down on the street, I said: 'Of all the idiots I've ever laid eyes on, that fellow is the worst!' That was in 1920. Well, a few days later, somebody sent me the galleys of *Main Street*. I was in Baltimore, and when I read it, I sat right down at the typewriter and wrote Nathan: 'Grab hold of the bar rail, steady yourself and prepare for a terrible shock. I've just read the book of that lump we met and by God, he's done the job!'

"Now, he's done it again with *Babbitt*. I guess there's no doubt about it, he's one of the good ones—not as good as Dreiser, but damned good. But he sure fooled us. So don't give up, Cain."

I began shaking my head, but he denied my obvious dejection.

"Hell, Cain, all young writers need to collect enough rejection slips to paper a room. Scott Fitzgerald told me he had a hundred and fifty of them pasted up on a wall. I myself accumulated a wheelbarrow full of them before I hit my stride. Now you've come out with pieces in some first-rate magazines and you've got some attention. It's no time to stop."

I was baffled by Mencken's manner of speaking and could not quite place it. But I finally decided it was pure Baltimorese, but spoken by a Baltimorean who used perfect grammar and pronounced every word clearly with no slurring. He had a rich voice, overlaid with the city editor's bark, but a bit facetious and terse, and high-pitched, as though he was talking to someone upstairs. But it also had a slight tendency to fade away at the end of a sentence, as though he was waiting to give you a chance to cut in—which he rarely did.

"I don't know," I replied. "I have another idea for a story about an opera singer who commits a crime—or maybe his girlfriend does—and then he can never start singing again, because his famous voice will lead the police to them. I've been toying with it ever since I taught school in Chestertown five years ago, but I don't feel like trying it now. Maybe I'll stick to magazine writing for awhile—which is why I was so excited to get your phone call."

The Smart Set had been started by Colonel William Mann in 1900. But Mann was no editor and the magazine had been taken over by Nathan and Mencken in 1908 when Mann sold it to John Adams Thayer, who soon lost interest in it. Now Nathan and Mencken, supported by Mencken's publisher Alfred A. Knopf, were planning to start a new magazine, to be called *The American Mercury*. It was all very much hush-hush and Mencken made me swear "on a stack of gottdam Gutenbergs" to keep the project confidential, at least for awhile. They were involved in a complicated scheme to sell *The Smart Set* to Hearst and did not want the word about a new magazine to get out until the deal was completed. When Mencken called me to set up this lunch at Marconi's, he mentioned the new magazine and said he wanted to talk to me about writing for it. His call came at the right time for me.

After working for awhile at the *Sun,* when I returned from trying to write a novel, I suddenly decided I was not really happy or very good as a reporter. I could never quite believe that it mattered a damn whether the public learned the full name and address of the fireman injured at the blaze.

My father had been fired as president of Washington College and was now vice president of the United States Fidelity and Guaranty Company in Baltimore, where he met Enoch Gary, president of St. John's College in Annapolis. Through my father, I met Gary, who offered me a job teaching journalism at St. John's. I will start teaching this fall.

I was studying the menu, when suddenly Mencken burst out: "Cain, m'boy, what this country needs is not a good five-cent cigar, as ol' Tom Marshall said, but a good fifty-cent magazine, one written and edited for William Graham Summer's 'forgotten man.' "

"Who dat?"

"You, me, the normal educated, well-disposed, enlightened citizen of the middle minority. The idea is to drive a wedge between the liberals, who are always chasing butterflies, and the *New York Times* conservatives. There must be lots of young fellows who are turned off by liberalism, but can't go along with *The North American Review*. I want to bring them out, to stir up the animals! The mere thought of it makes me young again."

"So, okay, granted we need a voice for the Forgotten Man, what's wrong with *The Smart Set*? You and Nathan seem to be doing all right with that."

"Huh! I don't like its title—never have! It sounds like a fashion magazine for just the kind of people who give me a pain in the ass. With its audience I'm restricted to literature and books. But I'm more interested in politics now and what we might call public psychology. Nathan, of course, would just as soon go on with *The Smart Set,* maybe letting me branch out a little into politics. But Knopf, who wants to publish the kind of magazine I'm talking about, says he won't buy *The Smart Set*. It has to be a new magazine or nothing, and I agree."

"Well, you got a point . . ." I said, but before I could continue, Brookes was back and we decided to order. Mencken had the German sausages.

"They may look like dog turds," he said, "but they taste wonderful." I ordered eggs Benedict. Then we settled down to the business of the day. I had typed up a list of article ideas—mostly profiles—and after looking at it for a few minutes, Mencken said they really added up to a continuing series of American types—labor leaders, Babbitts, ministers, feminists, professors, prohibitionists, editorial writers, do-gooders, etc. He liked the proposal, suggested we call the series "American Portraits" and that I write them in the same style and with the depth of my *Atlantic* piece.

I began to talk enthusiastically about the first one I wanted to do—on the labor leader, obviously an outgrowth of my West Virginia experience. "Most newspapers," I said, "portray him as a radical and the liberal magazines paint him as a burning idealist with lofty brow and glistening eye, ready to deliver the oppressed, abolish the sweatshop and set up the brotherhood of man tomorrow.

But what he really is is the toughest, craftiest, most opportunistic survivor who has slugged his way out of the rank and file of miners, steelworkers, assemblyliners or whatever."

"That's it, Cain m'boy. That's it, the labor leader. I've often argued against capital to the capitalists and they're usually polite and tolerant. But I've never encountered a union leader who would listen to an argument against unionism. They prefer to hear and read the same rubber-stamp balderdash they hear all day from their colleagues at the union hall and the reverent clergy who belabor them with pieties on Sunday. Try to get it done for the first issue, which we hope to bring out next January."

He paused to puff on his cigar, then removed it from his mouth, blew some smoke up in the air, and with his sparkling eyes staring at the smoke, he said: "What about some Washington types— congressmen, senators, cabinet members, all those phonies?"

I hesitated a minute: "I don't know," I finally said. "I never had a Washington assignment on the *Sun*. In fact, I haven't spent much time there since before the war when I worked in Kann's Department Store while I took voice lessons. I'm not sure I'd want to write about Washington without spending a little more time over there gathering some dope."

"Hell," Mencken interrupted, "why don't you go over and nose around? You can even wait awhile on the labor leader piece. Jeesus, investigating crooked politicians should be fun. I might even join you. I'm getting a little tired of the *belles lettres* world of *The Smart Set*. I know we reach some of the young intellectuals and brighter college students, but I think most of our readers are the fat ladies trying to keep awake on a Pullman car after a heavy meal. Nathan's happy with that, but I'm not. When I first started in this business, literature, books and ideas were my main interest—exposing the charlatans who were keeping this country in an intellectual cocoon. But things are changing. We have Dreiser and Lewis and Cabell and Hergesheimer and young Fitzgerald and there are others coming along. Our literature has finally been taken out of the flour barrel it was in for most of the nineteenth century. Also, I've made college professoring a disreputable profession. That's a real achievement!"

Having seen my share of professors at my father's college, I nodded in agreement.

"Politics, that's what's exciting me today." And suddenly Mencken became even more animated, his cigar tilted up a little higher and the Mephistophelean glint in his eyes virtually lit up the room. Removing his cigar and making an unsuccessful attempt to place its ashes in the ashtray, he prepared to launch one of his monologues, pausing long enough to take a bite out of his sausage, which had just arrived along with my eggs Benedict. "Ahhhhh, delicious," he said. Then after another bite, he launched: "Democracy, you know, is a sort of laughing gas: It won't cure anything, but it relieves the pain. Don't get me wrong. I'm not in favor of abolishing our government. We pay heavy taxes but we also enjoy a hygienic laugh in the cool of the evening. Our rulers are not demigods. They're just clowns and scoundrels to be laughed at even when they are most in earnest."

He stopped suddenly, momentarily deep in thought as he attacked his sausage. Then abruptly, his eyes sparkling, he continued: "Edmund Wilson says I have withdrawn from American life and watch the twentieth century from the seclusion of my house on Hollins Street. Maybe I ought to get out a little more. With you doing the legwork and me supplying the little gray cells which that British writer Agatha Christie's detective Hercule Poirot brags about having, we can find out the truth behind Cramer's death and what's going on in Washington. You know, the main objective of the Washington police and the Justice Department is to cover it up, not flush it out. Besides, I'd kind of like to try my hand at being a detective. I mean, if even those boobs down at Police Headquarters can figure out that most murders are perpetuated by angry, jealous, passionate or greedy spouses, then I ought to be pretty good at it."

"Well you probably would be a good detective—but not working for the local government, I see you as a private detective, like Sherlock Holmes, but playing the piano instead of the violin. And frankly, I'd rather be a Dr. Watson to your Sherlock Holmes than gathering dope for someone called Hercules Paro."

"Why's that?" asked Mencken, "and it's Hercuoole Pwahro, not Hercules Paro."

"Okay, Pwahro. I know you hate Conan Doyle, but . . ."

"A fatuous ass," Mencken interrupted. "A real charlatan, a mystic who believes in ghosts. How can anyone take him seriously?"

"So who takes Beethoven or Chopin seriously as human beings?

Their lives were hardly exemplary. But their creations achieved immortality—like Doyle's."

"You mean Sherlock Holmes?"

"Yes, I mean Sherlock Holmes," I said, "immortal, like the Ninth Symphony. You certainly can't believe that someone called Hercuoole Pwahro is going to achieve the same immortality."

"Posh, you can't compare Beethoven with A. Conan Doyle."

"I'm not. I'm comparing Sherlock Holmes with the Ninth Symphony."

"I guess more people are familiar with Beethoven's symphonies than they are with the man," Mencken admitted.

"And more people have heard of Sherlock Holmes than Beethoven's symphonies. That's immortality!"

"You may be right," Mencken said, blowing smoke from his cigar and staring at it as it rose to the ceiling. I thought I had made a point but I was not sure. In fact, saying "you might be right" often proved to be his way of politely bringing conversation on a subject to an end.

Before he could recover his verbal momentum, I decided I could use a respite. I had finished my meal so I excused myself to go to the men's room. Mencken waved me away, cigar in hand, and with his other beckoned Brookes to bring another round of pilsners. As I left the room I could see him pick up the *Sun* and begin to read about the death of Charles Cramer.

In the men's room, I could not help reflecting on my second meeting with Mencken. There was no doubt about his genius. The man was simply a gusher of words, ideas and observations. I had read enough Mencken to know that his thinking was a mixture of Darwin, Nietzsche, Julian Huxley and Shaw. But I also remember his saying in our first meeting at the *Sun* that he had never read *Alice in Wonderland*!

I could not believe it. *Alice* is simply a story about a little girl who followed a white rabbit down a hole—as unpretentious an idea as could be imagined. Whenever I feel an impulse to be important, I remind myself of *Alice,* one of the greatest novels ever written. Yet Mencken has never read it. It is also a book that Mencken could never have written. In fact, it is unlikely that Mencken could ever write a novel—yet he is perhaps the country's leading arbiter of our fiction.

He was also the leader among our young intellectuals of what some have called the second American revolution, the post-war revolt against the contemporary American culture, especially on the campuses. And he has quite candidly stated his aim: "to combat with ridicule and invective American piety, stupidity and tin pot morality, progressives, professional moralists, Methodists, osteopaths, Christian Scientists, socialists, single taxers, in brief the whole doctrine of democracy."

The editors of *The Liberator* and *Yale Review,* who, until recently, totally ignored him, now quote him regularly. *The New Republic,* while insisting it does not always agree with him, eagerly seeks his byline. *The Nation,* which had criticized his book on George Bernard Shaw and run articles by the leading Puritan, Stuart Sherman, attacking Mencken, was now carrying him on the masthead as a contributing editor. A host of writers have come forward to quote, praise or argue with him: Frank Harris, Aldous Huxley, Ernest Boyd, and Edmund Wilson. As one critic said: "It would be difficult to imagine anyone agreeing with everything Mencken said, but it is all but inconceivable that anyone could be indifferent to him." One who could not ignore him is Walter Lippmann, editorial page editor of the *New York World*. He describes him as "the most powerful personal influence on this whole generation of educated people." Lippmann refers to him as "the Holy Terror from Baltimore who calls you a swine and an imbecile and increases your will to live."

A fascinating character, no doubt about that.

When I returned to the table, Mencken was gone, and as I looked around to see if he might be table hopping among his friends in the room, Brookes passed by and said: "Mr. Mencken said to tell you that Hercule Paro . . ."

"Pwahro," I corrected him.

"Pwahro has gone to the telephone and will be back in a moment."

"Thank you, Brookes, you did very well with an impossible name."

"So who is Hercule Pwahro?"

"Hercuuuuul Pwahro," I said. "He is a detective in a new book by a British writer named Agatha Christie."

"Oh, I never read detective stories," Brookes said somewhat haughtily as he headed for another table.

"Well, I don't either," I said to myself. And while waiting for Mencken's return, I started to read the editorial page of the morning *Sun*. To tell the truth, I hate editorials and editorial writers. They sit alone in an office, high above the maddening crowd, and as they sit, soft voices rise from below. When they hear them, they pass into a long dream and, as they dream, their hands, which hold pencils, begin to write. The voices below are so soft that few could hear them at all, but these men hear them. They are the "Voices of the People." Or so the editorial writers claim.

And what the people of Baltimore were commenting on this morning was the recent announcement by Attorney General Harry Daugherty, who was Harding's campaign manager in 1920. Despite rumors to the contrary, the announcement said President Harding "will be a candidate for re-nomination next year." The *Sun*'s Voice of the People decided that perhaps it was a little premature for Daugherty to be nominating the president, considering all the scandals that seem to be just below the surface in Washington. Wouldn't it be prudent, the Voice speculated, to wait awhile to see what develops? After all, just why did the Veterans' Bureau legal counsel commit suicide? Or was it murder?

I was speculating about this myself when Mencken returned from making his phone call. As usual he seemed to have the answer: "Cain, as you know, when you want to find out something, a good detective, as a good reporter, goes to the source. So I naturally called Mary Rinehart to find out what she knew about Cramer's death. I reviewed her first novel, *The Circular Staircase,* for *The Smart Set* back in ought-eight. It caused a sensation then because, although a conventional mystery, it made some sense."

Mencken paused long enough to take a deep swallow of his pilsner, then continued: "But I haven't talked to her since Woodrow's folly and I wasn't sure how she would react to me. She is very patriotic. She would know—as most everyone does—that I favored the Germans during the war to make the world safe for democracy—one of the late Woodrow's most atrocious conceits."

He was, of course, referring to the former president, Woodrow Wilson, who was not dead yet, but pretty much confined to his house on S Street over in Washington. Mencken often called Woodrow "the late" possibly meaning the "former" president, although maybe he considered him already dead.

"Damned good idea, calling her," I said. "What did she say?"

"Well, she was rushing out the door, late for a luncheon date with Mark Sullivan. You probably don't know him. He's the former editor of *Collier's* and now the Washington correspondent for the *New York Evening Post*."

"I don't know him."

"Anyway, Mark wants to talk to her about Cramer, Forbes and the Veterans' Bureau. And Mary herself is digging into it. Says she might throw in a few deaths and use some of the corruption stuff going on in Washington as background for a mystery."

"How about Cramer? Will he be one of the deaths?"

"Didn't say. Mary knew the Cramers because her husband, Dr. Stanley Rinehart, works at the Veterans' Bureau. She couldn't go into detail now, but said if we come over and have lunch with her tomorrow at the Willard she'll tell us everything she knows."

Mencken paused for a good swallow of pilsner.

"So goddammit, Cain," Mencken rushed on, "I think we ought to go after 'em. Let's have lunch with Mary and hear what she has to say."

"What I think," I replied, "is that you've heard the bell ring and like an old firehouse reporter, you're straining to go."

"That, too," Mencken conceded. "But this story is something special. I tell you, Cain, corruption is inseparable from democracy. De Tocqueville pointed that out years ago. I went to the Republican Convention in Chicago where they nominated Gamaliel and everyone knew he was a stooge put there by the big money when the convention couldn't agree on Leonard Wood or Frank Lowden. Wood could have had it, but he refused to let the oil men dictate to him."

Mencken paused to take another healthy swallow of beer and order two coffees from Brookes. "But, by God, that 1920 Republican Convention was miserable! We had to bring our own liquor in suitcases and were afraid our rooms would be raided every day.

"But, ohhhh, the Democratic Convention in San Francisco, that was something else. As soon as the delegates were in their rooms, there appeared handsome, well-dressed young ladies asking what they would like to drink. Some of the delegates were suspicious and kicked the ladies out, fearing entrapment by the revenuers. But not me. In fact, one morning after an evening of heavy imbibing I woke up with a strange woman in my bed. At first I thought she was a harlot, but she turned out to be very respectable, although I had been either too tired or too drunk to use her carnally. I did meet a lovely young lady there, an *ass*piring—and she had a nice one— actress named Jane O'Roarke. One morning, I awoke on the beach at Half Moon Bay with this handsome Irish wench at my side. I fell head over heels for her. But the affair cooled—I don't know why, although she did become a little stout for my taste when she moved back to New York. Everyone who knew us thought we were fornicating, but oddly enough we weren't.

"Anyway, getting back to San Francisco, soon the word was out. No matter what you ordered to drink you got bourbon. Bourbon of the very first chop—and no bill attached. It was compliments of Mayor James Roph, who almost—but not quite—convinced me that God occasionally creates a good politician.

"Harding apparently serves good liquor too for the boys at his poker parties. Hell, Cain, I bet in a month we can find out everything that's going on in Gamaliel's tent show. What do you say, m'boy? Does the idea appeal to you?"

"Sure, why not? I've got time now, before I go to work this fall."

There was a period of silence as we contemplated what we had just agreed to do. Then I said: "How do you think we ought to start our little investigation?"

"One way would be trying to buy a liquor permit to take whiskey out of a government warehouse. That would show how the system works and, frankly, I need some more booze. Before Prohibition, I sold my Studebaker for three hundred and fifty dollars and stocked up on all kinds of liquor and beer for me and the Saturday Night Club—enough gin for two years and seven hundred bottles of beer. But between Red Lewis and the club, I've been just about drunk dry."

He paused long enough to note that two men sitting next to us were listening intently. Then, he continued his monologue: "I also had an early disaster with one of my batches of home brew. I bottled them too soon, then put them out in the backyard in the exact spot where the summer sun would hit the bottles at the hottest time of day." The men next to us shook their heads and made faces, indicating their sympathy.

"One Saturday evening," Mencken went on, "as the early club members began to arrive, we heard loud popping in the backyard like mines going off in Flander Fields. My brother August, wearing boxing gloves and shielded behind a screen, went into the breach and came back to report that almost the entire batch was ruined."

"So how come, Henry, you have the reputation of being the best brewmaster in the East?" one of the men at the next table asked.

"Despite that disaster, from which I learned a lot, I am. And I think it's safe to say that I was the first man south of the Mason-Dixon Line to brew a drinkable home beer. I give seminars now— ten pupils at a time. But on one condition, that each pupil agrees to teach ten more. That's my war against the Noble Experiment."

"I'll sign up, although my home brew ain't bad."

"No doubt," said Mencken. "It's simple enough to do, easy as having a tooth pulled. A batch of wort can be cooked in an hour and it's important to examine the yeast under a microscope. The fermentation is over in four or five days and two weeks after bottling—if you don't do it too soon and keep it out of the sun—the brew is ready to drink. But you'd be surprised how many dull dogs who took the course never got beyond a nauseous Malzsuppe, fit only for policemen and Sunday School superintendents.

"I tell you what, Cain. We'll start with lunch at the Willard tomorrow with Mary. I've got to run now, but we can talk on the train to Washington in the morning."

Then he pulled a big watch out of his vest pocket, looked at it, took a last swig of coffee, indicating I should do the same. It was time to leave.

Before departing, Mencken handed me a few pages of typed copy and said: "Here Cain, read this. It's a draft Nathan and I have done of our first editorial for the new magazine. It gives you some idea of what we'll be trying to achieve."

And we went our separate ways; Mencken took a taxi to the *Sun* office and, the cold drizzle having stopped, I decided to walk to my apartment on Linden Avenue, wondering all the way what it would be like digging into the Harding administration with the most opinionated man in America.

When I arrived at my brick townhouse at 2418 Linden, I poured a glass of home brew malt beer—superior to Mencken's I am sure—and settled down in my chair by the radio to read the editorial. It began by stating that the aim of the new magazine "is precisely that of every other monthly review the world has ever seen: to ascertain and tell the truth."

Nothing new about that, they conceded, but, they said, "the editors cherish the hope that it may be possible after all to introduce some element of novelty into the execution of an enterprise so old." And, they argued, the new magazine comes into being with at least one advantage over all its predecessors in the field of public affairs: "It is entirely devoid of messianic passion. The editors have heard no voice from the burning bush. They will not cry up and offer for sale any sovereign balm, whether political, economic or aesthetic, for all the sorrows of the world."

They went on to discuss the fact that most of the problems of the world are insoluble and that the *American Mercury* would be edited for "the normal, educated, well-disposed, un-frenzied, enlightened citizen of the middle minority. This man, as everyone knows," they said, "is fast losing all the rights that he once had. If we can't alleviate this forgotten man from the morass in which he now wanders we can at least entertain him.

"There are more political theories on tap in the republic than anywhere on earth, and more doctrines in aesthetics, and more religions, and more other schemes for regimenting, harrowing and saving human beings. Our annual production of messiahs is greater than that of all Asia."

And they conclude: "To explore this great complex of inspirations . . . in brief, to attempt a realistic presentation of the whole gaudy, gorgeous, American scene—this will be the principal enterprise of *The American Mercury*."

I can't deny that reading this was one of the most exciting moments of my life. So what if I couldn't write a novel. Writing for Mencken sounded like more fun anyway.

CHAPTER TWO

I arrived at the B&O station a little early for the 10:30 train that would take us to Washington and our luncheon with Mary Rinehart. Mencken was sitting on a wooden bench near the gate reading the *Baltimore Sun*. When he noticed me coming, he held up two tickets, then stood up and started walking toward the gate, where I joined him.

Once we were comfortably settled in the club car and Mencken had lit his Uncle Willie, I returned his draft editorial for the first issue of the *Mercury* and told him how much I supported what he was trying to do. "Just what the country and we journalists need," I said. "I'm looking forward to both reading and writing for it."

"Good, Cain. And I'm looking forward to working with you. You know, we just got to get back to common sense in this country. The forgotten man is being smothered by the liberals, pedagogues and Tories. The liberals suffer from a case of mental diabetes and think that a prairie demagogue, once promoted to the United States Senate, will instantly turn into another Metternich. The pedagogues believe that if you run a moron through a university and give him a Ph.D. he will cease to be a moron. And the Tories believe that capitalism is the only true faith and anyone who is against it should be hung by the thumbs until dead and damned in Hell for eternity."

Taking a long puff on his cigar, he abruptly changed the subject. "You get over to Washington often?"

"Practically never. No reason to."

"I don't much anymore, but I came over quite a bit as a kid. My father had a branch of his cigar business in Washington. At 7th and G Streets, as a matter of fact, near Union Station. He was grooming me to go into the cigar business and I did for awhile. Then suddenly he died. I loved him dearly and missed him very much, but it was, frankly, the luckiest thing that ever happened to me. It would prob-

ably have taken me years to get out of the business, alienated my
father and I would have missed those early newspaper days, some
of the best years of my life."

Then he pulled a big watch out of its allotted pocket and looked
at it: "We're running on time for our luncheon date at the Willard.
A great historic hotel. Most presidents-elect spend the night before
their inauguration there. They had to sneak old Abe Lincoln into
the hotel in 1861 because they feared a plot against his life. But no
sooner had they got him there, they had to whisk him up to Capitol
Hill where there were rumors everywhere that he had already been
assassinated."

"They were about five years early on that one," I interrupted, but
Mencken rushed on.

"Speaking of assassinations, I remember the night they nominated Coolidge for vice president in Chicago. After it was over I
went down to the catacombs below the hall to get a drink, which
was easy to do in the press quarters. I ran into an Irishman covering
for the *Boston Globe,* Michael Hennessy. He was in his cups but
making a speech to a handful of imbibing reporters: 'I offer you
four to one that Harding will be assassinated before he serves four
terms!'

"When we asked him why he thought that, he said: 'I'm not
saying anything against Harding. I wish him well. But I know Coolidge and he's the luckiest goddamn sonabitch in the United States.'
I ran into Hennessey recently at the Press Club in Washington and
he sticks to his story."

"That's the only way Coolidge could ever get to be president,"
I said, "But as to what might happen to the country I don't see
much difference between Harding and Coolidge except that one is
talkative and looks like a president and the other is silent and most
decidedly does not."

"That's right, both numbskulls. And Cal is a silent one, with a
lot to be silent about. But they weren't worried about Gamaliel
being assassinated before his inauguration. I went to the private
reception Harding gave the night before his inauguration at the Willard (where he and his wife were also staying) and I heard that what
the Secret Service agents were really worried about was that one of
the president-elect's lady-friends would show up.

"But the Duchess—that's what everyone called Mrs. Harding—was ready for her."

"Harding's girlfriend never appeared?"

"Later that night. But by then, according to Ray Clapper, a U.P. reporter, the Duchess had Harding safely in his room with secret service agents guarding the door. They knew his lady-friend was upstairs waiting. When Harding came tiptoeing out of his room, they forced him back in, then went upstairs and told the woman that Justice Department agents would be after her if she didn't leave the hotel immediately—which she did."

"Did Clapper know the woman?"

"No. But it was Grace Cross, who used to work in Harding's office when he was a senator. A lot of people knew that affair was going on. You've heard the saying, 'A senator is known by the women he keeps?' "

"Can't say that I have."

"Ever been to the Willard, Cain?"

"Yeah. My wife—Mary—and I spent our brief honeymoon there."

"That's right, I forgot you were married. How's that working out?"

"To tell the truth, not so well. We recently separated."

"I'm sorry to hear it, Jim," said Mencken. "But it doesn't surprise me. As I recall, she is a teacher, and frankly why any woman who has a career would want to be married is beyond me."

"Well, I'm not sure it was her career that caused the breakup," I replied. "I guess it's much more complicated than that. And it's been a very painful experience."

"Breaking up always is—which is one reason I'm against marriage. At least there are no children involved. I'm right on that, aren't I? You don't have any kids."

"No, we never got around to that."

"Well, from what you say, Jim, it was probably a good thing. You've got to consider your career, you know. There's been a lot of gabble about woman as an inspiration to the creative person, but there's very little basis in fact for that claim. Women not only don't inspire the artist to high endeavor, they actually stand against every high creation the artist conceives. What women invariably want, as

Mary obviously did, is for their man to be respectable, that he do something generally approved, that he suppress any sign of his genius."

"I don't think that was Mary's problem," I said. "Her trouble was that she flouted the basic principle that marriages are made in bed. One time, not too long ago, we took a little vacation from Annapolis to her home in Churchill, and on the first night I made romantic overtures only to be rebuffed. When I persisted, she explained her reluctance by saying that if I was on vacation she was, too. Vacation from what, I asked—the one thing that was supposed to make a marriage work?"

"Good question," Mencken answered. "If you can't spend a little time in bed on a vacation I don't know when you can."

"After we had been married awhile," I continued, "it was obvious that she was uncomfortable with me. She was quite refined and cultured and I think frankly I embarrassed her sometimes. She was also a born prohibitionist and did not like or approve of my drinking. You'll agree I'm not the best-looking man on the western shore and she was always annoyed at the way I talked—my city-room bark. After a time I actually began to think I agreed with you about marriage. I don't like domesticity, don't believe in monogamy and seem to be drawn to promiscuity. At least today I can admit it, whereas I couldn't have a few years ago."

"We can thank some of the young novelists for that—Fitzgerald, Lewis, Dreiser," Mencken responded. "People can say things like that out in the open now. But, as I've said, marriage is not just wrong for most men, but also for some women. No sane woman would want to be the wife of a man such as Nietzche or Beethoven or Chopin. His mistress, perhaps, because a mistress can always move on when the weather gets bad. Marriage, as I have said many times in the public print, is like hanging—worse than it's generally made out to be. As for myself, I think the man who marries best is the man who puts it off until it's too late."

"I've heard that you came close to getting married to Marion Bloom. Most everyone at the paper knows about her."

"That's right—I almost did," Mencken replied, crossing himself in mock appreciation to the Lord for delivering him from such a fate. "We saw a lot of each other before the war. She lived in New York and her sister, Estelle, was living with Dreiser. We partied together and sometimes Marion came down to Baltimore. Then she went to France during the war—she was a nurse—and when she returned, she became a Christian Scientist! Cheeeeeerist! She even thought she could convert me with that buncombe. Can you imagine me—the heathen missionary—living with a disciple of that Maryland Jezebel, Mary Baker Eddy? So I haven't seen Marion lately."

"Who you squiring now?"

"Nobody, really; it's mostly by mail." And he began staring at the blurred trees rushing by the window. The train must have been going sixty or seventy miles an hour now.

Shifting the subject, I asked: "Well, Mr. Mencken, how do you think we should start our Washington investigation?"

"Just call me Henry," he replied quickly. "Most everyone does. And don't call me 'Heinie.' First, of course, we talk to Mary and see what she's learned. And we've got to get into those houses we hear about where the deals are made and the women are laid. My booze comes from a bootlegger up in Pennsylvania—a good friend. Maybe he'll know who we see to get one of those liquor permits. Then we can pose as a couple of booticians. Maybe you can go as my bodyguard. You look big enough and tough enough. It'll cost us a little money to buy our way in, but there's no telling what we might find."

"Well, you've got to supply the money. I'm broke."

"Most men who are divorced or supporting women are," Mencken said before lighting up another Uncle Willie. "I did meet a very attractive young wench recently. She teaches English at Goucher. As a favor to my friend, Harry Baker, who teaches there, I agreed to award the prize for the best freshman short story. I also told Baker that I would take the winner out to dinner. She was a beautiful young seventeen-year-old named Sara Mayfield, who told Harry that going out to dinner with the Bad Boy of Baltimore would curl the blue blood of Goucher Dean Dorothy Stimson."

"I wouldn't blame the dean for being concerned."

"You're right. Harry told the young thing that she should have a chaperon. So she invited Sara Haardt, a young lady who taught Mayfield English at Goucher and also taught her in Montgomery, Alabama, where by odd coincidence they both know Zelda Fitzgerald, Scott's wife. To tell you the truth, I had noticed Miss Sara in the audience. Beautiful young woman. Tall, slender, willowy and

quite intelligent looking, a combination of the *femme savant* and
femme fatale. Bronze colored hair, deep brown, soft eyes and fair
skin. I abandoned my prepared lecture on 'The Trade of Letters'
and launched into a discourse on 'How to Catch a Husband.' It was
easy, I said, because a woman has precisely the same allurement
for men that Cape Hatteras has for the seafarer—enormously dangerous, hence enormously exciting. If women were taken away, man
could not survive and not just because the species would die out.
He would be bored to death. Only a disgusting cad avoids the game
of love."

"You've done a good job of avoiding it."

"Not on your life! I've had my innings and I'll have some more.
In fact, I've already exchanged a few letters with Miss Haardt,
who's back in Alabama until the fall. We're only at the lunch-at-
Marconi-Kaffy stage of the game now, but I see more exciting days
ahead."

"What about Mary Rinehart?"

"Not my type, Cain. But she's a damned good reporter. You
remember, she went to Europe during the war for the *Saturday
Evening Post,* and she also wrote a book about her experience, spent
time in the trenches, saw no-man's land, underwent a bombing raid
and interviewed General Foch, King Alfred of Belgium and Queen
Mary. To show you what a good reporter she is—and this is what
I really liked—she blew a hole a mile wide in the story about a
German cavalryman slashing off the hands of a little Belgian girl
with his sword as she raised them to surrender."

"I remember that one."

"In Belgium, Mary found that the child had been taken to England where she later tracked down the woman who nursed the little
girl. She had had her hands amputated after both had been mutilated
by a bomb that had fallen in Covent Garden. Mary did find that the
Germans had marched Belgian prisoners ahead of them into Belgian
villages, forcing the villagers to surrender or shoot their own people
if they tried to defend themselves.

"But she found that most of the German atrocity stories that
circulated here during the war were phony—as I always knew they
were. I know damn well they were put out by George Creel, that
slippery character who ran the government propaganda office for
the late Woodrow."

"Could be. I never heard any authenticated atrocity stories when I was in France."

The train was beginning to slow down as we approached Washington. Soon we were passing through some backyards and occasionally someone would wave at us from a window or back porch. I waved back. I don't know why.

We arrived in Washington at 11:10, right on time. As we were walking from the train platform to Union Station, Mencken said: "Welcome to your nation's capital, Cain, home of one hundred thousand miserable botches of ninth-rate clerks," a remark I chose to ignore.

Out front of the station there were several taxis, but we decided there was plenty of time for the streetcar ride up Pennsylvania Avenue to the Willard. "We'll tell Mary we're working on something for the *Sun* or maybe *The Smart Set* or maybe even a book," Mencken said. "By the way, have you got your notebook with you? I hope you can take notes. And if we ever manage to get a book out of this little investigation, you'll have to do most of the writing. We could use a joint byline, of course. But I don't have the time, what with the *Sun, The Smart Set* and trying to get this new magazine going."

I took my notebook and a couple of pencils out of my pocket and held them up for him to see.

When we reached the 14th Street stop and prepared to leave the streetcar, he was going on about some of the writers he wanted to bring in to the magazine—Eugene O'Neill, Sinclair Lewis, Edgar Lee Masters, Willard Huntington Wright, William Allen White, Ernest Boyd, Carl Van Vechten, Theodore Dreiser. I was flattered that Mencken would include me in that group.

When we entered the hotel lobby I was immediately conscious of its splendor. The huge marble columns and marbled front desk gave the whole room an ivory tone, which complimented perfectly the heavy red rugs and numerous comfortable-looking English oak and leather chairs.

As we passed the desk, I noticed a very good-looking woman who appeared to be checking out. She had reddish hair, but dark eyebrows. Her figure was tall and willowy and she was stylishly dressed. On our right, we saw the bar, which seemed a little forlorn and empty. Mencken was noticing the tall, handsome woman too. "Not bad," I said.

"Not bad, indeed," he replied.

Shifting the subject as we headed up the stairs and into Peacock Alley leading to the main dining room, I said: "Judging from the bar, I would guess you can't get a drink at the Willard."

"No, Cain, we won't be drinking today with Mary. I didn't even bring my flask for risk of embarrassing her."

"I did."

"Well, please don't bring it out," said Mencken. "We can drink later. Mrs. Rinehart may be an excellent writer, but she's also a solid Republican. I know she honors Prohibition, even if she's against it—like most Americans, who'll probably keep voting dry as long as they can stagger to the polls."

On our way through Peacock Alley, an elaborately appointed hallway that runs from E Street to the F Street entrance, Mencken said, "Despite all the presidents, Cain, the most distinguished guest the Willard ever had was Mark Twain. I assume you've read your Twain?"

"Some," I replied. "*Huckleberry Finn,* of course."

"Greatest American novel ever written. The story goes that right after the turn of the century, the first night Twain stayed at the Willard, he came down from his room into the lobby and started up Peacock Alley for the dining room. Then he noticed that at the other end of the alley was a much taller set of stairs coming down from the F Street entrance to the hotel. So Twain goes back up to the floor where his room was, walked through the corridor to the other side of the hotel, came down to the small F Street lobby, then descended the long stairs so all the people milling around in Peacock Alley could see him make his entrance. Do you think I ought to go up there and make such an entrance—out of respect for the author who had the greatest impact on my writing?"

"Go ahead. I see one young man who might see you coming down the stairs and I doubt if he ever heard of Mark Twain."

At the entrance to the huge main dining room we were greeted by the headwaiter who, not being able to ignore the cigar jutting from Mencken's mouth, said: "Gentlemen, if you prefer smoking I suggest the Pompeiian Room," and he bowed while pointing to a smaller dining room across the alley.

Mencken looked longingly at the Pompeiian Room, but said to me: "Well, let's see where Mary has us." Then to the waiter: "We're meeting Mrs. Rinehart for lunch. I believe she has made reservations."

"She has," the headwaiter replied, looking at a list on the tall, wooden reception desk at the entrance to the dining room. "The reservation is for two at noon in the main dining room."

"Ahhhh, yes. She didn't know I was bringing a friend. Do you think you could find us a table for three?" Mencken asked, quickly moving to put out his Willie in the circular, gold-plated receptacle containing white sand, placed conveniently near the entrance.

The waiter found us a table for four near a window looking out on 14th Street. We barely had a chance to be seated when I noticed a heavy bosomed, matronly but strikingly handsome woman in a large hat and light coat following the waiter, heading for our table. Mary Roberts Rinehart looked every bit the queen she was—queen of our popular lady writers. Her byline, on fiction and non-fiction, was everywhere: *The Saturday Evening Post, The Ladies Home Journal, Good Housekeeping, McClure's, American Magazine, Bookman, Colliers, Cosmopolitan,* on Broadway ("The Bat" and more recently "The Breaking Point") and books (*The Breaking Point* and *The Out Trail,* a travel book).

Rinehart was the kind of writer Mencken did not pay much attention to. But in that he generally admired anyone who was successful at what they did—except, of course, Prohibition agents, ministers and Grand Dragons of the Ku Klux Klan—he naturally respected her.

"Well, Henry, it's certainly good to see you again," she said in a cultured speaking voice. "When was the last time? Were you at the 1916 Republican Convention?"

"No, I missed that one," Mencken replied. "How about the 1920 one in Chicago?"

"I missed that one," Mary said, "although I did do some work for Harding in the campaign. In fact, that's when I first met Charlie Forbes—and frankly, I wish I never had."

"I'll bet the president feels the same way," Mencken said.

Then, noting that I was still standing there trying not to look like one of the potted plants in the huge dining room, Mencken quickly added: "Mary, I neglected to tell you I was bringing a friend. This is Jim Cain, a young reporter who is working with me on the Harding project. You may have seen his piece on West Virginia in the *Atlantic Monthly* last fall."

"I do remember that," Rinehart said, holding out her hand to shake mine in a masculine manner. "A nice article and well written. But you'd better stay away from this man. Every writer I know who has written for Henry on *The Smart Set* says he always tries to make them sound like him."

"I plead guilty," Mencken replied, "and what's wrong with that? If every non-fiction writer in the country wrote like H. L. Mencken—who, I might remind you, is now an acknowledged authority on the American language—it would be an overall improvement."

"Touché," said Rinehart, laughing.

Before she could continue, Mencken said: "Let me add, however, that Mr. Cain is developing a fine style of his own."

"I wish you well, Mr. Cain," Mr. Rinehart said. And then turned her attention to the table, beautifully set with two silver forks, two knives, an exquisitely designed plate, a glass of water and little matching butter plate with a folded napkin and fresh rose on top. "Oh, don't you just love dining at the Willard," she said, picking up the plate and studying the intricate design embedded in it.

Mencken lifted the rose to his nose and said: "Reminds me of the idealist who, noting that a rose smells better than a cabbage, concludes that it will also make better soup."

Rinehart gave an "Oh, Henry" shake of her head. I laughed and decided that Mencken was really a satirist, not a philosopher, and much funnier than that other spoofer of the system, Will Rogers.

Suddenly, a slightly-built gentleman wearing a dark suit and carrying a newspaper entered the dining room and walked toward a table partly hidden in the back of the room. Most heads turned to follow him to his seat and Mencken said: "I wonder who that is? He looks like a mortician from a small New England town."

"A lawyer, not a mortician," Rinehart said, as she rose from the table. "That's Calvin. I must say hello to him." Then she walked to the vice president's table.

"I should have known." Mencken said, "Just because he looks embalmed doesn't necesssarily mean he's an embalmer."

I stood up, deciding to take this opporuntiy to go to the men's

room, and Mencken said: "You going to say hello to the vice president, too? Better take your notebook. Maybe he'll say something
quotable."

"Nah," I replied. "I'm just going to the john. I'm sure Mary'll
give us a full report." On the way out, I asked the maître d' if the
vice president has lunch here often.

"Yes, all the time," he replied. "Usually by himself, although
sometimes Mrs. Coolidge is with him. They live here, you know."

"No I didn't. Was he here when they had that fire last year after
the Gridiron dinner?"

"They sure were. They both had to be awakened and evacuated."

When I went back to the dining room, Mary Rinehart was just
returning to our table, and Mencken, always the gentleman, rose to
help her with her chair and we all sat down together. Mencken could
hardly wait: "All right, Mary, was Cal silent, as they say, or were
you able to coax a few words out of him?"

"He was placid and unperturbable as usual, but he did confirm
what everyone says, that the president is very despondent and
concerned about the Veterans' Bureau and the rumors of scandal
in some other departments. But he did say one thing that was
amusing . . . and sad."

"Oh," said Mencken and I took out my notepad, but she shook
her head indicating I should put it away. "Mrs. Harding, as you may
have heard, likes to visit clairvoyants. In fact, she puts great stock
in them—especially a Madam Marcia over on R Street. And medium Marcia has told Florence that her husband will not live out
his term in office. Calvin just laughs at it but he says the Duchess
is very upset."

Before Mencken could reply, the waiter arrived. We all ordered
iced tea and the waiter left us to study the menus. The prices were
a little rich for me, but I figured Mencken would be picking up the
check so I decided on the $2.50 chicken and gave serious consid-
eration to the forty cent Neapolitan ice cream, which I love.

I thought Mencken would ask Rinehart to continue about the
medium predicting Harding's death. Instead, he surprised me by
saying, "Well, Mary, I am pleased that you agreed to meet and talk
about the Harding administration. I know how strongly you felt
about the war, and everyone knows I was on the other side in the
late unpleasantness. But despite our disagreement, I must say I ad-

mired your war reporting for the *Post*. It was first rate."

"Thank you, Henry," Rinehart replied. "You know, I got more mail for my war articles than anything I have written for the *Post*— or anywhere else. And, yes I was disappointed in you during the war—especially after we entered it." Then seemingly trying to shift the subject, she said: "By the way, I want to thank you for your kind words about me in your *Prejudices,* that I had 'unmistakably technical excellence and a certain civilized sophistication in point of view.' Some praise, coming from the most difficult-to-please critic in the country. Seriously, I don't know whether I've ever mentioned this to you, but I always appreciated your review of *The Circular Staircase*. It was one of the first and I'm sure it influenced other reviewers."

"Well," Mencken replied, "it was just a short review but what I said about it was well deserved. And I can quote it because I went back to the scrapbook Mother keeps and read my comments again— 'A mystery with both thrill and humor, a delicious lightness of touch, keeps you in good spirits until the unexpected denouement knocks you breathless at the close.' "

Rinehart, after thanking him again and saying that *The Circular Staircase* was the turning point in her career, was about to move on to another subject when Mencken returned to the war. He seemed anxious to explain to Rinehart—and perhaps me, too—what his position was. It is obviously a sensitive subject with him: "As the war got underway, I sensed the beginnings of a struggle to the death between the Germans and the Anglo-Saxons. And it was obvious which side I had to take. Like the leaders of Germany, I had grave doubts about democracy. And it dawned on me that the whole doctrine I had been preaching was fundamentally anti–Anglo-Saxon. So if I had any spiritual home it must be in the land of my ancestors. When the war started I instinctively began to whoop it up for the kaiser."

"But America entering the war should have changed all that," Rinehart interrupted.

"It did and I registered for the draft like everyone else. I couldn't endorse mutiny on the quarter deck so I went into retirement, sort of. I didn't join in the hysteria about the sinking of the *Lusitania* because I thought Germany was justified in trying to break the At-

lantic blockade. I also thought America's 'neutrality' had been dis-
honorable. And to get down to *realpolitic,* I thought it was in
America's best interest to side with Germany."

I interjected a question here just to let everyone know where I
stood: "I disagreed with you about the war and I was proud of my
service in France. But with your heritage, I can fully appreciate
your position. What puzzles me is why—considering your deeply
held pro-German and anti-American feelings—you continue to live
in America? I know you love Baltimore, but it's still in America
and most Baltimoreans are one hundred percent patriots. We have
a colony of expatriates living in Europe now. Why haven't you
joined them?"

"Why do I stay in America? Why do men go to zoos? But seriously . . ."

Before Mencken could continue the waiter arrived with the tea
and to take our orders. Rinehart had a lobster cocktail and roast
lamb with mint sauce. Mencken, loyal to his Chesapeake Bay country, had the Maryland crab flake cocktail and broiled bluefish, commenting that they were running again at Ocean City and in the bay.
I had the chicken but passed up an appetizer, saving myself for the
Neopolitan.

When the waiter left, Mencken said: "That was a good question,
Jim, about joining the expatriates. There was a time right after the
war when I gave serious thought to moving to Europe. But my
mother would never leave and I do love Baltimore very much—as
much as most of the patriots. But there's more to it than that. I also
love watching and writing about this glorious commonwealth of
morons, this Eden of clowns. Where is there a better show in the
world? I'm well-fed here, unhounded by sordid cares and taxes are
relatively low. I figure that my share of maintaining the Honorable
Mr. Harding in the White House for one year comes out to less
than eighty cents. Can anyone think of better sport for the money?"
Then he paused for just a moment before adding: "Besides, I
wouldn't swap the American bathroom for the Acropolis."

That brought laughs from both Rinehart and me and seemed to
relieve whatever tension had developed at the table. Then Mencken
added: "And don't forget, I planned to run for president!"

"That's right Henry, I forgot." Rinehart said. "You and Nathan nominated yourselves in 1920 for president and vice president."

"As Republican candidates. I could never have joined any party that that scoundrel Wilson belonged to."

Mencken was referring to a prank he and Nathan pulled in the last election. Their campaign was carried out exclusively in the pages of *The Smart Set*. Their platform included promises to:

- take the Statute of Liberty out beyond the three-mile limit and dump it
- abolish the Y.M.C.A.
- establish arenas in which to turn clergymen loose upon one another.
- give the Philippines to Japan

They attracted more attention in London than America and the *New York Sun* columnist Barton Braley summed up the opposition's position in a poem "Mencken, Nathan and God," which began:

There were three who sailed away one night
Far from the maddening throng
And two of the three were always right
And everyone else was wrong

"Well, I hope all that crazy post-war stuff is behind us now," Rinehart said laughing. "What we all need to do is get back to normalcy, as the president put it."

But I disagreed, on a technicality: "I think the proper word is 'normality,' as our expert here on the language must surely agree."

"No, Cain," Mencken replied, his eyes lighting up. "Although the word is much derided, 'normalcy' has a respectable ancestry. In my studies I found it used in a mathematical treatise dated, as I recall, sometime in the 1850s. The treatise also used the word 'abnormalcy.' But let's not give too much credit to Gamaliel. The president is still one of the worst practitioners of the language we have ever had in the White House."

"I concur," Rinehart said, "President Harding is no grammarian. But," she emphasized, "he is an honest man. And that's another reason I agreed to talk with you, Henry."

"Oh?" was Mencken's only response.

Rinehart explained: "I know you're starting an investigation of the corruption in the administration, and I encourage it. I know firsthand some of the things that are going on in the Veterans' Bureau and I've learned from Mark Sullivan, Will Irwin and others about shady dealings in both the Justice and Interior Departments. I hope you or someone exposes them. But I want to caution you not to link the president to any of this dirty business unless you find specific proof."

"Well, of course we wouldn't do that unless we had the evidence," Mencken replied, "and I put great stock in your endorsement of the president's honesty. But what do you know about the Veterans' Bureau?"

I had started taking notes and Rinehart looked only casually at my notebook as if to suggest that she had no objection. But before she could respond to Mencken's question we were interrupted by a heavyset man in a rumpled three-piece suit approaching our table. He had disheveled white hair and a blue polka dot bow tie and both Mencken and Rinehart seemed to recognize him immediately. As he neared the table he held out his open arms to Rinehart, who rose and said: "Why, Bill, what a surprise. I thought you were in Europe."

"I just got back," the distinguished-looking gentleman said, "and I'm going to see the president before returning to Kansas."

After giving him a big hug, Rinehart turned to us and said: "Henry, I know you know Bill White but perhaps Mr. Cain has never met our country's most eminent journalist."

Mencken, of course, knew William Allen White, author and editor of the *Emporia Gazette,* but I had never met him and we shook hands. I was curious to see Mencken's reaction to White because Mencken considered him one of the leading defenders of the literary and political establishment that he was constantly attacking. But Mencken greeted him warmly, shaking his outstretched hand and saying: "Bill, it's good to see you again."

"Same here, Henry," White replied. Then turning to Rinehart and mocking dire concern, he said, "But Mary, what on earth are you, a nice Republican lady and purveyor of literature for department store buyers and shoe drummers, as Henry calls us contributors to the *Post,* which, he says, buys literature like a soap factory . . ."

"Don't forget," Mencken interceded, "I said this method of buying stories was 'thoroughly American,' " which White ignored.

"As I was about to say, what are you doing dining with this
heathen anarchist?"

"Oh, you know we respectable ladies ignore Henry's rantings in
The Smart Set and he's always a pleasure to be with because he's
such a perfect gentleman."

"Thank you madame, but that is not precisely true. I have been
known to swear in front of ladies and archdeacons. The truth is,
Bill, Mrs. Rinehart graciously consented to have lunch with us to
tell us what she knows about corruption in the Veterans' Bureau,
where her husband works—and anywhere else in the administration
of the president you have lauded so in the public print."

"Hold on a minute," White replied. Then he pulled up a chair
from a nearby empty table and sat down next to Mencken, indicating clearly that he wanted to let us know exactly where he stood
on what was going on in Washington. "Henry, I'm not a Harding
man. You were at the 1920 Republican Convention where I was a
delegate. You remember when the convention was finally stamped-
ing for Harding, there were eight votes cast for Herbert Hoover?
Well, I cast one of those votes."

"Yes, I remember," Mencken replied.

And White continued: "And I've had my differences with the
president on a number of issues—the League of Nations and Prohibition, for example. Sure, as a Republican, I have written articles
in the *Post* and a number of other publications, praising Harding
for what he has achieved. But don't get me wrong. I could not be
more distraught at what that gang of crooks surrounding the president has done. Daugherty, as everyone knew from the start, is an
out-and-out scoundrel. And have you ever met Secretary Fall?"

Mencken shook his head indicating he had not.

"What a horrible man. Such a face and demeanor. He looks like
the patent medicine salesman of my childhood who used to stand,
with long hair falling on a long coat under a wide hat, a military
goatee and mustache, at the back of a wagon selling wizard oil.
How Hoover and Hughes must suffer being in the same cabinet
with that evil man."

White was quite upset and Mencken asked the obvious question:

"Well, Bill, what does the president say about these men? Does he know what they're doing?"

"He must," White replied. "Before I went to Europe, I had a brief meeting with him in the White House. In fact he asked to see me and I had the feeling he had something to tell me. But he wanted to talk—of all things—about a problem with advertising he had at the *Marion Star,* assuming I had the same problem at the *Gazette.*"

"What the hell was that?" Mencken said, obviously curious.

"This will interest you, Henry. He said that he got a lot of subscriptions from people from Maine to Oregon who thought, as he put it, that he took off two or three hours down here to write editorials for the *Star.* They were going to bust the paper he said because the local advertisers would not pay for readers so far away. He thought that because I was so well known now that I had the same problem on the *Gazette.* I told him that I had a little four-page weekly that took no advertising, so it was not a problem."

"Curious," I said, "that he would be concerned about such an insignificant thing with all the problems he must have on his mind."

"I think preoccupying himself with things like that is a form of escape," White replied. "It seems to have finally dawned on him that he's in over his head in that job. Judson Welliver, his press secretary and a friend of mine, confirms it. And in addition to that there are the scandals."

Rinehart interrupted: "So you see, Henry, Bill confirms what I've been saying: that the president himself is innocent of any corruption. It's the men around him who are doing the dirty work. And we all hope they are put in jail or run out of town as soon as possible."

White stood up and looked at his watch as he put the chair he had used back at the other table. "You never want to be late for a meeting at the White House, so I've got to run. Good to see all of you and a pleasure to meet you, Mr. Cain."

"So what takes you to Harding's lair?" Mencken could not help asking.

"I don't really know," White responded. "He just said he wanted to talk to me about something. Maybe he's going to ask me what I know about the rumors going around concerning corruption in his administration. I've certainly heard them, as I am sure all of you have. And, frankly, with people like Harry Daugherty, Jesse Smith

and Gaston B. Means loose in this town, anything could happen—
and Harding wouldn't necessarily know anything about it."

"I agree, Bill," Rinehart said.

"Well," Mencken said, waving good-bye, "tell the president I
voted for him."

When we were seated again, Rinehart said: "Don't you just love
Bill White? Such an old-school gentleman."

We all agreed that he was, and then Mencken, sensing that we
had better get down to business, said to Rinehart: "Well Mary, what
do you know about the Veterans' Bureau?"

"Well, it started with my meeting Charlie Forbes in Marion,
Ohio. I had been invited there after the convention because, as it
turned out, the Republican National Committee had discovered that
the GOP platform made no concessions to women."

"Pretty stupid," Mencken said, "considering that shortly after the
Republican Convention the ladies were finally given the right to
vote."

"Not too bright," Rinehart agreed, "but I was part of a large
delegation of women, including Alice Longworth, Ruth McCormick
and Mrs. Gifford Pinchot, who were supposed to correct that by
endorsing Harding's proposal for a new Department of Public Welfare."

"Oh, God," said Mencken, "see what the ladies are doing to
politics already? They even got Republicans thinking like do-
gooders."

"Don't worry, Henry," replied Rinehart, "we haven't heard anything about a Department of Welfare since they took office and I
don't think we will. Anyway, I had dinner that night with the Hardings, Alice Longworth, and little Doctor Sawyer, the president's
physician. And I'm sure that dreadful Harry Daugherty was there.
I remember everyone later urging Harding not to appoint Daugherty
to his cabinet. But he told people before the election that if he was
elected, 'Harry Daugherty could have any job he wanted.' What he
wanted was the Interior or Justice Department."

"And he just issued an announcement that the president will run
again in 1924," I said to Rinehart. "Do you think he did that by
way of assuring us that there is nothing to the corruption rumors
going around and the president's presumed despondency?"

"And," Mencken quickly added, "I wouldn't be surprised if

Daugherty put out that press release without Harding's approval. I'm sure Daugherty and his gang will do anything to make sure Harding runs again—to keep the graft coming."

"Well, I'm not sure that Daugherty did it entirely on his own," Rinehart answered. "But I do agree the press release was meant to be reassuring. Also at dinner that night in Marion was Charlie Forbes, who had already been promised the Veterans' Bureau. I got to talking with him and, in fact, he gave me a lift to the train station that night. I did not like the man but he seemed to have the president's ear and he could not be ignored. I recall that it was on the trip to the station that I told Forbes that my husband, Stanley, is a national authority on TB."

"Oh," said Mencken, showing his usual interest in anything medical or scientific. "I didn't know that. I'd like to meet him sometime."

"I would have invited him to join us today," she said, "except that he's up at Saranac, New York, looking at a possible new site for a Veterans' Bureau tuberculosis sanatorium. And I'm not sure how you two would get along, Henry. Neither of us likes the new realism in literature; in fact, Stanley simply could not stand *Main Street*. 'Doesn't the author know any likable people?' was his reaction."

"Lewis knows me and I'm surely a likable fellow," Mencken replied, adopting his choir-boy look.

At this point, the waiter appeared at the table wheeling a cart and Rinehart paused while the food was served. Then as we all commented on how delicious everything looked, especially the roast lamb, she continued her story: "I didn't see Forbes again until last fall. I had agreed to cover the Disarmament Conference in Washington for a national syndicate. Having just finished my novel—*The Breaking Point*—I felt like doing something different. I knew we would never put an end to warfare. Still I was interested in the conference. And while in Washington I met Forbes again."

"This was before anything had surfaced about the Veterans' Bureau," said Mencken.

"That's right," said Rinehart. "Forbes was in his element then. He was one of the president's poker playing cronies. . . ."

". . . And court jester to the best minds in government," I interjected, with some effort at jocularity. "Who are they?"

"The president has some strong men in his cabinet," Rinehart added, somewhat defensively. "Hoover, Mellon, Hughes, Wallace. Anyway, Forbes asked if my husband would consider coming to Washington to join the Veterans' Bureau as a special consultant on TB. I was stunned by the offer, but excited. I like politics and am well-connected with the Hardings. Our three sons were already in New York, so they were glad that we would be living closer to them."

"That's right," said Mencken, "some of your sons have gone into publishing, haven't they?"

"Yes," she replied, "Stanley, Jr., and Ted are the Rineharts in the new house of Farrar and Rinehart. Their father, however, was not very happy about leaving Pittsburgh, but he agreed to take the job. He still calls Pittsburgh home and assumes that we will eventually return."

"You probably will, if your roots are in deep enough," Mencken said.

"Well, we won't be going back for awhile," she replied. "But we are both disappointed in the Veterans' Bureau. In fact, Stanley is getting ready to leave. Under Forbes, the bureau simply became too corrupt. Because he was very friendly with the president's sister, Carolyn Votaw, he was able to get things done in the White House, although the president didn't know what was going on."

"I can believe that," Mencken said. "Frankly, Gamaliel is really too dumb to be a good crook."

"Whether it was stupidity or simply trust of his friends," Rinehart said, somewhat chillingly, "the president agreed that it would be more efficient if the construction of veterans' hospitals was transferred from the Army to the Veterans' Bureau. Once in charge of hospital construction, Forbes suddenly became a wealthy man living lavishly on his government salary of ten thousand dollars a year, apparently as a result of the kickbacks he imposed. He had raised the cost of constructing a hospital from twenty-nine hundred dollars a bed to thirty-nine hundred dollars."

"Even Gamaliel could figure out that Forbes appeared to be making a killing of a thousand dollars a bed for each new veteran's bed," Mencken said. "And remember the government is now taking care of three hundred thousand wounded veterans—which all those people who were so excited about sending the boys over there have forgotten."

Ignoring that comment, Rinehart went on for nearly fifteen minutes, uninterrupted even by Mencken. Forbes convinced the president that it would be more efficient if the bureau was given charge of the purchasing and disposal of veterans' supplies, which was being handled by the Army Quartermaster Corps. One company bought one hundred thousand pairs of pajamas valued at around a dollar twenty a pair for thirty cents a pair. Most of the difference between sales prices and the actual value of an item is believed to have ended up in Forbes' pocket. She also said it was the president's personal physician, Dr. Sawyer, chairman of the Federal Hospitalization Board, who finally blew the whistle on Forbes.

The president was crushed and absolutely furious with Forbes. In fact, he had a violent confrontation with him in the Oval Office, pinning him back against a wall and shouting, "You dirty, double-crossing bastard!" as he almost choked his old friend to death.

That night at dinner, Harding was so morose he could not talk. He declined a poker game and went into a despondency that lasted for several days, enough to start the rumors that the president was sick and probably would not run for the office again in 1924.

At this point in her story, the waiter arrived to see how things were going and to ask if we wanted dessert. We deferred to Rinehart who commented on her diet, but said "Oh, what the hell," and ordered a chocolate eclair; Mencken had a peach tart and I had the ice cream. We all ordered coffee.

When the waiter left, I asked, "Where does Charles Cramer fit into this horrid tale?"

"Let me say first," Rinehart replied, "I am absolutely certain Cramer was not murdered. Stanley and I are both convinced Cramer killed himself and that he had plenty of reason. He virtually ran the bureau for weeks on end while Forbes and Eliah Mortimer went cross-country with their wives entertaining lavishly while inspecting potential hospital sites." She stopped for a moment as the coffee and dessert arrived. When she continued, her demeanor had changed abruptly. Whereas she was clearly angry and disturbed when talking about Forbes, she seemed genuinely saddened by what she had to tell us about the Cramers. "We especially liked 'Bonnie,' as everyone calls his wife, Lila. She is quite attractive and obviously caught up in the Washington social life. She is openly flirtatious and frankly it would not surprise me if she was having an affair with someone. The night Cramer killed himself, he asked Bonnie to go to New York and deliver an important message. I never found out to whom. After driving her to the station around midnight, her husband went home, asked the maid to get him some stamps, then went into his study to write letters. He also wrote a suicide note. Then he took a book of Oscar Wilde's poems, opened it to the page on which the poem 'Resquiescat,' appeared and inserted a newspaper clipping about the emerging bureau scandals and the news that a congressional investigation was being planned. He had marked the lines in 'Resquiescat':

> *All my life is buried here*
> *Heap earth upon it.*

Then he went into the bathroom and shot himself."

"And you heard the shot?" I asked.

"Yes. From our apartment in the Wardman Park. Some windows, which were open, look out on Woodley Road. It was early in the morning. I ran across the street to the Cramer house, found the body and called the police. And one curious thing: there were several stamped letters sitting on the mantle. But when I came back later in the morning, they were gone!"

"That is curious," said Mencken. "Did you ever find out what happened to them?"

"No, I only know that William Burns' men from the Justice Department were there after I was. I learned later that one of the letters was addressed to the president."

"I wonder what was in it?" I asked.

Rinehart replied: "My guess is that it contained an admission of wrong-doing in the bureau, that Cramer stressed his innocence but took full responsibility. And I have heard no evidence that he was directly involved in any of Forbes' skullduggery or that he in any way profited from it. I call it a case of public humiliation, a destroyed career and maybe a deteriorating marriage. That would be enough to drive many men to suicide."

Mrs. Rinehart was clearly quite disturbed about Cramer. I think

Mencken sensed this. He said: "So you think we ought to forget about Cramer."

"Yes," she replied, "and probably the bureau corruption, too. A Senate investigation is now in the works and several reporters—including Sullivan, Will Irwin and probably your own Frank Kent—are already digging into the story. Frankly, if I were you I would concentrate your investigations on the Justice and Interior Departments where the corruption is just in the rumor stage. But it should be surfacing soon."

"Oh?" said Mencken, picking up interest again. "Tell us more."

"Have you ever heard of Teapot Dome?"

"The government oil reserve that former Interior Secretary Fall leased to private oil companies?" Mencken responded.

"That's right. It's a sandstone rock that actually looks like a teapot. It's perched on a dome towering over four hundred acres about fifty miles north of Casper, Wyoming. It's barren land but it contains government oil reserves. And there's another oil field that Fall leased to the oil industry—at Elk Hill in California. From the start it was known that oil money would play a big part in the nomination of a Republican presidential candidate in 1920. One Republican delegate, Jake Hamon, an oil producer from Oklahoma who is reportedly worth twenty million dollars, bragged that he wrote the check that enabled Harding to run for president.

"He also said he was ready to give up to four hundred thousand dollars to anyone who would cooperate with the oil men and he virtually offered the nomination to General Wood if he would let Hamon name the Secretary of the Interior. Hamon told someone that the Interior was worth one hundred million dollars in oil to whoever controlled it. Wood threw Hamon out of his room and I'm sure Warren would have done the same thing if Hamon approached him. But I'm not sure about Daugherty. I suspect he would have promised Hamon anything to get the votes Harding needed. . . ."

"In a smoke-filled room, as we all know," Mencken interrupted, his eyes lighting up.

"In a smoke-filled room," Rinehart repeated, "no doubt just as Daugherty has described it."

"So what happened?" Mencken asked. "Did Harding get oil money at the convention?"

"I don't know. Hamon told one of his friends that Warren Harding's nomination cost him a million dollars and after Hamon's death his son told Hamon's lawyers that he had been promised one-third interest in Teapot Dome. But he never got it."

"Didn't someone murder him?" I asked.

"Yes. Hamon had a drunken fight with his mistress in their hotel room in Oklahoma City shortly after the election and she shot him. Hamon lived for four days and, oddly enough, Warren insisted to the end that Hamon was a wonderful fellow. He was quite shaken by his death."

"Maybe Gamaliel was afraid Hamon might have gotten religious on his death bed and confessed his sins," Mencken said. "A lot of big sinners do, you know. Harding might still be worried that some priest is walking around with the knowledge that Hamon bought a president—or at least a cabinet secretary—and is just waiting for the right reporter to come along and make a large contribution to the collection plate."

Mrs. Rinehart ignored Mencken's comment, and I asked her what she knew about Secretary Fall. She replied: "Everyone knew from the start that Secretary Fall favored leasing the Navy's oil reserves to the oil companies. As a senator, he was even in favor of doing away with the Interior Department altogether. In his new job he persuaded Harding to transfer authority over the government oil lands from the Navy Department to Interior, then he leased Teapot Dome to oil tycoon Harry Sinclair and Elk Hill to another oil man, Edward Doheny. Now there are rumors around that there were pay-offs. I wouldn't be surprised at anything Fall might do, but I want to stress that if there was some kind of payment I don't think any money went to the president personally."

Mencken indicated agreement: "Like Grant, dumb but honest, as I've always said. That's Harding. So what about the Justice Department? What's going on there?"

"Again, just rumors," Mary replied. "But from what I've heard—and Sullivan confirms this—the corruption there is worse than at the Veterans' Bureau. In fact, they're calling Justice 'the Department of Easy Virtue.' "

"Most everything right now seems to be rumors," said Mencken.

"That's right," Rinehart responded.

"But there are times," said Mencken, "when a rumor is almost as important as the truth—and it is a journalist's duty to tell their readers not only what has happened but what is reported, what is threatened, what is merely said."

"But you must make certain you report what is fact and what is rumor," replied Rinehart.

"Wasn't there a motion to impeach Daugherty in the Congress?" I asked.

"Yes, It was brought by Minnesota Congressman Oscar Keller primarily for showing favoritism by not prosecuting some possible fraud and appointing unsavory people to jobs in the department. But nobody pays much attention to Oscar and the House rejected the impeachment proposals two-oh-four to seventy-seven."

Then Rinehart looked at her watch and took a last swallow of her coffee. Mencken and I took the cue and also finished our coffee, which was getting cool. And Mencken caught the waiter's eye with the time-honored signal of pretending to sign the check. He asked one last question, "Isn't Daugherty involved with illegal liquor licensing?"

"I've got to run. But briefly, *someone* in the Justice Department is apparently selling liquor licenses as well as protection from prosecution and pocketing the money. They even managed to make money off the Dempsey-Carpentier fight a couple of years ago, although I'm not sure just how."

I saw Mencken pick up his interest here. Although he rarely writes about sports, he had written two columns on that championship fight and they were among the best things he has ever done. I will never forget the way he refuted the general belief that Carpentier had really beaten Dempsey. Admitting that the Frenchman had landed one good blow on Dempsey, Mencken then described how Dempsey "shuffled amiably" after Carpentier, hit him, then moved in for the kill. I've always thought that "shuffled amiably" was the perfect description.

"Anyway," Rinehart continued, "the key people at Justice to investigate are Daugherty, of course, his henchman Jesse Smith, Smith's ex-wife Roxy Stinson and an incredible character named Gaston B. Means, who used to work for the department until his shady actions became so well-known around town that Daugherty had to fire him. I heard that once the new Assistant Director of the Investigation Bureau, J. Edgar Hoover, got so enraged at Means that he threw him out of his office and told him to keep out."

I underlined "Gaston B. Means" in my notebook. And then, as Rinehart continued, both "Smith" and "Stinson."

"Jesse Smith and his ex-wife go back to the Ohio days when Daugherty first discovered Harding and was grooming him for the Senate, mainly because he looked so much like a president. Smith is virtually Daugherty's shadow. They live together and he goes everywhere with Daugherty. And although he does not work for Justice, he has an office near Daugherty in the department. He is divorced from Roxy, but they are still very close and she comes to Washington very often to see and be seen and shop. In fact, Sullivan says she's in town now, staying here at the Willard."

"Very good," said Mencken. "We've got to meet her."

"Well, I don't know how much time you'll have. Smith seems to have fallen out of favor recently and I understand Roxy has been ordered to go home to Washington Courthouse in Ohio and stay there. She's quite attractive, but rather outspoken. The word around town is that they both know enough about what's going on in the administration to put them all in jail. But again, not the president! As near as I can tell, Harding doesn't know any of this stuff, except, of course, for Charlie Forbes and the Veterans' Bureau."

"Do you know Smith?" I asked.

"No, I've never met him. Everyone speculates about his role and influence. He's a good pal of the president, plays poker and golf with him. The Duchess also likes Smith. He often goes to the White House. He's not hard to find. He spends a lot of time at the corner of 15th and H Streets in front of the Shoreham Hotel, just watching people walk by. He usually greets someone he knows with: 'What d'ya know?' When he's not in front of the Shoreham, he's at a house on K Street or up at the Justice Department where he has an office next to Daugherty's. They say he's the second most powerful man in Justice, although he's not on the department payroll. Very strange. He's a big jowly man with horn-rimmed glasses, always impeccably dressed in a Chesterfield and Homburg. You can't miss him."

Then with one last glance at her watch, Rinehart stood up to leave. Mencken and I also rose and, as Mencken helped her with her coat, she lowered her voice so that the people at the next table who appeared to recognize her, could not hear, and said: "Remember, Henry, I think the people at Sixteen Hundred Pennsylvania Avenue know none of this and I hope you can confirm it in your investigation." Then she turned and walked regally to the door, while several heads watched her as she left. Whether they recognized her or not, Mary Roberts Rinehart was a commanding presence.

"Quite a woman," was all Mencken could say.

"Formidable," I said in my fractured army French. "So, what do we do now? By the way, would you like some brandy?"

"Cheeeerist, I'd love a drink! But I don't think we have time. We ought to find this Roxy Stinson before she leaves town. And if we find her, we have to start right off acting like we're Pennsylvania bootleggers trying to find her ex-husband. Which means I have to do something to look less like Mencken, the anti-Christ from Baltimore. A few of these boobs from Ohio may actually read some newspapers or magazines and you know my picture's occasionally in them."

"I see your point. So what are you going to do?" The waiter arrived with the check.

"First, I have to get rid of this high-collar shirt, which is sort of a trademark. I'll go across the street to Garfinkle's and buy a low-collar one. While I'm there I'm going to stop at Draper's Cigar store on F Street and buy a box of Willies. Then I'll come back to the men's room here, change my shirt and try to comb my hair different. And when you see me next, I'll be wearing my reading glasses. And don't forget, if you find Stinson before I get back, be sure to introduce me by some other name. How about Fritz Mercker?"

"That sounds like a German bootlegger from Pennsylvania. Maybe I'd better use another name too, though I'm sure none of them ever heard of James M. Cain. How about Jim Payne?"

"P-A-Y-N-E or P-A-I-N?" Mencken responded as he picked up the check and brought out his wallet.

"Take your choice. Just out of curiosity, how much is it?"

"Less than nine dollars for the whole thing, including tip. But don't worry, I can put it all on my expense account. We learned a lot."

"Yeah, but how much can we print?"

"Not much now."

Mencken went toward the headwaiter table to pay the check and

I headed for the marble-columned front desk. As I approached the lobby, I looked back and could see the bow-legged Mencken with his characteristic short steps walking rapidly up Peacock Alley toward the F Street exit. He almost looked like he was strutting.

When I reached the desk, I asked the concierge if he had a Miss Roxy Stinson registered at the hotel.

"Well, yes, or rather I guess, no," he answered in a European-accented voice befitting a concierge in a large fashionable hotel. "What I mean is, she checked out about noon. She's having lunch now at the Ebbitt Grill. But mademoiselle is coming back for her luggage which is still checked here."

"Good," I said, "when she returns would you tell her that Mr. Payne would like to meet her? That he's very anxious to contact Mr. Smith, her ex-husband. I'll be in the lounge. Also, a Mr. Mercker will be looking for me. You can tell him, too."

CHAPTER THREE

I was in the Willard lounge having a brandy and coffee when this woman walked in. She was the same woman we had seen at the front desk just before lunch. Everything about her said Roxy. Of course, I had no idea it was she. But after taking one good look at this tall, magnificent specimen, I just wanted it to be Roxy Stinson. It was.

Although she wore a turban-style hat and a sealskin coat, I could tell she had red hair and a good figure. Her dress was dark and long and the whole impression was very stylish. Whoever bought her clothes could afford the best.

I was the only person in the lounge, so she did not hesitate to walk immediately toward me, extending her hand as she approached. "Mr. Payne, I presume. The concierge—oh, I never can pronounce that right—said you would like to see me."

I was sitting on a long, cushioned seat against the wall, but as she walked toward me I stood up to greet her. With a closer look, I could see that her eyes were brown, her eyelids had a soft, bedroom look, her nose was a tad longer than it needed to be, but was classic in design, and her mouth, also, was slightly wider than you might expect and very inviting. Her coat hung open so I could see a low-cut dress revealing a gold choker with a single jewel in the center positioned just above the barely visible tops of her large, firm breasts. She spoke very confidently in a voice that suggested stage training. And, frankly, as I took her outstretched hand I felt like giving her a good hug and then pulling her down on the seat beside me as if we were old friends. Instead I mumbled: "Yes. And I presume you are Roxy Stinson—or should I say Mrs. Smith?"

"No, I'm back to my maiden name. But I am the ex-Mrs. Smith. And Jesse, my ex, will be along pretty soon. He's down the street at the *Washington Post*, seeing Ned McLean about something. You know, Ned owns the *Post* and is married to Evalyn Walsh McLean, who owns the famous Hope Diamond. Jesse just loves diamonds, don't you, Mr. Payne?"

I allowed that diamonds were everybody's friend, which brought a nice smile. Then I sat down and invited her to sit beside me. She did so rather quickly, settling just a little closer to my left than I might expect, which I found very pleasing. "Would you like me to order you some water or soda? I have a little brandy to go with it, if that appeals to you?"

"Oh, that's a marvelous idea. I'll have some soda. I was going back to Ohio this evening, but Jesse asked me to stay over so we could go to the ball game tomorrow afternoon. The Indians are in town and we're both big Cleveland fans, naturally, being from Ohio. Are you a baseball fan?"

I motioned the waiter over and ordered soda for Roxy and water for me. "I'm definitely not a Senators fan. You know what they say about Washington: 'First in war, first in peace, first in the hearts of his countrymen; last in the American League.' I kinda like the Yankees, but I don't really follow the game that closely."

"Oh, that's too bad. It's such fun. You ought to give it more of a try."

"Well, maybe I would if Babe Ruth still played in Baltimore where he started, where I live now. I guess he's the main reason I like the Yankees."

"Probably so," she replied. "So you're from Baltimore. Why do you want to see my husband? I know you didn't come all the way to Washington just to see me."

"Well I would have," I replied. I was about to explain the reason for wanting to meet Jesse Smith, when I noticed the waiter approaching with the water and soda, so I decided to wait. Then, after he had put the glasses on the little table in front of us and left the room, I said: "My friend from Pennsylvania, who should arrive any minute now, is in the cigar business and he wants to see Mr. Smith about obtaining a permit to buy some liquor. We understand he's the man in Washington to see about such things."

"He certainly is. You understand I don't get too involved in his business. But he works directly for Harry Daugherty, who is the attorney general of the United States—a personal friend of President Harding, like Jesse."

Before I could ask about her marital status, which intrigued me, I noticed Mencken coming in the door. He had his coat over his arm and was holding his wide-brimmed hat in his hand, which was too bad. He should be wearing it. He wore a low-cut collar and glasses which looked fine, but his hair was an absolute mess. (He later told me he had trouble parting it on the side, an understatement, which he rarely makes.) And as he approached us, it was apparent that he was attempting a limping shuffle, not that anyone would know how the Baltimore anti-Christ walked from seeing his picture in the paper or a magazine. "Miss Stinson, this is Fred Mercker," I said, "my friend from Pennsylvania who is anxious to obtain a liquor permit."

"Pleased to meet you, Mr. Mercker," she said, as she accepted Mencken's outstretched hand. "Sit down and join us."

Mencken took a chair on the other side of the table and laid his hat and coat on another empty chair. "I notice Miss Stinson, that you're sitting kinda close to Mr. Payne. Be careful, he's a leg pincher and—when possible—a garter-snapper."

"Oh dear," said Roxy, mocking a damsel-in-distress and quickly moving about a foot to my left. Then she asked Mencken: "How about a little drink? I'm sure Mr. Payne has enough brandy. My ex-husband, Jesse Smith, will be here shortly."

Mencken, to my surprise, declined, saying: "I never drink hard liquor in the daytime and I know we can't get a beer here—although I bet if I went up to Pennsylvania Avenue and down the street to that big white house on the other side of the Treasury Department I could."

"That's for sure, if you know the president well enough to be invited upstairs," Roxy said, laughing. After I ordered another round of water, Roxy looked at a stylish, bejeweled watch on her arm, and said: "I wonder what's keeping Jesse? How did you boys hear about him, anyway?"

"My bootician, or bootlegger, in Pennsylvania," replied Mencken, "recommended him or a Mr. Gaston B. Means as people who might help me obtain a liquor permit."

"Don't worry," said Roxy, "I know what a bootician is. I read *The Smart Set* too, although I'm the only one in Washington Courthouse, Ohio, that does."

Mencken and I looked at each other, smiled and nodded our

approval. "Well then," I said, "with that as a measure of your sophistication, you should know that a gentleman of my obvious re-
finement does not go around pinching ladies' legs and snapping
garters. So you can move back," I added, and gave her arm a gentle
tug in my direction. "And I think you ought to know that this, can
I say, 'gentleman,' sitting across from you is a confirmed bachelor
whom I have heard say, 'If I ever marry at all, it will be on sudden
impulse, as a man shoots himself.' He furthermore has said that
marriage is based on the theory that when a man discovers a particular brand of beer to his taste that he should at once throw up
his job and go to work in a brewery."

Mencken, knowing I was quoting Nathan here, affected a frown
as I concluded: "He also says that love is the delusion that one
woman differs from another, whereas I, dear lady, have always felt
that love is the discovery that one woman *does* differ from another."
The waiter had brought more water during my little discourse and
now I added the brandy, giving Roxy a little extra on this round.

Mencken, still frowning, quickly stepped in to defend his position. "It's true I've made some comments in the mood and attitude
suggested by Mr. Payne, usually in my cups and probably in the
aftermath of a disappointing love affair. But those who know me—
and even Payne, if he will admit it—have heard me express more
laudatory thoughts because I am convinced that the average woman,
whatever her deficiencies, is greatly superior to the average man.
For example, her intuition, her famous feminine intuition if you will.
It is far superior to men's."

Roxy, smiling, raised her brandy and soda in a salute to
Mencken, who, obviously encouraged, continued, really picking up
steam now, revealing what I was gradually becoming aware of, that
he talks almost exactly as he writes: "A man thinks he is more
intelligent than his wife because he can add up a column of figures
more accurately, understand the imbecile jargon of the stock market,
is able to distinguish between the ideas of rival politicians and because he is privy to the minutiae of some sordid and degrading
business or profession, say soap-selling or the law. But these empty
talents, of course, are not really signs of profound intelligence; they
are, in fact, merely superficial accomplishments and put little more
strain on the mental powers than a chimpanzee suffers in learning
how to catch a penny or scratch a match."

He paused for just a moment, trying to pat down the unnatural part in his hair, but when I started to comment, he rushed on, giving me my first taste of a real Mencken monologue: "The best and most intellectual, original and enterprising play-actors are not men but women; so are the best teachers and blackmailers. If the work of the average man required half the mental agility and readiness of resource of the work of the average prostitute, the average man would be constantly on the verge of starvation. They are the supreme realists of the race. It is a rare man, I venture, who is as steadily intelligent, as constantly sound in judgment, as little put off by appearances, as the average woman of forty-eight."

Then, he picked up his glass, saying, "A toast to Miss Stinson, a superb specimen of her species."

I was not sure how Roxy was reacting to Mencken's performance. At first she was amused. But by the time he had finished she seemed in wonderment that anyone could go that long on one subject. She obviously did not know many writers. But she clearly was amused. "Thank you for the compliment, Mr. Mercker, although I assure you I'm still a few years from forty-eight."

Turning to me, she said: "Well, what do you say to that, Mr. Payne?"

I was still laughing to myself and could hardly refrain from telling Roxy that Mencken was quoting from one of the most mistitled books in American literature, his *In Defense of Women*. I was just straining to quote one passage I remembered well: "The average woman, until art comes to her aid, is ungraceful, misshapen, badly calved and crudely articulated, even for a woman . . . As for ethics, women not only bite in the clinches, they bite even in open fighting."

Instead, I replied: "I can attest that he has expressed those views in one form or another many times. But I can document his views on marriage. So no matter how well you get to know him, do not expect a proposal from Mr. Mercker any more than you can expect a garter snap from me."

"Well, that clears that up," she said, indicating that as far as she was concerned we had exhausted the topic of women. "I just love staying at the Willard, it's so historical. Don't you agree?"

Mencken nodded and said: "It's the place where most Presidents-elect in recent years have spent the night before inauguration. I heard that when the Hardings stayed here just before his swearing-in that the Secret Service was not worried about assassins—as they were in Lincoln's first inauguration—but that one of his girlfriends would show up at the hotel. Any truth to that, Miss Stinson?"

"Oh, we all know the president has his girlfriends. Most gentlemen do, you know. But I can't tell you any names. I know a lot about what goes on in Washington that I can't talk about. My ex-husband is very close to Harry Daugherty. In fact, he lives with him now. And Harry is probably closer to Warren Harding than anyone in Washington. The president wouldn't be president if it wasn't for Harry Daugherty and Jesse is very close to the Hardings, too. He plays golf with the president and visits the Duchess—that's Mrs. Harding—in the White House all the time. I've been to White House parties a couple of times myself. So, you see, I have to be very discreet about what I say."

Suddenly Roxy stopped and looked at a large, jowly man wearing a gray felt hat and a gray chesterfield coat standing in the doorway of the lounge. As he quickly approached our group, Roxy said: "Here comes Jesse now," and she stood up to greet him. Mencken and I also rose waiting to shake hands with Smith. "Jesse," Roxy said, "this is Fred Mercker and Jim Payne. I think Mr. Mercker is from Pennsylvania and Mr. Payne's from Baltimore. They've been waiting to see you about obtaining a liquor permit. I told them you could take care of them."

"Good to meet you, Mr. Smith," Mencken said, "won't you join us for a drink?"

"No, I'm afraid I can't. Jud Welliver, he's the president's personal secretary, tracked me down in Ned McLean's office at the *Post*. Warren wants to see me and you don't keep the president waiting. Tell you what. Why don't you come around and see me at my office at 1625 K Street? I have an office in the Justice Department, too. But I also do some business at the K Street place. It's a little green house. You can't miss it. See you at ten o'clock tomorrow morning, if that's okay with you?" As he talked, he took a pen and a little green notebook out of his pocket and scribbled in it.

"That'll be fine," Mencken replied. "I have a reference, by the way," and he pulled Smith away from us and whispered something in his ear. I could hear Smith reply: "That's good. I'll have Gaston Means check it out." Then Mencken found out why they say: "Put up your umbrella when you see Jesse Smith coming." He was treated to a good spray of saliva. Smith seemed quite impressed with his own importance, but at the same time he seemed disturbed, as if he had the weight of all the administration problems on his shoulders.

He continued his spraying as he spoke: "Sorry I have to rush off, gentlemen. I know I leave you in good hands with Roxy. But if you don't mind, I'd like a word in private with her. I'll see you both tomorrow." With that, he took his ex-wife by the hand and led her out into the little vestibule beyond the door and perhaps out into the lobby. We could not see them from where we sat in the lounge.

After we had resumed our seats at the little table and I ordered some more water and soda from the waiter, I asked Mencken: "What was all that about—whispering something in Smith's ear?"

"Oh, I forgot to tell you. I talked to my bootician in Pennsylvania and told him I was going to try to get a liquor permit in Washington and could I use his name as a reference. I whispered it because I felt more comfortable not bandying my friend's name about in a public place. He does business with someone in Washington, too. His operation is just outside Bethlehem, where, incidentally, they're having their annual Bach festival soon. Joe Hergesheimer and I are going up. They have a great saloon in the area almost as good as the one at Union Hill, New Jersey, which Red Lewis, Phil Goodman and a few others frequent. You'll have to join us sometime. They claim to have a pipeline direct to Munich."

I nodded agreement that it would be fun to join them. The waiter arrived with the water and soda, and after he left, I poured more brandy into our glasses just as Roxy returned and sat down close to me again. Just to see what would happen, I pressed my leg against hers. She did not respond and but neither did she remove her leg.

Then Mencken said to Roxy: "You remember when I whispered the name of my reference to your husband, he said he would refer it to Gaston Means. Why Means?"

"Oh, don't worry about that. Gaston checks out all the liquor permit requests. He does a lot of work for William Burns and Harry Daugherty in the Justice Department. One thing he can do easily is make sure you're not a Prohibition agent."

"What!" Mencken almost shouted. "Me, a Prohibition agent! I'd more likely be a Methodist minister."

"Well if your reference is okay you won't have any trouble with Gaston." She took a long swallow from her glass and said: "Anyway, didn't Mr. Payne say you made cigars? Isn't that one of the businesses you can get alcohol for?"

"That's my business all right. Been in it for years; so was my father and my grandfather. I usually work on improving the cigar. I just love the aroma. The leaf is a precious article that comes from distant lands. It has to be handled with care. Blending a cigar is like mixing a drink. I tried to grow some tobacco in my backyard but it was a disaster. I do much better brewing my own beer. Once, I tried moistening the cheaper Pennsylvania tobacco with wine to make it smell like genuine Havana, but that didn't work out so well.

"Yeah, I can get some alcohol, but I'd like some better stuff than what they'll give me for cigars. And I have other uses for it—like drinking it. And I have a lot of friends. I understand from my bootician in Pennsylvania that it's not too hard to get if you know the right people. So here we are."

"Well don't worry. I'm sure Jesse will take care of you."

"That's good to hear. Your husband seems like a man with a lot on his mind. Must be something big—being invited to the White House for a special meeting with the president."

"Jesse thinks the president wants to invite him to join the group that's going on his trip to Alaska this summer. Anyone who is anyone in this administration is going. I think Harry's going. I don't see how they could leave Jesse out of it. But you know how politics are. You never know what's going to happen from day to day. You involved in politics much, Mr. Mercker?"

"Don't get my friend started on politics," I intervened, thinking we had better get out of here soon, before Mencken starts talking about Gamaliel and blows the whole thing.

"Jim's right," Mencken replied and quickly confirmed my concern by saying: "I don't think much of politics or politicians. I think it would be a good idea to hang a couple of congressmen chosen by lot, every year, right next to the Washington Monument. And one senator, every other year, only because there are fewer of them. You could throw two-thirds of them in the Potomac and they'd never be missed."

Roxy laughed and said: "Oh, Mr. Mercker, you say the damnedest things for a cigar maker."

Mencken seemed to catch himself, aware that he had easily slipped out of his role as a cigar maker in town seeking an illicit liquor permit. Instead, he took the large watch out of his pocket and announced that it was time for us to leave.

I knew I had to move quickly if I was ever to see this attractive woman again. More in the nature of a friendly gesture than an advance, I reached down, lightly touched her knee, and said: "It was a pleasure to meet you, Miss Stinson . . . Roxy . . . and we appreciate your introducing us to your husband. You said you were staying in town at least another day to go the ball game. Is there any chance we could see you again before you leave?"

"I don't know Mr. Payne, I'd like to stay indefinitely. I just love Washington. The people here are so interesting. But for some reason, Jesse seems to think I ought to be getting back to Ohio as soon as possible. Tell you what. You're going to be at Jesse's office in the morning. And I'm supposed to meet him there about noon to go out to Griffith Stadium. Walter Johnson's pitching for Washington. Maybe you could join us?"

"I'm not much of a fan," Mencken replied. "But Johnson always packs the stadium when he pitches. So it'll be a good day for my father, no matter who wins."

"How's that?" I asked, somewhat surprised at his remark. I also wondered how smart it was to mention his father.

"He owns some stock in the Washington Club."

"Well, I declare," said Roxy. "Is that a good stock? Jesse and I sometimes go into the market together. Would you recommend Senators stock?"

"Probaby not. I never heard my father talk about making any money from it. He just did it because he liked baseball so much."

"So does Jesse. He often takes his and Harry's clients to the game. Harry usually goes. But he's sick with the flu. I know you're not a fan, Jim, but it's a fun time. You know, peanuts, popcorn and Cracker Jack . . ."

"And we don't care if we never get back," I picked up. I was really beginning to fall for this woman, despite our age difference. "I agree it would be fun. How 'bout it Hen . . . I mean Fred. You going to join us?" I asked Mencken, hoping Roxy did not catch my slip and, frankly, wanting him to say no. I had visions of escorting Roxy back to her hotel room alone after the game.

"Come on, Mr. Mercker," Roxy said in a voice hard to resist, "you must like peanuts; they go good with beer."

"Well, if we could get some beer at a baseball game that would make it civilized and bearable . . ."

"I think that could be arranged," Roxy said before Mencken had a chance to decline. "We have our resources. They never check Jesse's party at the gate and we have a nice, Justice Department box where they leave us alone."

"That does it," said Mencken, looking at me as if to say "You're not going to get rid of me." "So we'll see you at Mr. Smith's office about noon tomorrow."

"Good," said Roxy with real enthusiasm as she rose to see us off. "I'll walk with you to the lobby. I want to find the newsstand and get something to read while I wait for Jesse. I think the new issue of *The Smart Set* is out. I just love that George Nathan and his Broadway reviews. Do you read the magazine, Fred?" she asked of Mencken who was walking closest to her.

"Madame, I might even compare it to the *Bible*. I read it religiously."

"I thought you did," she replied. "Sometimes you sound like them."

"What do you think of that other fellow who writes for the magazine?" I asked. "I think his name is Mencken, a name similar to Fred's. He must be German, too?"

"I know he's German. I think he even supported the kaiser during the war—which is one thing I don't like about him. But he can be funny, although sometimes he's sort of smart-alecky. Know what I mean?"

"I do indeed, ma'am. I do indeed," Mencken replied. And taking some coins out of his pocket, he added: "Let me have the pleasure and honor of giving you the thirty-five cents necessary to purchase this excellent publication."

"Well, thank you, kind sir," she said, taking the money without hesitation. "See you at the ball game."

CHAPTER FOUR

The next morning we were on the train again bound for Washington. Only this time we had small bags of clean shirts, underwear and shaving kits because we hoped to persuade Roxy and Smith to join us for dinner after the game. If we were successful we would be late that night so we had made reservations by telephone for a room at the Willard.

Mencken, in his effort to disguise himself and appear as a cigar maker, was wearing a low-collar, striped shirt, a flowered tie and a hideous plaid suit, which he borrowed from a neighbor who only wore it to church on Sunday. His hair, with the help of some kind of goo, was holding its unnatural part a little better today. He was wearing his dark, wide-brimmed felt hat and he had a pair of reading glasses he planned to put on when they arrived at Smith's office.

Needing no disguise, I was wearing my usual rumpled suit and a wide-brimmed felt hat.

"My office is on the third floor of our house on Hollins Street," Mencken said, after we had settled in our seats, "and the telephone is downstairs, and that means going down two flights of stairs whenever some swine who just wants to tell me that my comments in the column about some phony evangelist will surely get me in Hell for eternity calls me up. But those damned phones sure are handy for getting information."

He paused to light a Willie and stamp the match out on the floor: "I called my bootician in Pennsylvania and learned how the fraudulent permit system works. It's very simple. The Bureau of Prohibition is becoming a training school for bootleggers. For the right price, you are issued a 'B' permit enabling you to draw liquor from a government-controlled distillery for purposes other than imbibing or pleasure—usually for medical use or for some industry. Tobacco companies use it to treat their leaves, so my pose as a tobacco manufacturer is a perfect cover. You never know whom you're paying the money to; usually you just put it on the table in a rented hotel room. He also confirmed that Jesse Smith is the best contact, although he heard that Gaston B. Means can also take care of you. It'll cost us some good money, but that's no problem. The Saturday Night Club will foot part of the bill and I'll come up with the rest. Hell, I can make enough money off Red Lewis alone to make the whole deal worthwhile."

"Well, I'll put in a little if I can get a few bottles of brandy," I said.

"I'm not sure what we're going to end up with, but I'll keep that in mind. I also talked to Frank Kent—you know Frank, he's head of our Washington bureau now—and he said there's a Denver reporter in Washington trying to interest reporters in finding out how the former Secretary of the Interior, Albert Fall, can afford to spend so much money refurbishing his ranch in New Mexico. But nobody is paying much attention to this."

"We ought to." I had made some telephone calls myself. "One of my friends confirmed what Kent says. The Denver reporter's name is Stackelback, but the man we really want to talk to is Harry Slattery, a Washington lawyer who used to work for Gifford Pinchot when he ran the Bureau of Forestry in Roosevelt's Administration. What else did you learn?"

"That's about it, except for a little tidbit I picked up from George Nathan in New York. He called me this morning about a problem on the magazine. Awfully early for him, considering that he partied last night. In fact, she was still in his apartment when he called. The woman's in New York's artsy, money, social set in which Nathan likes to travel. He heard from her a rumor that Evalyn Walsh McLean's famous Hope Diamond has been stolen. It's not been reported to the police because people in the Justice Department think maybe someone in the Harding administration might have 'borrowed' it. And get this! Nathan's friend thinks the McLean dame doesn't even know it's missing! You know, Cain, the diamond is said to bring trouble to anyone who owns it."

"I wonder if Jesse Smith had anything to do with its disappearance?" I speculated. "Roxy made a strange comment to me after mentioning that Ned McLean's wife owned the diamond. She said

'Jesse just loves diamonds,' as if anyone would give a damn how much her ex-husband loves 'em."

The Hope Diamond, as every reader of the Sunday woman's pages in the newspapers knows, was named after Henry Philip Hope, a wealthy Dutch banker, whose company helped finance the Louisiana Purchase, a fact not generally known. Hope purchased it from a London diamond merchant named Daniel Eliason in 1830 for £18,000 (about $90,000, a pretty good sum, even today). At the time there were rumors that the diamond, which is blue and was described by Jules Jusserand, the French Ambassador to the U.S. during World War I, as "an ominous, unearthly stone with millions of sardonic winks," had actually been cut from a much larger blue diamond that had been stolen from the French crown jewels in 1792. But the legend went back three hundred years to India.

"You know," Mencken said, "the Gods are supposed to have put a curse on this trinket after it was stolen from a Hindu totem pole and when the Gods get in the act, you had better beware."

"Well, I read the Sunday papers and I can tell you that if the legends are true we had better watch out." And I recounted for Mencken as best I could the stories behind the diamond's curse: "The French jeweler who brought the diamond from India to France in 1668—John Baptiste Tavernier—and sold it to the French royal family lost his fortune and was said to have been torn apart by wild dogs in Russia. Louis XIV loaned it to his finance minister to attend a ball, then executed him the next day. Louis' death from gangrene was attributed to the diamond. The Princess de Lamballe, who had worn the diamond, was torn to pieces by a French mob. Louis XVI and Marie Antoinette, who inherited the diamond, both went to the guillotine. The Dutch diamond cutter who recut the blue diamond died of grief after his son (who later committed suicide) stole the diamond. A man named Beaulieu, who was said to have obtained the diamond from someone who committed suicide, was on the verge of bankruptcy and died of starvation the day after he was forced to sell the diamond to Daniel Eliason. Eliason, of course, sold it to Hope, who passed it on to his heirs, and the entire Hope family suffered an assortment of scandals and hardships too numerous to mention. One Hope married the American actress May Yohe who wore it for awhile until her marriage to Hope broke up."

"I remember her," Mencken interrupted, " 'Madcap May Yohe,' they called her. She created quite a scandal when she ran off with the son of a former mayor of New York."

"Yeah," I continued, "and her ex-husband had to have a leg amputated after accidentally shooting himself in a hunting accident."

"The Gods move in mysterious ways, their curses to perform," Mencken said.

I went on with the story: "After its time with the Hopes, the diamond ended up with a New York dealer who sold it to a French broker named Colot who went mad and committed suicide. Then a Russian prince got hold of the diamond and loaned it to a Folies-Bergère actress who was shot on stage by her lover while she was wearing the diamond. Then a Greek jeweller who sold the diamond to the Sultan of Turkey was forced over a cliff while riding in a car with his wife and child. They were all killed. Evalyn Walsh McLean bought it in 1911 for three hundred thousand dollars and then the stories about its curses and bad luck started appearing in the newspapers. And they intensified eight years later when the McLeans' nine-year-old first-born son, Vinson, was run over by a Ford touring car while playing in front of the huge McLean estate at Friendship—on the outskirts of Washington."

"So now we know all we need to know about the Hope Diamond," Mencken said when I finished. "You do do a lot of newspaper reading, Cain, and you have pretty good recall. You know what intrigues me is why wealthy men like to decorate their women with these gaudy, expensive baubles. Have you ever tried to read any Veblen, especially his *Theory of the Leisure Classes?*"

"Not much, but I read your essay in the first volume of *Prejudices.*"

"What a ponderous bore," Mencken said, his eyes lighting up as they often do when he talks about one of his pieces. "I remember quoting a Veblen paragraph which totalled two hundred forty-one words, of which two hundred were totally unnecessary. Just what did he really mean by this 'non-reverent sense of aesthetic congruity?' I studied the whole paragraph for three days, halting only for prayer and sleep, and I finally decided that what he was trying to say (or obscure) was that 'many people go to church not because they are afraid of the devil but because they enjoy the music, like to look at the stained glass, the potted lilies and the Reverend pastor.'

It took him a page and he could have said it all on a postage stamp. In another long section in his *Theory,* when boiled down, he seemed to be saying that rich men hung their wives with expensive clothes and jewelry for the same reason they drove expensive cars—to notify everyone that they could afford them and to excite the envy of the Marxists.

"So much for Veblen," he said suggesting he was ready to drop the subject. But he wasn't. "There's one passage in his *Theory* that exposes the whole thing for what it is—one percent platitude and ninety-nine percent nonsense! He asks two questions: One, why do we have lawns in our country houses? and two, why don't we use cows to keep them trim rather than hired hands? I'm sure you remember?"

I did; in fact, everyone who read Mencken at the beginning of the 1920s knew his Veblen cow theory as it was known on the campuses. But I made no effort to halt his repeating it and nodded.

"I don't object to his economic interpretation of history in E-flat to the effect that we delight in lawns because we are a descendant of pastoral people inhabiting a region with a humid climate. But why do we renounce cows and hire Jugo-Slaves? Veblen says we do it because 'to the average popular apprehension a herd of cattle so pointedly suggests thrift and usefulness that their presence would be intolerably cheap.' Can you imagine anything sillier than this? Has the good professor, pondering his great problems, ever taken a walk in the country? And has he, in the course of that walk, ever crossed a pasture inhabited by a cow? And has he, making that crossing, ever passed astern of the cow herself? And has he, thus passing astern, ever stepped carelessly, and . . .

"Well, why go on? Can this geyser of pishposh be relied upon to tell us why rich men give their wives expensive diamonds? I don't think so."

"Or why they give their cows bells," I said. "Maybe Smith or Roxy can enlighten us today."

We arrived at Union Station and, running a little late, decided to take a taxicab directly to 1625 K Street.

As we walked toward the waiting cabs, Mencken said: "Did you know this whole area was once called 'swampdoodle' where the pickpockets and bums and prostitutes used to hang out? And not too far from here," he said, pointing in the general direction of the

Mall, "was where the ladies of the honorable and oldest profession got their name during the Civil War, when General Joe Hooker created for his army a red light district and the ladies quickly became known as 'Hooker's Division.' "

"The city comes by its sins honestly," I said.

Pausing to light a cigar and stamp the match out with his foot, he replied: "Cain, m'boy, Gamaliel's sins against the American people are nothing compared to his sins against the American language. Setting aside a college professor or two and a half-dozen reporters, Gamaliel takes first place in my Valhalla of literati. He writes the worst English I ever encountered. It reminds me of a string of wet sponges. It's so bad, a sort of grandeur creeps into it. But I tell you, Cain, old Gamaliel, bad as he is, is still better than most of our presidents—that scoundrel Wilson, for example."

I dissented: "I'll take Wilson any day over Harding. After all, I recently went to war with his encouragement to make the world safe for democracy."

"Democracy!" he virtually exploded. "Don't get me started on that. I don't believe in it."

"Okay, our government isn't perfect," I said, "but it works and has for some time."

"Yes, the government goes on. . . ." But before he could continue, our taxi was making a U-turn on K Street and pulling up to the 1625 address.

It was, just as Smith had described it, a little green stone house with a nice magnolia in bloom in its front yard. I would learn later that it belonged to Ned McLean, who also owned another house on H Street that Smith and Daugherty lived in when they first came to Washington. Now they have an apartment at the Wardman Park Hotel. Daugherty's wife is in Ohio, although she spends a lot of time at Johns Hopkins due to her arthritis.

As Smith's secretary ushered us into his little office, Smith was hastily putting some papers in his desk drawer. He was dressed in a gray suit with white shirt and matching purple hankerchief and tie.

"Well, whadda you know; good to see you boys again," Smith said, spraying Mencken, who was shaking hands with him, with saliva. Mencken, who fears germs, noticeably showed his annoyance.

"Can I offer you some drinks?" Smith asked.

"No, too early for the hard stuff," said Mencken, indicating that he was speaking for both of us. "But I hope you'll bring something—preferably beer—along for the ball game. Roxy invited us, if that's all right with you?"

"Fine with me," Smith sprayed. "I've asked Gaston Means to join us. He's doing a little checking and he's anxious to meet both of you. I'll have plenty to drink at the game."

Good news about the liquor because we hoped to loosen Smith and Roxy's tongues, although Smith seemed tight as a drum, as if he expected a calamity at any minute. "Roxy and Gaston will be along before noon and we'll go directly to the game from here," Smith said, motioning us both to sit down in a couple of stiff, wooden chairs that were facing his desk. He seated himself in a soft, leather swivel chair and said: "You'll like him. Harry's mad at him now, but he's a good man. Gaston's been working up in New York, but Harry brought him back to Washington last fall. He got the attention of Assistant Attorney General Mabel Willebrandt, who runs the department's Prohibition program, with his work on the LaMontagne Brothers case. Have you heard of them?"

"Yeah," Mencken said. "A friend of mine who lives in New York told me about them. They were an old, highly respected wine importer before Prohibition and they had a store on Madison Avenue. After Prohibition, they moved down to West Thirty-fourth street, where they set up shop as society's bootleggers. My friend said they sold wine and whiskey to Vincent Astor, Mrs. William K. Vanderbilt, the First National City Bank and the New York Racquet and Tennis Club."

Mencken's friend must be Nathan, and he was referring to a liquor bust that everyone in New York was talking about.

"That's right," Smith continued. "Well, Gaston persuaded the LaMontagne Brothers' bookkeeper to show the company's records to the Justice Department. All four brothers were indicted, fined, banned from the liquor business for three years and sentenced to prison from two to four months. I can tell you, Daugherty and Willebrandt were really impressed with Gaston on that case."

Mencken was looking slightly puzzled as Smith told us about Means and the LaMontagne brothers. And I was too. Why was Smith, known on the street as one of the men to see about illegal permits to draw liquor from government warehouses, telling us, seemingly with some pride, about the work of another source of illegal permits who was applauded for busting some people whom Smith and Means must have been doing business with or protecting? Was he trying to show us what happens if we double-cross them or didn't go along with their prices? Were they blackmailing the LaMontagne brothers? Or did they just bust someone every now and then to pretend that they weren't on the take?

I could tell Mencken was also pondering this mystery, when suddenly one of the two telephones on Smith's desk rang and Smith nearly jumped out of his chair.

"Excuse me," he said, seeming to anticipate bad news as he picked up the phone: "Jesse Smith talking . . . Oh, hello, Harry. Hope you're feeling better." And he paused while obviously listening to a medical report from his caller.

"That's good," he said. Then another long pause as he listened, his face giving us no hint as to whether he was hearing good news— or no news.

"Well, I'm glad to hear that," Smith finally said. "Give my best to Warren. I'll see you in a couple of days." And he put the telephone earpiece back on its hanger.

"That was Harry," Smith said in a manner designed, I thought, to impress us that he was on a first-name basis with the attorney general and the president. "He's just getting over the flu. And he's going to the White House for a couple of days to rest up and be with the president. They have some business to take care of."

"Are the ramparts being threatened?" Mencken asked.

"No, nothing like that, just some housekeeping stuff."

Smith seemed to want to change the subject, but Mencken persisted: "You were called to the White House yesterday. I hope everything's all right with you and the president?"

"Oh, certainly. Warren and I go way back to his first days in politics. He just wanted to let me know that I might not be going along on his Alaska trip this summer. He wanted to tell me personally and assure me that the main reason is that I'll be needed here. No big deal. I do have quite a bit of work to do for Harry at the Justice Department."

"Speaking of work," Mencken said to Smith, "we would like to explore the possibility of obtaining a permit to buy some liquor from one of your government warehouses. Roxy may have told you, I'm in the cigar business and have need for this alcohol. But I could use a little extra, if you know what I mean."

"Sure do," Smith replied, "but Gaston handles most of these permits now. And as soon as he completes his security check, he'll be contacting you and let you know the fee. I'm certain there'll be no problem."

"Well, that was quick. I like the way you do business in Washington," Mencken said.

There was an awkward silence for a few moments, but before anyone could break the tension we heard a loud commotion in the outer office. Suddenly a short, heavy-set man wearing a derby, a light-colored suit and carrying a coat over his arm, burst into the room, and Smith said: "Ah, George, I was expecting you tomorrow."

"Well, this damned well can't wait 'til tomorrow," the intruder replied.

"George, I want you to meet Fritz Mercker and his assistant Jim Payne. They're in the tobacco business and we're talking about some permits," Smith said, introducing the new arrival as "George Remus, one of my clients."

"Smith, we have a little crisis," Remus replied, loudly. "If these guys are paying you more than I am then I'll wait a minute while you finish with them. If not, please ask them to come back tomorrow, because we've got some serious business to discuss."

Smith was obviously rattled. "Of course we can talk now, George. Will you excuse us, gentlemen," he said to us. Then to Remus: "Why don't we step into my private office. How 'bout a drink?"

"You know I just sell the stuff," Remus replied as they exited.

When they were gone, Mencken moved quickly to Smith's desk and began searching through the top drawer. He pulled out some papers, ruffled through them quickly, then separated one out, found a pad and pencil on Smith's desk and began making some hasty notes.

Mencken had just finished his note-taking and returned Smith's papers to the desk drawer when Roxy Stinson arrived. "Good to see

you two gentlemen again," she said cheerfully, and the very sound
of her voice brightened the room. She looked stunning, dressed in
a sporty sweater, skirt and jacket that did not hide the contours of
her full body. Then, surveying the room with her big eyes she asked:
"Where's Jesse? He should certainly be here by now."

"He's in the next room," I said, "with a man named George
Remus." We could hear them and although we could not understand
what they were saying, it was obviously an agitated, even hostile
confrontation. When I mentioned Remus, Roxy frowned.

Mencken was trying to hear what Remus and Smith were saying,
and Roxy, noticing this, made an effort to distract him: "You boys
ready for the game?"

"Ready as I'll ever be to watch grown men trying to hit a ball
going about ninety miles an hour with a stick," Mencken responded.

"Fred, these aren't grown men," Roxy replied, smiling. "They're
boys, even the oldest ones. And the fun is watching what these kids
do after the ball is hit. Frankly, I love to watch young, healthy boys
run around—like you men like to watch young girls dance in the
chorus at the Gayety."

Not bad. While I was silently applauding Roxy's reply, Smith's
secretary came in the room, bringing a huge, imposing man. "Mrs.
Smith," she said, addressing Roxy as her boss's wife, "would you
introduce Mr. Means to these gentlemen," and she quickly left the
room.

There was something compelling about Gaston B. Means. He
was holding a dark felt hat and a leather briefcase in his left hand,
a cigarette in his right. His large head was balding. He had dark
bushy eyebrows and seemed to have a perpetual smile, which ac-
centuated the two dimples on either side of his wide mouth. His
face was jowly, but not as soft and weak as Smith's. Means' chin
was strong and his eyes sparkled with intelligence. But there was
also a cunning in his face and eyes that put me, at least, immediately
on my guard. I don't know why. He was definitely a big man, heavy
but not chubby like Smith. He was dressed in a rumpled, dark suit
with matching vest, a white shirt and a maroon bow tie. His pockets
seemed to bulge with a variety of things including cigarettes. He
was smoking as he came in the room, and the first thing he did was
go over to the ashtray on Smith's desk and stamp out his butt. Then
he lit another.

Roxy introduced Means and said that Smith had already told us about him. When Roxy said that Jesse was in the next office with George Remus, Means, too, looked concerned. He seemed, at first, as if he were going to say something about Remus to Roxy, but then thought better of it.

"I just came by to tell you that I can't join you all at the ball game. I've still got a lot of work to do," he said, patting his brief-case. "Besides, I'm a New York Giants fan. Tell you what, Roxy, why don't you all come back to the Ebbitt Grill and join me for dinner? It'll be on me. I'd like to get to know your two friends better and maybe Mr. Mercker and I can have a little talk. You know where the Ebbitt Grill is, don't you Roxy?"

"I certainly do. It's right up Fourteenth Street from the Willard, on the corner. It's where all those newspaper reporters hang out. That would be fun. And it'll give me another excuse to stay over one more night. I'm sure Jesse won't mind."

Suddenly, Remus burst into the room, followed by Smith who was visibly distressed. Remus was just as obviously angry.

"Hello, Means. How do you do, Miss Stinson," Remus said to Roxy, tipping his hat. Then he stomped out of the room, saying: "What the hell is this, a gathering of the Harry Daugherty fan club?"

"We're headed out to the ball park, George," Smith said, almost defensively. "Won't you join us? Harry's not going. He's with the president."

"You better tell your boss that you guys are headed for real trouble if you don't start producing," Remus yelled back before chomping on his cigar and heading out to the street.

"What was that all about?" Mencken asked Smith cautiously after Remus had gone.

"Oh, George is a client involved in a case on appeal at the Supreme Court. He's angry that the case isn't going his way. He's naturally convinced he's innocent and deserves a better deal from the courts. It's in litigation, so I can't talk about it. I'm sure you understand." Smith had taken out his green notebook and was writing in it as he talked.

"Sure," Mencken replied.

I nodded my agreement and Roxy said, "Jesse, Gaston can't go to the ball game; too much work to do. But he wants us to join him for dinner; says he'd like to have a talk with Fred and Jim. Can I come, too? I don't mind staying in town another night."

"I don't know," Smith said, frowning. "You really should be getting home. But I guess it'll be all right."

Then Jesse Smith went into the next room for a few minutes and came back with two flasks which he said had bourbon in them. He handed me one and gave Mencken a small bag containing three brown bottles. "We won't have any trouble with these at the stadium. They don't have labels. I hope you don't mind warm beer, Mr. Mercker?"

"Not at all," Mencken said with a grin. "Real beer drinkers prefer it this way."

CHAPTER FIVE

Smith had a Justice Department car for the trip to Griffith Stadium, which took us out K Street to the dead-end at the city library at 9th Street, then up 9th to Rhode Island Avenue, then right on Rhode Island to 7th Street, and then left and up 7th to where it intersected with Florida and Georgia Avenues.

Roxy broke the initial silence by asking Mencken whether he had seen the latest issue of *The Smart Set*. Mencken shook his head and Roxy said: "Oh you must read it. It has the most wonderful story by F. Scott Fitzgerald. Have you read any of his novels, Fred?"

"Can't say that I have. I don't read much fiction. Don't have time."

"Too bad. You'd love it, Jesse. It's about a college boy who meets a young man at his school, who collects diamonds—just like you do. He claims his father is the richest man in the world and that he has a diamond as big as the Ritz Carlton Hotel in New York!"

Jesse, who had been staring rather glumly out the window suddenly came to life. "Oh come on, Roxy, that's impossible. The biggest diamond ever cut couldn't be much larger than a grapefruit."

"This one wasn't cut. You've heard of virtually whole mountains being all coal? Well, in Fitzgerald's story this boy's father out in Montana lives on top of a mountain that's all diamond. And the story is about the trouble he has trying to exploit his great wealth because be feels he has to keep the big diamond a secret. If the government found out about it it would take it away from him. So, as the college boy finds out, people who visit the site of the big diamond have to be silenced."

Which triggers Jesse's depression again. "That's just ridiculous," he said. "So what happens?"

"Not going to tell you. I'll give you the magazine tonight. I've finished with it, although I ought to give it to Fred. He bought it for me yesterday."

"No, no," Mencken said quickly. "I think you should give it to Jesse. It sounds like a story for someone who appreciates diamonds more than I do."

"That's me all right," said Smith. "I love diamonds. I once stayed at the Ritz Carlton with a woman who was wearing a very big diamond, Only this one was real—the Hope Diamond."

"Jesse," said Roxy, "you never told me you were having an affair with Evalyn McLean. Is it still going on?"

"Who said we were having an affair? It was just before the inauguration in 1921. I went up to New York with the Duchess—Mrs. Harding—and Evalyn. We stayed at the Ritz. The ladies were buying clothes for the ball. On our final night, I was escorting them to see 'The Green Goddess' on Broadway. Evalyn wanted to wear the Hope Diamond but the Duchess wouldn't let her."

"Why's that?" asked Roxy.

"The Duchess felt that whenever Evalyn was wearing the diamond it upstaged them both. One time in the campaign, the Duchess was giving a speech on the back of the train. Evalyn was sitting on one side of the car looking out the window, when suddenly people started leaving the back of the train and rushing to see Evalyn, who was wearing the diamond. Everyone wanted to see it—and the Duchess was furious."

"That's a great story," said Mencken. "Speaking of the big blue diamond, a friend of mine who lives in New York told me it has been stolen. And Mrs. McLean doesn't even know it's missing. Justice Department agents know about the rumors, but have not told the police because it's thought that someone in the Harding administration might be involved."

"Maybe the diamond has put a curse on the whole administration," I said.

"Or just someone who works for Harding," said Smith, with a rather odd look on his face. "But that's even more ridiculous than a diamond as big as the Ritz. I was out to Mrs. McLean's Friendship house the other day and she was wearing it."

"It could have been a fake," I replied. "Someone might have had an imitation made, then switched them."

"It's not likely anyone in New York would have heard that," said Smith.

"Why not?" I said. "The theft could have been leaked by a precious stone cutter hired to make the fake. Or maybe the jeweler who separated the big diamond from the necklace, which would have to be done to fence it."

"I can't imagine anyone doing that and getting away with it," said Smith. "But I'm going down to the McLean farm in Leesburg tomorrow. I'll tell Ned to have Evalyn's diamond checked. I'm sure there's nothing to the rumor."

Smith began to stare out the window again and I thought he was going to do it for the rest of the trip when suddenly he said to me: "I understand you fellows aren't big baseball fans, but you like to go out to see a game every now and then?"

"I guess that's about it," I said. "Baltimore only has a minor league team. I follow the Yankees some, but it's hard to keep up your interest in an out-of-town team. Fred, here, has very little interest in the game—or any professional sport, for that matter. Isn't that right, Fred?"

"That's right. But I tell you, I'd rather go see a game of baseball than have to read about it. Let me give you an example," and he pulled a rolled-up section of a newspaper from his coat pocket. "I'm reading from this morning's *Washington Post*. It's the sports page story about yesterday's game between Cleveland and Washington:

'And while Warmouth was passing nine Speakerites, Stan Colveskie, Cleveland pitching ace, was putting on an exhibition of airtight hurling.

'A single off Bluege's bat, after Evans, batting for Wild William, was down in the eighth, paved the way for Washington's first run. Bluege raced to third on a bingle by Harris and a fumble by Summa and scored on Goslin's liner to right after Fisher had fanned.'

"Then, a little later:

'The bases were full again and the tying run on when Harris hit a hot one toward third. But it was gobbled up by Lutzke, who sent it on its way for a double play at second and first.'

"And so on. Here we have Warmouth—a 'southpaw' pitcher, we are told, named William Wild (his real middle name), passing nine Speakerites. Now just what the devil does that mean? And what are bingles and how do you gobble up a hot one?"

"Whada you know," Smith said, suddenly becoming almost cheerful. "I think I can translate all that for you, Fred: A southpaw pitcher is left-handed and left-handers have a reputation for being wild, which means they can't get the baseball over the plate, which is called a ball. If they get four balls before three strikes (when the the batter swings and misses or doesn't swing when a ball is over the plate) the batter is given a walk to first base, which is also called a 'pass.' So wild William Warmouth walked nine Speakerites, who are the men who play for the Indians' center fielder, Tris Speaker, who's also Cleveland's manager. Bingles are basehits, usually one-base hits, also called singles. Gobbling up a hot one means successfully fielding a hard hit ground ball."

"Very good translation," Mencken said, putting down his newspaper and applauding lightly. "I can see you're a real baseball fan, Mr. Smith, so who do you think will win today?"

"I'm naturally rooting for Cleveland. But any day that Walter Johnson is pitching you got to bet on the Senators. We're pitching George Uhle, a pretty good pitcher, but he's no Walter Johnson."

"No one is," Roxy said. "I saw him pitch one time in Cleveland and I never saw anyone throw a baseball so hard. Late in the game, when the sun was going down, you could hardly see the ball."

Time for my one baseball story. "Did you hear about the time Lefty Gomez, a screwball pitcher for the Yankees, came to bat against Johnson late in an extra-inning game, when it was beginning to get dark?" Smith shook his head and Roxy looked surprised that I had any baseball stories.

"Well, when Gomez stepped into the batter's box, he lay down his bat for a moment and lit a match. The umpire said: 'Come on, Lefty, you can't see this guy's fastball in broad daylight. A match ain't going to help you now.' And Gomez replies: 'Look, ump, I'm not trying to see his fastball. I just want to make sure he sees me.' "

This brought a laugh all around, and as we reached the stadium even Smith was smiling. "Here we are at the stadium. There's plenty of time before the game. We can have some hot dogs and something to drink."

"Sounds good," Mencken said, quickly stepping onto the concrete sidewalk that led up to the gate and helping Roxy out of the car, beating me to it.

When we went through the gate Smith gave the attendant his special season tickets, spraying enough saliva to make us all wonder whether we would be getting rain checks. He let it be known that we were in the attorney general's box, seeming to be bragging about his connection to the attorney general. But perhaps he was just discouraging anyone from examining the paper bag with the three brown bottles Mencken was carrying.

Inside the huge ballpark and settled in our box seats behind the Senator's dugout, I decided we would probably not see any balls hit out of the park. The right field fence was about 328 feet from home plate, which was not too bad, but it was at least thirty feet tall. The left field bleachers had a lower fence—about ten feet—but they were 410 feet from home plate.

Griffith Stadium was famous around the country as the place where the baseball season was officially opened. When it was built eleven years ago, President Taft started the ceremony of throwing out the first ball. President Wilson continued the custom until he got sick, and I remember seeing the pictures of Harding, in his box draped with all the bunting, throwing out the first ball this year. Walter Johnson did not pitch that game, but as I recall, Washington won it, 2–1.

Smith said he always sat in front of Roxy at the ball game to protect her from any foul balls that might be hit their way. So Mencken and Smith sat in the two front seats in the box and Roxy and I sat behind them, which was fine by me. It was Friday, Ladies Day, so there was a nice crowd and lots of big hats sprinkled throughout the park. It was not a good day to have foul balls hit into the stands because the ladies were not always watching the man at bat. More often than not, they were looking at each other's hats.

We ordered our hot dogs, Mencken poured one of his beers into a paper cup, Smith did the same with bourbon from his flask and I made drinks for Roxy and myself. By the time the game got underway, we were all feeling pretty mellow. Smith, particularly, seemed to be enjoying himself, temporarily, at least, relieved of whatever was troubling him. Mencken and Smith were getting along amiably enough, but at one point Mencken brought up the death of Cramer and the troubles in the Veterans' Bureau—which seemed to send Smith briefly into another depression.

Mostly, however, their conversation was devoted to Smith explaining some of the fine points of the game to Mencken and discussing the trouble, oddly enough, Walter Johnson had getting through the first inning. With two men out and Speaker on first, Johnson hit the Cleveland first baseman (whose name, according to my scorecard, was Blower) with the ball, which must have hurt, but sent Blower to first base and Speaker to second. The Cleveland right fielder, Summa, hit a single, scoring Speaker. Then Cleveland shortstop Sewell hit a bingle, as the sportswriters would say, scoring Summa and Blower. Three runs were in. Third baseman Lutzke walked and their catcher, Myatt, hit a triple driving in Sewell and Lutzke. Cleveland had five runs.

As the game progressed, Roxy and I had a chance to talk, especially when Smith said he had to "say good-bye to some of this good bourbon" and Mencken said he would join him. The bourbon was having a warming effect on Roxy's thighs (one of which was tightly pressed against mine) and a loosening effect on her tongue. The more we talked the more it became apparent that not only was Smith very worried about something, but that Roxy was worried about him. "Although he tries not to show it," Roxy said, "the president's decision not to include Jesse on the Alaska trip upset him immensely. And not just the Alaska trip. He thinks some of the boys want him to disappear for good. And they want me to keep out of town, too."

"Who are 'they,' the boys?" I asked.

"Whenever Jesse says 'they' he always means Harry Daugherty and some of the men who work with him. Around town, they're becoming known as the 'Ohio Gang.' "

"You think they're really out to get Jesse?"

"Something's up, I know. Take today, for example. By now, there should have been half a dozen guys from around town coming by our seats to say hello and shake hands with Jesse. Everybody likes him and everybody know's he's a good friend of the president. But nobody's been around today."

"You're right about that," I said.

"Don't look now, but you see that very well-dressed gentleman up the stairs? He's standing in front of a seat on the right, an aisle seat. He just turned his head away because he saw me looking at him and he doesn't want to acknowledge me. His name is John King and he knows Jesse very well. I met him in New York, where he gave Jesse a two-hundred-dollar gold cigarette case as a token of his appreciation for Jesse's work in a deal they were in together. Well, I can tell you King should have been down here a couple of times already, slapping Jesse on the back and trading stories. Here come Jesse and Fred down the aisle and they're stopping by King to say hello. You can turn around now. See, King is acting like he barely knows Jesse."

I looked up the aisle and she was right. Smith was talking to a very smooth looking character who was almost a caricature of a Washington wheeler-dealer.

"The last time Jesse came out to Ohio," Roxy continued, "I went up to meet him in Columbus and without even realizing that he was doing something embarrassing, he grabbed me right there in the hotel lobby and threw his arms around me, and said: 'I never was so glad to see anyone in my life. They're going to get me.' I said, 'Jesse, are you all right? Nothing's going to happen to you.' And he said: 'Let's get home before dark.' "

When Smith and Mencken returned from the men's room, she quickly shifted the subject to an exuberant description of a play they had missed—where the Washington outfielder, Goose Goslin, made a running catch, crashing against the wall in left center field as the crowd also stood up and cheered.

After their return from the rest rooms, Smith's demeanor changed. He kept turning around and talking to Roxy, seeming to want to make sure she did not get back into serious conversation with me. Then, a little later when we all stood up for the seventh inning stretch Smith said: "Come on, Roxy, let's get some more hot dogs. You fellows want us to bring you anything?"

We said no, thanks, and they went up the stairs to the hot dog stand. "So what's with Smith?" I asked as soon as Roxy and Smith were out of earshot. "Since he came back with you from the can he hasn't been the same. He seems terribly preoccupied again, as he was earlier today."

"I think I pressed him too hard on Cramer's death and the Veterans' Bureau. I suspect he's getting suspicious. And it didn't help when we came back and he overheard you and Roxy talking about him. I know damned well he took her off to the hot dog stand to tell her to keep quiet. We're going to have to be very cautious."

"The liquor certainly loosened her tongue," I said, "She told me that Jesse is afraid the Ohio Gang is out to get him."

When they returned, Smith was still somber and he suggested changing our seating arrangement for the rest of the game. I would sit with him and Mencken would sit behind us with Roxy. In an obvious effort to keep the conversation off the problems in the Harding administration, Mencken started talking baseball, Mencken style—which probably made Smith even more suspicious. He and I both could hear him and he did not exactly sound like your typical cigar manufacturer, amateur bootlegger at the ball game.

"You know, Roxy, the popularity of athletics is grounded in the belief that heavy excercise makes for bodily health and that bodily health is necessary to mental vigor. Both parts of this theory are highly dubious, probably deleterious."

When he saw Roxy looking puzzled, he added: "Not good for you. The truth is, athletes, as a class, are not above the normal in physical health—and certainly not mental health—but below it. Take right now; it's a beautiful sunny day, but the fact is that for the higher varieties of civilized man, sunlight is often injurious and their natural inclination to keep out of it is sound. Man has sought the shade since his earliest days on earth."

"But Fred," Roxy said, "you can't deny that most of these young men on the field are marvelous specimens of mankind"—and in her lilting voice she made the remark sound positively sexy.

"Ahhh, that's true, Miss Stinson. But athletics didn't make them that way. They were simply better animals in the first place. And they would be just as vigorous and healthy if they had never gone into professional athletics."

Smith seemed puzzled, not quite able to follow Mencken's thesis but Roxy was enjoying every minute of Mencken on stage. In fact, the more she was exposed to the real Mencken, the more she seemed fascinated by him—which, frankly, made me a little jealous.

Washington had scored one in the third and two in the fourth. The Indians has scored another run off Johnson in the fifth, but neither side did much of anything after that. From the sixth inning on, Johnson looked like his old self. The score ended 6–3, but it was virtually over in the first inning when the Indians scored their five runs. Not a very exciting game. Only one foul ball came our way and fortunately it was not so close that Mencken—or I—had to go into action to protect Roxy, who probably could have handled it better than either of us.

We left the stadium and headed toward Florida Avenue where the Justice Department car was supposed to be waiting. Jesse walked with Roxy. Although they kept quite a distance behind us, we could tell that Smith was having an intense conversation with his ex-wife. "Looks like you're right about Smith," I said to Mencken. "I think he's lecturing Roxy now about being careful with us. I must say, I can't blame him. I don't think we're very convincing as a couple of booticians."

"No, and I doubt if we're going to check out with that fellow Means, either. He's no dumbbell. He's probably spent the afternoon looking into our backgrounds and I think the only thing he's going to believe about us is that we're not Prohibition agents. Incidentally, what do you think about dinner at the Old Ebbitt? There'll be a lot of reporters. Someone is sure to recognize us."

"That occurred to me, too," I replied. "Can you think of another place we can suggest?"

"How 'bout that restaurant at the top of the Hotel Washington, just a block from Old Ebbitt? It's right across the street from the Treasury Department and has a view of the city looking toward the White House and the Washington Monument. The people are dull but it's a beautiful city, especially in the spring."

"Good idea. I'm sure Roxy will go for that. Sounds very romantic. Do you want to suggest it or shall I?"

"You do it. It might raise Roxy's opinion of you."

"Thanks. But it probably won't make a hell of a lot of difference where we eat if Means doesn't give us clearance. What do you think we ought to tell them if Means confirms Smith's suspicions?"

"Good question. I guess I'd just confess that I'm H. L. Mencken the famous Wilson-hater and anti-Christ and we're working on a story for a new magazine, looking into the alleged corruption in the Harding administration. I'll tell 'em I voted for Harding, which I did, and I believe the president is too honest to have permitted the stuff we've been hearing rumors about. I'd lay it on just enough so as to not alienate Roxy, who I'd sure like to have a date with when this is all over."

"I had the same idea." I said quickly.

"Cain, my boy, you are way too young for Miss Stinson. How old are you? Just turned thirty, I'd wager," and I nodded that he would win his bet. "She's a mature woman, in her forties as I am. Leave her to this Jurassic."

"We'll see. Don't forget she showed considerable interest in the young men on the ball diamond today. What would you have done if that foul ball had come a little closer?"

"Yelled 'Watch out!' and ducked, just as you would have done."

By now we had reached the car; Jesse and Roxy caught up with us and Mencken and I jockeyed to see who would assist her into the waiting sedan. He won.

CHAPTER SIX

Driving down 7th Street toward the center of town in the Justice department car, Smith was mostly silent, even a little hostile. Roxy tried to keep the atmosphere friendly with some chitchat about the game and how exciting it was to see such healthy young men in competition. At what I thought was an appropriate moment, I said: "Fred and I have been talking and we're wondering whether it might not be more fun to go to the lounge and restaurant at the top of the Washington Hotel. It's near the Willard and they have a wonderful view. The Ebbitt can get pretty crowded and noisy. What do you think, Roxy?"

"Oh, that's a fine idea. Sometimes I stay at the Washington just so I can have breakfast in the restaurant. And we might run into some reporters at the Ebbitt. They would surely recognize Jesse and want to ask questions about Cramer and the Veterans' Bureau. What do you think, Jesse, is the Hotel Washington okay with you?"

"Good," he said, still in his sulk, which at least produced a minimum of slobbering. "Roxy's right about seeing newspaper people. Some of these Washington reporters can be a real nuisance."

"That's right," said Mencken. "By the time they've been in the capital for a couple of years, they think they're statesmen. But what they really are is a collection of dim-witted hired hands for a bunch of ignorant employers. There are managing editors in this country who have never heard of the Statute of Frauds. . . ."

Mencken was beginning to get carried away with his train of thought so I decided to try to derail it: "Remember, Fred, we might be engaging in a little fraud ourselves, trying to buy a liquor permit."

Smith looked at me seemingly surprised that anyone would mention such a thought out loud. "Yeah, have you ever thought of that, Mercker?"

"In my book," Mencken responded, "outwitting a fraud—and that's what the Volstead Act is—is not a fraud. The very fact that all of us, in one way or another, are engaged in outwitting this fraud is proof enough of its absurdity, even criminality. So why do we continue to engage in this asinine prohibition? It's the power that fanatical minorities have in American politics. As I've said many times, we'll have Prohibition as long as our dry congressmen can stagger to the halls of Congress and vote."

As Mencken wound down, Roxy seemed to be endorsing his remarks but was watching Smith, who was smiling weakly, which was about all he could do, considering that his boss, Warren Harding, had once been the editor of the *Marion (Ohio) Star*. And he could hardly acknowledge Mencken's observations about the law his boss had pledged to enforce.

Just as I decided that we had gone too far again Jesse suddenly had an idea that seemed to please him: "I know what. We'll let the driver continue to Old Ebbitt and you three go on to the Washington. I'll meet Means and bring him over to the hotel."

We all agreed that was a good idea, but despite Roxy's effort to lighten things up we rode pretty much in silence to the Ebbitt with Smith's despondency dominating the mood in the car. When we reached 14th and F Streets, Smith told the driver to take us over to the Washington, but to my surprise, Mencken quickly stepped out of the other side of the car and said: "Come on, why don't we walk over to the Washington? I'll bet you're all as stiff as I am from sitting through that ball game."

Soon we were escorting Roxy arm-in-arm down F Street, past Garfinckle's, heading directly toward the Treasury building. And Mencken got right to the point: "Roxy, your ex seems kind of depressed, as if something is bothering him. Do you think he's changed his mind about doing business with us? Have we done something wrong?"

"I don't think so," Roxy replied cautiously. "As for doing business with you, he wouldn't make up his mind about that until after Means reports to him that you all are okay. I assume he's been checking you out this afternoon. But there's no hiding the fact that he's feeling glum. Jesse is very upset that the president said he would not be going with them on the Alaska trip."

Then, quickly changing the subject, she said: "Let's talk about something else. How do you boys like Washington? I just love it here."

We both agreed we liked the capital city very much. When we reached the hotel, we took the elevator to the roof just above the tenth floor. No building can have more than thirteen floors in Washington, the idea being that nothing should be taller than the Washington Monument, which greeted us the moment we walked in the open cocktail lounge. Just standing in the entrance, we could see it, the Lincoln Memorial, the White House and the old State War and Navy Building, now the State Department. "Oh my," exclaimed Roxy. "This is such an exciting town!"

After Roxy finished oooohhhhhing and aahhhing about the view, we discussed at some length the pros and cons of making our own drinks here, deciding finally to leave it up to Jesse. We had not been in the terrace room long before a rather odd trio—piano, saxophone and drums—back in the far northern corner of the lounge—began playing the latest musical inanity, "Barney Google," the lyrics sung by the piano player.

I noticed the pained look on Mencken's face. Everyone in Baltimore knew of his love of the old warhorse classics—Beethoven, Brahms, Schubert—which he and the members of his Saturday Night Club butchered once a week, faithfully washing down the bad music with some good homemade brew or bootleg whiskey come ten o'clock. "Can you imagine, a saxophone as the melody instrument?" he asked no one in particular as he looked at the noisy trio. Then, to me: "Jim, did you know that the saxophone is the only reed instrument made out of metal? It was invented in Belgium in about 1840, by a man, unfortunately for him, named Saxe, unfortunate because the sax is well on its way to dominating American jazz, which means that perhaps for eternity people will be cursing the name of Saxe. And what's happening to American music is that it's more rhythm than melody."

Knowing where this line of thought was taking us because I had recently read his *Prejudices, Second Series,* I decided to get to the point before he did: "Well, Carl Van Vechten, who likes the new jazz, says that the ancient Greeks accorded rhythm a higher place than either harmony or melody."

"What of it?" Mencken said. "So did the ancient Goths and Huns.

So do the modern Zulus and New Yorkers. It's a reversion to bar-
barism. Carl's a good novelist, but he doesn't know a damn thing
about music."

Mencken certainly had the best of this debate, as we all were
forced to listen to a moaning saxophone and drums providing rhyth-
mic support for the pianist who was singing:

"Who's the most important man this country ever knew?
Who's the man our presidents tell all their troubles to?
I am mighty proud
That I am allowed
A chance to introduce
Barney Google with his goo-goo-googly eyes."

"Well, I don't mind a saxophone in a bigger band," Roxy said,
"and in a bigger room. But it's not right for a cocktail lounge.
Neither is 'Barney Google.' They'll probably be playing 'Mr. Gal-
lagher and Mr. Shean' next or 'Yes, We Have No Bananas.' "

"Let us pray," said Mencken.

"So how come you know so much about music, Mr. Cigar
Maker?" Roxy asked.

"Isn't a businessman allowed any culture?" was Mencken's response.

"It so happens he plays a pretty mean piano . . ." I cut in.

Mencken added: "Which I will gladly demonstrate for you at a
more appropriate time," as the trio brought "Barney" to a merciful
end:

"Barney Google is the luckiest of guys;
If he fell in the mud,
He'd come up with a diamond stud."

"And speaking of diamonds," said Roxy, who had been listening
to the end of the trio's first number and at the same time watching
the door for her ex-husband and Means, "here comes that well-
known diamond collector, Jesse Smith."

Smith (who incidentally was wearing a diamond ring on his right
hand and a diamond clip pin on his tie) and Means joined our big

table overlooking the city, leaving their coats on, not only because it was a little nippy but probably because wearing them made it a lot easier to bring out the flasks from their large pockets. And on the question that concerned me most, Smith did not leave us in suspense for long: "We've gone through our procedure now," he said looking directly at Mencken, "and you and Gaston can get together any time and work out your next move. It's a pretty routine thing."

I was surprised and I could tell that Mencken was too. Means had an odd smile on his dimpled face and once again I was impressed with him. He had obviously given us clearance and convinced what I am sure was a suspicious Jesse Smith that we were safe to do business with. Which meant to me that either Means was not a very good investigator—or more likely that he knew Mencken was not a cigar maker–bootlegger but wanted to do business with him anyway. I decided the latter was true, which meant, among other things, that we had to be careful dealing with Means. He was up to something.

Although Smith now acted more friendly toward us than he had in the car coming back from the ball park, he still appeared troubled about something. And he was obviously in no mood to observe Prohibition this evening. When we asked him about the propriety of mixing our soda water with whisky here at the Washington Hotel, he said: "By all means, let's have some fun," adding that Means had reinforced us with a couple of flasks of scotch and bourbon. Means patted the bulging pockets of his top coat by way of confirmation.

When the soda arrived, the whiskey added and we were, for the moment at least, comfortably relaxed, and browsing through the menus the waiter had also brought, we went through the usual amenities:

MEANS: Sorry I missed the game today. Did you enjoy it? Mr. Mercker?

MENCKEN: To tell the truth, except for boxing, I hate all sports as rabidly as a person who likes sports hates common sense. Better to be a second-rate bricklayer—which I am—than the best polo player on earth. I'm sure no one here agrees with that. You a married man, Mr. Means?

MEANS: Yes, with two children. Marriage is a fine institution.

MENCKEN: But who wants to live in an institution?

ROXY (laughing): Mr. Mercker has some strong opinions about women and marriage.

MEANS: I know.

CAIN: Now just how do you know that, Mr. Means?

MEANS: We investigators know everything. And you're not married, are you, Mr. Mercker?

MENCKEN: No. I'm a confirmed bachelor, set in my ways, as they say. In fact, I favor a dollar-a-day tax on bachelors because it's worth that to be free. Mr. Smith, you have been both married and divorced. What is your opinion on this matter?

SMITH: (fixing himself another drink): Well, to tell the truth, Roxy and I are fast friends. In fact we get along better now than we ever did when we were married.

ROXY: Nobody's asked me how I feel about it.

CAIN: How *do* you feel about it?

ROXY: I agree with Fred and Jesse. I prefer living out of wedlock. I like to be friends with lots of men—not married to one. How 'bout you, Jim?

CAIN: I like the bachelor's life.

MENCKEN: That settles it, four to one against marriage. It's a ludicrous comedy, a farce which is in fact an economic matter. Can any woman be truly happy if she has to dress less well as a wife than she did before she was married? And can any man be happy, married, who has to drink worse whiskey than he drank when he was single?

Everybody laughed as Jesse picked up his glass and said: "Whadayaknow. It's empty."

We started mixing another round of drinks, with Jesse slobbering all over and gaining on us in the race to deplete our flasks.

Then Roxy brought up the Fitzgerald story in *The Smart Set* again and reminded her ex-husband that she wanted to give him the magazine before they went home. "It's about a huge diamond," Roxy said to Means, "as big as a hotel. Don't you think he ought to read it?"

Before Means could answer, Jesse said: "Okay, so I'll read it.

Sure I like diamonds and I collect them. But I don't flash mine around like some people I know. Evalyn McLean doesn't care what she does with her Hope Diamond. She even makes jokes with it. Gaston knows about that. Once, she invited some people out to one of her homes to see the diamond and after they had been sitting around the big living room for awhile, Evalyn finally said: 'Oh, you wanted to see the diamond. What did I do with it?' Then she suddenly seemed to remember: 'Oh yes, I think Mike has it,' and she went to the window and called: 'Mike, Mike.' And pretty soon this Great Dane bounds into the room and it was wearing a big, blue diamond on a chain around its neck. It was the Hope Diamond. Evalyn was just playing a joke on her friends.

"You've heard about the curse? I know Gaston has. Evalyn says it doesn't bother her; that bad luck things bring her good luck. But she does take it seriously. She doesn't let any of her friends touch the diamond, and she did have it blessed by a priest. . . ."

"Well, that must have really put the hex on it," Mencken said.

Smith frowned momentarily, but continued his story: "Evalyn told me that the priest agreed to bless it if she never intended to sell it [I was afraid for a moment Mencken was going to comment that the priest would want a cut if she did, but he refrained]. The day they did it it was getting darker and darker as they approached the church and when the priest put the diamond on a cushion and blessed it, the street was suddenly struck by lightning. Evalyn's maid, who was with them, said: 'Jesus, Mary and Joseph' and fainted dead away. Evalyn said she was scared to death and the old priest's knees were shaking."

"I don't doubt it," said Mencken, "whole religions have been started on less than that. But I've heard that the Justice Department already knows it's been stolen but they're hushing it up because they think somebody connected to the Harding administration did it. Anything to that, Mr. Smith?"

"Absolutely absurd," said Smith, obviously annoyed. "I can't imagine anyone in their right mind stealing a diamond with a curse on it. I know I wouldn't."

"Then you believe in the curse?" Mencken asked.

"I sure do. Don't you?"

"I'd believe in a god first."

"You don't believe in God?" Smith replied.

"Which one?" said Mencken.

"Mercker believes in Voltaire," said Means.

"Oh, you must have read *Candide,*" said Roxy, looking at Mencken. "I read it in high school."

'Yes, I've read *Candide,* a wonderful story of a young man's trying to believe in Dr. Pangloss' best of all possible worlds while experiencing rape, pillage, murder, massacre, butchery, religious intolerance, earthquake, you name it."

"Getting back to the diamond," said Means, "I think a guy who stole it would have a tough time figuring out what to do with it."

"Just like the man who owned the diamond as big as the Ritz," Roxy intervened. "See what I mean, Jesse?"

"Okay. I'll read the story," Smith said, still annoyed. "I'll also take it to Leesburg tomorrow and let Ned read it. And I'll clear up this whole nonsense about it being stolen and that the Hope Evalyn's wearing is a fake!"

"I'm getting chilly," Roxy said abruptly. "Let's move into the dining room."

As the sun set behind this incredible view it had begun getting cooler to the point where it was not comfortable even with our coats on. But the dining room was quite comfortable and, if you were near a window, you still had a fine view. We were too late for window seats, so we ended up at a large table in the middle of the room. The dining area was also much more formal than the terrace lounge, which made me somewhat uncomfortable when adding whiskey to my soda. But not Jesse. He went right on mixing and drinking almost as if he felt he had special exemption from the Volstead Act. He probably did. At least he put his flask away when he saw the waiter coming.

Both Means and Smith ordered big filet mignons; Mencken decided on a two-pound lobster; Roxy had the chef's salad; and I had the Maryland crabcakes. We all agreed on coffee later, except Smith.

With everyone looking at everyone else waiting for someone to say something, Mencken broke the silence. Raising his glass in what I thought was going to be another toast to Andrew J. Volstead, Mencken said: "The bursting of spring in this beautiful city reminds us that July fourth cannot be far behind, which means that all across the country worthy young spinsters will be reading the Declaration of Independence again to their inattentive students. And no wonder they won't be paying attention. In their homes, they're used to a language that differs materially from standard English, in particular the standard English of the eighteenth century. Mr. Smith, what would the average soda fountain clerk make of such a sentence as this one from the Declaration—one of a number of complaints against George III of England? 'He has called together legislative bodies at places unusual, uncomfortable and distant from the depository of their public records for the sole purpose of fatiguing them into compliance with his measures.' "

I knew what was coming—a Mencken column of a couple of years ago. It was widely quoted in Baltimore but I don't think it had much of a play around the rest of the country. We were about to get a new version of the Declaration of Independence.

"Obviously not much," Mencken continued. "Let me humbly suggest a rewriting of the Declaration more along the following lines. I think that even the citizens of this great democracy could understand it:

> *"When things get so balled up that the people of a country have to cut loose from some other country and go it on their own hook without asking no permission from nobody, excepting maybe God Almighty, then they ought to let everybody know why they done it, so that everybody can see they are on the level and not trying to put nothing over on nobody."*

As Mencken launched into his "speech," I looked around the room and noticed that he had attracted quite a bit of attention. Fueled I am sure by the bourbon from one of Means' flasks, his voice had reached a level more appropriate to one of his Saturday night music and drinking get-togethers with the boys than to the sophisticated restaurant atop the Hotel Washington, one block from the White House.

> *"All we got to say on this proposition is this: First, you and me is as good as anybody else and maybe a damn site better; second, nobody ain't got no right to take away none of our rights; third, every man has got a right to live, to come and go as he pleases and to have a good time however he likes*

*so long as he don't interfere with nobody else. That any gov-
ernment that don't give a man these rights ain't worth a
damn. . . ."*

As Mencken continued I was looked around to see how his in-
creasing audience was reacting. I noticed two couples standing by
the door waiting for someone to give them a table. One of them, to
my horror, was Frank Kent, the *Sun*'s Washington bureau chief, a
good friend of Mencken's and an acquaintance of mine. I knew that
the moment he spotted us, Kent would come rushing over to our
table to say hello. Rising quickly to my feet, I said: "If you good
folks will excuse me, I'm going to retreat to the men's room. Anyway, I've heard Fred's speech before—in a Baltimore bar." And as
I left the table and headed for the door, I squeezed Mencken on the
shoulder and added: "Fred, you could turn it down a notch or two;
we may have a few patriots in the restaurant who might not appreciate you revising Thomas Jefferson."

I had to get to Kent before he came to us. As I approached the
party standing in the door, I recognized the other, older gentleman:
slender, balding, wearing round, steel-rimmed glasses, a white,
starched-collar shirt and a gray three-piece suit. It was Paul Patterson, president of the *Sun* papers, also a good friend of Mencken's.
I pretended that I just noticed that one of the group was Frank and
I went to him and shook hands.

After Kent introduced me to his wife and the Pattersons, I said:
"Frank, this may sound strange, but I wanted to intercede before
any of you came to our table to say hello to Mencken. We're involved with something that calls for Henry to try to hide his identity
and his disguise, such as it is, seems to be working. I can't tell you
what we're up to, but I'm sure Henry will eventually."

Then, looking at Patterson, I said: "While you wait for your table,
if Frank will step out in the corridor for a moment, I'll tell him a
little more about our project."

Patterson nodded his understanding and Kent and I left the room.
"Look, when you go to your table, just ignore Mencken and I'm
sure he'll ignore you. We came up here to the Washington because
we thought we'd see too many reporters at the Ebbitt."

"You're right about that. The Grill is packed. Boy, I'd love to
know what you two are up to; one of the guys at your table, Gaston

B. Means, he's the biggest crook in this town—and that's saying a lot. Who's the other guy and the woman? I didn't get a look at them."

"The other guy is Jesse Smith. Works for Daugherty in the Justice Department. I'm sure you know about him. That knockout of a woman is his ex-wife, Roxy Stinson. How she ever got mixed up with that jerk is beyond me."

"I know 'em both," Kent said. "That's some crowd you're with. Not one but two of the biggest crooks in town and the woman who knows enough to put them both and a few others in jail."

"That's what I heard. I also understand that Daugherty has ordered her back to Ohio," I said, wanting Kent to know that I was not totally ignorant of what was going on.

"Her and Smith, too," Kent said. "And with good reason. The word is that all the skullduggery that has been going on in this administration is about to blow wide open. And not just in the Veterans' Bureau; you've read about that—and Cramer's death. But there's also stuff going on in the Interior Department. And the Justice Department. Smith is Daugherty's bag man and no doubt Roxy knows a lot."

"Well, that's what we're working on."

"So is almost everybody in Washington. But let me tell you something, Jim. You'd better be careful."

"Why's that?"

"Some people think Cramer didn't commit suicide but was murdered to shut him up. And we've been doing a little investigating of Means. He's a liar and a complete crook who likes to brag about his illegal activities and his ability to avoid the law. He started working for William Burns, the chief of the department's investigative unit. But when Daugherty found out about some of Means' skullduggery, he ordered him fired."

"So how come he's still around?"

"Means had once done a favor for Burns; in addition, Means was valuable to Burns. His covert actions for the Justice Department included such things as breaking into the office of a senator who might be getting ready to investigate Daugherty and roughing up underlings who are threatening to cause trouble. So Burns kept him on a hidden payroll until the Number two man in the investigative unit, a young guy named J. Edgar Hoover, literally kicked Means out of his office and saw to it that he was fired for good. Means then started freelancing—promising gangsters pardons and favors he could not deliver and setting up for blackmailing people who could not afford to report what he was doing. But he kept doing some work for Burns."

I shook my head in disbelief and nervously looked back into the dining room to make sure Means was still at our table. Then I said: "Smith says Means is one of the best Prohibition agents, that he impressed Daugherty and Mabel Willebrandt with the way he busted the LaMontagne Brothers in New York and sent the four of them to jail."

"Yeah, I know all about the LaMontagne brothers," Kent replied. "And what we've heard, but can't prove, is that Means first set them up, then blackmailed them for about one hundred thousand bucks and when they didn't pay up he turned them in. That's the kinda guy you're dealing with.

"We're also pretty sure," Kent continued "that he literally got away with the murder of a woman named Maude King in North Carolina. He forged her will and milked her of thousands of dollars. Means was acquitted but the story was that two of the jurors had been intimidated and one had been bribed.

"And Mencken will like this. Before the U.S. entered the war, Means worked as a German agent. That's where he first started collaborating with Burns, who was a British agent. I think right now, Means, as a freelancer, is working *for* Daugherty through Burns and *against* Daugherty on his own because he hates Daugherty for getting him fired and not cutting him in on some of their deals."

Kent stopped abruptly and looked toward the dining room to make sure Means was still in place. "If you're playing some kind of game with Means, you don't want him to see us talking together. He's very sharp and knows a lot of reporters. He loves publicity. Like Smith, he wants to be seen as the big shot, man around town. I'm pretty sure he knows who I am, although we've never talked. Why don't you duck into the men's room here and I'll rejoin my party. You or Menck can call me next week if you want to know anything more about these people. By the way, the McLeans are giving a big party for the press at their estate, Friendship. I think it's late next week. You ought to meet them. They're part of the

Ohio Gang. Mencken probably has an invitation on his desk now. But you can both go along with me if you want."

"Sound good, I'll tell Mencken."

As he started toward the dining room, he said: "Be careful, you're involved with some tough customers."

I went into the men's room and was back at our table just in time for the conclusion of the new Declaration of Independence; Smith was almost out of it. Roxy and Means appeared fascinated by Mencken's recitation, which he was just finishing:

> *"The United States, which was the United Colonies in former times, is now free and independent and ought to be; that we have throwed out the English king and don't want to have nothing to do with him no more and are not in England no more and that free and independent parties can declare war, make peace, sign treaties, go into business, etc. And we swear on the Bible on this proposition, one and all, and agree to stick to it, no matter what happens, whether we win or lose and whether we get away with it or we get the worst of it, no matter whether we lose all our property by it or even get hung for it."*

Finishing with a flourish, Mencken raised his glass, pointing toward a couple at the next table who were listening to him. They responded amiably giving no indication that they recognized or cared to know who this character was. Smith tried to raise his glass in a manner suggesting "I'll drink to anything"—except that his glass was empty again. Means cautiously raised his glass and gave me a big dimpled smile. Roxy applauded lightly and I said: "Nice speech, Mr. Congressman. I'll be looking forward to your version of the Constitution, I hope you have it ready by the Fourth of July."

Standing up, he said: "I'll get to that in due time. Right now I'm working on the *Gettysburg Address*. Lincoln had it all wrong, you know. It was not the Union Army but the Confederate soldiers who were fighting for self-determination. They were the ones fighting for the right of people to govern themselves. The Confederates went into the Battle of Gettysburg absolutely free men and came out with their freedom subject to the supervision and vote of the rest of the country. Of course, my new version won't be as eloquent as Abe's but it will be more accurate. Well, I'm off to the men's room. I haven't washed my hands since we were at the ball park."

All in all, Mencken's ploy worked. This little group of Harding-ites seemed to be warming to the cigar maker as an amusing, harm-less guy who posed no real threat to them. After Mencken left the table, Roxy said: "He's some character, Jim. He looks like a busi-nessman, but he certainly doesn't sound like one. He can be quite funny. Have you known him long?"

"A little less than a year. I do some work for his cigar company in Baltimore. He is funny and very outspoken. As a businessman, he hates any kind of government regulation, especially Prohibition, which seems to have turned him against democracy in general. He told me he voted for Harding, but I don't think he's a Republican. And I know he's not a Democrat. He hates Woodrow Wilson and do-gooding liberals . . ."

"But in the field of economics I am the most orthodox man I know."

I had not noticed Mencken's return and I let him pick up the conversation: "I believe that the present organization of society, bad as it is, is better than any other that has ever been proposed. I'm in favor of free competition in all human enterprises and to the utmost limit I admire successful scoundrels and shrink from all socialists."

With his remark about successful scoundrels, I could see Means smile approvingly and I began to look at Means a little more closely. And I must confess it is hard to imagine this huge, good-natured caricature of a Southerner with his pronounced accent—"Bo'n on a plantation near Concord, Nawth Carolina"—doing the things Kent attributed to him. I thought it was time to try to draw Means out a little about his work. But before I could, it was Jesse's time to attract attention.

All of a sudden, and for no reason, except that Smith was dead drunk, he started to sing what Roxy said was his favorite song:

"My sister sells snow to
the snowbirds
my father makes
bootlegger gin
My mother she takes in
washing

My God! how the money
rolls in"

Before he could get into the second chorus, Roxy managed to
shut him down. Then the waiter arrived with our food. After he left
with our compliments to the chef on how beautiful everything
looked, I asked Means how he liked working as an investigator in
Washington.

"To tell the truth," said Means, "I like investigating crooks.
When you get something on them, you're in complete control. They
can't do a damn thing about anything you say or do—because they
can't retaliate. It's their Achilles heel. It will be their neck, too, if
what they're doing comes to light. Of course, once you put them
in jail, they can bad-mouth you. But it doesn't matter because a
convict's testimony never has any credence in court."

All this was said with an air of satisfaction, even smugness, as
if to suggest that Gaston B. Means was probably the smartest guy
ever to hit this town. In fact, he apparently decided that maybe he
was being a little too smart-alecky because he suddenly seemed to
clam up. Further questions about his work brought stock answers
about how exciting it was, a real challenge and very satisfying and
rewarding serving your country, etc., etc.

Nothing much of interest happened during the rest of our dinner.
When we were finished, Smith seemed somewhat revived, but Roxy
insisted that she was going to see him home. I offered to go with
her and she thanked me and said she would appreciate it. I hoped
that Mencken would say he was tired and going back to the Willard
when Means said: "Fred, why don't you walk me back to my house
on Sixteenth Street? It's not far, between K and L. We can discuss
the business we have to take care of. Besides, I understand we were
both on the side of the Germans before we entered the war. We
have a lot to talk about."

Now how in the hell did Means know that? There could only be
one answer: Means had, as I suspected, found out who Mencken
was, but had not told Smith, or if he had, he assured Smith that he
could handle us. Suddenly, I had the urge to tell Mencken what
Kent had said about Means and to warn him to be careful. But the
opportunity did not present itself. We all rode down the elevator
together and Means and Mencken waved good-bye and were on

their way before the driver had even opened the door of the waiting Justice Department car. First we went by the Willard and we waited at the 14th Street entrance while she went to her room to get *The Smart Set* with Fitzgerald's story for Jesse, not that he was going to read it tonight. But Roxy thought he might want to take it with him when he went to Leesburg tomorrow to see the McLeans.

Riding out Connecticut Avenue to the Wardman, we were all three in the back seat; Roxy was in the middle, Jess was slumped down half asleep or stoned on her left and I was on her right with my left arm around her shoulders. I kissed her slightly on the cheek a couple of times and moved my right arm over to her side so that I could just barely feel her breast. She very firmly but pleasantly said "Not now," and moved my hand away.

By the time we had crossed the bridge before Calvert Street and reached the Wardman it had started to rain heavily. At the hotel I offered to help Roxy escort Smith to his room, but she said, no, she would do it alone. When she returned to the car, there was obviously something wrong. I asked her what had happened and she shook her head pointing to the driver in such a way that he could not see that she was doing it. Moving her mouth close to my left ear, she said: "I'll tell you later. I'm getting as paranoid as Jesse."

Then she gave me a warm, very wet kiss on my ear and suddenly I had to adjust my shorts because of pressure from a previously dormant source. This was a real kiss—but at the same time she let me know that she did not want to get anything heavy going in the back seat of a Justice Department car. So we rode in silence through what had become a driving rain storm as the driver took another route to the Willard—across the Calvert Street Bridge, by the Knickerbocker Theater, which had had its roof cave in from a snow storm a couple of winters ago, down 18th Street to L, left to 14th and then down to the hotel. Although nothing much happened, it was one of the most exciting, sensuous moments of my life just holding her, aware of her expanding and contracting breasts, her warm, full body but mostly *the anticipation!*

When we reached the Willard, I naturally wanted to head straight for her room. But she asked could we go to the lounge for a nightcap and I said that was fine, I still had my flask from the afternoon. Once we were comfortable in the lounge and she was sipping a straight bourbon, I said: "Okay, what happened out there at the Wardman? Is Jesse all right?"

"The strangest thing," she said. "By the time we got to his room he was almost trembling, I think with fear. I don't know why. I didn't mind leaving him there alone because one of Daugherty's Justice Department aides, Warren Martin, was spending the night—at Harry's request. Harry's spending the night at the White House. But at the door, as I was leaving Jesse said: 'Roxy, they've passed it to me, the curse of the blue diamond.'

"I didn't know what the hell he was talking about but before I could ask him to explain, Warren was calling from the other room, 'That you, Jesse?' Jesse also said he had prepared a packet of papers that he was going to give to the Duchess before he went to Leesburg. They would support the fact that everything he did here in Washington, he did for Harry."

"And you have no idea what he was talking about—'passing it to him?' "

"No. When he was in Ohio—you remember, I was telling you about it at the ball game—he kept saying 'they passed it to me.' I kept asking him to explain, but he wouldn't. At that time he didn't say anything about a curse or a blue diamond."

"He must have been referring to the Hope Diamond in some way," I said.

"I don't know. It's funny him getting so drunk tonight. He hasn't done that for some time."

Then she paused. "Fix me another drink. I'm tired of worrying about Jesse. I'll try to talk with him in the morning before he leaves for Leesburg. If this storm keeps up, he may not even go."

"Good idea. Why don't I fix you another nightcap in your room? We can be more relaxed up there." She knew exactly what I meant. She set her empty glass on the table, pulled back her arms over her head, throwing out her breasts as if she was stretching for bed, and said: "Jim, that is exactly what I would like to do. How did you guess?"

"A Chinese fortune cookie told me recently that 'Something good is going to happen to you.' "

As soon as we were in her room and had locked the door, she turned to face me, dropped her coat and started taking off her dress, very deliberately, as if she was unveiling a statue. When she was down to her bra and panties, I slid to the floor, reached behind her, pulled that unbelievable body to me and and kissed her on the stomach. She pushed my head down toward its goal, but then thought better of it. She pulled me up, took my hand and walked me to a bed in the next room and with one quick swipe cleared it by knocking a small travelling bag to the floor. I have to say, I liked her style.

While she pulled the covers down, I managed to get my coat, pants and tie off but I couldn't wait to unbutton my shirt. I still thought this was all too good to be true and that she might change her mind and disappear into the bathroom. When I was lying beside her on the bed and doing my inevitable fumbling job to remove her brassiere, finally, in the interest of speed, she relieved me of that task. She did, however, let me handle her panties, which gently and fondly I did. Pretty soon, she had my shirt off and was beginning to gently kiss me about the waist.

I must say that reporting this scene in her room excites me considerably even now. I was naturally rushing to a climax, but Roxy persisted in leisurely foreplay, "like two civilized people," she said. So we were in the bed together for quite awhile, doing what two people do in bed, which usually produces an exhilarating climax. But the telephone rang!

She pushed me back abruptly, jumped up and rushed into the other room, without even trying to find a robe to put on: "That must be Jesse," she said. "Something must have happened."

I could hear her from the other room say "Hello." Then there was silence while she listened to whoever was on the phone. In a few moments, she said: "Well, I'll put the bastard on! He's right here." She threw the phone toward the chair next to the telephone table and came striding back into the room, obviously annoyed about something: "It's for you," she said coldly.

Whatever was bothering her, Roxy gave me no clue as she went into the bathroom and slammed the door.

I picked up the phone which had fallen to the floor and said, "Hello."

It was Mencken calling from our room at the Willard. But before I could ask him what the hell he had said to set Roxy off, he explained: "Cain, let me tell you, if I'm playing Sherlock Holmes to your Dr. Watson, we have found our evil Moriarity. That Gaston B. Means is a master criminal. A scoundrel, but a successful one, which makes him fascinating."

"It doesn't surprise me. I didn't get a chance to tell you before we left the hotel this evening, but when I went to the men's room, I also talked to Frank Kent and he told me a lot about Means. I wanted to warn you what kind of a guy he was but I didn't get a chance."

"Christ, he couldn't have been more cordial with me. And he knows who I am; he even found out who you are."

"How the hell did he do that?"

"I'll tell you later. Look, I'm writing up my notes on everything Means told me. You stay there and finish your evening with that fair wench. Then we've got to talk."

"Well it *was* a great evening, but I think it's over now. What in Christ did you say to her? She's made as hell at me now."

"Say? I don't know. When I called, I figured you were in bed and I think she is a very sophisticated woman, so, as a little joke, I said: 'This is the house detective, madame. Are you aware that you're entertaining a married man in your room?' Perhaps she has a thing about entertaining married men. A lot of women do."

"I guess so." And I slammed the hearing piece into the phone.

CHAPTER SEVEN

When Roxy came out of the bathroom in a robe and her pajamas, ready for bed, I tried to explain to her that, although technically I was still married, "Mary and I are separated. She lives with her mother in Churchhill, Maryland. We haven't talked about divorce yet, but that's coming."

"Well, technically and actually I am divorced," Roxy said, "and I'm not much interested in married men. There are too many attractive bachelors and divorcés and widowers around. So maybe we can get together sometime after your divorce. I'm going home tomorrow."

I reached for her trying to embrace, but she pushed me away. "No, I'm not in the mood. And I'm worried about Jesse. I'll call you in the morning and say good-bye." With that she escorted me to the door.

I took the elevator up a couple of floors to the 8th where our room was. The door was unlocked, Mencken was chewing on an unlit Willie and typing furiously on a typewriter he had requested from the hotel. He said he usually carries a small portable with him when he travels, but that he did not bring it on this trip because it might mark him as a journalist when he was trying to pose as a cigar manufacturer.

I told him I did not think his little joke was very funny, and without looking up from typing, he said: "I'm truly sorry, Jim, I guess she's not as sophisticated as I thought. I told you you were too young for her. Older women are tired of married men making promises and then walking away. How was she in bed?"

"None of your goddamn business."

"She must have been pretty good."

"You'll never know. So tell me, how did Means find out about us?"

"You have a nightcap and get ready for bed," he replied still typing rapidly. "I want to finish getting some of the stuff he told me down on paper. Then I want to do a quick column for next Monday while it's fresh."

"Column?" I almost shouted. "How are you going to get a column out of what this liar and crook told you?"

"Oh, don't worry. I'll just allude to the corruption that everybody in Washington seems to know is going on. But the column will be mostly about Lincoln's acknowledgement that politicians are 'taken as a mass, at least one long step removed from honest men,' that corruption is inevitable in a democracy and how they used to handle it in Prussia."

"And how was that?"

"Delinquent officials had not only to face trial in an ordinary criminal court but there was also a special tribunal in Berlin that would try them a second time for official corruption. And if found guilty the corrupt official could be punished in several different ways including jail. Any citizen of the state could bring charges against a crooked official. So how would you like to bring charges against the attorney general, Harry Daugherty?"

"How about Gaston B. Means?"

"I don't think so. He doesn't work for the government, at least not now. And that's the beauty of his operation."

When I was out of the bathroom and in my pajamas, he was still typing. We had a bedroom with twin beds and a sitting room, where Mencken was working. I decided to call Roxy and try to apologize for not telling her I was married, but the operator said she had asked not to be disturbed.

Then I settled into the comfortable chair in the sitting room, poured myself a shot of brandy from my flask and read the papers Mencken had brought to our rooms. I had just finished a story in Hearst's Washington paper, *The Herald,* about how Harding was annoyed by Daugherty prematurely announcing the president's candidacy in 1924, when Mencken pushed back his typewriter, and said: "That'll do for a first draft. I'll give it another look tomorrow. Now let me tell you about this Means," he continued. "He's one smart cookie. In the first place, he found out who we really are, which explains his comment about the Germans and the war. Turns out, that before the war he was working for a couple of German agents who dispensed with his services when they returned home. He had no feelings about the war, one way or the other. Just acting as a paid agent.

"Anyway, he told Smith that we were legit—not Prohibition agents. I think I convinced him that we really wanted to buy some whiskey, that I hated Prohibition more than Warren Harding.

"He said he knew how I felt, but that Prohibition was the best thing that ever happened to someone in his profession. He calls being a master rogue a profession. I like that.

"I said I could see what he meant, but that frankly I felt the world would be a lot better off if everyone went around half-stewed most of the time. That didn't surprise him, having figured out that I was H. L. Mencken, the famous Wet from Baltimore, and that I didn't give a damn whether he and Smith sold phony liquor permits or not. I told him that I've bought gallons of bootleg whiskey from bootleggers but that I wanted to cut out the middleman—especially in that Sinclair Lewis (the famous novelist, which impressed him) drank me out of house and cellar."

Mencken paused long enough to light another Willie and then went on: "He also told me how you get a liquor permit. It's quite simple. You are given a number of a room in a hotel not in Washington. For me, he suggested the Vanderbilt in New York, considering how often I go up there. You are given a room number, where you find a table on which there is your permit and a fish bowl in which you would normally place ten five-hundred-dollar bills (but he gave me a special price, three thousand dollars), which you count out conspicuously so that someone—no doubt Means—who is watching you from the next room, can see you and the money. The permit gives you permission to remove liquor from a specified government warehouse, which, for me, will be in Pennsylvania."

"So, how did he find out that you were the Baltimore Bard? I'll bet it had something to do with you mentioning that your father owned stock in the Washington Senators."

"That's right. Roxy told him about the stock, the fact that I was working in my father's cigar business and also that you were from Baltimore. When he couldn't find out anything about me in Pennsylvania, he checked the owners of Washington Senators stock and found that one was August Mencken, a name similar to Mercker, who had a cigar company, Aug. Mencken and Bro., which was in

Baltimore and that his son was H. L. Mencken, the *Baltimore Sun*
columnist and well-known author and editor. With that to go on,
he identified me in a photograph and quickly learned that I had
lunch recently with a James M. Cain, who used to work for the
Sun, and the next day I had lunch in Washington with you and
Mary Roberts Rinehart, whom he, of course, knew had been one of
the first to know of the death of Charles Cramer, which suggested
to him that we had, for some reason, an interest in the Harding
administration. All this was confirmed, he said, this evening at the
Hotel Washington when he saw you leave the table to talk with
Frank Kent, the Washington bureau chief of the *Sun.*"

"Obviously Means is a first-rate investigator."

"And a master crook who brags about it and loves publicity. He
had no hesitation telling me the most incredible things. And at the
heart of his role as the administration's most outspoken scoundrel
is the fact that, rightly or wrongly, he feels that he has total immunity from the law—because he has too much on the chief law
enforcement officer in the land, the attorney general of the United
States, who probably would be out of a job immediately if Gaston
B. Means spilled the beans. But would anyone believe him?"

"Jesus Christ, what power!" was all I could say.

"What power, indeed, which shows you the double whammy a
crooked government puts on us. We have not only the dishonest
elected officials and their appointees, but the rogues like Means who
are smart enough to figure out what's going on, usually by partic-
ipating in the corruption, then blackmailing officials into giving
them immunity.

"Means says quite candidly: 'With me, a man's just a number.
I'd just as soon investigate a tramp as anybody. I work for whoever
has money—just like a lawyer. Just put a memo on my desk and a
retainer and I go into action. You want to run for office? I'll find
the skeleton in your opponent's closet. I'll read his mail, bribe his
servants, make a plan of his house to facilitate a break-in.' For a
price he'll promise to fix anything with the Justice Department,
which is not so easy anymore. But he'll promise to fix it anyway—
drop a case, commute a sentence, help you buy back property confiscated during the war. He will also follow your spouse to see
whom he or she is keeping company with. He told me—in strictest
confidence, mind you—that he shadows both the president and Ned

McLean for the Duchess and Mrs. McLean when they go womanizing together.

"And, of course, he'll help you buy a permit to take liquor out
of a government warehouse. It's all the same to Means. He says
'The joke among us is that everything in Washington is for sale
except the Capitol Dome.' "

"So why was he telling you all that?"

"There are probably a number of reasons and it didn't hurt that
he was pouring us scotch of the first chop all evening, although
that was not what loosened his tongue. Means is too calculating for
that. He seems always in control. First he is a braggart. Second, he
craves publicity that shows him as smarter than the other guys.
Third, he really feels the standards are so lax in the Harding administration that he can get away with anything. He's convinced
the Justice Department can't touch him because he has too much
on Daugherty; the public doesn't give a damn and the press has not
been paying much attention—although that is beginning to change.
He knows that Frank Kent, Mark Sullivan, Samuel Hopkins Adams
and others are beginning to sniff around and we've all heard about
impeaching the attorney general for failure to prosecute bootleggers
and Secretary Fall for possible fraud in the leasing of the government oil reserves in Wyoming and California. It's even possible
that Means is the one leaking information about Daugherty because
Daugherty got tired of Means blackmailing him and refused to give
in to one of his demands. More important, Daugherty insulted him!"

"Insulted him? Hell, I don't see Means as the sensitive type."

"About some things. Means has always carried a grudge against
Daugherty since he first fired him. But then, more recently, Means
went to work quietly for Daugherty, through Burns, trying to find
out what evidence some senators who are considering impeaching
him had against him. Daugherty was furious because Means, after
investigating a couple of senators, told Daugherty that the Senate
had no evidence against him. Means says 'Daugherty sent an emis-
sary to tell me to "go to hell," that I've lost my cunning, that I'm
no longer a good investigator, and that I was fired—again!'

" 'No man,' says Means, 'can insult me at my most vulnerable
point—as an investigator. It's my only pride!' "

"Hell hath no fury like an investigator scorned," I said.

"So that's another reason Means is talking. Then, finally, there's the fact that like many very bright people, he's a little nuts."

"All very plausible. But it still doesn't explain why he picked you to unburden himself to about corruption in the Harding administration."

"There's a human element involved here. Frankly, I think he was impressed by me, with my reputation for being a rebel with little regard for established institutions, for which he, obviously, has even less. More important, I think, was the fact that we are journalists. He said that when he left Washington—which might be soon—he planned to write a book about his experiences in the Harding administration. He thought I might be able to help him get it published and he wondered whether you might be interested in ghost writing it—for a price, of course."

"I assume you told him not a chance."

"Certainly. I said we would probably be writing a book ourselves and that made his eyes light up even more. Braggarts love to brag to anyone, but even more to someone of stature. And then, when this nationally famous writer who is writing a book complimented him on being such a good investigator and such a competent con man, especially his ability to con the crooks in government—and you know how I admire competence in anything. Well, this kind of touched off his braggadoccio and I could hardly stop him crowing about how smart he was compared to such dopes as the attorney general, the secretary of the Interior, the head of the Veterans' Bureau—and, of course the president of the United States. He says he agrees with the Duchess—Mrs. Harding—that 'the president is just a plain fool.' "

"So what did he tell you about Harding's gang?"

"The most significant thing was that he thinks Jesse Smith has prepared a file which proves that he was just carrying out orders for Harry Daugherty. This won't exonerate Smith, but it'll at least keep the gang from setting Smith up as the fall guy."

Mencken's mention of Smith's file suddenly reminded me that I had not told him what Kent said about Means and Smith's strange comments to Roxy when she walked him to to his Wardman Park apartment earlier in the evening. "That jibes with what I learned from Kent and what Smith has been telling Roxy. Before you go on with Means' story, let me bring you up to date."

I told him everything Kent had to say, especially his conviction that incredible tales of corruption in the Harding administration were about to explode. Also that Smith told Roxy that they— meaning Daugherty—"have passed it to me." And he made some strange comment about them passing him the "curse of the blue diamond." Roxy also said she thought that Smith had prepared a packet of papers which he intended to give the Duchess tomorrow.

"Well, it's all coming together," Mencken said. "I suggested that Means might consider turning state's evidence, but he said: What good would that do? No one would believe him, which is the way he wants it. He made the point that I could go to the authorities tomorrow and tell them everything he told me tonight and he would deny everything on the witness stand and say he had his reasons for talking to me. Then everybody would be confused, they would say 'Gaston's such a liar, who can believe him?' that they wouldn't have anything except the word of known liar—case dismissed! What did Roxy make of that blue diamond comment?"

"No idea. So what else did Means tell you?"

"He started to run down as much as he knew or wanted to tell me about the Veterans' Bureau and Forbes. I told him we knew about them and he said he was convinced Cramer was silenced to keep him from doing what Jesse Smith is getting ready to do— blow the whistle. And you might ask, in this administration how do you blow the whistle when the attorney general and the head of the Bureau of Investigation can hush up almost anything? But Means says Daugherty will not try to block the VB investigation because Forbes wasn't playing by the rules and cutting Daugherty in.

"Then he was just starting to tell me about the American Metal Company, when one of the phones on his desk rang. He had been in a jovial amiable mood up to then, lots of sipping from the flask and laughing. But after he listened on the phone a few minutes his mood changed and he put the receiver to his chest and asked me to step into another room for a moment: 'This is a highly confiden- tial call,' he said. 'I won't be long.'

"The first thing I noticed about the room he indicated I should wait in was the fact that it had a telephone. I carefully picked it up, holding my hand over the mouthpiece, hoping that I could eaves- drop on his conversation. But this phone was dead.

"The next thing I noticed about the room was that it was big, for a basement room, and comfortably furnished. He lives with his wife and two children at Nine-oh-three Sixteenth Street in a large stone town house. His office is on the basement level and this room was next to it. But this was not a family room. It had a bar in one corner and near the center of the room was a poker table with several chairs grouped around it. It looked as if the table was permanently set up, but even so the room did not seem overcrowded. One thing for sure: this house did not come cheap. It is almost half again the size of my place in Baltimore and it's only a three-and-a-half-block walk to Sixteen Hundred Pennsylvania Avenue, a very fashionable address in this town. Mr. Means is doing all right for a private detective."

"Maybe his wife has money. Or remember what Kent said about his milking a widow for thousands of dollars a few years ago."

"Could be. But I think Mr. Means is making big money in the detective business. Anyway, Means beckoned me back into his office. I asked him if the president plays poker here and he said: 'No, the president usually plays at the H Street house that Ned McLean loaned Jesse Smith and Daugherty.' The H Street house is also known as the 'love nest.' That's another thing about Means; he wants to make sure you are aware that he knows *everything* that's going on in the underside of the Harding administration. I guess that's typical of private detectives."

"Or braggarts."

"Yeah. So, after the phone call we're back in Means' office and his mood has obviously changed. It's almost as if he sobered up in a hurry. I tried to draw him out about the phone call which had obviously rattled him. 'I hope that wasn't bad news,' I said. 'You look like you've seen a ghost.'

" 'Not yet,' he replied. Then, looking at his watch and changing the subject he said: 'I was telling you about the metal company; I'll have to make this brief, because I have some urgent business that needs attending to.'

" 'At this hour?' I asked him, and Means nodded yes. Still trying to get some idea what the phone call was about, I asked: 'Does it concern Daugherty?' Means smiled weakly and replied: 'Everything I do concerns Daugherty one way or the other. He's running the goddamn government.' "

Then, Mencken said Means shifted subjects and proceeded to tell him an incredible story about the American Metal Company, a German concern, which was liquidated by the U.S. government during the war. The money from the liquidation—about six-and-a-half-million—was put in liberty bonds, which ended up under the control of the Alien Property Custodian. After the Harding administration came to power, a man named John King . . ."

"He was at the ball park today," I said, interrupting, "but he ignored Smith."

"Interesting," Mencken replied. "King represented the metal company before the Alien Property Administration claimed the six-point-five million dollars should be returned because the company had been orally transferred to a neutral Swiss corporation. Such claims have to go through the Alien Property Custodian and then the Justice Department, which usually takes months. But King really knew how to grease the skids because this claim went through very fast. And all very legal—except the claim that American was really a Swiss company was a total fraud. On this little caper, not only a Harding henchman in the the Alien Property Custodian office was paid off, but the Justice Department was also cut in—for a total of fifty thousand dollars to one hundred thousand dollars. And Jesse Smith, Daugherty's unofficial assistant, knows all about it."

My first reaction was: And how much did Roxy know? Damnit, I thought. Do I really want to become involved with someone mixed up in this mess? Part of me, deep down in my groin, still said yes. But in my head I was less sure.

"Then there was Jap Muma and the film of the Dempsey-Carpentier fight," Mencken continued.

"Now, how in the hell did they make money on that?"

"Easy. You may remember that after the Jack Johnson–Jim Jeffries fight, Congress passed a law prohibiting movies of prize fights from being sold across state lines so that down in the Sahara of the Bozarts [Mencken's term for the Deep South, Bozarts meaning beaux arts] folks would not be subjected to the horror of a black-amoor beating up on a white boy. Then, along comes the Dempsey-Carpentier fight with its famous long count. The law did not prohibit the showing of the film, just the transporting of it across a state line. So Muma comes up with this ingenious idea; they'd get someone, usually representing a veterans' organization, to show the film, get arrested and go to court where he is given a small fine. The key was finding a federal judge who, for a price, would impose the fine rather than send the straw man to jail. Means said that Jesse boasted to him that he had fixed judges in at least twenty states. The total profit from this operation was over a million dollars. How much Smith and Daugherty ended up with after all the payoffs, Means didn't know. He knows that the money is usually split four ways when he's in on a deal—which is not often these days: Means, Smith, Daugherty and the Republican National Committee, they're still paying off their 1920 campaign debts. Daugherty takes care of any money that might go to Harding, who doesn't know what's going on and probably doesn't profit personally from the graft. But he says that Daugherty can get the president to sign most anything he wants him to, no questions asked. It's a form of blackmail because the president at least knows that Daugherty needs money to pay campaign debts. At any rate, Smith's share of the loot must be plenty. Means says he personally has seen Jesse wearing a money belt with seventy-five thousand dollars in it. But he also says that it could have come from George Remus."

"The angry little tough guy who barged into Smith's office this morning?"

"That's right. And, according to Means, he has a lot to be angry about. Remus has already given Smith anywhere from seventy-five thousand dollars to three hundred thousand dollars, first to keep from being indicted, which Smith failed to do, then prevent the trial, which has already taken place, then to keep from being sentenced to jail, which Smith will probably also fail to do. Most people think Remus is heading for jail if he loses his appeal now before the Supreme Court."

"Did you ask Means how much Roxy knows about all this?"

"Didn't think to."

"Anything else?"

"No. Means said he could give me some details about the stuff he had told me, but suddenly, he became anxious to get me out of there. He did offer to drive me back to the Willard in his big black Cadillac. I was going to walk but it was storming too much. In the short ride, he said he could get me a permit, but we would have to be very careful; things are getting hot. When I was getting out of his car at the Willard, he let me know that he was standing by to help us get—for a price, of course—any information we wanted about what was going on in Washington. Can you imagine that!"

"No wonder everyone says that scandals are about to break and they'll probably bring down the administration. Means sounds like a one-man wrecking team."

"Except you can't believe anything he tells you, let alone prove it."

"So what do we do now? By the way, I forgot to tell you, Kent says he's been invited to a press party the McLeans are throwing at their big estate. He says we can go along with him, but you'll probably have an invitation on your desk when you get back to Baltimore. It'll be a perfect chance to meet the McLeans and see what kind of reaction we get when we tell 'em what you heard about the blue diamond."

"Great. I have to go up to New York soon, but I should be back by then. How 'bout fixing me a drink? I've had a hard day."

It was the look on my face, I'm sure, that prompted him to pause and then say: "No. Better yet, I'll fix you one. You've had a harder day."

CHAPTER EIGHT

The next morning, Saturday, Mencken woke me, dancing around the bedroom mimicking Sherlock Holmes playing his fiddle. "Get up, Cain, the game's afoot. There's sleuthing to be done."

Then he threw a piece of paper on my bed: "What do you make of this? I forgot to show it to you last night."

It was the note in Smith's desk that Mencken had copied yesterday morning while Smith was out of the room.

To: JS
From: HMD
Subject: Pending matters of mutual concern

1. My sources tell me that GBR is enraged, especially after the last 30K, and has made threats against you.
2. JM is also unhappy, but with help from NM we may be able to stop proceedings.
3. I find what you hear about HD hard to believe but we can't believe GBM? Can you verify?

While I was pondering the meaning of this cryptic memo, Mencken picked up the Gideon Bible on his bedside table, scribbled something on the first page, then put it in his luggage. "What are you doing, stealing a Bible? Have you no shame?"

"Hell, I do it every time I stay in a hotel."

"Considering how often you go to New York, you must have one helluva Bible library."

"Are you kidding? I send them to my friends most in need of prayer." Then taking the pilfered Bible out of his bag, he said: "This one is, and I quote, 'For Louis Untermeyer, with compliments of the author.' Louis is a poet and they are in most need of prayer.

Anyone over thirty who claims to be a poet is palpably in an advanced state of arrested development, a sort of moron. If he's past thirty-five, he seems somehow unnatural, even a trifle obscene, I exclude Untermeyer of course. He's in his late thirties and a very sound fellow; I've known him for years. I have to send him this. He's in Johns Hopkins with a touch of grippe. I wrote him that he should ignore the doctor, drink three stiff glasses of *Gluhwein* and, most important, sleep on a stolen Bible. More effective than any voodoo I know, including the Hope Diamond."

"Well, now I read somewhere that you once published a volume of poetry—I believe it was titled *Ventures in Verse*."

"Which proves my point. I was a callow youth when I wrote my poetry; I may have even had a similar attack of piety. All of us pass through that stage, like a frog is a tadpole before becoming a frog. But I've been trying to make amends for years. There were only one hundred copies printed; half went to reviewers, most of the rest I gave to friends. Every time I go into a used book store, I look for copies and buy them up. It's only forty-six pages so they don't cost much. I even steal them back from my friends when I come across one of them in their library. Actually, the book got pretty good reviews, which tells you more about the reviewers than my poetry. I was really copying Kipling, who was my favorite as a youth. How do you like this?

Oho! for the days of the olden time,
When a fight was a fight of men . . .
When lance broke lance and arm met arm—
There were no cowards then . . . "

"I take it you don't like poetry much."

"Only at special times. Even Shakespeare I enjoy not on brisk mornings when I feel fit for deviltry, but on dreary evenings when my old wounds are troubling me, and some fickle one has just returned the autographed set of my first editions, and bills are piled up on my desk, and I am too sad to work. Then I mix a stiff dram— and read poetry."

It is very easy to get off the subject with Mencken, so I suggested that we focus on the note he copied. We had slept late, the morning was getting away from us and we wanted to spend some time at the National Press Club nearby in the Albee Building at 15th and G Streets. Even though it was Saturday, we hoped to find Stackelback there and question him about Secretary Fall.

Considering the note while dressing, we decided that "JS" was obviously Jesse Smith, "HMD" was Daugherty. Mencken, the connoisseur of words, remembered that his middle name was the odd one of Micajah. And GBR could be George Remus, if what Means had said about Remus giving Smith money for services not rendered was true. There was no doubt that "GBM" was Means, but we did not know what to make of "JM," "NM" and "HD." We figured it was unlikely that Daugherty would label himself "HD" after introducing himself as "HMD."

I thought Roxy could help us with this if we could figure out a way to tell her that we had gone through Smith's desk—which suddenly reminded me that before she left for Ohio I wanted to try again to explain last night.

I called her room, but received no answer. Then I called the front desk to ask if she had checked out. "No," I was told, but she has left the building: "Miss Stinson was picked up by a government car some time ago and has not returned."

Very strange, I thought. Mencken agreed when I told him, then he said: "By the way, do you think we ought to continue this charade with the buxom Miss Stinson or can I part my hair in the middle again? Sooner or later, Means will tell her who we are."

"Let's tell her. I doubt if she believes our story anyway. She's no dumbbell."

"Good. I wish I had a decent suit with me. I hate the thought of anyone seeing me in this booboise outfit. I guess I can always plead my partial color blindness."

"Just tell whoever comments, that you thought it was an appropriate dress for the capital of the boobs."

Rather than wait for room service to bring our breakfast, we went downstairs. I was looking at the menu in the dining room when suddenly Roxy Stinson appeared in the doorway. She saw us seated over near one of the windows looking out on 14th Street and walked quickly in our direction.

"Oh, I'm so glad I caught you before you left," she said. "I just tried to call you; something horrible has happened."

I pulled up a chair for her and she sat down while looking around the room, seeming to make sure that no one could hear her. Then she said softly: "Jesse is dead! I've been with Burns and some D.C. detectives all morning. They've decided to call it suicide and they told me that's the story and I better stick to it."

"So what was the motive?" I asked.

"They're going to say that he was in poor health, partly due to diabetes and an appendicitis operation that never healed properly, in addition to worrying about some corruption in the Justice Department they say he was responsible for. In other words, like he feared, they're going to pass the blame to him—although Jesse never did anything without Daugherty's approval. But even though he was afraid of guns and violence, I think that considering everything that has happened in recent weeks, he probably did shoot himself. I've never seen anyone so upset and afraid as Jesse has been lately."

"How's that?" asked Mencken.

"Well, right from the start, Jesse has been Harry's 'bumper' as he says . . ."

"Meaning?" Mencken interposed.

"Someone who stands between the attorney general and all the people who want favors from him. I remember he had not been in Washington more than four months, when he said, 'I'm not made for this! The intrigue is driving me crazy. If only I could come home. But I have to stand by Harry.' He loved that man. Would do anything for him."

"So what happened lately?" I asked.

"Not too long ago, that time I told you about at the ball game, Jim, when we were in Columbus, he acted like a man in mortal fear—not only for himself but for me. He wanted me to destroy all papers and letters I had that pertained to him—not his papers, but mine. He didn't want to stay for a dinner dance at the hotel, which he always loved, but wanted to get home before dark. He insisted we walk in the middle of the street; he thought every strange man we saw was following him. He had a briefcase he asked me to carry for him. He didn't want to be seen with it."

"Do you know what was in it?" Mencken asked.

"I can't see through leather and ladies don't go rummaging

through a gentleman's briefcase. I kept trying to assure him that he was going to be all right, that he was just imagining things. The next time he came home, he bought a gun—the one Burns says killed him."

"Oh," I responded.

"It happened this way: Jesse and Harry have a shack on a farm near Washington Courthouse. They often go out there alone to relax and talk politics. The last time they were home, just a few days ago, they went out to the shack. Harry was not feeling very good and he always takes a nap after lunch. Suddenly, a gentleman arrived from Columbus and insisted on seeing Harry. Jesse is supposed to keep people like that from disturbing the attorney general."

"Do you know who the guy was?" I asked.

"Jesse never told me and I never asked; I rarely asked him anything about his work. I usually learned more by not asking. But it was someone Jesse knew. He was very persistent and convinced Jesse that what he had to talk about was extremely important. If I had to guess, based on what Jesse told me, it was the bootlegger, George Remus. Jesse had promised Remus that even though the Justice Department would pretend to prosecute him, that he would never be indicted. And if he was indicted, he would never go to jail."

"And Jesse got some money for this?" I said.

"I guess so."

"But what if Remus was the man at the shack," Mencken said, "and Daugherty convinced him that Jesse was promising something the Justice Department could not give him in the present climate? Wouldn't that make Jesse the double-crosser in Remus' eyes and a target for revenge?"

"Maybe. Jesse told me that when he woke Daugherty, Harry went into a rage. He got dressed and was going to drive back into town without even talking to the man."

"But maybe Daugherty did talk to him and Jesse wasn't being truthful with you," I suggested.

"I just don't know. I'm so confused. Harry was just going to leave Jesse out there at the shack. He finally agreed to drive him back to Washington Courthouse, but wouldn't speak to him. Jesse got out of the car and went right to Carpenter's Hardware Store and bought the gun. People who were there later told me that Jesse

casually mentioned that it 'was for the attorney general.' Later that
evening when he came to my house, Jesse was holding his head up
for the first time in weeks. I said, 'Are things all right now, Jesse?'
And he said: 'Yes, they're all right now.' "

"Jesus," said Mencken. "What do you make of that?"

"I think he decided to shoot himself after he had been humiliated
and hurt by his best friend. I never did find out who the man was."

"Probably Remus," I said. "With or without Daugherty's authority, Jesse had been promising Remus protection from the Justice
Department that they could not deliver. Then, suddenly this guy
shows up and wants a showdown with the attorney general. And
Jesse is caught in the middle."

"And you could make a good case," Mencken cut in, "that when
Smith referred to buying the gun for the attorney general that he
meant for his protection or for Jesse's use in trying to give him
protection. If that was Remus wanting to see Daugherty he no doubt
left the shack mumbling a few comments as to what was going to
happen to a couple of hack politicians who double-crossed someone
like him."

"Possibly," Roxy said, "But I can't see Jesse or Harry thinking
they're going to have a shoot-out with a bunch of gangsters."

"What about his papers?" I said. "Did they find the packet of
papers Means said Jesse was going to give to Mrs. Harding? And
did they find his little green book he took notes in?"

"No, they found nothing like that. In fact, I heard Burns telling
one of the Washington detectives that they were to stress that no
papers of any kind were found, but that he had burned something
in the trash basket, which his head was half in. He apparently fell
to the floor and hit his head on the side of the trash basket. Burns,
who has an apartment at the Wardman himself on the floor below
Jesse's, got there before the other detectives or the coroner. After
Burns came Dr. Joel Boone, who's a naval officer and number two
doctor in the White House. Of course, Warren Martin was there all
night. But he was taking orders from Burns, who everyone knew
was taking orders from the attorney general, who didn't show up
this morning but was constantly talking to Burns on the phone.
Everything was arranged just like Daugherty and Burns wanted it."

"Burns is a well-known detective," said Mencken. "I wouldn't
think he'd participate in the cover-up of a crime."

"Don't kid yourself. He was appointed by Harry and is a childhood friend from Ohio. He'll do anything Harry tells him to do."

"So what happened in the apartment this morning?" I asked.

"As near as I could figure it out, Martin found the body about six A.M. He called Daugherty, who was spending the night at the White House. Harry told the president. One of them, probably the president, called Boone and told him to get right over to the Wardman. Harry called Burns and told him what had happened and told him to go upstairs to his apartment immediately. Burns took over and arranged things the way he wanted. Boone arrived and declared Smith dead, probably a suicide. The coroner, a guy named Nesbitt, and two D.C. detectives arrived. Martin called me at the Willard and said he was sending a Justice Department car to take me to the Wardman. I arrived after the coroner, but I heard Martin tell him that he found the gun in Jesse's right hand. But it was no longer there. They were just covering Jesse with a sheet getting ready to move him out."

"Could you see the wound?" I asked.

"Yes. It was not a pretty sight."

"Was it on the right side of the head or the left?" asked Mencken.

"It was the left temple that I saw,"

"And Jesse is left-handed—or right?" I said.

"Definitely right-handed!"

"Could have been an exit wound," Mencken suggested.

Roxy continued: "Then Boone went back to the White House to report. Nesbitt signed the death certificate, specifically citing cause of death as suicide. Then I heard Nesbitt assuring Burns that with the certificate stating 'suicide' there would be no inquest and probably no autopsy."

"How did they know it was Jesse's gun that killed him?" asked Mencken.

"Martin had seen it the day before."

"Well," I said, "it looks like they set it up so that there was no doubt about it being suicide because of Jesse's fear of being held responsible for the exposure of Justice Department corruption."

"And his health," Roxy added. "They claimed that he was failing because of high living, an unhealed appendicitis wound and diabetes. That will be in all the papers tonight."

"Obviously they wanted to make certain," Mencken said, "that no one would ever suspect murder."

"But it was murder, don't you see," Roxy answered. "If he shot himself it was because he knew he was being targeted to take the rap."

"Roxy, I understand your feeling for Jesse," I said, "but don't you think there's a possibility that Jesse did engage in some graft on his own—like Means—without telling Daugherty? Knowing that Daugherty had taken some illegal earnings—like his share of the money from the Dempsey-Carpentier fight—Jesse could have thought: 'Okay, what's a little more? I deserve it and have earned it for all I've done for them.' "

"I don't think Jesse would do that. He loved Harry and the president, he wouldn't have done anything that might hurt them—unless Daugherty told him or approved."

"But Means says he personally saw Jesse with seventy-five one-thousand-dollar bills in a money belt he wore. You must have seen that.

"Did they find Jesse's money belt?"

Roxy looked surprised, as if she hadn't thought of that. "I don't know. Nobody mentoned it."

"Did Jesse have a will?"

"Yes. He has one on file in Washington Courthouse with Mal Daugherty, the attorney general's brother, a banker who handles all of Harry's and Jesse's financial affairs. However, there's another will. By way of emphasizing it was suicide, Martin told me that that evening Jesse had scribbled a new will on a sheet of Wardmam Park stationery leaving everything to a sister and niece. Martin also said that somebody—probably Harry—will contest it because it's not witnessed. Maybe that will tell us what to do with the diamonds."

"What do you mean?" I asked.

"We also found Jesse's diamonds. They were in a small box that he usually keeps locked and hidden in a chest of drawers. It had either been pried open or was broken. But Martin, who has seen the box, said it didn't look like any of the diamonds were missing. I tried several times to get Jesse to put them in a bank safe deposit box, but he said no, that he liked to get them out from time to time and look at them."

"The box didn't by chance contain a large blue diamond did it?" Mencken asked.

"You mean the Hope?" Roxy replied.

"Yeah," I said. "We're assuming his comment about passing the curse of the blue diamond on to him must have had something to do with the Hope. I tried to call you last night—to apologize again and see what you thought he meant by that. The operator said you had gone to bed."

"That's right. I was very tired and I thought you might be calling. I agree Jesse's comment must have referred to the Hope, but I know he had nothing to do with its disappearance. For one thing, the McLeans are good friends and two, he believed in the curse. He wouldn't have touched that diamond with a flagpole."

"So where did Jesse get that money belt full of thousand-dollar bills?" I asked.

"Probably from a fight film they put on," Roxy replied.

"Yeah," Mencken said, "Means told me about that."

"Daugherty definitely knew about it," Roxy said. "And I'm sure he got his share. What about you? Are you still going to try to get a liquor permit?"

"I don't know," Mencken answered. "Even before Smith's death, Means thought things were pretty hot. And I guess there's one thing you ought to know."

"What's that?"

"In running his check on us, Means also found that we're not exactly what we appear—or at least have been trying to appear. My father *is* in the cigar business, but I'm not. And Jim, here, does not work for me—although I hope he will soon. I did want a permit to buy some liquor and still wouldn't mind having one. But mostly for my own use, not to sell, because I am not a bootician; I'm a journalist, as is Jim. His real name is James Cain. Although he's a writer, he's going to start teaching college in Annapolis this fall. We pretended to be businessmen and amateur bootleggers as a way to begin an investigation of the Harding administration for an article for a new magazine I'm going to edit—maybe even for a book."

I thought this was going to catch Roxy off guard, but she took it completely in stride: "Well, I'll be damned! I guess I shouldn't be telling you so much. But it doesn't surprise me, you not being a businessman. You remember, Jim, I told you I thought he was a little unusual for a cigar maker."

"You may not believe this, but Fred—Henry—really is H. L. Mencken the author. I'm sure you know of him. He's also co-editor of *The Smart Set,* that magazine you like so much."

"That does explain a few things—like why you never sounded like a cigar maker."

"Well, I once was, for a couple of years in my youth. And I guess we want to apologize for deceiving you. I promise we will not reveal your name as the source of anything we might write."

"I appreciate that. And I've come to like you boys, even Jim, who deceived me more than you did, Mr. Mencken."

I shook my head as she said this, but did not try to defend myself now.

"I'd like to help you, especially in your book. A book is a permanent record; it records our history. And I'll do anything I can to help get it down in history that it was Harry Daugherty who killed Jesse and that anything they claim Jesse did was really done for Harry Daugherty. Even if Harry didn't actually approve of it, Jesse knew he was doing something that Daugherty wanted to have done, just like Harry did a lot of things he knew the president needed to have done, even though he never told the president. That's just the way the system works."

"That may be the way the political system works," I said, "but not the legal system. Under the law, the guy who did something wrong is just as guilty as the guy who ordered or approved it."

"I'll accept that, but I just want it to go down in history that poor Jesse did whatever he did—for Harry Daugherty."

"Maybe you can help us with this," Mencken said. He took the note he had swiped from Smith's desk out of his pocket and showed it to Roxy. "I won't burden you with how we happen to have it, but it's obviously a memo from Harry Daugherty to Jesse Smith."

As Roxy looked at the note, she said: "Well, of course you stole it from Jesse's desk yesterday morning."

"He did it," I said.

Ignoring the impropriety of his theft and with a tone of "we have more important things to concern us now," Mencken said: "We figure 'GBR' is George Remus and 'GBM' is Means, but we're not sure about the other initials. Any ideas?"

After studying the memo for a moment, Roxy said: "Yes. I'm pretty sure 'JM' is Jap Muma and 'NM' is Ned McLean."

"Owner of the *Washington Post*?" Mencken said.

"Yes. And the *Cincinnati Enquirer*. And good friend of President Harding and Jesse. The reference to an 'investigation' probably refers to an investigation of the showing of the Dempsey-Carpentier film across the country. You know about the film?"

"Means told me how they—including Jesse—made money off it," Mencken said. "How come they had an Oriental involved?"

" 'Jap' is not Japanese; that's just what they call him. He's from Cincinnati. Mainly he works for Mr. McLean and Jap was the lead organizer of the plan to market the film of the fight across the country. McLean had the first showing here in Washington—a big affair with a lot of top people in the government invited. Naturally, no one said anything about this showing. But Muma finally got caught and they couldn't bribe the judges—one of them was Judge Kenesaw Mountain Landis in Illinois—and he was indicted. And he was furious.

"I remember being at a small party at the H Street house when Jap was raving about the injustice being done to him: 'Fine! Jap Muma, general manager of the McLean newspapers. Personal friend of the attorney general. Old acquaintance of President Harding; called him "Warren"; calls me "Jap." Fine. On my way to Atlanta as a conspirator. The mastermind.'

"But he doesn't have to worry. Jesse told me that Daugherty and Burns have buried the evidence in the files and the Muma case is closed."

"Very good," I said. "Any thoughts about who 'HD' might be?"

"No. I know Harry would not be referring to himself as 'HD.' He always used 'HMD' in memos."

"You referred to the 'H Street house,' " said Mencken. "Is that like the K Street house—where the gang does business?"

"No. H Street is where they have their drinking parties and—at least some of them—take their girlfriends, especially the president. That's why they call it 'the love nest.' It's at Fifteen-oh-nine H Street and it's a safe place because it's also owned by Ned McLean. I've been there a couple of times. I heard that at one party, which the president attended, a girl, of shall we say questionable reputation, from New York was accidentally killed by a flying whiskey bottle. They got the president out of there in a hurry and hushed the whole thing up."

"How about the famous poker games?" I asked. "Are they played there?"

"Depends on who's playing. If there's top people in the game, it's usually played at McLean's I Street House or upstairs in the White House. If it's middle-level guys and public relations men, Washington lawyers and fixers, people like that, they'd more likely play at the H Street house or maybe Means' Sixteenth Street place. You got to remember that the poker games are an old Ohio custom, a way to pass money to politicians. You make side bets that the giver is sure to lose and the politicians are sure to win. Jesse told me about one time the president won a pearl stickpin worth about four or five thousand dollars. He won it spading, which is betting on the side that one person's hand will have a higher spade than another hand. The president put up one hundred dollars against the stickpin and when he won, went around bragging about it."

"Great subject for a column," Mencken said, lighting up a Willie.

Then I suddenly had an idea. "I got it! The 'HD' in the Daugherty note does not refer to a person. It's the Hope Diamond! And that means both Smith and Means heard the same thing Nathan heard in New York. That the diamond had been stolen."

"You're right, Jim. That has to be it. And that's what Jesse was talking about when he told the McLeans he had something to tell them when he came to Leesburg."

"Which means," I added, "that the McLeans still don't know their diamond is missing because we can assume Smith didn't want to tell them over the phone."

"Well maybe we can tell them when Kent takes us to that press party at Friendship," Mencken suggested.

"Oh, won't that be fun. I wish I could go," Roxy said.

"Can't you come back for it?" I asked, showing my overeagerness.

"I could, but that's one party I wouldn't be invited to."

"Miss Stinson is right. You won't see many gals at a press party."

"Especially the notorious Roxy Stinson," she inserted, "whom everyone says knows enough to put all the Ohio Gang behind bars."

"Just who makes up the Ohio Gang we hear so much about these days?" I asked Roxy.

"Oh, it's about a dozen top guys in the Justice Department, all part of the political clique that came from Ohio with Harry. And they don't mind being called the Ohio Gang, they're proud of it. I know Jesse was."

"Means told me a lot of stuff about what's going on in Washington," Mencken said. "I'm sure a lot of it was baloney, but a lot of it sounded very plausible. Why do you think, Miss Stinson, Means wanted to leak that stuff to me?"

"That's easy. Means has gone too far in some of his operations and some lawyers in the Justice Department want to bring him to trial. Daugherty says he can't defend him and Means is threatening to blow the lid off everything if Daugherty doesn't get the Justice Department to drop the case as he has done for so many others. I think Means is trying to let everyone know that if he goes to jail everyone goes with him. One of the things Jesse has been worried about is that Daugherty—who has told Means to 'go to hell'—is just going to say 'Jesse did it' when Means starts blowing the lid."

"And Means could have spread the word that Jesse was going to turn state's evidence," I said, "which endangered Jesse with both Justice Department Investigator Burns and the bootleggers—or anyone else who might have contributed to Justice Department corruption."

"True enough," said Roxy as she abruptly looked at her jeweled watch and then said that she must leave. I offered her a brandy but she said: "No, thanks, that would relax me too much and I have a lot of things to do. Once I get on the train, I'll have a drink in the club car. There's alway some gentleman in there to offer me one."

"I'm sure of that," I said.

She said Jesse's funeral would be at Washington Courthouse in a few days and she had to see Mal Daugherty—the attorney general's brother in Ohio who handled Harry Daugherty's and Smith's business affairs. Standing to leave she said: "I have so much to tell you; I havn't even gotten into what's going on at the Interior Department. I know Jesse knew all about that too and he and

Daugherty were mad that they were not cut in because there are millions of dollars involved."

When she stood up, I did too, offering to see her to her room. I hoped I would have a chance to clarify my current marital situation and reestablish the relationship that was developing last night. She agreed to let me escort her upstairs, which greatly encouraged me.

Mencken stood up as Roxy prepared to leave and, grabbing her hand, said in fractured German: "*Ich küss die hand.* I understand that you prefer unmarried men, which is very sensible. It's a sure sign that you prefer superior men. In all history, you will not find six first-rate philosophers—or iconoclasts for that matter—who were married. The ideal state for these superior men is celibacy tempered by polygamy. When you tire of this callow youth, as you surely will, I would like very much to take you out to dinner and—whatever."

"Well thank you very much, Herr Mencken. I do like your magazine and you are cute. We'll just have to see. I'm not sure yet when I can get back to Washington. But I hope soon."

Except to comment that I, too, would soon be a bachelor, I ignored the competition from my fellow reporter and told him to go ahead and order and that I would not be long.

In her room, the first thing Roxy noticed was that someone had been searching it. "They're looking for Jesse's papers." she said. "They think I have them."

"Don't you?"

"Of course not."

Somehow I did not believe her. Then she apologized for last night, saying she should have given me a chance to explain. We exchanged phone numbers and addresses and I kissed her good-bye.

When I returned to the dining room, Mencken said: "You know, Cain, I like 'em like Roxy with a little beef on 'em. Broomsticks are for Harvard professors and George Nathan."

"So what do you make of all this?" I said, nodding agreement, but declining to talk about her now. "We could have a first-rate mystery story here. Can you imagine, all the people in this town, from the president on down, who benefit from Smith's death?"

"The main thing I make of all this," Mencken replied, "is that democracy has finally blossomed under Gamaliel. When the colonists overthrew a bad king they set up a system that gave every man a chance to be a rogue on his own account. And under Harding, dozens of them have gravitated to the capital, including the one I think had the most to gain."

"Who?"

"Jesse Smith himself."

"In other words, it probably was suicide?"

"Why not? In the first place, he was in poor health. Second, he was afraid something terrible was about to happen to him. If he wasn't killed by someone, then he was probably headed for jail. This would be even more distressing if he—Smith—was homosexual, perhaps emotionally in love with Daugherty and afraid of what might happen to him in jail. Assuming he disposed of papers incriminating him and the attorney general, he may have figured there was a chance that the corruption rumors would die with him and his destroyed papers and the whole thing would blow over and be forgotten, which was really about the best he could hope for."

"No doubt about it. He was a candidate for suicide."

"You know, Cain, I am told by an intelligent mortician that suicides are going up—especially on campuses, it has been reported, which is not surprising. Suicide always gets a bad rap. But what could be more logical than suicide? In other words, what could be more preposterous than keeping alive? Yet all of us cling to life with desperate devotion, even though the length of it remaining is palpably slight and filled with agony. Half the time of all medical men is wasted keeping life in human wrecks who have no more intelligible reason for hanging on than a cow has for giving milk."

Here comes a column, a *Prejudice* or a *Smart Set* editorial I thought, which is what makes working with Mencken on this story such a unique experience.

"Man tends to hang on in such terrible shape because he visualizes death as something painful and dreadful. It is, of course, seldom anything of the sort. The proceedings to it are sometimes (though surely not often) painful, but death itself appears to be devoid of sensation, either psychic or physical. It is true that suicide is more unpleasant than natural death if only because there is some uncertainty about it. The person wishing to leave this vale of tears hesitates to shoot himself because he fears with, some show of reason, that he may fail to kill himself."

"This would certainly be true in Smith's case."

"Yes, but that problem is bound to disappear with the progress of science. Safe, sure, easy, and sanitary methods of departing this life will be invented. But returning to the present, an increase of suicides on the campuses, if the reports are true, should surprise no one. During my late teens when I might have been in college—but was spared this intellectual humiliation—I more than once concluded that death was preferable to life. At that age a sense of humor is in a low state. Later on, by the mysterious workings of God's providence, it usually recovers. What keeps a reflective and skeptical man alive? In large part, I suspect, it's his sense of humor."

"Which Smith gave no evidence of having. On the other hand, he was not reflective or skeptical."

"No. But there is another thing: curiosity. Human experience is irrational and often painful, but in the last analysis remains interesting. One wants to know what is going to happen tomorrow. Does Harding know what's going on in his administration? Will the desirable Miss Stinson be amenable to your advances the next time you see her? Such questions keep human beings alive. . . ."

"But in Smith's case," I said, "he was deathly afraid of what might happen tomorrow."

"Precisely. But even for the normal, healthy man, there comes a time. I have had what must be regarded as a happy life. I work a great deal but working is more agreeable to me than anything else I can imagine. But it remains my conclusion, at the gates of senility . . ."

"At forty-three? Come on!"

"I said gates—where He is keeping me waiting—that the whole thing is a grandiose futility, and not even amusing. As for the poor college students, what I would like to see would be a wave of suicides among college presidents. I'd be delighted to supply the pistols, knives, poisons and ropes. A college student, leaping uninvited into the arms of God, pleases only himself. But a college president, doing the same thing, would give keen and permanent joy to a great multitude of persons."

I laughed, then suddenly realized that time was running on and we hadn't had breakfast yet. Looking at my watch, I said: "We ought to be getting to the Press Club. It's almost noon."

"You're right. We don't have time for one of my discourses on the futility of life. The game is still afoot and we must pursue the oddly named Mr. Stackelback."

Part 2

CHAPTER NINE

A$_s$ we walked to the Press Club in the Albee Building, just a couple of blocks over to 15th Street and then up to Pennsylvania Avenue, we speculated on all the people who were better off with Jesse Smith dead.

"Of course, the president probably had nothing to do with it." I said. "Daugherty has a perfect alibi, spending the night at the White House, where everyone logs in and logs out. And he could have convinced the president that Smith, apparently getting ready to talk, had to go. And he may even now have convinced the president that Smith was responsible for the corruption in the Justice Department."

"So, we start with Burns," Mencken said, "probably acting directly on orders from Daugherty who might have had at least a tacit understanding with the president."

"But we have to include Means," I added, "who has been known to do their dirty work and who had a special relationship with Burns. We know he works for whoever will pay him and he could have been hired to do this job by Burns. . . ."

"Or by Mrs. Harding! It doesn't make much difference to her who was crooked in the Justice Department. If what they did became public, her husband's reputation was ruined and his political career probably over. She had the motive to try to silence anyone who might damage her husband."

I agreed, then added: "And Forbes! He could have known that Smith was about to go public with information about corruption, including some detailed evidence concerning fraud in the Veterans' Bureau. And having silenced, as some people believe, his chief counsel, Cramer, he was ready to silence Smith."

"And if we're going to include Forbes," Mencken concurred, "then we have to add whoever is involved in the Interior Department sale of government oil reserves to private industry. Remember,

Roxy said Smith and Daugherty were angry at Secretary Fall for not including them in the deal, which brought millions of dollars to the oil industry. Maybe the word got out that Smith, out of revenge, was about to blow the whistle and one of the oil magnates hired someone to silence Smith."

"The list goes on—and we haven't even mentioned the most obvious suspects."

"Right," Mencken concurred again. "Any of the crooks—beginning with George Remus—who were promised things by Smith that he did not deliver. We heard Remus virtually threaten Smith with retaliation. And if that was Remus with Daugherty and Smith out at their shack in Ohio, we can assume threats were made then."

"Yes! And by the way, maybe Smith really did buy that gun for the attorney general, at his request, because Daugherty was scared."

We paused for a few minutes, speculating in silence as to whom else we might include, and watching the traffic as we crossed G Street. Then, as we neared the Albee Building, Mencken said: "There's one other person I am sure you have not thought of."

"Who's that?"

"When in doubt, *cherchez la femme.*"

"There's not any evidence that Smith had a girlfriend," I said. "In fact, just the opposite. It appears that he may have liked men. He gave some impression of being in love with Harry Daugherty; at the very least, Smith was extremely devoted to Harry. Could be that this whole thing is some kind of a jealous lover's quarrel. But I don't think you mean that."

"No, I don't. You're right. Smith doesn't seem to have a girlfriend. But he does have an ex-wife. And one thing I learned when I worked the police blotter is that in any murder you look for the domestic angle. Maybe she knew Smith was getting ready to change his will and she feared that he would leave her out of a new one. I tell you, if any real detectives get involved in the Smith case—which I doubt—the first thing they're going to start asking is where was Roxy Stinson late that night. Do you know?"

I shook my head. I could not believe Roxy would kill her ex-husband. She seemed genuinely fond of him. And too smart to commit a crime she knew would be in the public spotlight. But the more I thought about it, any impartial appraisal of Smith's death had to include her, which I finally and reluctantly conceded to

Mencken: "I must say, I do find it odd that Roxy sticks to the theory that Jesse shot himself, despite her awareness that Burns framed the perfect suicide scenario and despite all the circumstantial evidence that points to murder. Even with your upbeat philosophy of self-destruction, I suspect you lean toward murder.

"Remember, last night he wanted to get the papers that would implicate Daugherty to Mrs. Harding this morning before he went to Leesburg. He also wanted to tell the McLeans about the Hope Diamond. It hardly seemed like an ideal time to shoot himself. Surely, he knew that if he did, someone working for Daugherty would find the papers, and they would disappear forever—and the gang would be free to pin everything on him."

"Cain, my boy, you make a good case. If I didn't need contributors to my new magazine, I'd urge you to give up writing and become a detective."

We entered the Albee Building, heading for the elevator and the Press Club, as I replied: "No chance. I'm as eager to write for your magazine as you are. Furthermore, I need the money. Divorces are expensive. Are you a member of the Press Club?"

"You kidding? I don't belong as a matter of principle." As we waited for the elevator, he looked around to make sure no one else was in the lobby, then he elaborated: "I will exempt this club and a few others, but at least three-fourths of the press clubs across the country are run by newspaper men of the worst type—many of them so incompetent and disreputable that they cannot even get jobs on newspapers. Not only that, but the average club has too many shyster lawyers, quack doctors and minor job holders. Yet in how many towns do decent newspaper men take any overt action against them? I propose that they be shut up—east, west, north and south."

"Well, they can't be all bad. Press club bars have the reputation of being an easy place to get a drink of whiskey."

"Not this one. Believe it or not, it's the driest bar in the country. Too damned many Republican members from the Midwest who are dries themselves—or at least profess to be—and would snitch on anyone being served a drink. Better be careful with your flask, Jim. And here comes one of the better sort of press club members who will confirm what I say."

I looked around to see Frank Kent approaching: "What am I

going to confirm, Henry? I'll bet anything you are complaining to Cain about not being able to get a drink here."

"Absolutely correct," I said, as we entered the elevator and started the slow climb to the club. "He also had a few unkind words about press clubs."

"Oh, I've heard all that. So, what brings you slumming here today, Henry? I guess you've heard about Jesse Smith? That's why I'm in town. You must have been among the last to see him alive."

"Yeah, we just heard a little while ago. From Roxy Stinson."

"What does she think—murder or suicide?"

"She's convinced it's suicide," I replied, "but that Daugherty drove him to it. That was told to us in confidence, but she might talk with you if you move fast. She's on her way back to Ohio."

"Thanks, I'll try to reach her. You meeting someone in the club or just here for lunch?"

"Matter of fact," I said, "we're looking for a reporter from Colorado named Stackelback. He's supposed to be going around town telling tales about former Secretary Fall and the U.S. oil reserves. Have you talked to him?"

"He'll probably be here," said Kent, "and you won't have any trouble finding him. He usually takes up his position at the bar here about noon and will talk to just about anyone who'll listen. You can't miss him. He'll be wearing a Stetson, boots and a string tie with that metal clasp."

Entering the club, we went immediately to the bar, which was not as crowded as it usually is at noon. But there were several reporters there trying to figure out how to inconspicuously get the contents of their flasks into their drinks. And, of course, everyone was talking about Jesse Smith. We could see a Stetson hat and string tie at the end of the bar and Kent confirmed it was Stackelback. But he was talking to someone, so we waited.

The men at the bar seemed to be divided about equally on murder vs. suicide and I was surprised at how many in the Washington press corps seemed genuinely fond of Smith. But almost everyone knew he was up to his neck in the corruption: "Come on," one reporter shouted across the bar, "Smith died from Harding of the arteries and you know it!"

While waiting for Stackelback, we gave Kent more details about

what we were doing and why we wanted to talk to Stackelback.
After we finished, Kent said: "You'll find his story incredible.
Seems like a pretty good man. A reporter for a sheet called *The
Denver Post*. Everybody knows by now, of course, that the first
thing Fall did after taking over the Interior was to persuade the
secretary of the Navy to transfer the administration of the government oil lands to the Interior. Shortly after that, Fall leased the oil
rights at Teapot Dome in Wyoming to Harry Sinclair, owner of the
Mammoth Oil Company, and part of the Elk Hills reserve in California to an old friend, Edward Doheny, owner of the Pan American
Oil Company."

"Didn't Harding have to approve the leases?" I asked.

"He did and it was all very legal and followed traditional Republican policy. The companies promised to build some storage
tanks at Pearl Harbor for the Navy and fill them with oil. Navy
Secretary Denby claimed his main concern was that the government
was losing oil through leakage at both Teapot Dome and Elks Hill
and that leasing now might put a stop to that. One thing we do
know: the oil companies stand to make hundreds of millions of
dollars on the deal."

When Kent finished his little backgrounder he looked down at
Stackelback, who seemed to be winding up his conversation with
another reporter. "I'll let him take it from there. And I got'ta rush.
There's a press briefing at the White House right after lunch."

We could see that Stackelback would soon be free so we decided
to hurry down the bar to make sure no one got to Stackelback ahead
of us. As we departed, Kent said: "Nice suit, Henry, but it's definitely not you."

He called himself D. F. Stackelback. He was tall and wiry, as
you would expect of someone from cowboy country, and he
drawled like a Texan, which I won't try to duplicate here. We
started the conversation by saying that, although we had to be careful in this very dry bar, if he was really thirsty we could fix him a
bourbon and water. He thought that was a fine idea. Mencken declined, but I decided to have a drink, too. I don't think anyone saw
me fix them. I had thought that a little bourbon might loosen him
up, but he needed no urging to tell his story, especially after I told
him we were a couple of reporters from Baltimore. He had heard
of Mencken but he didn't seem to know much about him. He said

he was in town to tell his story to as many reporters as possible:

"It all started one day," he said, "when Clinton Anderson, a young reporter for the *Albuquerque Journal,* heard that Senator Fall—we still call him Senator out there—had received a shipment of cattle and a fancy racehorse from someone back East. Anderson was dogging Fall because the *Journal* and the *Chicago Tribune* were fighting his efforts to get hold of some government forestry lands."

"So, what's that got to do with oil?" I interrupted to ask.

"Nothing. At this stage nobody was thinking about oil."

Stackelback paused for a long swallow. "Anderson, who, I might say, has a great future in New Mexico, telegraphed the *Chicago Tribune* to see if they knew how Fall suddenly could afford a racehorse and some cattle from the East. You got to understand, now, that everybody out there knew that Senator Fall was broke, in debt and owed about eight years' back taxes. The *Tribune* replied to Anderson, saying that Fall's friend Ned McLean—I'm sure you know who he is—sent Fall the racehorse and cattle as a gift."

Mencken and I exchanged knowing looks and Mencken asked: "That's odd. Did Anderson and the *Journal* buy that one?"

"Not for long. At the same time Anderson wired the *Tribune,* he also wired my paper, *The Denver Post.* Now you also have to understand about the *Post.* It is run by two guys—Frederick Bonfils and H. H. Tammen—who don't know much about publishing. But they know a helluva lot about blackmailing. Tammen is an ex-circus promoter and performer; Bonfils is a former gambler. And they decided that Fall was a likely prospect for some blackmail. So they sent their star reporter—me—to Three Rivers, New Mexico, where Falls' ranch is to see what I could find out. I'm not very proud of working for that paper, but I needed the job. Still do."

"I know what you mean," I said, raising my glass in a mock salute of sympathy before taking a long swallow.

Before Stackelback could continue, Mencken took his watch out of his pocket, looked at it and said: "No wonder I'm getting hungry; it's almost one o'clock and we haven't even had breakfast yet. How 'bout it, Stackelback, will you join us for lunch? It's on me."

"Well, thanks. Don't mind if I do."

We left the bar, found a table and, after studying the menu for a few minutes, I said to Mencken: "Here's one good reason for not shutting the press clubs down: the prices are right."

"You can get a good steak sandwich or pork barbecue in Denver a lot cheaper than anything here," Stackelback said, after looking at the menu.

"You mean this H.C.L. that's sweeping the country hasn't reached the West yet?" asked Mencken. He was referring to the current term for "high cost of living." But this menu was quite reasonable. You could get a complete luncheon for sixty cents, including a lettuce salad, vegetables, pudding and coffee. I chose the broiled Spanish mackerel; Stackelback and Mencken ordered the broiled spareribs and sauerkraut—"and thank God we can now call a kraut a kraut," said Mencken. "Couple of years ago and we'd have had to order 'liberty cabbage' to get some sauerkraut!"

"No kidding," said Stackelback. "You took that war pretty seriously back here, didn't you?"

"Some did," said Mencken.

"So, where were we?" I said to Stackelback, thinking this was no time to start fighting the war again.

"Oh, yeah. Well, when the *Post* sent me to Three Rivers I made friends with the station master who showed me the bill of lading and receipts for, to be exact, six heifers, one yearling bull, two six-month old boars and four young sows. The racehorse was for Fall's foreman. And they didn't come from McLean. They came from a farm in New Jersey owned by Harry Sinclair, who Fall has been working for. And now we are talking big oil—big, big oil."

"So maybe the rumors about a payoff are true," I said.

"But," Mencken said, "a horse and few cows don't seem like much of a kickback for a lease to government oil lands worth millions!"

"Wait, there's more. With that lead, I started investigating another rumor—that Fall had recently bought a big ranch next to his property. I didn't get very far; some of Fall's friends threatened me if I didn't leave New Mexico immediately, which I did. But not before I learned that Fall had bought about sixty-five hundred acres to add to his farm, built a new hydroelectric plant, installed new wiring and fencing; improved his irrigation and power systems; and rebuilt his ranch house."

"That's a lot of digging," I said, "for someone who was being threatened with a tar-and-feather escort out of town."

"They were threatening worse than that. Some of the facts I mentioned were dug up by Anderson, who did not back down. In fact, one time Fall came into the *Journal* office, shouting, 'Who's the sumbitch who wrote those lies about me?' And Anderson stood up and said, 'I'm the son of a bitch and I don't tell lies.' Fall left the office quietly.

"And we found something else. Fall's adding to and improving his property began after Harry Sinclair, traveling in his private railroad car, *The Sinco,* arrived at Three Rivers and put it on a siding for three days while he visited Fall at his ranch, coming back to *The Sinco* every night. Now you don't do that sort of thing out on the prairie without causing a lot of talk."

"You obviously got out of New Mexico in one piece," I said.

"Yeah, I did okay. But Anderson and Carl Magee, who owned the *Albuquerque Journal* had their problems. Magee originally bought the *Journal* from Fall, and as soon as Anderson began publishing his stories about the senator's new-found wealth, Fall began putting the pressure on the *Journal*. Fall also came into Magee's office and said: 'I'll put you on the rack and break you!' But Magee threw him out of the office. But soon Magee's bank loans were called and Fall began filing libel suits against the *Journal*. So they had to be very careful about libel and couldn't print everything that Anderson and I had dug up."

He paused when the waiter brought the food, and after he left I fixed the western reporter another drink.

"Well, things went from bad to worse for Magee," Stackelback continued. "A judge friendly to Fall sent him to jail for two days for contempt of court—and his friends brought him food because they thought he would be poisoned. Then another judge sentenced him for a year as a result of one of the libel suits. But Magee was pardoned by Democratic Governor Hinkle. He was finally forced to sell the *Journal* to an Albuquerque bank run by a crony of Harding's, although Magee was convinced that Ed Doheny, Fall's old friend, actually put up the money. After that, the *Journal* and the other paper in town, the *Herald*—also owned by Fall's friendly bank—started publishing stories favorable to Fall."

"So what did you do when you left New Mexico?" Mencken asked, while savoring what he called "Woodrow's cabbage."

"Went back to Denver," said Stackelback, "where Bonfils and

Tammen suddenly became crusading journalists totally ignoring the libel laws. Even before I got back with my report (which they locked in their safe) the *Post* had begun printing flaming stories about Teapot Dome accusing Harry Sinclair of pulling off one of the boldest public land grabs of the century. We mailed every congressman and senator copies of these stories, which I'm sure helped inspire the resolutions by Senators Kendrick and LaFollette asking the attorney general to look into the affair."

"Which Daugherty ignored," Mencken said.

As Stackelback nodded agreement, I said: "Bonfils and Tammen don't look so bad here. How come you're not proud of working for them?"

"Oh, I'm proud enough of the work I did on that story, but you haven't heard everything. And here's where it gets a little complicated. There's this Denver politician and oil prospector named John Leo Stack, who had some unsubstantiated claims on the Teapot Dome reserves. When Sinclair's company offered Stack peanuts—around fifty thousand dollars I heard—for his claim, Stack went to Bonfils and Tammen and signed an agreement promising them a percentage of anything he got for his claim if they would start publishing stories about the Sinclair-Fall connection. So that's how Frederick Bonfils and H. H. Tammen became crusading journalists. And they continued being crusaders for quite a while—until one of Sinclair's lawyers convinced Sinclair that the smart thing to do would be to pay off Stack. The deal, I heard, was two hundred and fifty thousand dollars plus half the profits on three hundred and twenty acres of Teapot Dome land. And suddenly the great *Denver Post* Teapot Dome campaign came to an end."

"Don't tell me," I said in disbelief of what I was sure Stackelback was about to say.

"That's right. The stories about Fall and Sinclair suddenly disappeared from the *Post* and my bosses started printing nice, friendly pieces like the one headed 'The Gripping Story of the Sensational Rise to Fame and Fortune of Harry F. Sinclair, One of the Most Spectacular Men of the Present Day.' "

"Wow," was all I could say.

But Mencken's reaction surprised the western reporter. "My young friend here has faith in newspapers, whereas I have very little. He points to the *New York World* as his model and I agree the *World*'s one of the good ones and Swope is a good man, a friend of mine. In fact, I was best man at his wedding, which Cain, knowing how I feel about marriage, will have a hard time believing. But most papers today aren't much better than the *Denver Post* and a lot less honest about their interests. The trouble with most newspapers is that they are run fundamentally not to make money but by men who already have money and want something else. In this case, Bonfils and Tammen didn't have enough money so they used their paper and the Fall-Sinclair crusade to make some. Maybe not a helluva a lot different than your average owner using his paper for friendly stories about their advertisers who are paying them money, which is more or less what your bosses did when they started running friendly stories about Sinclair."

Stackelback was looking a little confused but seemed to acknowledge that maybe Mencken had a point. I was fascinated. "That's nothing," I said to Stackelback hinting that he doesn't have to believe all of Mencken's exaggerations. "You should hear what he thinks of us journalists."

"The truth is," Mencken continued, "this crusading business is one of the worst curses of journalism and perhaps the main enemy of that fairness, accuracy, and intelligent purpose which should mark the self-respecting newspaper. It trades upon one of the sorriest weaknesses of man—the desire to see the other fellow jump. No newspaper carrying on a crusade against a man ever does it fairly and decently; not many of them even make a pretense."

At this, I could see Stackelback beginning to bristle a little.

"I speak here," Mencken said, "as one who has engaged in such doings. But when I get to hell I shall at least be able to file two caveats against my incineration—one that I signed my name to every line I wrote and was physically and financially responsible for all stretchers; the other that I gave every aggrieved man, absolutely without condition, full liberty to strike back in my own paper at any length and on any terms. And they had just as much display and were printed promptly. Sometimes I got the better of it and sometimes I got a good pummeling. The gallery was pleased in both cases. Oh, and one other caveat: I was never converted to anything.

"The point is that, so far as I know, there is not a single newspaper in the whole United States today that offers any such fair play to its opponents, especially allowing a countercharge. Did Bonfils and Tammen do that?"

"Not really," Stackelback said, "But then Fall mostly responded with threats to me."

"I assume you quit as soon as the *Post* reversed itself and had you writing stories favoring Sinclair," Mencken said.

"I sure did. And I came here to the capital hoping to persuade some of the big papers and Congress to look into Fall's relation with Sinclair and Doheny."

"Any success?" I asked.

"Some. I talked to a few congressman and senators and one— Senator Walsh from Montana—seems ready to begin an investigation.

"Good." said Mencken. "Let me ask you this: I assume you've heard that one of the attorney general's close associates and a friend of the president, Jesse Smith, has been found dead under some very strange circumstances."

"Yeah. I heard that this morning, here at the club. But I don't know much about the circumstances."

"The official story is suicide," I said. "But there are indications that it might have been murder. . . ."

"And our question is," Mencken said interrupting me, "Do you think Secretary Fall could have had anything to do with the death of Smith if Fall had heard that Smith, in an effort to protect himself, was about to give information to the president concerning corruption in the Harding administration, including the Interior Department?"

Stackelback thought for a minute before answering: "He couldn't do it himself today, he's too frail. But he is known to have shot a man once in his youth. And he's certainly capable of having it done either by a hired killer or some of his buddies. Remember, it was friends of Fall who threatened me in New Mexico—and they weren't kidding."

The reporter did not have much more to add to his story, but he did confirm that one person who could help us was the Washington lawyer Harry Slattery. He also reminded us that Archibald Roosevelt, the late president's son, worked for the Sinclair Oil Company in New York.

So we agreed that I would interview Slattery in Washington and Mencken would talk to Roosevelt in New York. Mencken had to

go up to "Babylon," as he called the city on the Hudson, on Monday
to spend a few days putting *The Smart Set* to bed and talk with
some potential authors for his new magazine.

Mencken terminated the discussion rather abruptly because we
had to get back to Baltimore for the Saturday Night Club meeting,
to which he had invited me. Naturally, I was quite honored. He
knew I did not play any musical instrument, but I had once studied
to be an opera singer. "Let me get one thing straight, Henry, I'm
no opera singer, but I have a pretty good barroom bass."

"Just what this club needs," he replied, "a singing bartender."

CHAPTER TEN

As we walked back to the Willard to check out, Mencken had an idea: "You know, Cain, we ought to call the McLeans in Leesburg and tell them what we heard about the Hope Diamond. Smith was going to tell them when he went down there today, which means that unless he mentioned it on the phone last night, Mrs. McLean does not know that the big blue diamond she is wearing may be a fake."

"Good point. Do you know McLean?"

"Met him a couple of times—at a press affair and briefly at the 1920 Republican Convention. I should be able to get through to him."

We picked up our pace and when we reached the hotel we obtained some change from the cashier and went directly to a pay telephone off the lobby. Mencken thought this would be better than going through the hotel switchboard. "Those telephone girls have nothing better to do than listen in on those phones," said Mencken, "in fact, I think some of them take the job just for the oppotunity to hear some good gossip."

"Or they're paid by someone like Gaston Means or one of Burns' investigators."

The pay phone was enclosed in a small booth with a door on it and I stood outside with the door open just enough for me to hear Mencken's end of the conversation. "I wonder if Mr. Ned McLean is still there. This is H. L. Mencken calling from Washington. It's rather important."

While he waited, Mencken put his hand over the mouthpiece and said: "Well, they're still in Leesburg. The butler is giving him my message."

Then, after a few moments: "Good to hear your voice, too, Ned. And I want to say how sorry I am to hear about Jesse Smith. I'm sure you've heard about his apparent suicide. I know he was a very good friend of both you and Mrs. McLean."

Silence.

"Well, the reason I'm calling concerns something I heard from my partner in New York—something I passed along to Mr. Smith when we went to the ball game with him yesterday. He said he was going to tell you or Mrs. McLean when he came down to Leesburg this morning, but unless he called you last night and told you, you probably have not heard it—or maybe you already knew about it."

Longer silence.

"Well, Roxy Stinson, his ex-wife, says the official story is suicide, but I think I agree with Mrs. McLean. However, what I'm calling about concerns some substantial rumors going around New York that the Hope Diamond has been stolen and the McLeans do not even know it—meaning that if your wife still has it somebody has substituted an imitation for it. There are also rumors that the theft has not been publicized because someone in the Harding administration might be involved."

Silence.

"Well, that's what Jesse thought. Do you know if it has been out of her possesion lately or left unguarded where someone might have access to it?"

Silence.

"Well, here's the strange part—and this is not just a rumor. Roxy Stinson, Jesse's ex-wife, who went to the ball game with us Friday and to dinner after the game, rode with him out to the Wardman Park the night he died because he had had a lot to drink and was afraid to be alone. When she was leaving him at his door, Smith said: 'They've put the curse of the blue diamond on me!' "

Silence.

"All I know is what she told me. And all that stuff I heard about a stolen diamond could be nothing but rumors. But I thought I ought to tell you what we heard."

Silence.

"I'm not sure that's such a good idea. From what I've heard Mr. Burns might not be the best man to put on the case—especially if it's an 'inside job' as the rumors have it."

Silence.

"You're welcome. And I have heard about the party. Thanks for the invitation. I'm looking forward to it." And Mencken hung up.

"Come on," Mencken said, as he hurried out of the phone booth. "We're really running late. The club is meeting at my house tonight, which means I have a lot to do to get ready. I never lay these musicals on Mother. I'll tell you what McLean said when we get checked out."

We were out of there in a hurry and in the taxi to the station Mencken did not want to share what McLean said with the cabbie. But once we were settled in the privacy of the club car, Mencken said: "Okay, here's what McLean told me. First, Smith did call them a couple of times last night, but he said nothing about the diamond. He did say he had something important to tell them, but didn't want to talk about it over the phone. He was very upset and quite frankly sounded scared to death."

"What did they think of his death?"

"Mrs. McLean is positive Jesse Smith was murdered and intends to tell the president that when they come back to D.C. tomorrow. They're going to spend Sunday evening at the White House with the Hardings and Daugherty. Mrs. McLean still has the diamond and was planning to wear it this weekend. He says it couldn't possibly be an inside job, which is one reason he thinks the rumors are crazy."

"What did he say when you said there might have been a switch?"

"He's been traveling a lot lately, some of it on a golfing trip with the president. So he doesn't know if the diamond has been accessible lately. But he does say that his wife is very casual about the diamond, often taking it off and hanging it on a picture hook or something and letting her dog wear it. So it wouldn't be too hard for someone to make a switch—especially, he implied, if Mrs. McLean had had a few drinks."

Mencken paused to light a Willie, then continued: "The idea that someone had given Jesse Smith the curse of the diamond is absurd, he says. This whole business of a curse is a lot of nonsense. He didn't believe too much of what Roxy Stinson had to say; said she's been reading too many Sunday magazine sections. He said he was going to put Burns on the case, but said, 'We'll see,' when I said that was not such a good idea. But he thanked me cordially for calling him and reminded me of his party next weekend."

After Mencken finished we both remained silent for awhile trying to put it all together. And I made some extensive notes. Then we began to rehash what we learned about the Harding administration in just two days. We were quite overwhelmed that, in addition to all the corruption, we had stumbled into a possible murder mystery with so many plausible suspects.

"And don't forget the cursed diamond!" I said.

"What a story we're gonna have," Mencken replied. "But right now, I'm sick of the whole bunch and ready for a little relaxation.

"Jesus. That reminds me. As I told you, because of Red Lewis and the club, I'm getting a little low on bourbon. I guess I ought to call Gaston Means soon and set up an appointment to buy one of his liquor permits. The club will want to chip in. And Lewis should put up something."

We spent the rest of the trip talking about the club members and Mencken telling me some of his views on music, very opinionated, as he is about everything else. Because he does not especially like opera and I love it, we were about to start a real argument when, fortunately, the train pulled into Baltimore.

"Right on time," said Mencken. "Tell you what, Cain. Why don't you come a little early tonight and I'll take you to my wine cellar and show you where the beer is. We'll be serving mostly my home brew."

I arrived at the red brick rowhouse at 1524 Hollins Street on Union Square at about ten minutes of eight. As I neared the top of the white stairs, gripping the metal handrail, I noticed the replica of a lyre fastened to the metal. I rang the bell and Mencken greeted me in his undershirt: "Welcome to the home of the four Bs— Beethoven, Bach, Brahms and beer. Please excuse my attire. But I need a certain looseness around the shoulders for a proper performance, especially of the fourth B."

Escorting me into the house, through the living room and into a hall leading to the back of the house, he said, "Before I introduce you to anyone, let me take you downstairs and show you where I keep the liquor." In the basement, he unlocked a door on which there was a sign bearing a skull and crossbones. The sign read:

THIS VAULT IS PROTECTED BY A DEVICE RELEASING CHLORINE GAS UNDER PRESSURE. ENTER IT AT YOUR OWN RISK

"As you can see, I enjoy every known alcoholic drink and many more of them would be collected here if it wasn't for our noble experiment, and I drink them all when occasions are suitable—wine with meat, the hard liquor when the soul languishes, beer to let me down gently of an evening. In other words, I'm omnibibulous, or, more simply, ombibulous."

"Nice word. You must also have a cast-iron liver."

"Maybe so. But let me tell you something I've never told anyone but Nathan: I've just about reached the age where I think I'd rather drink than diddle."

"Good. I'll buy you a first-rate bottle of bourbon from my bootician if you leave Roxy alone."

"I'll think about that one. Come on. We got to get upstairs. It's music time."

The musical part of the evening consisted of the first movement of the "Eroica," the first two movements of Beethoven's Eighth, finishing up with the Brahms F Minor Piano Quintet. At first, the music was disturbingly ragged, so much so that at one point Mencken, who played piano, stood up and with a voice that drowned out all the instruments, yelled: *"Maul halten!"* And I began to wonder if the music of the famous Saturday Night Club wasn't vastly overrated.

Nothing much was said. The players simply put their scores back together and started over. The second time around there was considerable improvement and Mencken threw himself into the music, sometimes standing up and pounding the keyboard while keeping his foot on the loud pedal.

He proved to be an accomplished, sight-reading pianist. Also, I was quite familiar with the Quintet and had heard it not too long ago at a concert in New York, which had made no impression on me even though their performance was faultless. Which itself seemed a fault. The professional musicians seemed more interested in the Quintet as a performing challenge, not as music. On the other hand, these slightly stewed amateurs shook me up. It seemed almost as if I was hearing the Quintet for the first time. Though less gifted than the professionals, these men really felt the music. The men were transported into the world, maybe even the mind, of Brahms and by the time they finished, with Mencken standing up and shouting "yoooooooh" at the end, I understood what these evenings were all about.

But they were also about drink, food and camaraderie. When they finished the Quintet, Mencken tapped a glass sitting on the piano and said: "Time for the anthem" and everyone began to sing:

"I am one, I am one
I am one hundred percent American.
I am a supe, I am a supe
I am a super patriot.
A red, red, red, red, red. I am
a red-blooded American.
I am a one hundred percent American
I am, God damn, I am."

Mencken then said that, because of our patriotism, he had an opportunity to obtain a permit to take some whiskey out of a government warehouse. But it would be expensive, so he was passing the hat and expected everyone to kick in if not what he felt his whiskey or gin would cost for the next couple of years, at least what he could afford. Everyone, including me, put something in the pot but I am certain they did not come close to contributing what Mencken would need.

Then it was time for the food, drink and jokes—which began as close to 10 o'clock as they could. The ribaldry ended with a beer drinking contest, which Mencken won easily. From then on the wit and humor went decidedly downhill. And I knew everyone was going to have a rip-roaring hangover in the morning—me included. As I waited for a taxi which Mencken called, he handed me a piece of paper and said: "Be sure to take this when you get up in the morning. It's a recipe for a miraculous cure for the common hangover given to me by a doctor at Johns Hopkins. It's mostly Epsom salts, but I guarantee it."

The next morning, I mixed and drank Mencken's cure, sat down in my comfortable chair, leaned my head back against the cushion and waited for the miracle. Instead I was immediately as sick as I have ever been. So that evening, after I had recovered enough to sit at my typewriter, I drew up an affidavit concerning a "remedy

for the hangover consisting of common salt in aqueous solution to
be taken the morning after imbibition" and which I quote in part as
follows:

**WHEREAS, the said Henry Louis Mencken represented
that the said remedy had been given to him by a practicing
physician, and represented further that the said physician regarded it as his greatest contribution to the science of medicine, and represented further that he had tried it himself and
found it efficacious, and**

**WHEREAS, I, James M. Cain, in good faith and believing
the said remedy of the said Henry Louis Mencken to be a
good and efficacious remedy, did take inwardly common salt
to the amount of one tablespoonful, in aqueous solution, and**

**WHEREAS, the said remedy not only failed to relieve the
original complaint, but greatly aggravated it, causing me,
James M. Cain, to become violently ill and swoon at intervals,
and afflicting me with violent thirst, so that I drank water
until I swelled up like a balloon fish, and afflicting me with
nausea and vomiting, and causing me during swoons, to
dream of caravans of camels, each camel carrying seventeen
spare stomachs filled with brine, and leaving me with an intolerable and apparently permanent gustatory affliction, so
that I now taste salt in my tonsils, uvula and teeth, and all
the fillings thereof,**

**NOW THEREFORE do I, James M. Cain, proclaim the
said Henry Louis Mencken, in so far as he pretends to knowledge of the healing art, to be dishonest, false, fraudulent, and
a common nuisance, and denounce his whole therapeutic system as null, void and without sense.**

I sent it to Mencken, he ultimately took it to New York and
gave it to his publisher, Alfred A. Knopf, and *that,* I believe, was
the real beginning of our friendship, cemented by an even stranger
incident the following week.

CHAPTER ELEVEN

Monday morning I was still slightly ill and weak from Mencken's remedy. In addition, I had developed a cough, which I thought was also due to too much beer and salt. But it worried me as all coughs do because of my assumed susceptibility to tuberculosis. But I ignored it, at least for awhile, and spent the morning lining up an interview with the Washington lawyer Harry Slattery and learning a little about his background.

It turned out that, although he was a practicing attorney, his main concern is conservation and has been since he graduated from Georgetown University Law School and went to work in the Roosevelt Administration as a clerk for the Inland Waterways Commission. There he met a number of pioneers in the conservation movement, including Gifford Pinchot, who inspired Teddy Roosevelt's interest in the subject and is considered the country's leading conservationist. From 1909 to 1912, Slattery was secretary to Pinchot when he was chief forester in TR's Department of Agriculture. He is a quiet bachelor, known to shun publicity and love the political life in the capital as well as the city in which it is located. I told him I was an ex–*Baltimore Sun* reporter working with Henry Mencken on a book or magazine article about the Harding administration. He said to come right over, he would be free all morning.

When ushered into his book-lined office, I was greeted by a rather prosaic, likeable gentleman in his late thirties who put me immediately at ease: "I understand, Mr. Cain, that you want to know what's happening to the government's oil reserves. Well, you've come to the right man. And I don't mind talking about it— especially to writers and reporters—because, frankly, Warren Harding gave me and Mr. Pinchot the greatest political double-cross we ever had."

"How's that?" I asked. I had prepared a series of leading questions, but it quickly became apparent that I did not need them. Slattery seemed as eager to talk about oil leases as Stackelback was.

"Very simple. The conservationists only agreed to back Harding in 1920 after he assured us that he supported the movement. We had written the conservation plank in the Republican platform and Pinchot came out with a strong endorsement."

"For Harding?"

"For his conservation policy. The conservationists, of course, opposed the exploitation of the government's oil reserves, which many Republicans favored. But we felt we had Harding's pledge and felt very good when he won the election with sixteen million votes of the twenty-five million cast." Slattery paused momentarily to light up a cigarette, which soon joined the many cigarette stubs in the large ashtray on his desk.

"Right after the election, Pinchot was again invited out to Marion to discuss conservation and was again assured that Harding supported it. Pinchot gave Harding five names he would support for Secretary of the Interior. Senator Fall was not on the list. We had, of course, heard all the stories about the oil men in the smoke-filled room at the Republican Convention. But we thought we had Harding's pledge."

"Why do you think Harding appointed him?"

"I don't know. We have never been able to confirm the rumors that it was a payoff to the oil industry for supporting Harding at the convention. But Pinchot, after studying Fall's record, wrote me that it would 'not be easy' to pick a worse man for Secretary of the Interior. Almost as bad, for Secretary of the Navy they picked Congressman Edwin Denby, known to favor exploitation of government oil lands."

"I guess you're familiar," I asked, "with the stories circulating in the *Albuquerque Journal* and *Denver Post* about Fall suddenly improving his property in New Mexico—and the suspicion that the money to finance these expenditures came from the oil interests?"

"I am. We've confirmed the expenditures and the gifts of some cattle to Fall. We've also investigated the source of Fall's money but can't prove it came from Doheny or Sinclair. We have also suggested a Senate investigation which Senator LaFollette is pushing."

"So what's going to happen?"

"I'm not sure what the next move is. When I first heard that the right to lease the oil reserves was transferred from the Navy to the Interior Department I decided to talk to the assistant secretary of the Navy, Theodore Roosevelt, Jr. I felt he was a good man concerned about oil policy But I couldn't believe Roosevelt's reaction when I went to see him. He said Fall had been a Rough Rider with his father in Cuba and that I couldn't say anything derogatory about his father's good friend. He said he personally had carried the executive order transferring the oil—which Fall had written—to President Harding.

"When I predicted that Fall would give the oil companies leasing rights, he became even angrier, saying that Fall would not do that without consulting first with Denby or him. Then he showed me to the door."

"Did Fall consult with them?"

"We don't know. All we know for sure is that the reserves at Teapot Dome and Elk Hills have been leased to Sinclair and Doheny and the leases are worth millions of dollars. I also know that Fall is watching me carefully. Not long after my meeting with Roosevelt, one of Fall's gunmen from New Mexico showed up in my office and openly threatened me if I did not stop my campaign against the oil leases."

Slatterly paused long enough to enhance the full impact of what he had just said.

"Shortly after he resigned from the Interior, Fall went to work for Sinclair; he went to Russia with him, in the hope that he could help Sinclair obtain leasing rights on Sakhalin Island. The communists said Sinclair could have drilling rights, if the United States would recognize the Soviet Union within five years. When Sinclair and Fall returned to the U.S. the former secretary said that the situation in Russia was not as bad as it had been made out to be and that he looked forward to someday recognizing the Soviet Union."

"Good God," was all I could say.

"Although Fall was well paid for his trip to Russia—around twenty-five thousand dollars plus expenses—it was all very legal. What was not legal was Harding's executive order transferring the government oil reserves to the Interior. It had never been published and was not filed in the appropriate section at the State Department. And there had never been bidding on it."

"How's that?"

"Fall claimed he had the right not to seek bids because the oil reserves concerned national defense. The government would receive royalties from production of the wells. But a very unusual clause called for royalties to be paid, not in cash, but 'oil certificates,' which could be exchanged for fuel oil land storage tanks, but only with the Mammoth Oil Company owned by Harry Sinclair. Fall granted Edward Doheny's Petroleum and Transport Company a similar lease, which called for his company specifically to build Navy storage tanks at Pearl Harbor in exchange for 'oil certificates.' This meant that the government was giving these two companies run by friends of Secretary Fall exclusive contracts—again without bidding—for providing oil and tanks."

"Wouldn't the Navy be concerned about all this?"

"Many among the top brass were, but they were reluctant to speak out. Admiral Griffin, who was retired but still a member of the Naval Consulting Board, told me that, 'If they get into this thing, they will find stranger things in heaven and earth than we have dreamed of.' "

"Surely somebody could do something."

"You would think so. Stories appeared in the press but no one sounded an alarm and they quickly faded. However, we did manage to get Senator LaFollette interested and after initial opposition from Republicans in the Senate, especially Senator Smoot—incidentally, he's one man you ought to talk to—LaFollette pushed through a resolution calling for a Senate investigation of the Teapot Dome lease."

"Whatever happened to that and why should we talk to Senator Smoot?"

"Smoot has become Fall's defender in the Senate and he'll give you Fall's side of the story. The LaFollette proposal is still locked up in the Senate Committee on Public Lands and there wasn't much in the press about it, but after the LaFollette resolution, the president sent Congress a mass of documentation supporting the leases and a letter stating that Fall had his complete support. That was about a year ago and God knows when and if the Senate will act. Incidentally, Smoot, too, has given us the double-cross. He used to be an avid conservationist."

"Let me ask you something, Mr. Slattery: You said that Senator

Fall sent someone around to threaten you, and a reporter we talked to who investigated Fall in New Mexico, said he was threatened and virtually run out of the state by Fall's men. I'm sure you've heard the rumors that Daugherty's right hand man—Jesse Smith— might have been murdered, although the official story is sui- cide. . . ."

Slattery nodded.

". . . Do you think Senator Fall would be desperate enough to kill Smith or have him killed by one of his henchmen?"

Slattery paused for a minute or so and I could almost see the wheels in his brain shifting gear: "I have heard the rumors and I don't discount them. But I don't connect Fall. Whether it was sui- cide or murder, I would think Smith's problems were related to the corruption in the Justice Department rather than Interior. If there were payoffs for Teapot Dome and Elk Hills I think they went to Fall personally and exclusively. I'm pretty sure he has kept Daugh- erty out of his affairs—and I am almost certain the president did not profit by the leases."

"I gather from our sources that Daugherty and Smith were not cut in on the oil deal. But that's the point. Daugherty and his chief investigator, Burns, seem to know everything that's going on in this administration; in fact, we've heard that Daugherty and Smith were both mad at Fall for not cutting them in on what is probably the most profitable deal this gang has pulled off. Either out of jealousy and spite or to protect himself from being accused of any involve- ment with the oil leases, Smith might have been ready to squeal on Fall. What do you think?"

"I think you know a helluva lot about what's going on under the slimy rocks. Who are your sources?"

"I'd rather not say. But one of them is very close to the scene and, for several reasons, has been very forthright with us."

"I think I can guess who that is. Roxy Stinson?"

I did not respond.

"Well, let me tell you something. If you know Miss Stinson, advise her to be very careful. If Smith was murdered, then she's logically next on the list. And, yes, I do think Secretary Fall is capable of killing or having someone killed. When he wants some- thing he is relentless. He comes from the West where settling things by force rather than the law is often the rule and when he thinks he's right, he is the law. Remember, even though he might have been paid off for the government leases he gave Sinclair and Doheny, in his mind, he didn't do anything wrong. He absolutely believes he is right about letting private oil companies make a profit extracting oil from government lands. In his wing of the Republican Party, that's gospel."

"So, you agree that Fall is a suspect in the Smith case?"

"Yes. And I'll tell you something you probably don't know. We keep close tabs on Secretary Fall and since he resigned from the Interior earlier this year, he has been quietly coming into town from time to time, talking with senators dealing with the Interior investigation, especially Reed Smoot. He was in town last week and guess where he stayed?"

He paused, but did not wait for me to answer: "That's right. At the Wardman Park where Smith and Daugherty live. And he was in town the night Smith died. He left town the next day and is on his way back to Three Rivers."

"Now that is interesting," I said, standing up and indicating I was ready to terminate the interview.

"But wait. There's more," Slattery said. "Last week I got a call from Jesse Smith. He said he wanted to talk with me about something very important, and we made an appointment for him to come by my office this week—tomorrow, to be exact."

And that really got my attention: "Did he give you any idea what he wanted to talk about?"

"No. But I've never had any dealings with Smith on any subject, and he knew that I am the most actively concerned non-political type in town on the subject of government oil leases. It's well known that Daugherty doesn't like Fall. He's jealous of Harding's friendship with him, going back to their Senate days, and the fact that Mrs. Harding adores Fall and does not like or trust Daugherty."

"I can't believe that Smith was getting ready to come in here and expose Fall."

"No, it wouldn't happen exactly like that. What he would have done is discreetly inquire as to how much I knew about Teapot Dome, etc. Then if I told him I knew quite a bit and had heard the same rumors he had, he would point out that both he and the attorney general were worried about anything that might reflect on the president and have assured me that if there was anything shady about the oil leases deal, that Warren Harding had absolutely nothing to do with it and would be more shocked than anyone else, because of his long friendship with the senator, etc., etc. That alone would tell me that they knew, or at least thought, Fall had been paid off."

Then Slattery, the Washington insider, smiled that look of complete satisfaction at having encouraged a journalist to keep inquiring into the government oil leases. As we shook hands before I left, Slattery said: "I'm sorry Mr. Mencken was not able to join you. I'm one of his fans, although I often disagree with him."

"Don't we all," I said laughing.

"I was just reading his last *Prejudices* over the weekend and I was impressed with his two remarkable essays, 'Sahara of the Bozarts' and the 'Autopsy' of President Roosevelt. I worked in the Roosevelt administration and am a TR loyalist. And I was surprised at Mencken's favorable assessment of Roosevelt, despite the fact that he tried to rally the country to war in the 1916 election. And we all know where Mencken stood on the war."

I nodded agreement and Slattery said: "Tell me something. Where does Mencken find time to read so much? In the introduction to his essay on Roosevelt, he laments on the state of presidential biographies, mentioning at least seven of the Lincoln biographies as being downright failures. Then he says that in preparation for his Roosevelt essay, he read at least ten biographies of the late president with most of them containing vastly more gush than sense."

"He reads all the time," I said "and very fast and, unlike the rest of us, he remembers most of what he reads. You have to understand that Mencken's relationship to words is not like yours or mine. It's more like Mozart's relationship to musical notes. Words and thoughts just flood into Mencken's brain and come gushing out in well-formed sentences and paragraphs. And he talks almost like he writes. When I first read Mencken I knew I wanted to write like him. But I soon realized that I never would be able to any more than the average composer could ever write a symphony like Mozart. Mencken and words and Mozart and music defy analysis. He's on the train right now going to New York and I bet by the time he reaches Babylon on the Hudson, he will have absorbed the contents of two books."

"I don't doubt it," Slattery said.

"Incidentally," I said, "that's why Mencken couldn't join us this morning, which is too bad because he would very much like to have heard you on the subject of Fall and the oil leases. But he's going to try to see Archie Roosevelt in New York. As you no doubt know, he works for one of Sinclair's companies up there."

"I know all about Archie and the sinecure his family got him working for Sinclair. And I'm glad you reminded me. Someone in Sinclair's office in New York claims to have made reference to sixty-eight thousand dollars being given to the foreman of Fall's ranch in New Mexico at about the same time Sinclair sent him some horses and cattle. If you talk to Mencken, tell him to ask Archie about that."

After bidding him another good-bye, in his outer office, I asked his secretary if I could use her phone to call the Senate Office Building. I wanted to get an interview with Senator Smoot.

Much to my surprise, Smoot's press assistant said he could see me now. It seemed like all of a sudden everyone wanted to set the record straight on government oil leases. It was only a short taxi ride from Slattery's office in midtown to Capitol Hill and soon I was being ushered into the Utah senator's office. Reed Smoot was a well known figure in Washington, having survived a three year effort after the turn of the century to deny him a seat in the Senate because of the country's opposition to Mormonism. But he was now in his fourth term and one of the senate's leading advocates of a high tariff. He was also a staunch Republican and supporter of Harding.

He was a tall, thin gentleman who still had the rugged looks of a western pioneer. The interview did not last long and consisted primarily of the senator giving what seemed like his stock speech setting forth official Republican doctrine on the oil leases, i.e.— there was no bidding because national security was involved; in return, the nation got royalties from the wells and storage tanks at Pearl Harbor; something needed to be done soon because the government oil fields were losing oil through drainage to neighboring oil fields; President Harding had approved the transfer of the oil fields from the Navy to the Interior and approved of Fall's leases. And he conceded that he was doing everything possible to prevent the proposed Senate investigation of the oil leases.

I decided I would get nowhere. Furthermore, my cough was getting worse and I was anxious to get out of there. But before putting away my notebook and thanking him for taking the time to talk to me, I said: "By the way, you've probably heard the stories going around town that Senator Fall is spending substantial amounts of money improving his property in New Mexico. As an old friend of his from the Senate, do you have any idea where he might have gotten the money, considering his modest salaries in the government? Is his wife well-off?"

"I hope, sir," Smoot replied, visibly bristling, "you are not insinuating that there is any connection between the oil leases and Senator Fall spending money in retirement to improve his ranch?"

"Well, some newspapers out West have been trying to find the source of his money."

"That's just local politics. I don't know anything about Senator Fall's personal finances, but I do know that he is a substantial person and has many powerful contacts all across the country. He's a good friend of the president's friend, Ned McLean, who throws money around lavishly. I'm sure McLean would loan the senator money immediately if he needed it."

By the time I returned to my Linden Avenue apartment that afternoon, I was coughing continually. I bought some medicine and that helped a little, but I finally called my doctor and after I told him about being exposed to mustard gas during the war, he said I ought to check into Johns Hopkins in the morning; that he wanted to make some tests.

That evening, I called Mencken at Nathan's apartment at the Royalton in New York and caught him before they went out to dinner. I did not have to tell him about my cough, which was quite evident, but I did tell him about the doctor wanting me to check into Johns Hopkins.

He commiserated with me and countered by reciting his own long list of ailments—a sour stomach, a pain in the prostate, tired eyes and a sprained back from helping a taxi driver disentangle himself from a collision. "Too bad, because I've been running along for nearly a week with no ailments except, of course, for a new type of dermatitis caused by the plates I wear for my arches. No one seems to know how to cure it. Now I am limping all over New York and will probably go shuffling off to the crematory. Now, if you want, I'll put Nathan on and he can tell you what's wrong with

him. But you can discount most of what he says because he's a
hypochondriac."

"No thanks," I replied continuing to cough. Mencken insisted he
was not a hypochondriac because all of his ailments were real. He
also said: "I lined up a fine writer—Ernest Boyd—to do an article
on the phony Greenwich Village aesthetes, products of a superficial
American university education, who went to Europe with the late
Woodrow's crusade and after the war, sat around the Paris cafes
long enough to pick up the ideas being spouted by the left wing
French intellectuals, then returned home and started repeating this
nonsense in the *New Republic*. Should be a good piece."

I agreed.

"I've got an appointment to talk with Archie Roosevelt tomorrow. After that, I'm going to the Vanderbilt to buy one of Means'
liquor permits. Pray for me because that makes me a sinner for
breaking the law. But then we've all been breaking the law regularly
since that abomination of a law was passed. By the way, Means
gave me a good price. He must be cutting out Daugherty now that
Jesse Smith is no longer around to collect their share."

I told him about the interview with Slattery and said to be sure
to ask Roosevelt about the guy in his office who is said to have
seen a check for sixty-eight thousand dollars made out to the foreman of Fall's ranch. With that, I was ready to hang up and give my
throat a rest.

"Well, we're off to Luchow's, where they serve genuine *Wurz-
burger* in tea cups. I've got to get out of this damn apartment.
Nathan has it furnished and lit like a bordello and it's more smoke-
filled than any room at the last Republican Convention. He has a
cigarette in his mouth from the moment his man turns on his ma-
tutinal showerbath in the morning. By God, I hate this town! Already I'm eager to get back to Baltimore. Cain, the very richest man
in New York is never quite sure that the house he lives in now will
be his next year. The intense crowding and the restlessness that goes
with it, make it almost impossible for anyone to accumulate the
materials of a home. The charm of getting home. I have lived in
one house all my life. If I had to leave it I'd be as certainly crippled
as if I lost a leg."

"Well, that would be one way to get rid of your dermatitis," which brought a loud laugh as he repeated my remark to Nathan.

When Mencken hung up, I wanted to call Roxy, but decided to wait until I had been to the hospital. But in a few minutes, the phone rang and it was Roxy calling from Ohio. "Jamie, I've been trying to call you for some time but the line has been busy."

"I know. I've been talking to Mencken in New York. And I'm going into the hospital about my damned cough. The doctor wants to take some X rays. Whenever I get a cough, everybody, including me, starts worrying about TB because of my inhaling some gas during the war. We'll know tomorrow."

Roxy said she just called to say "hello" and to let me know that she was coming back to Washington tomorrow.

"Will you be staying at the Willard?"

"No. At the Wardman. I have an appointment with Daugherty to discuss things. And incidentally, somebody ransacked my house here, too, while Mother was away. They're still looking for those papers."

I did not know what to say to that, except: "You be careful now." But talking to Roxy made me feel considerably better.

The next day, I checked into Johns Hopkins for some X rays and tests. My cough was a little better and seemed to have settled in my chest. I didn't know whether that was good news or bad. But after a couple of days the doctor decided that I did not have TB, just a bad cold which had turned into bronchitis.

In the hospital, I mentioned to the doctor my theory of voice, that it actually depends on the mass of bone in the skull rather than the chest. "I often thought," I told the doctor, "if I ever had the chance, I'd like to weigh some skulls and check them by means of a tuning fork against their actual resonance."

"That's easy," said the doctor and he soon appeared with a gunnysack full of skulls and a set of scales. I had asked my mother to bring me in a tuning fork. I went to work testing my theory, and then Mencken appeared with a bottle of red Spanish wine in a brown paper bag. When I told him what I was doing and demonstrated that my theory was correct, Mencken's face lit up with astonishment. He was intensely interested in the experiment, especially in the variation in the sizes of the skulls. When I explained that two or three of the skulls were women's, he said, "How do you know?"

and I replied, "Because they had no frontal sinuses." Mencken simply glowed with admiration. I couldn't have invented anything that
raised me higher in his estimation.

After I put the skulls back in the gunnysack and Mencken found
two paper cups for the wine, I told him all I had learned in my
conversations with Slattery and Smoot.

Mencken then told me about his adventure in New York. "The
morning after I talked to you on the phone, I went to see Archie
Roosevelt. He was very cordial because he knew I had written some
nice things about his father. But he is a terribly dim-witted and
naive young man. He acted as if he didn't know which Sinclair
company he was vice president of. He had heard the rumors about
the relationship between Fall and his boss and that Fall had been
spending a lot of money in New Mexico."

"Which Slattery confirmed," I said.

"He did know that Sinclair had sent Fall some cattle and confessed that he had given some thought to resigning from his job
with Sinclair; and that a couple of employees involved with the
Teapot Dome lease had already resigned.

"When I asked him, as you suggested, about the gentleman in
his office who was supposed to have mentioned sending Fall's foreman sixty-eight thousand dollars, Roosevelt said: 'I know all about
that because I was the source. Why don't you ask the gentleman
himself?' and he picked up the phone and invited a Mr. Gustav
Wahlburg into his office.

"Mr. Wahlburg turns out to be one of Sinclair's private secretaries, a very nervous man who probably wouldn't know the truth
if it came gushing up out of an oil well and hit him in the face.
When I asked him about having been heard to say that Mr. Sinclair
had sent sixty-eight thousand dollars to Senator Fall's ranch foreman in New Mexico, he replied—and you won't believe this: 'What
Mr. Roosevelt heard was "six or eight cows"—not sixty-eight
thous.'

"Well, that would have made my day, except it wasn't nearly as
bizarre as what happened next. After a quick lunch of sauerbraten
and cabbage at a nearby German restaurant—that's one thing you
have to say about Babylon; it has a good restaurant on almost every
block, sometimes two or three—I appeared at the Vanderbilt Hotel
promptly at the allotted hour, two-fifteen, and went immediately to

room five-fifteen as told. The door was unlocked and there was a table in the middle of the room with a fishbowl on it. Under it was an envelope. I carefully counted out three thousand dollars—making sure that whoever was watching from an adjoining room could see it—and placed it in the fishbowl. Then I opened the envelope and it appeared to be a permit authorizing me to buy liquor from a government warehouse somewhere in Pennsylvania.

"I put the envelope in my pocket, quickly went to the elevator and took it down to the lobby, where I was immediately accosted by two of New York's finest plain-clothesmen, who took me to the nearest police station. And, believe or not, they had never heard of H. L. Mencken, a practicing journalist who, I assured them, was working on a story.

"But they did let me use the telephone and soon Knopf and Nathan and a lawyer arrived and convinced the police that my credentials were valid. I told them the whole story—that I had paid a Mr. Gaston B. Means, who operates out of Washington, three thousand dollars for the liquor permit I had on me when I was arrested. The two cops may not have heard of H. L. Mencken, but I could tell from the look on their faces, that they had definitely heard of Means. They assured me that they would investigate but they were not very encouraging about the possibility of getting my three thousand dollars back."

I was trying to keep from laughing because it made my chest ache, when suddenly the curtain around my bed was pulled back and in walked Roxy carrying a big bunch of flowers. There were hugs all around, but I cautioned Roxy that the cold that put me in the hospital might still be contagious.

Mencken went over his stories again and I had to tell Roxy all I had heard and we were well on our way to finishing the bottle of red wine, when Roxy said: "I finally saw Jesse's will and he named the people who were to get his diamond collection—one went to me, one to Harry, one to Harry's brother, Mal, one to John King, who worked with Jesse on the American Metal Company deal and the last one to a Republican National Committeeman from Connecticut, whom I don't know. There was no mention of a big blue diamond."

"It's none of our business, but did Jesse leave you any money in the will?" I asked.

"Twenty-five thousand. He also left Harry, Mal and a couple of relatives the same amount."

"Do you think that was fair?"

"Oh sure. Jesse has given me lots of money and he left me his Cole automobile and helped me build my house. We had a ten-thousand-dollar joint account, which I think Harry is going to challenge. But I feel very comfortable. So if you can get out of here, Jim, I'll take you both out to dinner and we'll celebrate my inheritance."

"How 'bout it, Cain?" Mencken said. "They going to let you outta here tonight?"

" 'Fraid not. Doctor says he wants to keep me one more day. I still haven't thrown off my cough. But you two go ahead—and hoist one for me. Maybe we can have a date tomorrow night, Roxy, if my cough is gone."

"Too bad there's no 'R' in the month," Mencken said, reaching for the wine bottle, "or we could have oysters. They're the greatest aphrodisiacs in Christendom. I understand that Methodist Ministers cultivate their own."

"Now wait a minute," I interrupted, producing a copy of *In Defense of Women,* one of his books I had brought to the hospital. "I want to read Roxy some of your choice comments on women. You can borrow this if you want, Roxy. You'll find it illuminating; let me quote: 'The average woman, until art comes to her aid, is ungraceful, misshapen, badly calved and crudely articulated, even for a woman. If she has a good torso, she is almost surely bowlegged. If she has good legs, she is almost sure to have bad teeth. If she has good teeth, she is almost sure to have scrawny hands or muddy eyes, or hair like oakum, or no chin. Their so-called beauty, of course, is almost always pure illusion. The female body, even at its best, is very defective in form. It has harsh and very clumsily distributed masses; from the side, it suggests a drunken dollar-mark. Putting it in uniform, as we did during Woodrow's recent folly, was almost like stripping her. Compared to it, the average milk-jug, or even cuspidor, is a thing of intelligent and gratifying design—in brief, an *objet d'art.*' " And I slammed the book closed.

Mencken was looking slightly subdued until Roxy said: "Oh, isn't that marvelous! And how true! But somebody's going to have to show Mr. Mencken a *real* torso. I'm sure the Rennert has some cuspidors for comparison."

"Not only a real torso, but a dowry. Until Prince Charming comes along, she could do far worse than a gentleman of her own age who is an expert on women; in fact, has written a book on the subject."

"Look," I replied. "Some mature women like younger men, in fact, prefer them. Isn't that right, Roxy?"

Before she could respond, Mencken said: "Cain, that sounds like a challenge that can be settled only in bed. What do you say, Miss Stinson? Are you prepared to settle this competition?"

"Well, certainly not here and not with both of you at once, although that could be interesting. But I might be persuaded to begin the playoffs tonight. Besides, I've never slept with a famous writer and editor before. It might be sort of like sleeping with a movie star, although you certainly don't look like one. Pour me another cup of wine, Mr. Author. Let see if the mood hits me."

The trouble was the more she went on like that the more I loved her. With everyone but me in good spirits, we finished the wine and then, after a nurse had put her head in the door to request that we make a little less noise, Mencken and Roxy left to have dinner with all of us toasting:

> "It was six or eight cows
> Not sixty-eight thous.
> We'll drink a lot
> of tea from the pot,
> Not sixty-eight thous.
> But six or eight cows
> But there was twenty-five thous
> And who needs cows?"

CHAPTER TWELVE

Next day, while I was still in the hospital, Mencken phoned: "Good morning, Cain—just calling to see how you feel. They going to let you out today?" He seemed especially joyful, which annoyed me.

"Yeah, I'll be outta here by noon. My cough is almost gone and the doctor says there's no sign of TB. But I have to keep watching it. How did it go last night?"

"Lots of wine and beer—in teacups, of course, except in her room. She had lobster and I had the crabs and we both had terrapin soup."

"That's nice. How did the rest of the evening go?"

"We did make several jokes about what she called 'our competition,' but you know, Cain, a gentleman never discusses his intimate relationship with a respectable woman. As the evening wore on, the conversation naturally got around to marriage, love-making and lovers, et cetera, et cetera."

"Et cetera, et cetera."

"And I told her, find a man over forty who heaves and moans over a woman in the manner of a poet and you will behold either a moron who ceased to develop at twenty-four or a fraud who has his eye on the lands, tenements and hereditaments of the lady's deceased first husband. With her having a deceased husband and me being over forty, that certainly ruled out any talk of marriage and love."

"That's good news."

"But," Mencken added, "whatever the future of monogamous marriage, there will never be any delay in the agreeable adventurousness which now lies at the bottom of all transactions between the sexes. In short, women will never cease to be women and as long as they are women, they will remain provocative to men. And she's certainly provocative. I'll say that."

"Okay. So how's her torso—unveiled?"

"That you will have to find out for yourself. She's obviously quite proud of it and I didn't see anything to contradict that."

"What time did you get home?"

"To tell the truth, I'm still at the Rennert. I just woke up. Roxy's on her way back to Washington."

"You spent the night with her?"

"Of course. And speaking of lovers, et cetera, Roxy told me something very interesting. It seems that last week Jesse tried to set up a party for tonight in what they call 'the love nest'—you remember; she told us about it—a little house on H Street, down the block and across from Lafayette Park. The president vetoed it, telling Jesse he wanted the house for his use that night and didn't want to join in any party. Which means that he's meeting his girlfriend tonight at Fifteen-oh-nine H Street. It's an early date—around seven P.M."

"Don't you think we ought to go over there?" I asked.

"What do you mean?"

"To do a little detective work?"

"You want us to become a couple of peeping Toms? Look, the public acts of a man I consider fair game, and if in his lunge for the taxpayer's trough he violated the standards of decent conduct, I stand ready to raise high my strap and render him a smarting blow. If he jollies up the American public from the podium, I shall descend upon him with the glorious whoop of the calvary sergeant spying redskins, or the caretaker of a violated nunnery.

"But," he said with emphasis, "if he jollies up to a damsel in the privacy of his boudoir, or anywhere—even in the White House— no matter. The woman knows what she's doing and the act will get no criticism from me. I am busy enough defending the republic and my war wounds prevent me from undertaking other activities."

"What's her name?"

"Nan Britton. The president has been seeing her for some time."

"How does Roxy know all this?"

"Jesse—and Daugherty—were primarily responsible for taking care of what they called 'the Nan Britton problem.' "

"There might be some blackmail involved," I said, "which would explain the Ohio Gang's continuing need for money over and above their sheer greed. I definitely think we ought to go over there tonight."

"And spy in the window?"

"No. The Secret Service would never let us get that close anyway. But we might learn something."

"All right. I'll see you at the station in time to take the four P.M. train. And we can have a leisurely dinner in Washington before it gets dark. How does that sound?"

"I don't know. I had hoped to get a date with Roxy. I'll let you know."

"Well, good luck," Mencken said. "Hope you measure up, if you know what I mean." And he hung up before I could respond.

When I left the hospital, needing exercise, I walked to Marconi's for lunch, then to my apartment, trying to kill time until Roxy was back at the Wardman. When I finally reached her, she sounded depressed. "Just a little hangover," she said, "Too much wine and beer."

"You must have had some night."

"I suppose you want to hear all about it?"

"No. But I was hoping we could get together tonight. It'll have to be late because Henry and I are going to do a little detective work first. In fact, why don't you join us for dinner? And then after our sleuthing I'll come back to the Willard and we can go dancing."

"Oh? You seem anxious to get your turn at bat."

"Well, to hear Henry tell it, it sounded like he hit a home run the first time up."

"You can ignore everything Mencken says, especially on this subject. Look, I'm setting the rules in the competition and under my rules, one competitor doesn't talk about the other's game. Got that?"

"Yeah."

"I'd love to join you for dinner and go dancing later. And I bet I know what you two are doing this evening. You ought to be ashamed of yourselves."

"It's all part of the job, if we're going to learn about everything that's going on in Washington now."

"Even in the bedrooms?"

"Even in the White House closet."

"Henry told you about that, eh?"

"Naturally. Where would you like to go for dinner?"

"How about Harvey's? It's at Pennsylvania at Eleventh Street. You can't miss it. It has an incredible cast-iron façade and a sign that says 'Restaurant of Presidents.' They're famous for their seafood, especially oysters."

"Too bad they're out of season," I said.

"You won't need them."

"So, what does that mean?"

"Wine's enough. See you later. I have an appointment here this afternoon with Harry Daugherty. He's not feeling well enough to come to his office. I'll come down to Harvey's after that."

I called Mencken who had arrived home and told him Roxy was going to join us for dinner at Harvey's at five o'clock and that I was going dancing with her later in the evening.

We boarded the 4 P.M. train to Washington and the first ten minutes or so of the trip was given over to rehashing what I had learned from Slattery and Smoot and Mencken's experience in New York. Then Mencken seemed to drift off, staring out the train window as we sped through the bleak Maryland landscape. Suddenly, he said: "By the way, Cain, another thing I learned in New York. The negotiations with Hearst for the sale of *The Smart Set* broke down, but they found another buyer. Nathan and I will be announcing our departure in the October issue."

"So we can talk about the magazine now?"

"Right, in fact, we want to spread the word because I'm looking for new writers."

"Good," I said, as he seemed to drift off again. After awhile, but not sure I should be interrupting his daydreaming, I said: "How's the column coming? Have you got a subject yet?"

"Yes, I have. A good one. 'The telephone.' "

"I imagine you'd be all for it, considering how many calls you make."

"At the office, yes. But at home it's an abomination. Not too long ago, I sat down to dinner in my own house without any impertinent and imbecile jackass summoning me from the table to the phone. You will never convince me that it could have been possible without divine intervention. For the first time in years, I wallowed in the luxury of a meal eaten in peace, with no abominable shrilling of a bell to interrupt my engulfing of my victuals, and no choleric conversation with a moron to paralyze my digestion. There is in the whole world no more villainous enemy of civilized decency than the modern telephonomaniac."

He paused to light up a Willie and take a long, loving look at the smoke he blew toward the train window. Then he continued: "In my office, it is even worse. Let's say at nine A.M. I start to compose a treatise upon the disarmament buffoonery and am interrupted at nine-ten by a woman who wants me to subscribe to some brummagen charity, and at nine-seventeen by another woman who wants to know if I will read her poetry, and at nine-twenty-seven by a life-insurance solicitor, and at nine-thirty-three by a strange simian who wants to know who publishes this or that book and at nine-forty-one by a misdirected call for some neighbor, and at nine-fifty by another, and at nine-fifty-six by a third, then it is a bet of at least one hundred to one that I have very little on paper by ten o'clock, and that what is there will be blowsy and puerile stuff. It is simply out of the question to do any decent writing under such circumstances—and yet those are the circumstances under which most writing has to be done in America today."

"I guess that's what you get for being famous."

"I guess so. I thought of having my telephone taken out, but that would make it difficult for my friends or persons who have legitimate business. I've also thought of having my name taken out of the telephone book, making my phone what is called 'silent.' But that would also annoy my friends and the bores seem to have the numbers of all 'silent' phones. Friends who have them say they are annoyed as much as I am."

"Have you tried taking the receiver off the hook?"

"I have, and it works, of course. But it's open to all the objections that lie against the other two plans and has one of its own. It makes the exchange girls swear like sailors and causes them to send repairmen to find out what's wrong. He comes in, jangles the bell for ten minutes, holds long conversations with colleagues somewhere else, and pockmarks the parquetry with his spikes. And I dislike putting an honest man to so much trouble. To the last telephone repairman who came to my house, I offered my apologies and a bottle of Erbacher 1913. It's almost better to stand the ringing of the telephone—except that I work in a remote part of my house, removed by a flight of stairs from the nearest telephone."

"Can't you have a phone installed at your desk?"

"What a question! Would I be any more comfortable if the infernal machine were directly under my nose? Frankly, I should install the damn thing in my basement, then the three flights of stairs up and down will rid me of all temptation."

"It sounds like an invigorating column. I'm looking forward to reading it."

"You just heard it all," he said, confirming what I have often noticed, that when you talk to columnists about something they are working on they sound like they are reading it almost verbatim. He was about to offer his views on another household menace, radio—the programs of which, he said, were worth precisely what they cost you, nothing—when the train decreased speed as it pulled into Washington's dreary railroad yards that preceded the station, coming from the east.

We had to wait a few minutes for a taxicab, which took us to 11th and Pennsylvania, and Roxy was right—we had no trouble spotting Harvey's unusual cast-iron facade. When we entered the restaurant, we saw Roxy seated on a bench close to the maitre d' stand and reading the new magazine, *Time*.

She stood up as we approached and after we both gave her a hug, she said: "I just love this new magazine. They do a wonderful job of summing up last week's news. This issue has a good story about how Washington is still surprised that President Harding agreed to run again, considering all the rumors about his being tired of his job and not in good health. What it didn't say was that Daugherty pushed him into announcing. Everybody knows Harding is overwhelmed by the job, but the gang can't stand the thought of the president quitting after this term. I just love the way the magazine is written so sprightly. Have you seen it?"

"I've seen it," Mencken said. "The two publishers came to me to talk about starting it and I said they had too much competition from the *Literary Digest*. If they had followed my advice you wouldn't be reading it now."

"Oh, you just thought they'd give *The Smart Set* some real competition," Roxy replied. "And this issue says that George Horace

Lorimer—not H. L. Mencken—is considered by many the greatest
editor of his day. The *Post* has two-and-a-half million circulation
every week."

"And why's that?" Mencken asked.

"Because he edits the *Saturday Evening Post* for working men
and women?"

"That's right," replied Mencken. "And Nathan and I edit for the
thinking man—and a few women."

"Oh, you're impossible," Roxy said, as we were led to our table.
After we were seated, a waiter appeared and started pouring glasses
of ice water. Mencken quickly asked whether we were going to be
able to obtain any drinks improved by alcohol for his unspecified
medical condition, and the waiter replied quite firmly that there
would be no liquor available, seeming to imply that revenue agents
might be in the vicinity, perhaps even dining here tonight. After all,
we were only about four blocks from the Treasury Department.

So Mencken shrugged, took a long swallow from his glass and,
making certain the waiter was listening, said "Ahhhh, that's not too
bad. The first glass of water I've had in over two years. You know,
that well-known Prohibition agent, Izzy Einstein, says that Washington is the driest city in the country. It took over two hours from
the moment he arrived in town to find a drink—and he finally had
to get an address from a policeman. Whereas, in New Orleans it
took only thirty-five seconds. That was the time it took Izzy's first
cab driver to respond to his question, 'Where can I get a drink?'
by taking out a pint and offering to sell it to him."

We all laughed and the waiter started to leave when Mencken
tugged at his sleeve. "Wait a minute, young man. Your implied
concern about revenue agents is well deserved. Izzy himself may
be in town. He's only five feet tall and weighs two hundred and
twenty-five pounds, so you'd think he'd be easy to spot. But that's
the point. He doesn't look like an agent and, besides, he's a master
of ruses and has more disguises than Sherlock Holmes. One of his
favorites is to pose as a cosmopolitan gourmet and order his dinner
in French. He speaks several languages, but delivers what he calls
his C.O.D.s ('Come On Down' to the Federal Building) in plain
English. He also plays the violin and disguises himself as a concert
violinist. He can do a Polish Count, street car conductor, a beauty
contest judge, black face (in Harlem) and a fisherman. He once went

into a Sheepshead Bay fisherman's bar carrying a string of just-caught fish."

Then Mencken picked up his glass of water and poured just a little into his top coat pocket: "And whenever Izzy is sold or given a drink he pours it into a little funnel he keeps in his coat pocket, which is connected by a tube to a bottle sewn in the lining of his coat. He sometimes works with a co-agent named Moe, and one winter night, dressed up as a couple of bums, they knocked on a speakeasy door and when the doorkeeper looked out, Moe pointed to Izzy, whose teeth are chattering, and yells: 'Can't you give this guy a drink! He's frostbitten!'

"One of his favorite opening gambits is to ask a bartender, 'Care to sell a pint to a deserving Prohibition agent?'—and then whisper to the bartender, 'I'm Izzy Einstein'; which the bartender repeats to everyone in the bar and, amid the laughter, produces a pint. But he's also quick to pick up an opportunity. One bartender refused to serve him because, he said, 'You look like Izzy Epstein,' and produced a picture of Izzy to prove it. Apologetically, the bartender said, 'And I hear Epstein's in town.'

"When Izzy said, 'You mean Einstein, don't you?' the bartender insisted it was Epstein. So Izzy offered to bet the bartender the price of a drink. The bartender said 'Okay,' and poured a shot, which Izzy emptied into his coat pocket and gave the bartender a C.O.D. So let's bow our heads in silent lament for a very talented man who is wasting his life in a scoundrel's job."

"I'm going to do better than that," I said, cautiously producing my flask. "I'm going to drink to him—a real drink—even though he may be in the room right now, possibly disguised as the sage of Baltimore."

"Me, too, but one of my own," Roxy said, lifting her skirt and producing a small flask a little larger than a cigarette package, held to her leg by a very tight garter.

"Yeah, Cain," Mencken said smugly. "That's one thing I forgot to mention. Roxy's flask. I ran into it last night, quite by accident, in search of something else."

"And here's your evidence, smart aleck," Roxy replied, pouring some of the liquor from her flask into Mencken's coat pocket. Then, as she looked at the maître d's desk, wondering who, if anyone, might have seen her, she said: "Well, look who's here."

Mencken and I both turned and saw two men waiting to be seated. One was the unmistakable, huge, large-headed Gaston B. Means, wearing a bow tie, homburg and dark gabardine topcoat. He was with a shorter, heavy-set, hatless man whose face was dominated by a large black moustache.

"Who's the guy with Means?" I asked Roxy.

"That's Billy Burns, the Bureau of Investigation Director. He's running the Jesse Smith investigation, although it's not much of an investigation anymore. Harry says it was suicide and that's that."

I noticed that Burns started to follow the maître d' to a table, while Means ambled in our direction. When he arrived, he went directly to Roxy, bent over to give her a hug, and said: "I'm so dreadfully sorry to learn about Jesse. He was one of my favorite people in this town. I know you're going to miss him."

Roxy nodded and said, frostily I thought: "Thank you, Gaston. I know you'll miss him, too."

Turning to Mencken, Means said: "And how are you two gentlemen of the press? Good to see you again. I'm sorry I haven't returned your calls this week, Mr. Mencken, but I've been traveling. What were you calling about?"

"You know damn well what I was calling about," Mencken replied, pulling a chair from the table next to ours. "Sit down for a moment. I want to talk with you."

"All right, but just for a moment. I have to join Bill Burns. We have a lot of business to discuss and I have a job tonight."

"Look," Mencken said, leaning closer to Means and lowering his voice, "right after I left the Vanderbilt last week, I was nabbed by two New York plainclothesmen, who seemed to know exactly what I was doing and where. If it hadn't been for some friends, I'd probably still be in jail. I told the cops, frankly, that I was authorized to get my merchandise from Gaston B. Means, who is well connected to the Justice Department, and they just looked at each other. Did they call you?"

"Never heard from them. Lots of guys use that alibi when they get caught—that I, or Jesse Smith, authorized it."

"All right. So how about giving my money back?"

"Look, I didn't tip them off!"

"You've done it before, we've heard."

"That's a lie. Anyway, the money's gone. It's been distributed.

I gave you a bargain price and you know it. Sorry this happened, but being a bootlegger is a risky business and I can't be responsible for everyone who gets caught."

"So you don't mind us putting this in our book?"

"What? That H. L. Mencken got taken on a liquor permit scam by Gaston B. Means? Most people would just laugh and say 'What the hell did Mencken expect?' "

Then with Mencken fuming but aware that Means was right, Means rose from his chair, and prepared to leave.

"One more thing, Mr. Means," I said, also lowering my voice, "Since we talked last week, we have some pretty good evidence that the big blue diamond is indeed missing."

"Yes, I've heard that, too. That's the word on the street. Can't imagine what anyone could do with it—unless they cut it up into a couple of stones. But then, the two pieces wouldn't be nearly as valuable as the Hope."

Then Means walked to where Burns was sitting and the waiter, who had been keeping his eye on our table watching for Means to leave, quickly appeared to take our orders. Mencken had flounder and Roxy joined me in having lobster, insisting she would pay for mine because I missed her inheritance celebration dinner the night before.

When the waiter left, I said to Roxy: "Okay, who's this Nan Britton we're hoping to meet tonight?"

"She's the president's lover and has been since about 1917 when he was in the Senate. She's from his hometown in Ohio and had had a crush on him since she was about six years old. She used to hang around campaign headquarters when he was running for governor and the Senate. She also worked for the Republican National Committee during the 1920 campaign. I'm sure Harding or someone in the campaign got her that job—probably to keep her out of Marion, where Harding was running his front porch campaign. By then they had been lovers for three years. And Harding saw her several times during the campaign when he was in Chicago."

"How did it start?" Mencken asked. "She must have been pretty young for Gamaliel."

"She was. Twenty, to be exact, when they first got together. Jesse knew all about the affair because he and Harry had to keep it quiet and pay for keeping her. After his 1916 campaign for the Senate, she was living in New York when she wrote to Senator Harding seeking a job and asking whether he remembered her. How could he not? She was very well developed, even as a young girl, and she used to dress in short skirts and tight sweaters. Her father was a doctor, a good friend of Harding. Nan used to keep pictures of Harding cut from campaign posters on the wall in her room. It was well known around Marion that she had a crush on the local hero. In fact, as she grew older and more developed, some of her parents' friends suggested that their daughter was making it a little too obvious how she felt.

"Anyway, Harding wrote back that he did, indeed, remember her, that he would do what he could about finding her a job and that he made lots of speeches in New York. The next time he was in the city he would call her. He did and that's when the affair began. And it's been going on ever since, mostly in New York, although she has often been to the White House, where they make love in a little broom closet off the president's anteroom."

"My God," said Mencken. "This assignation would make Don Juan proud."

Roxy replied: "He has at least three people in the White House helping him: a Secret Service agent (whose name Jesse would never tell me), George Christian, the president's secretary, and Arthur Brooks, the president's valet whom Harding inherited from President Wilson."

"Is he a blackamoor?" said Mencken.

"Yes. The agent always remains on guard in the president's office while Harding and Nan retreat to the broom closet. Christian and Brooks handle the correspondence. Nan and the president are continually writing each other and the president's letters are sometimes very long."

"Jesus," said Mencken. "Someday there's going to be a monumental scandal."

"I doubt if they'll ever be found," Roxy said. "The president keeps her letters and everything pertaining to Nan in a particular drawer in his desk and has instructed Christian to burn everything in the drawer if anything happens to him. And George, in turn, told Jesse to burn the stuff if anything happens to the president and him. And Jesse said the president told Nan to burn his letters to her."

"Fat chance," said Mencken.

"Do you think Britton's blackmailing the president?" I asked.

"She doesn't have to. The president, through Jesse, gave her at least five hundred dollars a month."

"Are there others?" asked Mencken.

"Over the years, yes. And it was Jesse's job, with Harry's guidance, of course, to pay off the blackmailers and buy back letters or other incriminating evidence they might have."

"No wonder Daugherty needed money—and not just to pay off campaign debts," I said.

"Now you're getting it," replied Roxy. "And a great part of the money they took in went right into 'Jesse Smith Account Number three,' which Jesse kept in Mal Daugherty's bank in Washington Courthouse, Ohio. That's where they kept the blackmail fund."

"How 'bout the president?" Mencken said. "Doesn't he realize the problems his womanizing causes?"

"I'm not sure. But I do know that Harry tried to discourage the president from getting involved with women. Harding once told a group of reporters off the record—at the National Press Club—that it was good that he was not a woman 'because I could never say no.' Harding thought that was very funny, but Harry didn't. Jesse did say that because the president understood the need for money— and not just to pay off campaign debts—he could let his conscience be very elastic."

"How about the Duchess? Does she know about the president's philandering?"

"I'm sure she knows about Carrie Phillips, the woman he had an affair with before 1920. Everyone in Ohio knew about her, although the Republican National Committee managed to hush it up. And she almost caught her husband and Nan in the Oval Office, although I don't think she knew it was Nan."

"When was that?" I asked.

"About a year ago. The Secret Service agent, who was in on the Nan situation, brought her from the railroad station to the White House. He took her to the president's office and then stood watch outside his door. Nan's coming to the White House in itself did not raise eyebrows because her family and the Hardings were friends and everyone knew Nan worked in the campaign—and that she was a big fan of the president's."

"Very big," Mencken said.

"Yeah. But Mrs. Harding has at least one Secret Service agent loyal to her, and one day he told the Duchess that the president was seeing a woman. So she goes rushing down to the president's office and demands to be let in. But the agent says no. He has his orders. If she wants to see the president, she has to go around the other way, through George Christian's office. The Duchess takes off for the secretary's office and the agent guarding the president's office rushes in and warns the president and Nan, who by this time are in the broom closet. And the agent managed to get Nan out of the White House and into a car before the Duchess could get through Christian's office. A very close call."

"But Mrs. Harding didn't know who the woman was?" I asked.

"I don't think so. On the other hand, the Duchess may know everything that's going on because Mrs. McLean—with the Hope Diamond, you know—owns the house on H Street you're going to stake out tonight. And, believe it or not, she sometimes lets Harding and Nan meet secretly at Friendship House out on Wisconsin Avenue—usually before or after a golf game. Ned McLean built a golf course there, just for the president. They also go woman-chasing together—at least, they did when Harding was in the Senate. But I think they've also done it some since Harding has been in the White House. I know Ned has set up a couple of one-night stands for the president. . . ."

"Which could easily lead to blackmail," Mencken said.

"Easily. I don't think Mrs. McLean gives a damn what her husband does. He's usually drunk or doped up half the time, anyway. In fact, Mrs. McLean drinks quite a lot herself. How much of all this she knows is hard to say."

"This is not exactly what we had in mind when we started out to investigate the corruption in the Harding administration," said Mencken. "It's more like a romance novel."

"But don't you see how it all ties together?" Roxy replied. "Whenever you start to investigate anything you run into sex, one way or another. That's just life."

"You're right, it does tie together," Mencken agreed. "The average man is far more virtuous than his wife's imaginings make him out. And one of the main reasons is lack of funds. It usually takes more money to finance it than he can conceal from his consort. A man may force his wife to share the direst poverty, but even the least vampish woman of the third part demands to be courted in what, considering his station in life, is the grand manner, and the expenses of that grand manner scare off all save a small minority of specialists in deception. So long, indeed, as a wife knows her husband's income accurately, she has a sure means of holding him to his oaths. I dare say, many, maybe even most men, would pursue women the way Gamaliel does if they had the attorney general of the United States financing their assignations."

"True enough," said Roxy.

"On the other hand, I sympathize with old Gamaliel. He has an above-average sex drive, as do most politicians, and let's assume he is, for one reason or another—and it's really none of our business—estranged from the Duchess. So what does he do in that fishbowl of an office to satisfy his sexual urges? He takes risks, which, if unearthed by his opponents, will bring on charges of immorality and cries for resignation."

"But not exactly grounds for impeachment," I said.

"No. But probably grounds for voting against him next year. If any of these womanizing scandals surface before the election, I suspect he will resign. Which is exactly what worries Daugherty. . . ."

"And the Duchess," Roxy added.

"They will do everything in their power to prevent it," Mencken said, taking out his big watch and looking at it. Then, glancing at the window, he said, "We had better be hurrying up. It's beginning to get dark and we ought to be leaving for our rendezvous with history."

Roxy waved good-bye to Means, who for some reason, was leaving ahead of his dinner partner. Burns appeared to have finished his meal but was enjoying a second cup of coffee. I kept my eye on him, and when he ordered a third cup of coffee, I had the uncomfortable feeling that he was waiting for us to leave first.

When we left Harvey's, we waited with Roxy on Pennsylvania Avenue until a cab came along. "You boys have fun," she said. "If the show runs late, Jim, give me a call. And if I don't hear from you at all, I'll know the Secret Service arrested a couple of peeping Toms in Lafayette Park. They might even think you're homos. That's where they hang out, you know."

"That's what I hear. But we won't be wearing matching hand-kerchiefs and ties," I replied.

"They might arrest you anyway. If they do, I can bail you out by telling them that you're both in heated competition for a woman's hand. . . ."

A taxi pulled up at the curb and we said good-bye to Roxy. "Remarkable woman," Mencken said. "She might even change my mind about marriage."

CHAPTER THIRTEEN

After saying good-bye to Roxy, we walked casually toward 15th and H Streets, but arrived before it was completely dark. Killing time, we walked west on H Street until we reached Madison Place, which we crossed to put us on the edge of Lafayette Park. Standing there, waiting for it to darken, I turned toward the Lafayette Square and, pointing to a bench close to the middle of the famous park, I said: "Well, there it is. Perhaps the most significant site in my professional career, where I made one of the most important decisions in my life."

"No kidding," Mencken replied. "I had no idea the Marquis de Lafayette had such an impact on you, Cain."

"He didn't. But a few years ago, before the war, I was selling Victor Records and Victrolas in the phonograph record department of Kann's, down on Seventh Street at Pennsylvania Avenue. I had just resigned after the skinflints refused to give me a well-deserved thirteen dollars-a-week raise. I started walking slowly up Pennsylvania Avenue, wondering what I would do next. In a previous job working for the Maryland Roads Commission, I had written some reports I was proud of. And I enjoyed writing. But I had no idea what to do about it. So I came back to Washington and quit my job. Walking up Pennsylvania Avenue to Fifteenth Street, I ended up sitting on a bench in Lafayette Park. I was twenty-two years old and had no more idea what I wanted to do in life than I had four years earlier when I graduated from college. With help from my father, who was president of the college, I had entered college quite young—which I don't think was a good idea."

"I agree with that," Mencken said.

"That's another story. So I'm sitting on this bench and suddenly I hear my own voice saying: 'You're going to be a writer!' Since then, I've thought about it a thousand times, trying to figure out

why that voice said what it did. There must have been something
that had been gnawing at me from the inside. Nor did I have any
realization that the decision I'd made wasn't mine to make. It would
not be settled by me, but by God."

"I'll pray for you, Cain, because I'm counting on you to be a
regular contributor to our new magazine, and that's a helluva lot
more than God will do to get you established. And you're right.
Good writers are born, not made. But aspiring writers can learn a
lot studying professional writers."

"Like you."

"Why not? Have you ever had any regrets about your decision?"

"No. But I was looking at it from the wrong end of the telescope.
If I had a story idea, then wrote it up in secret, then sent it to some
magazine—like yours—and then when it was accepted I told my
family, friends and well-wishers about it—if it happened that way,
it would have made more sense."

"You're probably right. Well, I think it's dark enough now. Let's
go back to our station," Mencken said, as he started to walk back
toward 15th Street.

It was a three-story stone house, next to the Shoreham Hotel
which had entrances on H and 15th Streets. Both the Shoreham and
1509 H had canopies from their doorways out to the curb; H Street
was quite wide, with two sets of streetcar tracks running east and
west down its middle. We walked slowly along H Street across from
the two entrances and it was immediately obvious that we were not
going to find a place where we could remain hidden while we
watched who came and went from the McLean house. We would
have to keep moving and look inconspicuous.

On our side of the street was the Union Trust Company, a couple
of houses similar to McLean's, an office building—the Wilkins—
and the Cosmos Club on the west corner of the block, which was
bounded by Madison Place. Across the street from Madison was
Lafayette Park. There were plenty of trees and bushes in the park
where we could hide, but they were too far away from 1509 to be
of much help. Roxy had warned us about the entry area, which had
a one-way mirror enabling someone inside to see out the front door
but preventing someone outside from looking in. This meant we
could not appear directly in front of the house very often, even
across the street.

The house had been decorated by Evalyn McLean. Roxy said its main salon and dining room, both lined in buff satin, were on the second floor. The bedroom, which Jesse used when he and Daugherty occupied the house, was done in pale pink taffeta with a gilt bed; Daugherty's in chintz.

Roxy was not sure which one Harding would be using; probably Daugherty's. There was a vault for the liquor, which was plentiful and delivered under the full protection of the Justice Department. The house was two blocks from the White House and the Justice Department and right next door to the Shoreham, where Jesse had liked to stand on the corner and greet friends with his "Whaddya know?"

After walking slowly on the south side of H Street by the stone house (which was on the north side) and looking carefully for any sign of Secret Service agents, we positioned ourselves in the doorway of the Wilkins Building, far enough away from the nearest streetlight so that it would be difficult to see us from the doorway of 1509. Mencken produced a small pair of opera glasses which he focused on the front door of the house across the street. "All clear," he whispered. "I wonder where that one-way mirror is?"

I shook my head, not wanting to break the silence any more than I had to. Mencken turned his little binoculars up and down H Street: "Can't see anyone, except a couple of gentlemen standing together on the edge of the park," he said quietly.

Suddenly, a truck, approaching at a good rate of speed from the east on H Street, came to an abrupt stop directly in front of the H Street house and two men alighted, walked quickly to the front door and appeared to ring the bell. We could see the writing on the vehicle from a streetlight on the other side of H and, much to our surprise, it was a Wells Fargo armored truck. "Good God," Mencken said, a little too loud for my comfort. "Looks like they're delivering cash from the Treasury Department."

I whispered in his ear, "That's the way they deliver their whiskey. Damned clever."

"I hope it doesn't cause the president a *coitus interruptus*," Mencken said, training his glasses on the front of the house: "It would me. The guy that opened the door looks like he might be a Secret Service man. He has his topcoat on inside the house, which suggests to me that the president is already here and the agent is guarding the front door, ready to step out at any time if he has to."

The truck stayed long enough for the two men to take about ten cases of liquor into the house and then the truck drove away. "Cheeerist," Mencken said, softly as he could, which was not very soft. "I sure as hell don't intend to write about Gamaliel jollying his lover at a love nest across the park from the White House. But delivering ten cases of what I am sure is booze of the first chop there, while the rest of us have to risk going to jail to get stuff that is often no better than swill! That's too much! Maybe I ought to do a column tipping Izzy Einstein off to what's going on here. He could come disguised as a Wells Fargo driver."

"Let 'em have their whiskey," I said. "Can you imagine having to run this country *without* having a drink now and then? Anyway, you don't think the *Sun* would print it."

"I guess you're right. Maybe I'll talk to Nathan about doing something in the magazine, although he'll probably agree with you. I know he wouldn't have any objection to Gamaliel sneaking away from the Duchess every now and then to bed an attractive younger woman. Gamaliel's probably not that well taken care of at home and you know, like whiskey, every man needs a sexual outlet. The Puritans like to say that the sex instinct, if suitably suppressed, may be sublimated into esthetic idealism. But look at the great artists of the world; they are never Puritans or seldom even ordinarily respectable. No moral man—that is moral in the Y.M.C.A. sense— ever painted a picture worth looking at, or wrote a symphony worth hearing, or a book worth reading. And, of course, it's highly improbable that the thing has ever been done by a virtuous woman."

"Politicians certainly need their sexual outlets?"

"Maybe more so. Picture this, if you will. It is the close of a busy and vexatious day—say, half past five or six o'clock of a winter afternoon. He has a cocktail or two, and has stretched out, smoking, on a divan in front of a fire, perhaps in his office or perhaps in her apartment or even a little house on H Street in the nation's capital.

"At the edge of the divan close enough for him to reach with his hands, sits a woman not too young but still good looking and well-dressed and, above all, a dancing, musical voice, like Miss Stinson's, for example. She talks of all the things that women talk of. But no politics. No business. No theology. Nothing challenging and vexatious—but remember, she is intelligent, again like Miss Stinson. What she says is clearly expressed and often picturesquely so. As he observes the sheen of her hair, the glint of her white teeth, the graceful curve of her arms and listen to the exquisite murmur of her voice, gradually he falls asleep—but only for an instant. At once, observing it, she raises her voice ever so little, and he is awake. Then to sleep again—slowly and charmingly down that slippery hill of dreams. And then awake again, and then asleep again, and so on.

"I ask you seriously: could anything be more unutterably beautiful? The sensation of falling asleep is to me the most delightful in the world. I relish it so much that I even look forward to death itself with a sneaking wonder and desire. Here is sleep set to the finest music in the world—it is enchanting and ennobling."

"It is, indeed. But it doesn't sound all that great for the woman."

'True. But he returns to his sorrows somehow purged and glorified. But he is a better man. He has gazed upon the fields of asphodel and is genuinely, completely and unregrettably happy. Do you think Gamaliel is still awake in there?"

"I hope so. I'm getting a little tired peeping at nothing. I'm not sure politicians look at feminine companionship the same way you do."

"They don't. But every politician I ever knew was alert to the women who are attracted to power and position, beginning with those handsome young wenches that come from states all across the country to work in their capital offices."

"But what if the politician falls in love with one of these women?"

"That's a good question because, to hear Roxy tell it, apparently Gamaliel is really in love with Nan Britton. There seems to be sexual passion involved and no man caught in its throes is in any mental shape to cope with the daily problems of the presidency or lay out abstract policies. Passion is the most dangerous of all the surviving enemies of what we call civilization, which is based on order, decorum, restraint, formality, industry and regimentation."

"Jesus!" I said. "I fear for the nation. We better get in there and break this thing up."

"Not on your life," replied Mencken. "I'd much rather see our ridiculous civilization fall to an excess of passion than the outlawing of one of its most essential ingredients—whiskey."

I looked at my watch, trying unsuccessfully in the dark to make out what time it was. "Maybe Harding has gone to sleep," I said impatiently. "Looks like we're in for a long evening. Why don't we walk slowly down to Madison Place and then back to Fifteenth? You know any good jokes?"

"Yeah. Here's one suitable for the occasion," Mencken said, as we started to walk along H Street. At about that time a streetcar approached us from the east, stopped on H Street across 15th. Then it passed us, going west on H Street. "This Irish cop got married, and the priest poured holy water all over him and did the same to the girl. After the ceremony and the big feed, the cop and his Maggie, he in his tuxedo and she in her borrowed pair of silk pants, rush over to their hotel room and in a jiffy they go at it. He pounds away at her and she eggs him on for more. You know these insatiable Irish maids. I had one in Baltimore once. Quite an experience!

"Well, suddenly, Maggie mumbles something to the cop and he sits straight up in bed and starts to beat the living daylights out of her. The poor girl spends the night recovering from her wounds, while the cop snores away in his bed. In the morning, he wakes up and looks at her, recalling what she had said the night before. 'I have a mind to give you more of the same,' he said to Maggie, 'except that I'm a gentleman. But I'm going to get rid of you all right. I won't be married to no Protestant.' Maggie was silent for a moment, then whimpered: 'But darling, I'm no Protestant.'

"He turns around and looks at her, surprised: 'But isn't that what you told me last night?' Still whimpering, Maggie replies: 'No. What I said was, "I used to be a prostitute." ' So the cop starts crying, embraces Maggie and says: 'Oh my darling! I thought you said you were a Protestant. Will you ever forgive me?'

"I told that to one of our high-toned Episcopalian priests in Baltimore and it brought a big laugh."

"No doubt," I said, trying to laugh as quietly as I could.

"You know, Cain, maybe the Irish cop was right. It's a funny thing about prostitutes. Now everyone knows that just as some men have a drink problem, some men have a sex problem. And there is no half-baked ecclesiastic, bawling in his temple on a suburban lot, no fantoddish old suffragette sworn to get her revenge on man, no shyster district attorney, ambitious for higher office, who doesn't have a sovereign remedy for it. And yet, there is not a man who has studied and pondered the problem who doesn't believe that it is eternally insoluble. Hence, prostitution. And no prostitute was ever so costly to a community as a prowling and obscene vice crusader or dubious legislator or prosecuting officer."

By this time we had walked casually to Madison, back to 15th and H and were standing on the corner acting as if we were in serious conversation, which we were. Mencken seemed about to continue his discourse on the superiority of prostitutes, when a large black sedan pulled up in front of 1509 H Street and stopped, heading west. Two men dressed in topcoats and wearing hats got out. One went to the front door of the house and the other stood near the right-hand rear door of the big car looking up and down the street. We walked toward Madison Place, hoping not to attract attention. When we reached the corner, Mencken looked around and noticing that the man by the car, presumably a Secret Service agent, was looking toward 15th Street, ignoring us, he pulled his binoculars out of his coat pocket and focused them on the front door of the house. Soon, a gentleman wearing a homburg and a chesterfield coat, with its collar turned up, and the man who had gone into 1509, came quickly out of the house and got in the car.

"Ah ha!" said Mencken. "I'm pretty sure that's Gamaliel. I see a lot of white hair under that hat. Quick. Give me your hand. They're going to be driving right by here soon. If we're holding hands, they'll just think we're a couple of queers."

Taking Mencken's hand, I said: "I have this idea for a novel about an opera singer who is a latent homo who loses his powerful voice when he goes with a man but regains it when he makes love to his Mexican whore. Some doctors I talked to think it's a plausible thesis."

"Sounds cuckoo to me," Mencken replied. "I wonder if I lost my great voice holding hands there?"

As he predicted, after the two men and the man who looked like Harding were all in the car, it headed west toward Madison Place, where it turned left in front of us and went south to Pennsylvania Avenue and then right toward the White House. We could see it turn left into the White House gate, confirming Mencken's belief that it was the president.

"Nan should be coming out soon," Mencken said. "Let's go back to the Wilkins Building. She'll probably head toward Fifteenth to catch a cab on the corner. Or maybe she's staying at the Shorham. It would be very convenient."

"Maybe too convenient. If I were the president, I wouldn't want her that close to McLean's house."

"I hope you're right. If we're in luck, she'll be staying somewhere like the Willard or the Washington. Let's hope Gamaliel doesn't send a car or we'll lose her for sure." We walked slowly back to the Wilkins Building, pretending to be engaged in conversation. And this time we were pretending. Mencken said, "I'd hate to make a living doing this."

"I'd starve."

We had not been back in the doorway long, when we heard a streetcar heading east along H Street. We both held our breath as the car stopped at the corner of 15th and H. If Britton suddenly burst out of 1509 and ran to get on the trolley, we would have a hard time catching up with her and boarding the car without being noticed. But she did not come out and the streetcar moved on.

Then, almost as if she had been waiting for the streetcar to clear the area, a woman wrapped in a white cloak came out of the house, looked up and down H Street then crossed it and headed toward 15th. We let her get to the corner and when it appeared she was going to go south on 15th, we began to follow her. But suddenly, a man came out of the shadows on the other side of H Street. He appeared to have been standing, hidden, under the Shoreham Hotel H Street entrance canopy. He was a big man wearing a dark trenchcoat and a homburg.

"I wonder if he's a Secret Service agent escort?" Mencken said, as we paused to see what he would do. Then, as the man reached the corner and appeared to be following the woman, Mencken trained his small binoculars on him. "By God," he mumbled, "It looks like Means! I'll bet he's been around here all evening. Remember, he said he had a job tonight and he left Harvey's before we did. Take a look," he said, handing me the glasses.

"Yep. That's Means all right. We got to be careful."

"Hell, he knows we're here. He just came out ahead of us because he can't afford to lose the woman. I'll bet he wants to talk with her. Christ, Cain! When we started this little investigation, did you ever imagine we'd end up following a man who sells government liquor permits, who might have murdered a semi-government official, and who, in turn, is following a mysterious woman in white who is coming from an assignation with the president of the United State . . . ? As Holmes and Watson, we're trailing an A. Conan Doyle villain who is following a Wilkie Collins heroine.

"And I wanted to get away from literature and into politics."

Then, taking back the glasses and focusing on the two people ahead of us, Mencken said: "The woman does not appear to know she's being followed and Means seems to be gaining on her, purposely. He's not lurking back, trying to stay out of sight."

When they reached the intersection where New York Avenue runs into Pennsylvania, the woman in white crossed over to the east side of 15th and then continued south, passing the Home Life Insurance Building, then crossing G Street past the Albee Building and the Keith Theater, continuing south. We followed, and about the time we were in front of Keith's, the woman was near the corner of F and 15th, where Means overtook her and said something, which startled her. She turned around quickly to face Means and, according to Mencken, who had her in the glasses, she seemed terrified. "Come on, let's see what's playing at Keith's," Mencken said, by way of suggesting a reason for us to slow down until they continued. We walked over to the front of the building where there was a glassed-in box listing some coming attractions. We tried to act like two gentlemen out for a leisurely evening stroll, although I don't think it was necessary. Means had not looked back once since he left H Street. And I agreed with Mencken that he probably knew we were watching the McLean house and did not care whether we were following him or not.

"Look," Mencken said, "they're bringing back the *The Sheik* for a Saturday matinee. You know, I recently had lunch with Valentino; can't remember exactly why. Oh yeah, it was to talk about that new book of his—*Daydreams*—a volume of messy poems that helped confirm the rumors, started when his first wife said they never slept together, that he was a pansy. Remember, the *Chicago Tribune* called him a pink powderpuff?"

"No," I replied, taking a quick look at Means and the woman to see if they were still standing on 15th Street, talking. They were.

"Well, he should have passed it over and kept away from the New York reporters. The mischief was done; he was both insulted

and ridiculous. But there was nothing he could do about it. He felt
it was infamous. But I told him nothing is infamous if it isn't true.
A man still has inner integrity. We discussed these lofty matters for
some time, when, suddenly, it dawned on me that what we were
talking about was not what we were talking about at all. Valentino
is a curiously naive and boyish young fellow, not handsome, but
attractive. There was an obvious fineness in him. When talking
about his home and youth, his words were simple and yet somehow
very eloquent. I could still see the mime before me, but now and
then, briefly and darkly, there was a flash of something else—what
is commonly called, for want of a better name, a gentleman. And
it was apparent that Valentino's agony was the agony of a man of
relatively civilized feelings thrown into a situation of intolerable
vulgarity destructive alike to his peace and his dignity. It was not
the *Chicago Tribune* remarks and their aftermath that were riding
him. It was the whole grotesque futility of his life. Had he achieved
out of nothing, a vast and dizzy success? Then that success was
hollow as well as vast—a colossal and preposterous nothing!"

I noticed that Means and the woman were now walking rapidly
down 15th, headed for the Washington Hotel and I tugged on
Mencken's sleeve indicating that we should follow them.

"Valentino," Mencken said, as rapidly as we were walking, "with
that touch of fineness, was only the hero of the rabble. Imbeciles
surrounded him in a dense herd. I confess that the predicament of
poor Valentino touched me but provided grist for my mill. But I
couldn't quite enjoy it. Here was a young man who was living daily
the dream of millions of other young men. Here was one who was
catnip to women. Here was one who had wealth and fame. And
here was one who was very unhappy. I think I'd almost rather be
a politician."

"I like the idea of being catnip to women."

Means and the woman crossed F Street and were definitely heading toward the Washington Hotel. When they entered it, we quick-
ened our pace, but were not sure what we would do when we
overtook them. There was a first-floor lounge in the hotel and when
we entered the lobby, Mencken went over to a group of chairs and
a sofa, behind some potted plants, and I walked over to the lounge,
approaching it from the side so that most people in the lounge could

not see me. At the door I looked cautiously in and could see Means and a young lady sitting in one corner of the lounge, placing an order with a waiter.

"We're in luck," I said to Mencken, joining him in the sitting area. "They're having something to drink, which will give us a little time to plot our next move. What'll we do now?"

"If they come out together, we'll confront them and say we're friends of Roxy Stinson and Jesse Smith. You say you would like to have a word with Means on a business matter and I'll offer to walk Miss Britton to the elevator. If Miss Britton comes out first, as I think she will, I'll intercept her on her way to the elevator while you go into the lounge and keep Means there long enough for me to make contact with the young lady. If you can find out what Means is up to, so much the better."

We had been there just about long enough for the woman we assumed to be Nan Britton to have a coke or some coffee, when she suddenly appeared in the lounge doorway and headed for the elevators. Mencken went into action and so did I. When I reached the lounge, Means was paying the check and I went over to his table and sat down before he had a chance to get up: "Good to see you again, Means. Can I buy you a cup of coffee, or offer you a drink?"

"No thanks. I've got to be leaving, I wondered when one of you would show up. You're the worst couple of gumshoes I ever saw. You don't even know how to do a simple surveillance or follow someone. You were so amateurish the Secret Service just ignored you. They figured you were just a couple of reporters who saw the president come out of a house where he sometimes plays poker. So what?"

"Well, I must say you're pretty good. We never once saw you until you came out from the Shoreham awning and began following Miss Britton. I assume the young lady is Nan Britton?"

"Yeah. I guess Roxy told you about her?"

"And Nan's date with the president."

"I tell you, that Roxy better be careful. She's got to stop blabbing her mouth, the gang is well aware that she knows almost as much as her ex-husband did about what's going on here. And look what happened to him."

"So you think Smith was murdered?"

"Certainly! You heard about the bullet on the left side of his head—and he was right-handed?"

"Does your friend Burns agree?"

"Billy's sticking with suicide. It's easier for him. For everybody. What does Roxy think?"

"I'm not sure. She seems to think he might have killed himself. But even if he did, she thinks it was murder because he was driven to it by Daugherty—who turned against him and seemed to be setting Smith up to take the rap for a lot of the corruption that is surfacing. So what are you up to? Who you working for tonight?"

"Normally, a good investigator never reveals who his clients are. But I'm going to make an exception in this case. You're working for Mencken and I respect him. Besides I'd like to have someone of his stature—and yours, of course—on my side in the unravelling of this administration, which is already beginning to happen."

"Yeah, the House and the Senate are going to be launching hearings; the attorney general can't prevent them much longer and the press is waking up. But that's not what you're working on tonight, This is bedroom stuff."

"You're right. This is not your everyday corruption. But it's related. And before I tell you anything, I need to know what *you* were doing spying on the president's little tryst. In this business, when you give up information you get something in return."

I decided I couldn't tell Means anything he didn't already know or could figure out. "All right. As Mencken told you, we're working on a magazine article—and maybe even a book—on the shenanigans in the Harding administration. When Roxy told us about the president's date tonight, we decided it was interesting but not something we wanted to get into. But it might prove relevant."

"Let me ask you something," Means intervened. "Why is Roxy telling you all so much? You two seem to know a lot more about the administration than most reporters. It must come from Roxy."

"A lot of it. She wants to help us with our book—not to make her look good, but to make sure everybody knows that whatever Jesse did—and she knows he was involved in many of the frauds— he was just carrying out orders of the attorney general."

"Well, she better watch out."

"Anyway, Mencken, especially, didn't like the idea of prying into someone's love life. But I convinced him that this might be something that could lead to blackmail, which might in turn, explain the Ohio Gang's voracious need for money. We thought if we could somehow get to meet Miss Britton after her meeting with the president we might learn something. Mencken is talking to her now, I presume. And we certainly didn't count on running into you, which is very interesting."

"I can tell you, you won't learn much from Miss Britton. You're going to learn a helluva lot more from me. I'm working for none other than Mrs. Harding herself, which I, of course, will deny. Nobody would believe me anyway and, from what you say, you wouldn't be interested in printing it. I'm also working for another woman (a friend of the Duchess, whose name I will *not* reveal). Mrs. Harding knows about Nan Britton—in fact, she almost caught them once making love in a little room off the Oval Office."

"We heard about that."

"I have several assignments: One, to confirm that the affair was going on by obtaining letters from the president to Miss Britton and bringing them to Mrs. Harding (which I have done) and, two, catching them together and confronting Nan. And three, warning Nan to stay away from Harding, that, frankly, it might be dangerous to both her and the president if this affair is continued."

"Does Mrs. Harding think blackmail is a possibility?"

"Yes. But not in the conventional sense. She thinks Attorney General Daugherty, who Mrs. Harding hates, *is doing the blackmailing!*—making the affair possible by supporting Nan and then telling the president that certain of their money-making scams are necessary for her support."

"Do you think that's what's going on?"

"Yes. That's why Jesse Smith was never officially given a Justice Department job, even though he had an office there and spent a lot of time at the department. He could take care of the president's women much easier as a private operator."

"Harding seems to have been a womanizer all his life. Does Mrs. Harding know about them?"

"Most of them. You got to remember she's a great believer in clairvoyance. When Harding was in the Senate, Mrs. Harding, with some other Senate wives, went to see Madam Marcia, the well-known Washington clairvoyant up on R Street. Later, while her

'Wurren' was still a senator, she went back anonymously and asked
for a horoscope reading for a man born on November second, 1885,
at two P.M.—her husband's birthday."

"Did Mrs. Harding tell you all this?"

"No, it came from a friend of hers, who I also work for. Madam
Marcia, having no doubt figured out who was the man in question,
told Mrs. Harding that her husband would rise to great prominence,
that he was sympathetic and kindly, intuitive, free with promises
and trusting of friends, enthusiastic, impulsive and perplexed over
financial affairs."

"Pretty safe predictions, depending on how you define 'great
prominence' in Washington."

"Madam Marcia also told Mrs. Harding that the man had had
many clandestine love affairs. After Harding became president, she
also predicted that he would not live out his term—that he would
have a sudden death, 'peculiar and violent.' More recently, Madam
Marcia told her that some of the men her husband had confidence
in dealt with death. My friend insists that Mrs. Harding devoutly
believes in astrology, which means she is obviously a very upset
woman."

"I would be too if I were a believer," I said, looking at my watch.
It was getting late and I decided that if I was going to see Roxy
tonight I had better get out to the Wardman in a hurry. "What did
Miss Britton say to you when you told her she had better stop seeing
the president?"

"She said that when her sweetie says that he can no longer see
her, she will stop seeing him. And tell Mrs. Harding to speak to her
husband about that."

"Britton sounds like a tough cookie."

"She is. So I told her that they would be discovered sooner or
later and that it would ruin the presidency. You'll never guess what
this little girl said to that?"

"What?"

"She replied with great righteousness: 'My sweetie doesn't care
about the presidency. He hates that job. He says he would much
rather live with me on a farm where there aren't so many reporters
and he doesn't have to make decisions.' "

Means had been looking at his watch, too. It was time to go.
"Mr. Means, talking with you is always instructive and I'd like to

hear more. But I have a date and you seem pretty busy yourself. Maybe we can talk again in the future."

We rose from our seats almost simultaneously. As Means walked me to the street, he said: "I'll bet your date is with Roxy. I envy you. Don't forget to tell her to be careful."

"I will and that's the third time you've said that." We parted in front of the Washington Hotel. He got into a chauffer-driven, black Cadillac sedan which drove slowly north on 15th Street.

As soon as Means' car was out of sight, I returned quickly to the hotel and called the penthouse lounge. I asked the headwaiter who answered the phone to page a Miss Nan Britton. He said she had just left.

I called her room and when Britton answered, I said: "This is the Secret Service. I understand you have a gentleman in your room. He had better be leaving immediately."

"Ohhhh, er, uh. We've been having coffee in the penthouse lounge. He saw me to my room and he's at the door now. He's just leaving."

"He better be out of there in a hurry."

"I'll tell him."

I did not wait to see Mencken rushing out of the lobby elevator and short-stepping to the lounge looking for me, but it is an imagined scene I will cherish for the rest of my life. He never mentioned it.

CHAPTER FOURTEEN

I phoned Roxy from the lobby of the Wardman and soon this tall, gorgeous, red-haired woman stepped out of the elevator and started walking toward the couch where I was sitting. She was not wearing a coat because we would spend the evening dancing in the Wardman lounge. She had on a black, two-piece suit with a jacket which was tight around her breasts, the tops of which were temptingly revealed by the low cut of her silver blouse. She wore a simple, black velvet choker around her neck with a small jewel that dangled at the top of her bosom. It was no Hope Diamond, but I couldn't take my eyes off it or its resting place. Finally, she held out her hand with outstretched fingers: "You might be interested in this, too," she said, diverting my attention to a sparkling diamond ring.

"From Jesse, no doubt."

"No doubt," she said, as we started walking to the lounge, where we could hear what turned out to be a small band with a blonde vocalist singing "Blue Skies." "He always had excellent taste in everything, especially jewelry. Incidentally, I'm glad you didn't tell Means about Jesse saying they had put the curse of the blue diamond on him."

"Did you ever figure out what he meant by that?"

"No, except that perhaps he might have been exposed to it in some way. But I'm sure he didn't steal it from the McLeans."

"Why?"

"First of all, Jesse's no crook. He may have done some shady things here in Washington, but that's just the way the game is played as he saw it. And everything he did had the approval of the attorney general of the United States. He's the real crook, as someday President Harding, who's not a crook either, is going to find out. Second, Jesse really believed in the curse on the Hope Diamond. He would have been scared to touch it, let alone steal it."

In the lounge, we chose a table back in the corner away from the dance floor. By the time we were seated the band was playing "Valencia" and I suggested we wait for something a little slower and softer to dance to.

She agreed and said she wanted to hear all about our spying on the love nest. "After the president left the house," I said, "Nan came out and we followed her as she started walking down Fifteenth toward the Washington Hotel. All of a sudden, a man appears out of the shadows and starts following her, too—ahead of us. Guess who it was?"

"Probably Gaston B. Means, working for the Duchess."

"Exactly right. In the lobby of the hotel after they had a cup of coffee, they separated and Mencken followed Nan while I confronted Means who was still in the lounge. He said he had been instructed to confirm that the affair was going on and to threaten Nan that it would be dangerous for both of them if she continued seeing the president. I haven't seen Mencken since we split. I was too anxious to get out here and keep my date with you."

"That's nice. Henry won't get much out of Nan. How did she respond to Means' warning?"

"Simply that it wasn't up to her. When the president says it is time to stop, she'll stop."

"Don't look for that to happen soon."

"Why?"

"Because, as Jesse used to say, 'Warren loves young women like a cat loves cream.' "

"I prefer older, more mature women. How about you and the president? Did he ever make a pass at you?"

"Once, at a Christmas party before he became president, he played kneesy with me. But I never gave him any encouragement. It would have been a disaster. Daugherty doesn't like me much as it is. And the president's womanizing drives him crazy. Jesse, too."

"By the way, Means says to tell you to be careful, that the Ohio Gang thinks you know almost as much as Jesse did—and look what happened to him."

"Don't worry; they'll never pin any of that stuff on me. I'm not worried or thinking about suicide, just about a pleasant evening with a nice young man."

"Good. But Means doesn't think Jesse committed suicide."

"A lot of people agree. But I still have to think he did—and Harry Daugherty drove him to it. I never could see what Jesse saw in that evil man. But he just loved him."

"For that matter, I don't understand what you saw in Jesse. He just doesn't seem like your type, to say nothing of the fact that you are so much more attractive than he was."

"Well, back when we were first married—and that was quite a few years ago—he was one of the most dashing young men in Washington Courthouse. A flashy dresser, nice looking, good dancer, witty in a corny, Ohio sort of way and a successful businessman—in dry goods. He opened up a department store and made a lot of money long before he got mixed up with Harry and politics. For an unsophisticated young lady like me, he was quite a catch. All the girls thought so."

"So how did your marriage go? How did you get along in the bedroom, if you don't mind my asking."

"I do sort of. I think two people's sex life is absolutely nobody else's business. But I will say we were not compatible, which I guess is obvious from the fact that we divorced."

"Do you think Jesse is—was—a homosexual?"

"I was never really sure. He didn't seem overly interested in women, he lived with Harry in Washington and they spent a lot of time alone together at their cabin out in the country. Harry is married but he hardly ever sees his wife, who is either in a hospital somewhere being treated for her arthritis or bed-ridden out in Ohio. It does look suspicious."

"So why did you stick with Jesse so long—as his friend?"

"Well, I have to be honest. It was kind of exciting seeing Warren Harding's career progress, from the Senate to the White House. And come to Washington and be on the inside. I definitely got Potomac Fever."

The band was now playing "My Blue Heaven" and I said: "Shall we, Miss Stinson?"

"I'd love to, Mr. Cain."

On the dance floor, I held her as tight as I could without creating a spectacle. She pulled me close and rubbed her hand up and down my back, while I held mine steady, resisting the urge to let it wander down behind her. Finally, I felt the inevitable pressure that would have made it difficult for me to return gracefully to our table and I pushed her away a little. She smiled and said: "I see you're in good shape for the next round of the playoffs."

"That's right. And I was assuming it would take place tonight on your home field. Is that correct?"

"Who knows. Depends on my mood, which right now is very good. But if I forfeit, you win nine to nothing."

"I'd rather loose after a fair turn at bat. How about Henry? Did he forfeit?"

"Interesting you should say that. I said I wouldn't discuss the competition. But maybe I will. Ask me later."

I decided to change the subject. "You said you had Potomac Fever. I hope that doesn't mean you want to go into politics. No attractive woman should, you know."

"Well I have given it some thought. But that sounds like a male politician talking."

"I'm no politician, In fact, I'm apolitical. And my reasons for thinking you ought to forget politics are pretty complex, but I'll try to oversimplify for the sake of brevity."

"Please do."

"It's my observation that there is only one situation in which a singular woman can look completely ridiculous. And that is when her husband and her lover shake hands, fill the glasses and pledge each other's health. But this thesis breaks down when women operate in the mass. A woman is like a harmonica. She shines best as a solo instrument. When she attempts to play *ensemble* the result is often disastrous. The reason is simple."

"This better be good."

"Her appeal is to the imagination and it must carry something of the sinister to it. No woman was ever remembered for smug, tame little attributes. If her charm is beauty, there must be a suggestion of snakes, skulls and fatal elixirs around. If her charm is intellect, there must be a menace in it. You, of course, have both charms."

"And that ain't all, Buster, which, if you get lucky and don't mess your game up with a lot of anti-feminist nonsense, you may find out."

"But if your charm doesn't have that menace to it—like being the woman who could send all the Ohio Gang to the jug . . ."

"That's not exactly what I had in mind," Roxy interrupted.

". . . then she is merely that most banal of God's creatures, an

interesting conversationalist. But this capacity to suggest the sinister
for some reason, inheres only in one woman at a time."

The band finished "My Blue Heaven" and the musicians began
adjusting their instruments for a short break. I continued my thesis
as we returned to our table in the corner: "But his concept does not
work in the plural. A gosson . . ."

"What's that?"

"A young man. When his beloved calls on his sisters he is surprised to find out how usual she seems. A nun, in the singular, is
full of romance; one thinks of a broken heart, rosaries, and long
hours alone with misty dreams. But when a bevy of nuns issue from
a convent, one is conscious only of clacking tongues, flapping
gowns and shiny faces. And right from the beginning a lady politician is faced with this problem. She must cooperate, she must go
to meetings, engage in shrill debates, have her picture taken in
groups of fifty on the White House lawn. She has to do all those
things no woman should do, she bustles, she talks loud. Her utter-
ances become banal: 'Madame President, don't you think we ought
to have a committee on publicity, too? We women must remember
it's organization that counts, et cetera, et cetera.' *We women!* What
a hideous phrase. It reeks of church suppers, charity and card parties; no breath of elusive perfume hangs about it, no memory of a
sidelong glance, no delicately curling cigarette smoke, a tremulous
languor. Females in wholesale lots."

When we were seated, Roxy spoke: "Do you have a cigarette so
I can exhale some delicately curled smoke, she said, giving him a
sidelong glance as he, in turn, inhaled that elusive perfume hanging
in the tremulous languor."

"I made my point."

"You did, indeed."

"Am I still in the game?"

She paused, straightened up, extending her chest as far as she
could and said: "I want you to look directly at the diamond hanging
from my choker. What do you see?"

"Heaven."

"Next, in a few moments after I pull up my skirt, I want you to
casually and discreetly reach under the table and remove the small
flask from the garter just above my knee."

I followed instructions explicitly and when I had removed the small flask, I held the top between two fingers so that the bottle did not touch her leg and slowly moved my hand up her thigh for a few inches before removing it.

"Ummmmmmm," she said. "You handled that very well. You're still in the game. In fact, you may have pulled ahead a little."

"In all fairness, it was Henry who started me thinking about women in politics for an article I'm going to do for his new magazine. He would be more disturbed about your going into politics than I am."

"All right. But you're a little ahead in the game, not because of your view of women in politics—which I don't disagree with—but because of the way you dance and remove a flask from a lady's garter. That, I really enjoyed. Now your next test is to discreetly fix me a drink. And you can stop worrying. There's no chance of my running for office. Harry Daugherty would shoot me down immediately."

"How did your meeting with him this afternoon go?"

"Horribly. He's going to contest my joint bank account with Jesse, claiming that it should go into Jesse's estate and be split like the rest of his assets. He also said that the thousands of dollars in the 'Jesse Smith Extra' account in Mal's bank in Washington Courthouse—which Jesse had told me about—was political money to cover Republican Party expenses. And he said he would do his best to ruin me if I testify against him in the Senate investigation."

"Did he threaten you physically?"

"Not directly. That's not his style. But the implication was there. I also asked Harry about the American Metal Company case and he said: 'That was all between John King and Jesse—and Jesse made a mistake. And he never breathed a word to me that he had done such an idiotic thing, although technically, he had as much right as King to represent the claimants. But it was morally wrong and I didn't know anything about it. Still don't.' "

"How does he account for the actions of his great and loyal friend, Jesse Smith?"

"Simple. And this is the worst part. Harry is going to say—in fact, he's already started it—that Jesse did it because he was sick. He said that Jesse's mother died of complications from diabetes and that 'diabetes plays sad tricks with the human brain, causing loss of memory, even breaking down the moral fiber of character.' Then he went on to say that Jesse had told him that if he ever got diabetes there would be a shorter way out for him.

"I accused him of driving Jesse to suicide by dumping him and setting Jesse up to take the fall."

"Looks to me," I said, "like you still think Jesse committed suicide, despite all the evidence suggesting that the Ohio Gang very much wanted Jesse out of the way."

Roxy just stared at her glass as tears came to her eyes. The drummer had returned and begun adjusting his snare, indicating the band was about to play again. Roxy rose from her seat and said: "Jamie. I still have to call it suicide. I'll be right back. I'd like to dance another set, if you would."

"I'd love it." When she had been gone a few moments, I rose and headed for the lobby to do something I had been thinking about all evening: see if I could find a bellboy who had been on duty the night of Jesse's death. I located the captain of the bellboys standing near the front desk and I pulled him aside and asked him if there were any bellhops on duty tonight who happened to work the night Jesse Smith committed suicide. After I gave him a twenty-dollar bill, he said there was one, Carl. "The police spent some time with him. He's on duty tomorrow all day, starting at eight A.M."

Returning to the lounge I found an impatient Roxy wondering where I had been. The band had started playing again—"Kiss in the Dark," a lovely song from *Orange Blossoms* on Broadway. Taking her hand and leading her to the dance floor, I said: "I located a bellboy who was on duty the night Jesse died. He apparently knows something, because he's been talking to the Secret Service. He's on duty tomorrow and I'm going to talk to him."

"Oh. Can I come with you?"

"I'd rather not."

"I understand. Be sure to let me know what he says."

"I will." We were on the dance floor and as her soft body pressed against mine, I felt the usual stirring. I couldn't help but think about what might lie ahead. But I knew better than to talk about it: "What'll we do tomorrow?" I asked.

"How 'bout being tourists and taking in the sights—the Washington Monument, the Capitol, the White House, the new memorial to Abraham Lincoln? It's wonderful. Like a Greek temple. Have you been down to see it?"

"No. Sounds like fun. I havn't been up in the Monument for a couple of years. The thing to do these days is take the elevator to the top and then walk down. You know, at five hundred fifty-five feet, it's the tallest phallic symbol in the world."

"I knew you'd think of that. Hmmmmmmmmmm, it seems like you have your own monument rising," she whispered softly as she pulled me closer to her.

"Shall we make this the last set?" I suggested.

"Okay, if you're in a hurry. You have to go back to Baltimore tonight?"

She must be teasing. "Well, it is getting late. I sort of thought I might spend the night here at the Wardman. Remember, I'm going to be seeing that bellboy tomorrow."

"Oh, that's right. Do you have a room?"

"Well, again, I kind of thought we might spend the night together, at least 'till the competition is over. I know we can't talk about it, but you did spend the night with Henry at the Rennert."

"That's true. I guess we should keep the playing field level and also have your innings in a hotel. I'm ready when you are."

In the elevator, she said: "When are you and Henry going to start working on that book?"

"Well, actually, we're working on it now gathering information with your help—and Gaston Means'. But it's too soon to start writing. We need to talk to a lot more people and dig out a lot more dope."

When we reached her room and were inside with the door bolted, I pulled her to me and kissed her, while trying to cope with the buttons on the back of her dress. Pushing me away, she said: "For a married man, you are hopeless as a disrober of ladies."

"That's what marriage will do to you."

"Well, if you'll excuse me, I'll be back in a second. You just get in that bed, wait patiently and try to get your clothes off—although you might have some difficulty with your pants."

It took longer than a few moments, but while she was in the bathroom I had plenty to time to think erotic thoughts as I undressed, got into bed and waited. Finally she came into the room, wearing only a thin robe. But as she walked toward me, the telephone rang. Damn! I thought. If that's Mencken, this could be the end of a beautiful friendship. She turned and went quickly to the sitting room where the phone was. I could not hear anything she said, but in only a few minutes she came back into the room walking slowly to the bed. "Who was that?" I asked. "Not the hotel detective, I hope."

"No. Just a friend from Ohio in town. I promised to get together with her before I go home."

When she reached the foot of the bed, she paused for a moment and said: "Speaking of playing fields, I just want you to see yours." Then she dropped her robe to the floor and all I could think of was a poster of Lillian Russell I had once seen, which was mostly curves and bulges in all the right places.

"It's incredible," I said. "But I'd hardly call it level."

"Good. Move over," she said, pulling back the covers. "Oh my, the Washington Monument. Let the games begin."

They did. And there will be no details. That's part of her rules— and mine. Sometime later, when we were both lying there just staring at the ceiling, exhausted, I couldn't help but ask: "Well, madam referee, when are you going declare a winner? Or have we just been in the semifinals with the finals still to come—like right now?"— and I moved down kissing her on the stomach and thereabouts.

"No," she said gently, lifting my head. "Let's wait awhile. And I don't know that I'm going to have to declare a winner. You may take it, nine-to-nothing."

"How's that?"

"You'll never guess what happened."

"Don't tell me! You had a lovely dinner, lots of wine, pleasant conversation—but no politics or business, et cetera—and then he drifted off to sleep. . . ."

"How did you know?"

". . . Muttering something about having gazed upon the fields of asphodel . . ."

"Meaning what?"

"Lilies."

"Oh. But it was more than just lilies, good dinner and the wine. Somehow I think he suspects that I'm really husband-hunting and his hatred of marriage is no joke. He says it is impossible to reform or rebel against the institution. 'Who are happy in marriage?' he says: 'Those with so little imagination that they can't picture a better state, and those so shrewd that they prefer quiet slavery to hopeless rebellion.' He does not include himself in either group."

"I know. But I can't understand why he doesn't consider you a kindred spirit."

"Maybe I'm not. But there was more to him not being drawn to me. He thinks I'm intelligent enough, but I'm no intellectual. I never went to college; I studied to be a singer."

"So did I. No wonder I love you so much."

"That's not why you love me; in fact, I'm not sure you're capable of real love or a sustained relationship with a woman."

"Maybe. But right now, I think I could spend the rest of my life in this bed with you."

"Nuts. Like most men, in the morning you'll be ready to move on, to get back to work, start writing, play golf . . ."

"Or go up in the Washington Monument with my best girl. Golf is a stupid game."

"So is making love, when you think about it—except for a few minutes of sheer joy."

"Then, maybe I won, even without the forfeit?"

"Going away. But as I said, it was more than the wine and marriage. I really think Henry is a one-woman man, at least when it comes to emotional involvement, which seems to frighten him a little. Disrupts his mental process. And right now, he seems emotionally involved to some extent with three women."

"Really?"

"Yes. One named Marion Bloom, although that affair seems almost over; another named Sara . . ."

". . . Haardt. She lives in Alabama. But she recently was teaching at Goucher in Baltimore."

"And a third. Her name is Anita Loos. A screenwriter who lives in Hollywood, but spends a lot of time in New York. And Henry is planning a trip to California to see her sometime in the next year or so."

"I know the name, but I didn't know Henry was involved with her."

"Very much so. She's married, but the marriage is more of an arrangement. You know how people are these days, especially with artists and intellectuals? All these women are intellectuals in one way or another—especially Anita Loos."

"How's that?"

"According to Henry, she's very smart and witty—and a good writer. Incidentally, he told me a very amusing story about her. At one point, while she was living in New York, she had to go back to Hollywood to write a picture for Constance Talmadge. Just before she left for the coast, George Jean Nathan introduced her into his crowd of drinking buddies, which included Henry and a sexy blonde named Mae Davis. Loos said Miss Davis was what she called 'an old man's darling,' with a rather naive, stupid viewpoint on most everything, which intrigued Mencken."

"It would. He's fascinated by real dumbbells, especially their impact on the American language. But that's interesting about Anita Loos. He's never mentioned to me that he's involved with anyone in Hollywood."

"Well, he is. In fact, he says she insists that she's in love with him and he has strong feelings for her, too. Anyway, in the few times they saw her before Loos left for California, Mencken spent a lot of time goading Miss Davis into making idiotic remarks, which Loos interpreted into thinking Mencken had a sexual interest in the blonde, which he denies . . ."

"But which, of course, he may have."

"Of course. So by the time Loos boarded the Twentieth Century for Los Angeles, she was intensely jealous of Davis and worried about leaving Mencken alone with her in New York. But her fears were unfounded and not because Mencken had no interest in her."

"Oh? How's that?"

"Much to Loos's surprise, on her first night in the club car, she learned that the blonde, Miss Davis—with a mountain of luggage— was also on the train bound for Hollywood for a screen test for Charlie Chaplin. She also noted that the blonde was waited on, catered to and cajoled by almost every gentleman in the club and dining cars. When she dropped a magazine, two men leaped to pick it up for her. When she had to move a suitcase, she was immediately helped while Loos had to haul her own heavy luggage. Finally she began to wonder what the difference was—in that she figured she was about the same age as the blonde, that they had the same degree of comeliness, and in mental acumen, there was no contest. Miss Loos knew she was much smarter. And it really annoyed her that not only all these men, but Mencken, who likes smart people, seem to prefer types like Mae Davis. What was the difference?"

"Obviously . . ."

"That's right. The hair. It finally dawned on her that, like Samson, Miss Davis' strength was rooted in her hair—beautiful, natural blonde, whereas Loos' is jet black, which she wears in what she claims is the first boyish bob of the twentieth century. So one night in the club car, she took out her yellow pad and pencil and began sketching out a character she called Lorelei Lee that would be the nucleus of a novel she is working on now—which she naturally is calling *Gentlemen Prefer Blondes*. And Mencken even played a part in determining where Lorelei came from."

"How's that?"

"She wanted to make her blonde a symbol of the nation's lowest possible mentality, which recalled to her Mencken's essay in which he called Arkansas the 'Sahara of the Bozarts.' So she decided that Lorelei would be just a little girl from Little Rock."

"Very clever, and a great idea for a comic novel. I'll have to ask Henry about it."

"When you do, tell him I'm a little jealous. But I understand. I'm not a blonde and I'm no intellectual."

"Thank God. But I'll bet you're a good writer."

"Well, people do say I write good letters. But most everybody can do that."

"Don't kid yourself. I've read hundreds of letters sent to the *Baltimore Sun* and you'd be surprised how poorly most people write, even well-educated people, especially academics."

"I'll write you a letter soon and you can grade it."

By now, Roxy was half asleep, so I turned out the soft bed-light we had had on during the game, climbed gently into bed, threw one arm around her so that my hand slightly touched one of her breasts and went to sleep thinking of the most wonderful night I have ever spent with a woman. Talk about fields of asphodel.

I woke about 8:30 and Roxy was still asleep. I whispered that I was going down to the lobby to find the bellboy and asked her if she wanted to join me in the dining room for breakfast later, or for me to bring her something. Still seeming half asleep, she said: "Just bring me some coffee and a roll. I'll be fine."

In the lobby, I found the captain of the ushers, reminded him that last night he told me about Carl and asked if Carl was around now. "He will be soon. He's upstairs."

In a few minutes an elevator door opened and a young man dressed in a bellhop uniform approached the desk. "That's him," said the captain. I approached Carl and said I wanted to have a word with him. As we walked down the hall, I slipped him a twenty-dollar bill and said I understood he was working the night of Jesse Smith's death and that he had been talking to the police about it.

"It wasn't the police. It was mostly Department of Justice investigators. The District police haven't been very involved."

"Oh?"

"Yeah. And they're not happy about it. They're getting questions from reporters all the time and they don't have anything to tell 'em. Makes them look stupid."

I told him that I was going to have breakfast in the dining room and asked if he would he join me. "No. I'm not allowed to. But we can keep walking like this down the hall."

"Did you see anything unusual that night?"

"Well, one thing. But, you know, this Justice investigator I was talking to said it would be best if I didn't say anything about it to the press."

"I'm not a reporter. I'm doing a little investigating for Smith's ex-wife." And I slipped him another twenty-dollar bill.

"Yeah, I know who she is. Tall, redhead, great body. She came in that night."

"She brought Smith home from dinner," I said. "He was pretty drunk."

"Sure was. But she also came out to see him again, later that night."

"Yes, of course," I said, trying to act as if I knew that Roxy had come back to the Wardman later that night—which, naturally surprised the hell out of me. "But that was much later."

"Yeah."

"You naturally told the Justice Department people about that?"

"Naturally."

"Anything else?"

"Yeah, but they seemed most concerned about her coming back late, as if they really wanted to keep that quiet."

"I can certainly appreciate your position. But you should understand how upset his former wife is. She wants to find out everything she can about that night." This cost me another twenty dollars.

"Well, much later that night, I was coming down the back stairs from a late night get-together with one our guests—a very attractive mature woman. Happens all the time. They invite you to their room for a drink and a little hanky-panky if you know what I mean."

I assured him I did.

"She was on the sixth floor. So I was coming down the stairs and after I went by the fifth floor, where Mr. Smith lives with the attorney general, I pass this big heavy man, huffing and puffing up the stairs. I remember it occurred to me that it was strange, him walking up the stairs when he was having such a difficult time and could have taken the elevator."

"Did you know him or recognize him?"

"I recognized him. He's a private investigator and I had seen him around the hotel. He would sometimes ask the bellboys and maids to do some spying for him or give him information—for which he paid very well."

"But you never had any direct dealings with him?"

"No. But some of the other guys have worked for him."

"What did he look like?"

"Tall. Wore a hat and a topcoat. Kind of sloppy looking. Smoking a cigarette. He smiled at me as we passed and I noticed the big dimples in his cheeks, which got bigger when he smiled."

"Do you know where he went? What floor?"

"No. But he continued going up."

"Could he have gotten off at Smith's floor?"

"Yep."

"Anything unusual about him? Was he carrying anything?"

"A large, leather briefcase."

"Anything else?"

"Nope."

"What did the ex-Mrs. Smith do when she came in that night—the second time?"

"Why don't you ask her? She came in, talked with some guy in the lobby for awhile, then went up in the elevator. In a little while, she came back down and went out the front door. Funny thing, this time she came down the back stairs."

"Did the guy she talked to go upstairs with her?"

"Don't remember."

"How long was she up there?"

"I don't know. A good while. Long enough for her to screw someone. Although, funny thing, she seemed to be crying."

"How late was it?"

"Pretty late. But before midnight."

"And the agents know everything you told me?"

"Yep."

"Anything else?"

"Can't think of anything. Except that the D.C. Police say that the Justice Department guy, Burns, misplaced the gun."

I thanked him very much for talking to me and told him how much the ex-Mrs. Smith appreciated it—wondering all the while just how much Roxy would appreciate my knowing that she had come back to the Wardman that night. She has had plenty of opportunities to tell us why she came back and what happened when she was here. But she had not.

I went to the dining room, ordered a good breakfast, bought the *Washington Post,* and read it for awhile, especially a long story on all the rumors going around that Jesse Smith did not commit suicide but was murdered. Why the hell had Roxy not told me? I did not hurry at breakfast, wanting to give Roxy a little more time to sleep and to think about the ramifications of her actions that night. She was definitely hiding something from us—but I still could not believe that she would kill Jesse. She keeps insisting she thinks Jesse committed suicide, when there was so much talk about murder. The truth was, I really didn't want to ask her, to maybe catch her up in a lie and perhaps even force her to tell me something about that night I didn't want to hear—or want Mencken to know. I decided that sooner or later I was going to have to ask her so I might as well do it now.

After ordering coffee and a roll for Roxy, I went up to her room. I had forgotten to take a key, so I knocked gently on the door. There was no response. Figuring Roxy was still asleep, I knocked a little louder—but not too loud, because I really did not want to attract attention. Still no response or sound from inside. So I knocked again, quite loudly. She did not answer, although an obviously irritated woman two doors away looked out her door with the implication that I ought to go away, which I did.

In the lobby, I called Roxy. No answer. Then I checked the dining room, thinking she might have become tired of waiting and come down for breakfast, passing me in the elevator as I was going up. But she was not there. Now I was really concerned. However, I could not just walk away and go back to Baltimore as if Roxy had decided to go out for a walk, forgetting about me on this beautiful spring morning. After all, we had talked about going sightseeing today. I returned to a seat in the lobby and pondered my problem. There was nothing to do but go to the front desk.

"Sir, I'm a friend of Miss Stinson who is registered here. We have a date for breakfast this morning, but I can't seem to wake her. She may have taken a sleeping pill and overslept. Could someone go check to see if something happened to her?"

"No need," the concierge behind the desk said: "Miss Stinson checked out about a half-hour ago. She left no message and I must say, she did seem in a hurry."

"Do you know if she checked any luggage?"

"No. She was carrying one medium-sized bag. It didn't look very heavy."

"Do you know where she went from here? Did she look around the lobby for someone or go right out the front door?"

"Can't say. I was quite busy at the time. Why don't you ask the front doorman?"

"Thanks."

The doorman said he did not see a tall, red-headed woman carrying a bag come out of the hotel and he knew no one of that description took a taxicab in the last half hour or so.

Roxy Stinson had suddenly decided to disappear in a hurry, making it obvious that, for some reason, she did not want to say goodbye to me. I didn't know whether to worry or be mad. But I knew I had to see her again.

Part 3

CHAPTER FIFTEEN

I took a cab to Union Station, and when I found that I had about twenty minutes to wait for the next train, I called Mencken at home. He said he was very busy, working on his Monday column, which he wanted to finish before the club met that night. They were starting early because they had decided to play all the Beethoven symphonies except the Ninth. "It'll be a historic session. We're meeting at Willie Woolcott's out in Catonsville. He's got a large living room. You going to join us or do you have another date with Roxy?"

"No. But I guess I'll pass tonight. I don't feel much in the mood for music. I think I'll stay home and type up my notes."

"You sound a little glum. Did Roxy pronounce me the winner last night? What do you think I'll get? A silver statue of a man and a woman *flagrante delecto*? Just joking."

"I hope so. Look, I need to get some of this stuff we've learned on paper. We've got a real obligation to Roxy."

"You mean, you think she's getting into bed with us just to make sure we do the book?"

"I don't know what she's up to. But I'm convinced she's right about one thing: They're going to try to lay all the skullduggery in the Justice Department on Jesse Smith."

"Sounds like you've got some new information."

"I've got plenty. And I'm anxious to hear about what happened with you and Nan Britton. But you finish your column and we'll talk tomorrow on the train. Remember, we're going to the McLean brunch."

"Yeah, I remember. Frank Kent is going to meet us at the station in Washington around ten A.M. and take us out. It'll be a nice drive, if this good weather holds up."

"Another reason I'm going to pass on tonight is that I want to stick by the phone. I'm hoping Roxy will call."

"Oh. Something wrong?"

"I don't know. But she disappeared this morning—while I was down talking to one of the Wardman Park bellhops. We were going to have breakfast and then go out and see the sights in Washington. But suddenly, she disappears without even leaving me a note. It was a strange thing for her to do and, frankly, I'm a little worried."

"Don't blame you. We do have a lot to talk about."

"We'll do it tomorrow, I got to run now. My train will be leaving soon." And I hung up.

Next morning I felt horrible, mostly because I couldn't sleep—not hearing a word from Roxy. But Mencken looked even worse than I felt. "What happened to you?" I said. "You must have the world's biggest hangover."

"I wish I did. We had to cut the drinking short last night to take on the Beethoven symphonies. But we only got through five, even though we started early and played to well past midnight. They were dropping all around me like we were in combat. I was the last one standing, literally, banging out the closing chords of the mighty Fifth. It was a sight to behold. But then I couldn't get to sleep at all, with Ludwig's melodies running through my head like I was in a Beethoven parade. The club also gave me a rough time for being conned by Means. I'm dead!"

"I don't feel so good myself. We're going to be a lively twosome. I wish we could sleep on the train, but we have too much to talk about."

When we were comfortably seated in the club car, I said to Mencken, who seemed barely able to stay awake: "Okay. You go first. Did you get to talk to Miss Britton?"

"Yeah. We went up to the penthouse lounge and talked awhile. She didn't want to sit in the lobby and risk having to see that 'dreadful Gaston Means' as she called him. But she didn't have much to say."

"That's what Means said. She wouldn't talk."

"Well, you can't blame her. She insists she was at the H Street house doing business with some of the men from Ohio—she mentioned a Howard Mannington and Buddy Martin. She still considers herself a sort of unofficial employee of the Republican National Committee, where she used to work full time. She even gets paid a little now and then—plus expenses. When I told her we knew the president was there that evening, she said: 'So what.' She often sees the president when she's in town; even visits at him at the White House. I told her that I had no intention of writing anything about it, but that some newspaper men might not be so circumspect and it might hurt the president. She said 'Let them write anything they want; my family and the Hardings are old friends.' Then she said she was tired and wanted to go to her room."

"Did she recognize you?"

"No, but I introduced myself. She had heard of *The Smart Set* and me, but hadn't read any of my books."

"She more or less admitted to Means," I said, "that she was having an affair with Harding, but that she wasn't going to stop it until her 'sweetie,' meaning the president, told her to stay away."

"Her sweetie, eh? What else did you get from Means?"

"First of all, he said he warned Britton that it would be dangerous for her to keep seeing the president"—and I went on to give Mencken a complete run-down of my conversation with Means.

"And he warned me several times that Roxy should be careful—that she knows almost as much as Smith did and look what happened to him."

"So Means still thinks Smith was murdered?"

"Absolutely."

"And Roxy? I don't blame you for being worried about her."

"She seems a little closer to accepting murder as a possibility. She had a very ugly meeting with Daugherty." I told Mencken about it in detail. "He's very obviously setting Jesse up to take the fall and suggested that if Roxy disputes the suicide theory, she might be implicated in his death herself."

"Not too surprising," Mencken said. "Remember, you tried unsuccessfully to call her later that night. And when the attorney general of the United States starts talking like that you know you're in trouble."

"She may be. And here comes the most interesting part of my sleuthing last night." Then I told Mencken everything I had learned from the bellboy and the details of Roxy's mysterious disappearance.

"So Roxy and Means were both out there late that night."

"Yep. And the attorney general knows all about it, but insists on sticking to the suicide theory. . . ."

"Knowing," Mencken interposed, "that any investigation into Smith's death would bring up the question of why Smith was killed. And even though he had two good suspects in Roxy and Means, Daugherty could jump to the top of the list of suspects that had the most to gain from Smith's death."

"Right."

"Sherlock Holmes never had a case this complex. You know something? It seems obvious to me why Roxy disappeared on you."

"Why?"

"The bellboy says that he told the Justice Department everything he told you?

"Yes."

"Which means that Daugherty knows it. And he told Roxy he knew about the bellboy's revelations by way of supporting his hints that she would be a suspect if the question of murder came up. Did Roxy say the AG *had* mentioned that he knew she was out at the Wardman late that night?"

"No. And I see what you're getting at."

"I'm sure. Roxy disappeared when you told her you had found the bellboy who had told Daugherty about her—and Means—being out there. And she didn't want to have to explain to you what she was doing there that night when you came back to the room and confronted her with the bellboy's statement. So she just vamoosed."

"That has to be the only explanation—unless there was foul play."

"Meaning somebody kidnapped her?"

"Something like that."

"But if she's okay, unharmed, then sooner or late she's going to return, once she works out her story. Or alibi."

"We'll just have to wait and see. There's not a helluva lot I can do right now. I'll probably call her mother in Ohio in a couple of days, but I don't want to start spreading the word that Jesse Smith's ex-wife has disappeared. That would make her look very suspicious, maybe even suggesting that she was in on some of Jesse's deals."

"Which maybe she was. And we can't ignore that, Cain."

"I'm afraid you're right."

Mencken was now puffing on an Uncle Willie and staring out the window, engulfed in smoke and thoughts about the mess we had uncovered in just a few days. As his eyelids began to close, I slowly removed the cigar from his hand before it slipped to the floor.

Frank Kent was waiting for us at the station in his new, 1923 Ford sedan. A nice car. Mencken sat up front with Frank and I was in the back seat as we started up Massachusetts Avenue, heading for its intersection with Wisconsin Avenue about twelve miles northwest. "Let me tell you about this brunch," Kent said, stopping at the first of several traffic lights we were going to hit.

"Don't you hate these traffic towers?" said Mencken. "Pretty soon every principal street corner will have one. Where three or more streets come together there'll be whole clusters of them. Now they flash two colors—white and green. Five years from now, they'll range the whole spectrum, like the new Christmas tree taxicabs. And the cops will add pinwheels and roman candles. I read the other day that so many people were herded for trial in the traffic court it took three judges to dispose of them. Nine-tenths of the criminals are persons who would not otherwise fall into the toils. Traffic regulations tap whole new categories of victims. Time was when the cops seldom got a chance to nab a white woman. Now they take them by the hundreds. It's almost Utopia for the *polizeii*."

"Okay, Henry," Kent finally said. "So we all hate traffic towers. But think what would it be like without them. You'd wreck a car a week."

"I don't drive anymore," Mencken replied. "I sold my Studebaker to stock up on booze."

"Getting back to the party, it's going to be an odd affair," said Kent.

"That's what I figured," said Mencken. "Anything the McLeans do is sort of odd. But then, I guess the rich can do what they damn well please."

"Especially when they're close buddies with the town's leading citizens," I added, "who in this case, happen to be the president of the United States and the First Lady of the land."

"It will be well attended because it was scheduled as an informal press conference for Harding, a chance for the president to talk to some of the press before he takes off on his Alaska trip in a few days. And that was before the death of Jesse Smith and all the rumors about corruption in the Justice and Interior Departments. The frauds in the Veterans' Bureau, of course, are beyond rumors. The president's one-time buddy, Charlie Forbes, is gone, the Congressional investigation of the bureau is expected to flush out the whole story, and everyone in Washington has heard about Harding grabbing Forbes by the throat in the Oval Office, pounding him against the wall and calling him 'a double-crossing bastard.' "

"Best thing I've heard about ol' Gamaliel," Mencken said, "except for him jollying his young lady friend in the White House broom closet. Can't say that I blame him. She's a looker."

"What's this?" Kent said turning his head to ask Mencken directly. "You know something I don't know?"

"Probably, although we've got to keep it confidential. But it shouldn't surprise a Washington reporter that Gamaliel has a girlfriend. And keep your eyes on the road, Kent. You're a worse driver than I am."

Frank turned his head back just in time to keep from swerving into a Ford coupe with an open rumble seat. When he was settled, Kent continued: "Anyway, Judson Welliver in the White House has been quietly telling some of us that the president may not be able to make an appearance. Too soon after Smith's death—which really shook him up. But it's assumed by most of us covering the White House that Harding doesn't want to talk to the press right now, especially about Smith's death and corruption in his administration. It's well known that Smith had fallen out of favor with the president, dropped rather unceremoniously from the Alaska trip and asked to return to Ohio."

"Speaking of Smith," I said to Kent, "we understand that Roxy Stinson, his ex-wife is in town. Have you seen her?"

"No, but I did hear she was staying at the Wardman. The word at the water cooler is that if Smith was murdered, then Roxy—who is assumed to know almost as much as Smith about what's going on in Washington—had better watch out. In fact, yesterday I heard a rumor that she's a marked woman."

"God, this town is really buzzing," said Mencken.

"A new rumor every day," Kent replied, "most of them started by or concerning Gaston B. Means. I tell you, that guy is going down in history."

"I must say, you got to admire his audacity," said Mencken.

"Yeah. And there's always just enough truth in what he says so
you can't ignore him. Right now he's spreading stuff about the
attorney general hoping to force Daugherty to drop a Justice Department investigation of him."

"So why is Daugherty threatening a Means investigation?"
Mencken asked.

"Because Means' roguery has gotten so out of hand. He thinks
that because he has so much on Daugherty and the Justice Department, and is in so good with his old friend Billy Burns, that he has
virtual immunity to deal with bootleggers on his own—double-
crossing them whenever it's profitable, as apparently Jesse Smith
was doing, too, although most people believe Smith worked only
on Daugherty's orders."

Most of the rest of the forty-minute trip we spent talking about
Means and Smith. We did get briefly into the Teapot Dome oil deal,
with Kent saying he had heard the same thing that Senator Smoot
told me—that it was Ned McLean who lent Secretary Fall the
money he was spending to improve his ranch in New Mexico. Like
Daugherty, Smith and the Justice Department, the Interior Department and Fall were inspiring a new rumor every day, and Kent
helped pass the time by reciting the latest parody going around:

> *"Absolute knowledge have I none,*
> *But my aunt's washerwoman's sister's son*
> *Heard a policeman on his beat*
> *Say to a laborer on the street*
> *That he had a letter just last week—*
> *A letter which he did not seek—*
> *From a Chinese merchant in Timbuktu*
> *Who said that his brother in Cuba knew*
> *That a wild man over in Borneo*
> *Was told by a woman who claimed to know*
> *Of a well-known swell society rake*
> *Whose mother will undertake*
> *To prove that her husband's sister's niece*
> *Has stated plain in a printed piece*
> *That she has a son who never comes home*
> *And who knows all about the Teapot Dome."*

"That's just where our project stands now," Mencken exclaimed. "Mostly rumors! And God knows how much of this stuff we're going to be able to print."

"That's what occurred to me when I was typing up my notes yesterday," I said. "Even our source doesn't know anything for sure."

"And everyone says Means is a colossal liar," Mencken added.

"But it's all going to come out eventually," said Kent, "when they get some of these people before a Senate or House investigating committee."

"But not Jesse Smith," I chimed in.

"Which is probably why Jesse isn't here," Mencken said.

"He's much better off to them dead," I said. "Now they can say the seventy-five thousand bucks in the money belt stopped with Jesse."

As we approached the iron gates, set between two stone pillars that helped wall off the Friendship estate, Mencken asked Kent: "Who do you think'll be here today? What kind of crowd?"

"A strange mixture, I guess. All of the fourteen reporters scheduled to go with Harding on his trip; some *Post* people, of course, including the managing editor, John Spurgeon. "I don't know how many of the reporters will show now that the president may not be coming.

"Who else?" Mencken asked.

"An interesting bunch: Mark Sullivan, Will Irwin, Samuel Hopkins Adams, Mary Roberts Rinehart, Bruce Bliven, William Allen White. Maybe Walter Lippmann. You know him. Editorial page editor of the *World*. And maybe those two guys who started that new magazine, *Time*—Henry Luce and Britton Hadden. What do you think of *Time,* Menck?"

"I'm surprised how successful it's been. But they do the one thing that's essential for getting readers; they keep it interesting, which is more than their competitors in the daily press do. But it reads like it's all written by one man."

"Maybe it is," I said. "That's not a bad idea."

"Sound like fun," Mencken said. "They ought to have plenty of booze, although I don't feel much like imbibing after last night."

"There'll be booze," Kent replied, "especially if Harding doesn't come. I understand the president is getting a little sensitive about his drinking, although the public doesn't seem to give a damn. They're putting out the story now that the president's doctor has ordered him to take a drink occasionally."

"My doctor certainly agrees with that," said Mencken. "Occasionally every day."

Friendship was situated on about eighty acres—of ponds, golf and tennis courts, streams, riding trails and parks. There was a large parking space for automobiles over to one side and the number of cars there indicated that many of the guests had already arrived. The two-story white wooden and brick house was large enough, but rather modest looking, at least on the outside.

We entered the house from a large doorway situated under a second-floor deck which provided a covered driveway for getting in and out of automobiles in the rain. As we entered the house, it was immediately apparent that it was quite comfortable. The ceilings were low and there were paintings and tapestries on most of the walls. There were also thick rugs, comfortable chairs, tables, couches and what my mother called loveseats, everywhere. It seemed like every room had a fireplace and they all looked well-used; even in June there were aromatic traces of wood smoke filtering through the pervasive smell of gardenias. Friendship was virtually a professional arboretum and conservatory. And a miniature zoo; I looked everywhere for Mrs. McLean's pet monkey and Great Dane but couldn't see them. They were probably locked up in some distant room for the party.

As we entered a big living room, Kent went off to join a group of *Washington Post* staffers and I could see that Mencken did not have to worry about the booze; there were lots of people standing around talking and nearly everyone had a glass in his or her hand. I looked for Ned or Mrs. McLean, but did not see anyone I could identify as our hosts. Soon, a butler was guiding us to a bar off in the corner of the big room where we were offered a choice of martinis, scotch or bourbon highballs, or beer. I asked for a pilsner, but to my surprise Mencken ordered a glass of tomato juice— "without the gin."

When he said that, a large woman who was standing at the bar but with her back to us, turned and said: "I thought that was your unmistakable, cultivated voice, Henry. And I can't believe its owner is passing up an offering of a free drink. Good to see you again. And you too, Mr. Cain." It was Mary Roberts Rinehart.

Shaking her hand, Mencken said: "To tell the truth, I never drink when I'm on a case and Cain and I are working today. Besides, I have a dreadful hangover. But from too much Beethoven, not beer."

"You still have those musicals every Saturday night?"

"The high point of my week."

"By 'working,' I presume you mean you've started on that project you mentioned when we had lunch last week?"

"We have," I said, "and you wouldn't believe how much we've unearthed in such a short time."

"Yeah," Mencken interrupted. "And, incidentally, we want to thank you for guiding us to Roxy Stinson and Gaston Means. I don't know where we'd be if we hadn't gotten them to talk to us."

"Wasn't that terrible about Jesse Smith's suicide," she replied, "coming so soon after Charles Cramer's?"

"So you think it was suicide?" asked Mencken.

"Yes, I'm sticking to the official version, at least for now. But I'm open-minded. I've heard all the talk about murder," she said, lowering her voice and looking around, apparently uncomfortable talking about murder.

"Might make a good mystery for you?" Mencken suggested.

"I have thought about it, as I told you at the Willard. But Jesse Smith is too close to the Hardings, as I am. Writing about it would make me uncomfortable. Anyway, somebody's already working on a novel."

"Oh! Who?" Mencken asked.

"Sam Adams. He's over there, talking with Bruce Bliven, managing editor of the *New Republic*. Adams is probably doing a piece for him. I'm sure you know him, Henry."

"Never met him," said Mencken. "I don't know Bliven, either. But I know who Adams is. He did that great series of articles a few years ago for *Collier's,* exposing the corruption in the quackery in the patent medicine business, that led to the creation of the Food and Drug Administration. Remember? He sounds like a perfect candidate to do a novel about this administration. I think I'll see if he's interested in doing something for us. By the way, Mary, I couldn't tell you when we had lunch at the Willard, but Nathan and I will be leaving *The Smart Set* and starting a new magazine next year. We won't be able to afford you, but you can spread the word. We're looking for new writers."

"It's not the money and you know it, Henry. You don't cater to *Saturday Evening Post*–type writers. But I'll spread the word. I'll bet you've already signed up Red Lewis and young Fitzgerald."

"They can hardly wait," Mencken replied, as Rinehart turned to order a drink and we drifted away from the bar. As we did, Mencken, noting that Adams and Bliven had come to a lull in their conversation, said: "Let's say hello to Sam."

We approached the two men—Adams: gray-haired, rumpled looking and obviously older than any of us, probably in his fifties; and Bliven: much younger, about my age, dark eyebrows and a mustache, glasses and extremely intelligent-looking. After Mencken introduced himself and me, he went right to the point: "Well, Mr. Adams, we have it on good authority that you're writing a novel about the Harding administration."

"*Thinking* of writing a novel," he corrected, "and I've only been doing that for a couple of days. Good God! I just mentioned it to a couple of friends and it's already talked about at Washington parties and spread among the heathen in Baltimore. But things do get around in this town, Henry. I've heard that not only are you working on something about the Ohio Gang, but that you and your cohort, George Nathan, are starting a new magazine."

"We're doing more than thinking about it," Mencken said. "But the first issue won't be out until early next year. If you have any article ideas drop me a letter at the *Sun*. Got a title for your novel yet?"

"Nope. But it will be something suggesting merry-making and high jinks in the capital. Got a name for your new magazine? I hope it's better than *The Smart Set*."

"We have a great name. But I'm not telling what it is—especially in this crowd. Somebody might steal it."

"Very wise," said Bliven.

"I'm not sure I'd call Cramer's or Jesse Smith's death high jinks," I said. "A lot of people think Smith's was murder."

"Or Harding of the arteries," Bliven added.

"We heard that one at the Press Club," I said. "Do you think it was murder, Mr. Adams?"

"To tell the truth, I'm not sure. It looks suspicious. But, of course, in my novel I can make it anything I think might intrigue my readers. The truth will come later when the Congressional investigations and the trials that are sure to follow are finished and the investigative articles we're all working on are written. I'm already thinking about a non-fiction book on this incredible period, but it will be a long time coming. As for Smith, if I had to guess, I'd say murder. What do you think, Bruce? I know you're preparing a series on the Ohio Gang. Do you think it was murder?"

"Well I'd say it was not," a tall, very distinguished looking silver-headed gentleman said, joining our little group. It was Mark Sullivan. After we shook hands all around and I was introduced, Sullivan continued: "But I must say, I was shocked. Jesse was such a wholesome, optimistic fellow. I always thought of him as someone who got immense pleasure out of devotion to his friends. And, frankly, I considered myself a friend of his. I was out of town when it happened, but my first thought was that if I had been in touch with him, I might have learned what he was thinking and might have been able to argue him out of it. I really feel sympathy for Harry Daugherty. They were so close."

"A lot of people think Daugherty or somebody in the Ohio Gang might have killed him or had him killed," Adams replied.

"I've heard all the rumors—that they wanted to silence him or set him up to take the rap for something we don't know about yet, or both. But one thing I know for sure: Harry Daugherty didn't have anything to do with Smith's death. He spent the evening watching a movie in the White House."

"What do you think, Henry?" Sullivan asked with a touch of sarcasm. "Because that'll no doubt determine what the country will eventually decide. I was just talking with Walter Lippmann over there and he said: 'Oh, there's H. L. Mencken, the most powerful influence on this whole generation of educated people, and a prophet.' I think he was serious."

"I doubt it," Mencken replied. "Walter also has called me a 'near Machiavelli' and we have violent disagreements about democracy. As for Smith, don't you think he might have been done in by one of those bootleggers he's rumored to have been dealing with—and maybe double-crossing?"

"If that's more than rumors, then I guess it's a possibility. And if I recall your *Smart Set* piece last year correctly, you think some crimes are justifiable. Sounds like you might include Smith's justified. Right?"

"Maybe. Practically all so-called crimes are justifiable on occasion, and nine-tenths of them, to certain kinds of men, are unavoidable on occasion. It's a platitude that you will find as many intelligent and honest men in the average prison as you will find in the average club, and when it comes to courage, enterprise and determination—in brief, to the special virtues which mark the superior man—you will probably find a great many more."

"In other words," Sullivan retorted quickly, "a bootlegger, no doubt by your definition a superior man, was free to kill a man who had double-crossed him. Henry, there may be some justice in that kind of revenge, but this is the nation's capital, not Chicago. Here we right wrongs not with guns, but the law and a trial. . . ."

"With a crowd of poltroons in the jury box," Mencken said, "venting their envious hatred of enterprise and daring upon a man who at worst, is at least as decent as they are; with a scoundrel on the bench lording it over a scoundrel in the dock because the latter is less clever than he is."

"No wonder you have arguments with Walter about democracy."

Then, obviously irritated at Mencken, and looking at a sharply dressed man and woman, accompanied by two young men, who had just entered the room, Sullivan said: "Oh, there are the McLeans. I want to have a word with them before they get too busy." And he rushed off in their direction.

"Although I don't agree with you about the futility of a jury trial," Bliven said, "your average gangster, living by his code, certainly would be justified in killing Smith if he had accepted cash for something he promised then failed to deliver."

"But we can't let the gangster's law govern the United States government," Adams said.

"We invited it by enacting a stupid, illegal act—Prohibition," Mencken replied. "Don't you see—if there was no Volstead Act most of the liquor business in the country would still be conducted by honest American businessmen."

"Well, Smith's murder may have been justified," I said, "but his ex-wife doesn't think so. She says that if anybody deserved to die, it was 'the general,' as Smith called Attorney General Daugherty; he was only carrying out his orders."

"Of course, she's a suspect herself, " Adams said. "I understand she inherited quite a bit of money."

Trying, I guess, to defend Roxy, I said: "Not that much, I heard."

"Some say she knows where there's much more loot stashed away," Adams replied. "And there might have been insurance."

We went on like this for awhile, talking about what most everyone was talking about in Washington until we heard someone tapping a spoon on a glass trying to get attention. It was Evalyn Walsh McLean, and as we edged our way closer to her, I could not help but notice the big, blue stone she wore around her neck.

CHAPTER SIXTEEN

Evalyn Walsh McLean had a trim figure, black hair, nice legs, a narrow waist and a solid resting place for the diamond—real or fake. She wore a white, sleeveless dress with a V neck cut low enough to enable the diamond to rest on flesh, but not show any cleavage. Her bare arms revealed three jewel-studded bracelets, one on each wrist and one, which looked like it might have been a jeweled watch, above her left elbow. She also wore a dark bandeau across her head which was studded with conventional diamonds. The chain that carried the Hope also contained several small diamonds and this one-woman Tiffany display was rounded out with two large, pearl earrings. If someone had thrown her in the Tidal Basin she would have drowned immediately from the weight of her jewels.

Her husband, at around six-foot-two was taller than his wife and by contrast, wore a simple white cardigan sweater over a dark polo shirt and a pair of plaid knickers, suggesting that he had just come off his golf course—or was planning to go on it as soon as this brunch was over. He held a glass half-full with what appeared to be bourbon and judging from the glistening in his eyes it was not his first. He was wearing a cap, but later, when he took it off, I could see that his dark hair was parted on one side, brushed straight back in the middle and on the other side and was really too short to stay brushed for long. He had grown a scraggly moustache, which he might have hoped would distract from the fact that his hair was receding in front on both sides.

"We want to welcome you all to our little playland here that we hope is appropriately named 'Friendship,' " Mrs. McLean said after taking a sip of her glass and tapping it again with a very expensive-looking silver spoon. "I know some of you in the press prefer to call it the Harding Country Club, which is not really a bad name since we have always offered the Hardings friendship, and we rejoice from time to time in watching the president get some relief from what we all know is the toughest job in the western world. Just ask William Allen White—who has been telling some of us here today about the strain the president seems to be under right now." Quite a few heads turned in the direction of the white-haired gentleman who was standing not too far away from the McLeans and looking a little uncomfortable with the attention.

"With all the games we have available here—golf, swimming, handball, tennis, cards, riding, croquet, you may be surprised to learn that Friendship was once a monastery. I'm sure you will agree that it—or we—would not be as popular with this administration as it is now if we had left it that way, although the right Reverend Billy Sunday might applaud such reverence."

She paused for a ripple of laugher and then continued: "Before turning you over to my husband, I have one little announcement to make: I hope this 'hideous piece of light-blue coal,' as some have called it, that I am wearing around my neck will put to rest the recent rumors that the Hope Diamond has been kidnapped. It is safe and sound right here where it belongs on my neck and has rarely been out of my sight."

"How can we be sure that's the real Hope?" someone asked. (I later learned it was Stephen Early, who covered the president on his Alaskan trip for the Associated Press). "What I heard was that a fake diamond had been subbed for the real Hope and that even you did not know it was missing."

"Well," McLean replied, "if I couldn't tell the real Hope from a large hunk of blue costume jewelry, what difference does it make? I was enjoying it just as much no matter what it was. And Mike, my Great Dane, who also wears it occasionally, as I'm sure you heard, never noticed any difference. At least, he never said anything to me about it."

She paused for the laughter, then continued: "Seriously, I've had this piece of coal examined and it is the real stone. But if you want to keep reporting that this is a fake, that's fine by me. That will discourage anyone from trying to walk off with it.

"Now, Ned would like to say a few words. Many of you here

today already know Ned and some of you *Post* editors can remember back to when he was learning the business as a young reporter and covering his beats in a yellow convertible."

"I remember," a voice from a cluster of men standing in a group yelled.

"And you probably remember that Ned wasn't the greatest reporter the *Post* ever had. He did not recognize news even when the man who bit the dog also bit him. But he gave it the old college try—even though he never went to college—and I think you'll all agree he's turned into a pretty good publisher."

There was a sprinkling of applause, mostly from the *Post* clique, as McLean set his drink down on one of the ever-present tables and stepped a little more toward his audience. "I want to join Evalyn in welcoming you to Friendship; many of you have been here before and you know how much we want you to enjoy yourselves. The first thing I want to say is that, unfortunately, the president will not be able to make it today, as some of you may have suspected. He had planned to be here to talk about his trip across the country and up to Alaska, but that was before poor Jesse Smith's death. That hit him pretty hard. In addition, he just has too much work to do before leaving town. But I didn't want to cancel this nice party; and, in fact, I hoped right up to the last moment that I could persuade the president to be with us, to no avail—which explains why that little bar over in the corner there is wetter than it might be otherwise."

"Aren't you worried about Izzy Einstein?" someone popped up from the rear of the room. "He might even show up disguised as the president. . . ."

"Or maybe he's in the room now," Mary Rinehart suggested, pointing to Mencken. "You might ask him why he's not drinking today. No one ever heard of the real H. L. Mencken turning down a drink."

Picking up the cue immediately, Mencken stepped forward and said: "Anyone holding a glass is automatically under arrest. My assistant, Mr. Cain here, will pass among you handing out the C.O.D.s."

"You will note, Izzy, that I'm not actually holding a glass," Ned McLean said, laughing and looking at his half-full glass on the table. "Bartender, will you wipe the fingerprints off this glass before this imposter from Baltimore can seize it? And while you're at it, fix him a real drink.

"Seriously, gentlemen," McLean continued, "I have one more comment I would like to make before I present two special guests today. Most of you have heard, I'm sure, that Senator Reed Smoot and others have been suggesting that Secretary Albert Fall's recent expenditures on his ranch in New Mexico were financed by a loan I made to the secretary. I want to go on record as officially confirming that. I have known Albert Fall for years, going back to the days when both Senators Fall and Harding were the closest of friends and they were—and still are—frequent guests at Friendship. The secretary often said how much he envied me this pleasant estate and that one thing that he sometimes regretted was going into politics and passing up the money he could have made in the private sector which would have enabled him to make his ranch more comfortable. So, yes, I did loan my old friend some money—one hundred thousand dollars to be exact—that would make it possible for him to expand and improve his property."

"Do you have a signed note from Fall or any check stubs to verify the loan?" Bliven asked.

"No, I don't, Bruce. I didn't need a note from an old and trusted friend. And I never fill out the stubs in my checkbook. I just write the checks and rely on my monthly bank statements to let me know where I stand. Frankly, that is one of the perks from substantial inherited wealth . . ."

"And a good marriage," Mrs. McLean added, lightening the mood a little and seeming to suggest that she, too, was in favor of loaning their friend the money.

"Gentlemen," her husband continued, "let's not turn this pleasant occasion into a press conference on Teapot Dome. Senator Fall is about to write a letter to Senator Lenroot, who is on the committee investigating this matter, explaining in detail my loan to him."

Then quickly, before anyone could ask another question, McLean said: "I invited two young men from New York to join us today. I thought you would like to meet them. They are the founders and editor-publishers of the new magazine, *Time,* that everyone is talking about. I know lots of us have some misgivings about their rewriting the daily press without doing much—if any—original reporting themselves. And, frankly, I've been a little concerned myself. But to hear them tell it, I think in the long run their magazine will help expand the number of people who keep up with national and international events, which can't help but be good for our business. I'd like you all to meet Britton Hadden and Henry Luce."

There was some polite applause. Then Hadden stepped forward. He was of average build and height, had dark brown hair combed to his right side and a dark brown moustache. He looked very alert and was extremely intense, walking lightly on his feet as if he were a baseball shortstop ready to break in any direction.

"I want to thank Ned for inviting us here today to meet this distinguished group and to say right off that I can assure you this is the real H. L. Mencken here today—not Izzy Einstein, about whom *Time* reprinted the story in which he said Washington was the hardest city in the country for finding a drink of whiskey. Izzy obviously didn't get invited to the right parties. But we can confirm that it is the real Baltimore bard with us today because when we were planning our new magazine we made a special trip down to his hometown to seek his advice. . . ." Then Hadden waited for a moment before saying: "And if we had followed it we wouldn't be here today and there would be no *Time*."

"You mean the great H. L. Mencken can be wrong on occasion," yelled William Allen White.

"On occasion," Mencken answered. "But I think Mr. Hadden will confirm that I did not try to be discouraging—just remind them that they had some tough competition in the *Literary Digest* and *Current Literature*. But that didn't bother these young men. They assured me *Time* would be different from the *Digest* because that treats a few subjects at great length, whereas *Time* would print all the week's news in a brief, organized manner. That's what they've done and I think they're doing a great job. Most important, they're following the number one rule of good communicating—keep it interesting."

"Thank you, Mr. Mencken," said Haden. "I'm a great fan of yours. And let me say that over half the people we went to trying to raise money to start the magazine turned us down because they agreed with you—they didn't think we could compete with the *Digest*."

"Let me ask you one thing," Mencken replied. "Although the copy is lively, the whole magazine reads like it was written by one man . . ."

"You mean, like *The Smart Set?*" Mark Sullivan interrupted.

"Touché!" Mencken responded. "Is that true, Mr. Hadden, and, if so, who is the man?"

"No. We have several good writers, and the trick is to match the right writer with the right story. That's the job of the editor, who is the one most responsible for the uniform *Time*-style. And at present that editor is me—although I don't like to pencil-edit a bad story. I try to find another writer. But Henry, who is the business manager now, and I, plan to rotate regularly. Trouble is, Henry is a better businessman than I am, and, although he shows promise, I'm a better editor than he is. Of course, he won't admit it."

"I certainly won't," Luce said. Hadden's partner was about the same height and build but better looking. He had no moustache and his hair, which he parted in the middle and brushed back, was already receding at the temple. He was much more serious in manner, looking at times as if he was carrying the weight of the western world on his shoulders. They both wore three-piece suits in sharp contrast to the casual wear of many at the party.

"There is one thing I would like to say," Luce continued and as he started to speak I noticed that Mrs. McLean was walking toward where Mencken and I were standing. When she reached Mencken, she gave him a tug on his coat sleeve, pulled him over to one side and whispered something in his ear. They talked quietly for a moment, then she returned to where she was standing next to her husband.

"We understand the concern you have for our lifting the news from the daily press," Luce was saying, "but we talked to Melville Stone, the retired head of the Associated Press, and he assured us that news was in the public domain after it had aged a few days. Also, we know some people are saying that our intent to summarize the week's events in as short a space as possible will result in people becoming even less interested in the news. But we think it's going to work the other way around. Our magazine is not for people who really want to be informed; it's for people willing to spend a half-hour to avoid being entirely uninformed. The biggest communication bottleneck today is not the amount of information available but the relatively small amount that is getting into people's heads. By making the news interesting and less pompous, we think, over time, we will help increase the number of people who follow national and international events. I hope you gentlemen will agree with us.

"But we didn't come here to lecture on communications in the modern world—and I need another drink. Anyone who wants to discuss this subject further can meet us over there."

As Luce and Hadden headed for the bar, I asked Mencken what Mrs. McLean said to him. "She suggested that we stay on after the brunch; that she wanted to talk to us about the diamond. When I told her our ride was Frank Kent, she said we could let him go home when the party was over and that she would have her chauffeur take us into town later."

The brunch continued in the usual manner with people forming little groups, then drifting apart to form new groups with almost everyone talking about the same thing—Secretary Fall, Teapot Dome, Jesse Smith and the Justice Department. At one point, we paused briefly to talk with William Allen White and Mencken reminded the Kansas editor that the last time we met in the Willard he was heading for a meeting with Harding in the White House. "Did the president have anything interesting to say?"

"Not much, Henry. It was a strange meeting. The president just seemed depressed. We enjoyed a good cigar and he obviously wanted somebody to talk to, but he didn't have much to say. I probably learned more from his assistant, Judson Welliver, than I did from the president."

"Oh? How's that?"

"Well, I'm sure you'll keep this confidential—particularly the source—but Judson was terribly distressed at what the president is going through. . . ."

"You mean about the scandals, the corruption?"

"No. It's the fact that the president is coming to an awareness that he's not up to the job, that there are a thousand things he ought to know that he doesn't. He realizes his ignorance and is afraid. He listened to both sides on the tax bill and didn't have any idea who or what to support. 'My God,' he told Judson, 'this is a hell of a place for a man like me.'

"My own brief meeting confirmed it. I've never seen a man having such a hard time trying to decide what he should do. I remember how Roosevelt used to click into truth with a snap of his teeth and how your friend, Henry, Woodrow Wilson sensed it with some engine of erudition in his cranium, but this man cries out for it—to no avail."

"Curious," Mencken replied, "when I was in New York recently, my old friend Nicholas Murray Butler told me something similar. Nicholas had seen the president recently and Harding seemed to be trying to get up his nerve to tell him something, but couldn't do it. I forgot to tell you that, Jim."

"One wonders why Harding has decided to run again next year," I said.

"That was Daugherty," White replied. "Everyone knows he wrote that announcement throwing Harding's fedora in the ring. That gang can't stand the thought of having to go back to Ohio where the pickings are slim compared to Washington."

A buffet lunch was served on the terrace and after eating, several guests began wandering around the huge estate. Mencken and I, coffee in hand, took one path and soon found we were approaching the first tee of the golf course. There was a dark-haired young man there sitting on a bench near a number of bags of golf clubs. "What's your name, young man?" said Mencken. "You look like a caddy who has been stood up by his employee."

"I guess I have. My name is Shirley Povich and believe it or not, this is my first day on the job. Mr. McLean said to make sure to be here today because I might be caddying for a very important man. Nobody's showed up yet, but I'm going to sit right here until somebody tells me to go home."

"I think I know who that man might be," I said, "but they say he probably won't be here today."

"Well, I don't care. I'm staying till dark unless someone tells me otherwise."

"Good luck, Shirley," Mencken said and we continued our stroll.

After lunch the party began to wind down and as we said good-bye to Kent and the cars started to roll down the long driveway, we went back to the house looking for Mrs. McLean. We did not see her, so I decided to take this opportunity to visit the men's room, to which I was directed by one of the waiters—up the stairs and around to the right. The second floor consisted of a long row of rooms facing each other, probably small dormitory bedrooms for the monks who lived here once upon a time. As I came out of the bathroom and started for the stairs, I noticed a woman emerge from another bathroom down at the other end of the hall, walk rapidly toward me, then disappear into another room. She wore a white bonnet and a white cloak—and looked eerily like the woman in white Mencken and I followed Friday night.

I returned to the first floor and found Mencken waiting for me at the bottom of the stairs. Friendship seemed empty now and I barely had time to tell Mencken what I had seen when, suddenly, Mrs. McLean appeared from a doorway and ushered us into a large, comfortable parlor. Ned McLean was sitting, drink in hand, over by a fireplace with a set but unlit fire. Mrs. McLean was the first to speak. She was not wearing the Hope Diamond now. "I'm so glad you were able to stay on for a little while. We just wanted the opportunity let you know how much we appreciate your efforts in helping us find the diamond. After we talked to you we had it checked by a jeweller and it was, as you suggested, a fake. Someone had substituted a very good imitation for the real Hope."

"Well," I said, "apparently all's well that ends well. Right?"

"Not exactly," she replied. "I was not telling the truth out there."

"You mean, the Hope hasn't been found yet?" Mencken asked. "You're still wearing the fake?"

"Yes. But I decided not to let on that it had ever been missing. That would just start the Sunday papers writing about the curse and possibly linking it to Jesse's death and my son's."

"So who's working on the case?" Mencken asked.

"Billy Burns." Mrs. McLean responded. "We more or less had to go with him."

"Why's that?" I asked.

At this point Ned McLean spoke up: "I don't know whether you've heard or not, but Director Burns is actually my 'boss.' I'm a dollar-a-year special agent in his investigative division of the Justice Department. I've done a lot of intelligence work for Billy and he would have been furious if I had turned the case over to a private detective or the police, especially one that might in some way embarrass the president."

"I guess you know," Mencken said, "that Gaston Means works directly for Burns now, despite the fact that Daugherty fired him some time ago?"

"We're well aware of that," Ned McLean responded. "But de-

spite Daugherty's loss of confidence in him, Billy has told me that
he considers Means the 'most wonderful operator' he ever knew.
Those were his exact words."

"What he really is," Mrs. McLean interceded, "is the best crook
I've ever known. He's completely different from ordinary people.
Always in hot water and always getting out. Loves to do wrong and
loves to brag about it. He has the real criminal mind—such a clever
one. Which is why Burns wants him on this case. Gaston is in touch
with the underworld and should have no trouble getting the Hope
back—for a price, of course."

"You mean you paid Gaston B. Means for getting back something he may well have stolen himself?" I said.

"It will be well worth the price. I paid a hundred and fourteen
thousand dollars for it, but it's worth a lot more now."

"How much are you paying Means?"

"I'd rather not say."

"One thing you ought to know," I said. "Smith's ex-wife, Roxy
Stinson, says that the night Smith died, he told her 'they have put
the curse of the blue diamond on me.' That would seem to suggest
that Smith at one point had the diamond in his possession."

"That is strange," Mrs. McLean replied, looking unsettled for the
first time that day. "But I know Jesse didn't take it. He believed in
the curse and even hated to be in the same room when I was wearing it."

"What about you, Mrs. McLean," Mencken asked. "Do you believe in the curse?"

"I'm not sure. The death of my son, after I had bought it, upset
me horribly—and I naturally couldn't help but think about the diamond. It was such a strange way he died. I've had some other
tragedies in my life, but they're the kind of things that probably
would have happened anyway. But I do think it's a talisman of evil.
I never let my friends or my family—except Ned, who thinks the
curse is a bunch of nonsense—touch it. . . ."

"And you've had it blessed, I heard," Mencken said, with obvious sarcasm.

"Yes. I've had it blessed. Maybe that's why my Great Dane
hasn't had any troubles."

"And you, Mr. McLean?" I asked. "Aparently you don't think
much about the curse?"

"I think it makes good reading for the Sunday papers. We always get a lot of letters at the *Post* when we run a piece on the Hope."

"So does the *Sun*," Mencken concurred.

"Anyway," Mrs. McLean continued, "Burns says the diamond was not in the apartment the morning of his death, although they did find a box of smaller conventional diamonds. . . ."

"One of which he left to me," Ned McLean said. "I wonder who Jesse meant when he said *they* passed the curse to him?"

"Roxy says that whenever he referred to 'they' he meant Daugherty," said Mencken.

"I know Roxy. Mrs. Harding doesn't like her, but I do. And I don't trust Daugherty any more than you trust Means. And I don't think Harry had anything to do with Jesse's death. We were at the White House with him and the Hardings right after Jesse died. They played a movie that night to try to take everyone's minds off the tragedy. And all during the film, Daugherty slumped down in the dark, letting out these horrible moans. I've never seen anyone so upset. Besides, Harry doesn't believe in the curse, so I don't think he planted the diamond on Jesse."

"But it's not whether the planter believes in the curse, but the plantee," Mencken said. "The question right now might be: 'Does Gaston B. Means believe in the curse?' "

"I doubt it very much," Ned McLean replied, "which is one reason we thought Gaston was the man to get it back. And we want to thank you again for tipping us off. If there's any way I can reward you, just say the word—money, favors, special seats at the 1924 Republican Convention. And, of course," Ned continued, starting to chuckle, "extra tickets to the next Harding Inaugural, which I presume I'll be handling again."

With that offer, McLean rose to his feet and went to another bar in the corner of the room and started to pour himself a drink.

"Don't you think you've had enough, Ned?" Mrs. McLean asked. "Don't forget your golf game. But I'll have one."

Ned returned carrying only one drink, which he gave to his wife. I was still pondering his curious offer, thinking that ten thousand dollars would certainly be nice right now—or any time—and that they've probably already paid Means much more than that. But Mencken was thinking in a different direction.

"That's very kind of you Mr. McLean. . . ."

"Call me Ned; everybody does."

". . . but we wouldn't think of taking any money and the *Sun* can get me pretty good seats at the conventions. But there is one thing: Cain and I are working on what will be either an article or a book on the Harding administration and its present trouble and frankly we've dug up some real interesting stuff. There's a staggering amount of corruption just below the surface here in Washington, as I'm sure both of you are aware—at least of the rumors, some of which, we can assure you, are true.".

Both McLean and his wife remained silent, but Mrs. McLean nodded her head in apparent agreement.

"What I'd like to ask," Mencken continued, "as a very special favor is that you help us to try to get an interview with President Harding, preferably before he leaves for his Alaska trip. Also with Secretary Fall and Attorney General Daugherty. Neither of them, probably with good reason, are anxious to talk with the press now. Maybe you could help."

McLean was shaking his head negatively but Mencken persisted: "One thing we can assure you, Ned, is that whatever we write will be totally unbiased and non-partisan. I voted for the president and have maintained in the public print that Harding, with all his faults, is a significant improvement over the late Woodrow. Normally, I don't like to meet the people I write about because I might get to like them. But some of the stuff we've dug up warrants a response—especially from the president, but also from Fall and Daugherty. It would be only fair."

Mencken paused for a moment and then said, "One more thing. We will not bring up the question of the president's women— including his current girlfriend, although we know about her. What he does in the bedroom—or the White House coat closet, for that matter—does not interest me one bit. Public servants are entitled to their privacy just as private citizens."

Ned McLean was staring at the fireplace as if it were an evening in January and there was a warming fire. But he said nothing. Then Mrs. McLean rose from her chair, put her glass on a table, walked over to where her husband was sitting and pulled him to his feet: "Will you gentlemen excuse me for a minute? I'd like to talk with Ned alone."

The two of them left the room. Mencken looked as puzzled as I was but we remained silent, waiting to see what would happen next. In a few minutes, Mrs. McLean reeentered the room. She was now wearing the blue diamond around her neck and I couldn't tell it was a fake.

"Ned will be back in a moment," Mrs. McLean said. "Can I fix either of you another drink?"

We both shook our heads but she poured another—a large one—for herself. When she returned to our cluster of seats, Mencken said: "Mrs. McLean, I know you've heard the rumors about Jesse Smith. A lot of people think he was murdered. What do you think?"

"I'm sure he was! When he called us that night at Leesburg—twice—he was scared to death, terrified, like he feared for his life. Not morose, like he planned on taking it. You know who I think did it?" And without waiting for us to reply, she went on: "That bootlegger the Justice Department has indicted—George Remus. He's from Ohio and we've heard that Jesse had taken some money from him, trying to get evidence in a sting operation—at least that's what Daugherty claims. I don't trust Daugherty worth a damn, but Smith might have been double-crossing Remus, taking money from him, promising to keep the bootlegger out of trouble, then not delivering. Maybe Remus had threatened Smith and Jesse knew he meant business. That's why he was so afraid that night."

"Might also have been a good reason for comitting suicide," I said, "if he knew he was a marked man."

"Jesse was a real coward," Mrs. McLean responded. "He was terrified of guns and didn't have the guts to shoot himself. I can assure you that if he did, he had to have help."

But before Mrs. McLean could continue, Mencken suddenly shifted the subject: "I assume that stone you are wearing is the fake Hope Diamond."

"Yes. It's a marvelous likeness. I never would have known the real one was missing if you hadn't alerted me."

"Well, I'm amazed," said Mencken, "that you think Gaston Means is going to get it back. You know he was seen out at the Wardman that night Smith died."

"Yes, by a bellboy. Roxy Stinson too. Billy Burns told Ned about them both."

"And if Jesse Smith had the diamond in his possession, Means could have retrieved it that night," Mencken said.

"Or so could Roxy," she replied. "If Means took it, I'd have it back by now."

"Not necessarily," I said. "He could be waiting awhile before telling you he needs more money to get it back."

"That's exactly what I'd expect from him," Mencken said, "I think he's the most completely dishonest man I have ever met. But I have to admit there is a charming honesty to it—being so honest about his dishonesty."

Before she could respond, I said: "I ran into Means the other night, in connection with a little investigation we were both working on, and he said a woman he was working for had told him about Mrs. Harding and Madam Marcia, the clairvoyant on R Street in town. Is Mrs. Harding seeing a medium?"

"Yes. And going to Madam Marcia was the worst thing she ever did. It got the Duchess all worked up—about oil leases, Jesse Smith, Secretary Fall, Daugherty, and Harding's womanizing. Madam Marcia's even got her convinced that the president will not live out his term in office!"

Then looking anxiously toward the door to the next room, she added: "Of course all this is confidential, very much off the record—as is everything you might hear this afternoon."

Suddenly, there was a noise at the door and both Mencken and I turned to look. A tall, strikingly handsome silver-haired gentleman wearing a cap, polo shirt and knickers ceremoniously entered the room as if he were accustomed to ruffles and flourishes. If he had been wrapped in a white robe instead of dressed for golf, he would have looked like a Roman Senator. As it was, even in knickers, he looked like a president. It was unmistakably Warren G. Harding.

CHAPTER SEVENTEEN

Right behind the president was Ned McLean, seeming a new man, as if basking in the presidential glow had brought him to life. "Mr. Mencken, Jim Cain, I would like you to meet my friend President Warren Harding—although you may have met him before. You've probably heard it said that Warren Harding has shaken more hands than any president in history."

"We did meet, briefly, sir," Mencken said, shaking hands. "At a press reception for you at the Willard at your inauguration."

"Ah," the president said, in a strong voice, easily expandable to fill an auditorium. "I do remember the occasion, but there were so many there that evening and I was quite overwhelmed, being not even on the job yet. But I do love to meet people. In fact, it's the most pleasant thing I do, maybe the only fun in this job. It doesn't tax me and it seems to be a very great pleasure for the people."

"Well, you certainly have a pleasurable, presidential handshake. I can't blame the people."

"You know what else I like to do," Harding said, not seeming to hear Mencken's remark.

"Before you go on, Warren," McLean interrupted, "I think Evalyn and I will withdraw. I'm going to hit a few golf balls in preparation for our game and Evalyn has to see that the servants get cracking, cleaning up after this affair and getting ready for tonight's dinner and poker party. We'll leave you gentlemen to your business."

As Ned McLean left the room, Evalyn approached the president and greeted him with a big hug, which he returned. "I see you're wearing that beautiful diamond. Is that the real one—or a fake?" the president asked.

"Guess," Mrs. McLean replied.

"How would I know? All diamonds look real on you, my dear."

"Oh, I bet you say that to all the girls."

"No, just to beautiful millionairesses with a closet full of jewelry."

"You always say the right thing, darling," and she gave him a kiss on the cheek before following her husband out of the room.

"Wonderful couple," the president said.

Before he could continue, I said: "Mr. President, if you'd feel more comfortable just talking with Mr. Mencken alone, I would certainly understand and be glad to leave."

"Not at all, Mr. Cain. And, incidentally, you might be wondering what I'm doing here, having declined an invitation to Ned's press party. Well, we had a golf date this morning and I came out here fully prepared to play golf and join the party. But I just didn't feel up to it and I had a tremendous amount of work to do—which I brought with me—before leaving on my Alaska trip. So, at the last minute, I decided to stay upstairs, read my papers and take it easy. I'm glad I did. I feel much better."

Recalling my glimpse of a woman in white coming from a room upstairs, I was sure the president was feeling more relaxed.

"But Ned asked me, as a special favor, to have a talk with you. He also said that you have uncovered some things going on in my administration that, perhaps, I don't know about and should. I understand you and Mr. Cain are working on a book. Of course, everything we talk about will be confidential and off the record."

"Understood, Mr. President," Mencken responded. "Our project might turn into a book—or an article for the new magazine George Jean Nathan and I are starting next January."

With the mention of the magazine, the president seemed to pick up interest. "A new magazine, eh? What's it about, what are you going to call it?"

"I think we finally hit on *The American Mercury*."

"I like that," Harding replied, "but does it suggest what kind of magazine it will be?"

"Mainly, it will be devoted to politics and national affairs, rather than literature and culture. That's what interests me today—politics. We want to publish a magazine devoted to just plain common sense presented in as readable and entertaining a manner as possible. It will also be our duty to try to keep government employees honest."

"I certainly commend that, and how I envy you. I really miss

my paper. You know what else I like to do? Mencken, as a news-
paperman, you'll appreciate this. Every day in the midst of the affairs of state, I go to press on *The Marion Star*. I wonder what kind
of layout the boys have got on the first page, how much advertising
there is, whether they are keeping up with this week last year. There
never was a day in all the years that I ran the paper that I didn't
get some thrill out of it. When I first took this job, I had a lot of
fun. I got a kick out of it every day for six months or so. But it has
fallen into a routine. And then there is . . ."

The president did not finish his sentence, seeming to wander off
into a brief reverie. Then he said, smiling: "Shoot, Mencken, I know
you didn't request this interview to write a human interest piece
about me."

"Well, I might surprise you," Mencken replied. "I think you're
honest and have an eye for the well-turned ankle. And, any man
who likes a good shot of bourbon can't be all bad. However, I do
want to discuss some the rumors about what's going on in your
administration—behind your back."

The president's smile gradually left his face and he leaned back
in his chair and crossed his arms over his chest. "I've heard that
you refer to me as 'Gamaliel the Stonehead' and have described my
cabinet as 'three highly intelligent men with self-interest, six jack-
asses and one common crook.' I've always wondered: Who is the
common crook?"

"That's easy," Mencken replied. "Your old friend Harry Daugherty. Everyone now knows that in that little green house on K
Street, Daugherty's friend Jesse Smith—before his untimely death—
collected money for liquor permits, friendly settlements on foreign
property confiscated during the war, squashed indictments and handled other favors your government is able to disburse. Incidentally,
do you think Smith committed suicide—or was he murdered, as
some people around town are saying?"

The president was silent for a moment, then he said, sadly: "That
was a tragedy and we haven't recovered from it yet. Harry Daugherty says Smith was worried about his health. I'm sure the investigation will uncover the truth."

"Not if it is left to William Burns, who works for Daugherty,"
said Mencken. "The Washington police say that he even managed

to misplace the pistol that killed Smith. Do you know who Roxy Stinson is?"

"Jesse's ex-wife."

"She says that Smith was shot in the left temple, but that her ex-husband was right-handed. Still, she agrees it was suicide. Smith was also depressed at being dropped from the Alaska trip."

The president's face dropped, his bushy eyebrows tightened and he turned in his chair to look at the cold fireplace. Finally, he said: "Quite frankly, I did wonder whether my decision to drop Jesse from participation in my administration played a part in this tragedy. But Jesse had started running with a fast crowd—lobbyists, lawyers, fixers, et cetera. And he seemed to like bragging about how big a shot he was and how close he was to Harry, which was true. It was becoming very difficult for Harry and it made me uncomfortable, too. So I made my decision."

"I guess you've heard the rumors," Mencken said, "that, to save his own neck, Smith was getting ready to tell what was going on in Daugherty's Justice Department. According to Miss Stinson, whatever Smith did it was with the full approval and knowledge of Harry Daugherty, whom he loved."

The president appeared crestfallen for a moment. Then he moved around in his chair to face us, and said: "By the way, who is Cain?"

"James M. Cain is an ex–*Baltimore Sun* reporter who will be teaching this fall while working on this story with me."

It was obvious that the president had never heard of me and was not much interested, except that maybe he was becoming a little nervous talking about such sensitive things in the presence of a reporter completely unknown to him. But he made no indication that he wanted me to leave.

"There are apparently," Mencken continued, "a lot of people in this town who wanted to keep Smith silent. And maybe a few from out of town—like the bootlegger, George Remus, who had his own motives. We've heard that he was pretty mad at the Justice Department for indicting him after he paid Jesse Smith a lot of money to make certain that it didn't happen. Just the other day, we heard Remus threaten Smith that somebody in your administration would be in trouble if he went to jail, which is probably where he is headed."

"I do not believe that what you say about George Remus is true. But I'll ask the attorney general."

"You might also ask him about the deal-making that goes on in a little green house on K Street and the parties at the little house on H Street across Lafayette Park from the White House that, we understand, you sometimes attend yourself."

"Mr. Mencken," the president replied stiffly, "it's true that the Duchess—my wife—and I occasionally go over to H Street for a poker party with our friends from Ohio. And as the country's most vocal and persistent wet, I cannot imagine you have any real objection to a little refreshment with our cards. But I can assure you I have no idea what, if anything, goes on in a K Street house."

"Well, we've been there and know the kind of things that go on. Wouldn't that kind of thing explain Jesse Smith's suicide? Maybe he was afraid that someone like Remus was going to get him or expose him?"

"Harry says it was his health that caused the Smith tragedy," the president replied.

"I think it was more like the Cramer suicide," Mencken replied. And it would appear from the sudden change of expression on the president's face that he had struck home. "Most reporters in this town think that Charles Forbes, your Veterans' Administration Chief, has been selling hospital supplies out of a VA warehouse in Perryville, Virginia, at bargain prices and taking his cut. They also think the suicide of his legal aid, Charles Cramer, was directly related, that Cramer knew the skullduggery at the VA was going to be exposed. It seems like a reasonable guess. In fact, isn't that why you sent Forbes to Europe this spring, to get him out of town?"

"I've heard the same rumors about Charlie Forbes," Harding said, "and I have asked Dr. Sawyer to look into the matter. But nothing has been proven yet and I think it's unfair to assume Cramer's tragedy was related to a scandal until we know all the facts. But before I sent him to Europe, I seized Charlie by the collar, shook him against that wall and told him he was 'a double-crossing rat' if he did anything like that. Then there's Prohibition. I told Congress last year that conditions relating to its enforcement savor of nationwide scandal. Those were my very words."

"You're right, Mr. President, you can expect corruption in every government, at every level. But this last thing I want to talk about is pretty big and could concern national security."

Mencken paused to measure the president's reaction. His face revealed nothing.

"As you know," Mencken said, "your former Secretary of the Interior, Senator Albert Fall, obtained authority from the Secretary of the Navy, Edwin Denby—with your approval—to lease the Navy's oil reserves at Teapot Dome in Wyoming and Elk Hill in California to oil magnates Harry Sinclair and Edward Doheny. . . ."

The president interrupted: "I know about that decision. And I also know why there was no bidding for the leases—because Secretary Denby felt the arrangement should be kept confidential for security reasons. You may or may not know it, but part of the deal is for the oil companies to build and fill oil storage tanks at Pearl Harbor in the Pacific and on the Atlantic Coast. For several reasons, we do not want to publicize this. And Denby did not want to have to go to Congress for the money to build storage tanks; he preferred to have it done using the Navy's own resources."

"That may be true, Mr. President. But Secretary Fall, who is not a wealthy man, seems to have come into a lot of money since he left your cabinet. He bought a ranch adjoining his place in New Mexico, made a lot of improvements on his property, and suddenly paid his back taxes, which he has owed for more than twenty years. Does that not seem strange?"

"I've heard these rumors about the oil leases," the president answered, "but if Albert Fall isn't an honest man, I'm not fit to be president of the United States. When he left the cabinet, he went to Russia with Harry Sinclair to assess that country's oil situation and bid on oil rights. I remember when he left. We talked on the phone and I said I hoped he made a lot of money. And I know that Sinclair paid him twenty-five thousand dollars as a consultant."

"Fall has spent a lot more than twenty-five thousand dollars in recent months; it's been more like one hundred and fifty thousand dollars," said Mencken.

"I happen to know he borrowed the money," the president replied firmly, "from Ned McLean."

"Yes, we heard all about that loan today. But McLean can't document it."

The president was silent.

"Mr. President," Mencken continued, "a lot of people do not think it is very surprising that your administration is making friendly deals with the oil tycoons. Everybody knows that five months before your were nominated, in 1920, Harry Daugherty predicted—and I quote from the man who reported it: 'I don't expect Senator Harding to be nominated on the first, second or third ballot, but I think about eleven minutes after two o'clock on a Friday morning of the convention, when fifteen or twenty men, bleary-eyed and perspiring, are sitting around a table in a smoke-filled room, some of them will say, Who will we nominate? At that decisive time, the friends of Senator Harding can suggest him.'

"Isn't it true that some of those 'friends' were oil tycoons— James Darden, Harry Sinclair, Edward Doheny and Jake Hamon? And didn't Hamon tell everyone that whoever got Interior in your cabinet would be worth half-a-million dollars and that Harry Sinclair beat him and got the job for Senator Fall?"

President Harding was noticeably ruffled: "Mencken, Harry Sinclair had nothing to do with my appointment of Senator Fall, an old friend from Senate days. And everyone knows that I fought to keep Hamon out of the cabinet, even though he was one of my strongest supporters. It really stunned me when he was killed."

"Yeah," said Mencken, "a bad way to go, shot by a girlfriend in a hotel room."

"What a wonderful fellow Jake was," Harding said. "Too bad he had that one fault—that admiration for women."

Mencken refrained from commenting on that one, and the president went on: "The Teapot Dome and Elk Hill leases were very good for the country. In addition to the storage tanks, there was the possibility of drainage or runoff from those reserves with serious loss to the Navy. Surely you must have heard that?"

"I have heard that is what Fall and Denby are saying," Mencken replied. "But a lot of oil men and Navy officials disagree. There was a time, of course, when profiteering at the expense of the government served a purpose. Where would we be if those nineteenth-century tycoons hadn't looted the Treasury, in one way or another, and opened up the West—built railroads, canals, factories? Someday a historian will write the history of the republic from the point of view of the Rockefellers, Harrimans and Vanderbilts and will give them a lot of credit. They probably played a more important role than those preachers in Boston. But I'm afraid that time is past."

The president seemed to relax a little when Mencken began praising the tycoons, but it did not last for long. "Did it ever occur to you, Mr. President, that the reason the attorney general did not agree to investigate Teapot Dome—as Congress demanded—was because he knew how many men made money off that deal, that he was holding off while trying to force Secretary Fall to cut him in? Miss Stinson says that her husband and Daugherty were mad that they were not let in on that deal—that Jesse knew several men who shared in some millions of dollars profits brought about by the big increase in Sinclair and Pan American stocks after the leases were granted to those companies by Fall."

The president was slowly shaking his head.

"This may surprise you, Mr. President," Mencken continued, "but I voted for you! You are—and I have said it in my column many times—exactly the man the American people deserve. Furthermore, I think you're an honest man, no matter what some of your friends might be doing, and far superior to your predecessor, the late Woodrow, a congenital liar and the perfect model of a modern Christian cad."

Then, pausing a moment, Mencken said: "Considering everything we've learned about the corruption in your administration, I'm surprised you're running next year. I presume you made your decision to run again next year before all the rumors started about your administration."

The president said: "No, I made the decision *after* the rumors started; in fact, they encouraged me to run again. I think the best way to establish my integrity is to be reelected, despite the rumors. The people will believe me when they hear my story. And, frankly, I wish Harry had not announced my candidacy for next year yet because now the people will think this is a campaign trip I'm taking, which it's not."

After a moment, he continued in a somewhat different vein: "The truth is there are times when I'm not sure I'm right for this job; it's so demanding! Do you know what happened recently? I asked Bill White to look up an old boyhood friend—Dr. Marcellus Bowen, head of the American Bible Society—in the Near East, when he was going out there. Well, when White came back, he told me that

Bowen had died, and I remember saying, 'God, have I been that busy, that he could die without my knowing it?' What a life! Frankly, I think if it hadn't been for the rumors about these scandals, I would have gone back to editing *The Star,* which I really loved."

The president paused and Mencken looked at his watch. It was almost three P.M. but Harding continued his monologue: "But here I go again. I'm about to start across the country on a trip that will take me to Seattle and then up to Alaska. We're calling it a 'Voyage of Understanding,' in which I will explain my policies to all the people who have been so kind and supported me."

Mencken waited a moment before he said: "Mr. President, I feel sorry for you because by the time you return from Alaska, some of these scandals I have mentioned will be openly discussed in the press. And what I think we are going to find is that since the Grant administration, the American people have grown less tolerant of corruption at the national level. They still accept some hanky-panky at the State House in Columbus or Annapolis, but they expect more of their representatives in Washington. Attorney General Daugherty reminds them too much of Boss Penrose and Mark Hanna. And the people Daugherty brought with him—his friends and yours—are quite frankly too dumb to see the difference between courthouse politics and how they play the game in Washington."

The president was frowning. But Mencken continued: "Don't get me wrong. There was plenty of corruption here in Washington before your gang came to town. Of the nearly four hundred representatives of the people on Capitol Hill there are maybe forty who cannot be bought, even with votes. The rest are absolutely indistinguishable from a convention of garage keepers. But their chamber is the shrine of government and their absurd proceedings result in the enactment of what is called law, and that law we are asked to revere as something almost sacred—even the Volstead Act, which everyone, including most of the people in the highest offices in the land, ignore. At the same time, you brought to Washington people who are making big money off of lots of things, especially Prohibition—which I personally can attest to. And, Mr. President, if you do not understand this, you will by the time you return from your 'Voyage of Understanding.' "

Rather abruptly, the president's mood changed, as if he knew that what Mencken had been saying was true. Very firmly, he replied: "Mr. Mencken, the people may think I don't work hard, but the White House is hell at times. And I curse Harry Daugherty for getting me in that job. But I'm doing my best to give the country a good administration. People think I don't know of some things going on in my administration, that I'm weak and too tolerant and all that. But they'll find out. When I get back to Washington, there will be a shake-up in some places which will show that they have misjudged me."

Then, standing up as if to say the interview was over, he added: "I have no trouble with my enemies. I can take care of them. But my damn friends, my goddamn friends, they're the ones that keep me walking the floors nights.

"Again, everything we've discussed here is off the record." And as he walked out of the room. I detected moisture in the president's eyes.

CHAPTER EIGHTEEN

Mencken and I were sitting there sort of staring at each other, trying to absorb what we had just experienced, when Mrs. McLean returned: "Well, how did it go? I hope you got everything you wanted." She was not wearing anything around her neck.

"Very informative," Mencken said. "But it confirms my policy of not wanting to meet the people I write about because I might get to like, or at least feel sorry for them."

"Don't worry, you'll get over it," I said.

"I hope so. But I do feel sorry for the president."

"Why?" Mrs. McLean asked.

"Because he's so obviously a man in way over his head and the poor fellow knows it," Mencken said.

"He also knows he's in deep trouble because of his friends," I said. "And there's not much he can do about it. . . ."

"Except try to convince the people that he knew nothing about what was going on," Mencken added, "which he might actually be able to do. This is a defining time in his presidency. How the people react to him on this trip and what he does when he returns will be significant."

"If he returns," Mrs. McLean said. "He's not feeling at all well right now. He told me he does not think he will survive this journey. And *that* is confidential!"

Mrs. McLean remained standing, which indicated to me that it was time for us to leave. Mencken assumed the same thing and, rising to his feet, he said: "We want to thank you and your husband not only for this pleasant luncheon, but for persuading the president to talk with us for a little while. You said you could arrange a ride for us back into town."

"Yes. My car and chauffeur are waiting for you out front. And I thank you again for trying to keep that stupid diamond from bringing anyone else bad luck. We will certainly let you know what Detective Burns finds out."

"And we'll do the same if we learn anything," I said, as we went out the door.

Not wanting to talk in earshot of the chauffeur about what we had learned today, we did not discuss anything significant on the way into town. But as we reached Massachusetts Avenue and turned left, Mencken asked the chauffeur: "You've probably heard about the curse on that big jewel—the Hope Diamond—Mrs. McLean wears sometimes? How do you and the others on the staff feel about it? Do you all believe in the curse?"

"Some do, some don't. I didn't pay it much heed—until young Vinson's accident. That really spooked me. You probably heard about dat?"

"Yes." said Mencken. "How did it happen?"

"I was out at de house that Sunday. Mr. and Mrs. McLean in Louisville at de Derby. Little Vinson and Mr. Ned's man, Megget, were walking on the grounds when Vinson said: 'Let's go outside the gate.' Meggett thought, 'Why not?' It was such a nice morning, just like today, and there's very little traffic on dat road any time— especially Sunday morning. They got out and cross da street and they saw a farmer they knew—named Goebel—driving a wagon loaded with ferns. So Vinson, actin' just like a little boy, ran over to Goebel, says 'How are you, Goebel?' then grabbed a few ferns and ran back across de road t'ward the gate. Goebel yelled: 'Hey! You can't have dose ferns' and started to run after him. So little Vinson suddenly changed direction but didn't see one of those Tin Lizzies comin' right at 'im. And one thing I can say fer sure, no matter what you might've heard. That Lizzie wasn't going fast, no sir. It just barely hit him, but hardly enough to push him over. But he did fall and the Lizzie never even run over him. Vinson didn't seem hurt at all and he walked into de house holding Meggett's hand. Soon he was talking to Grandma Walsh and she sent for a doctor. And a couple came. They didn't think he was hurt, but said he might have a fractured skull, which would be bad. He might be bleeding in his head. And that must have been it. Later that day, he 'came paralyzed. And once he asked his grandma: 'Is it wicked for me to love Mother more than God?' At six o'clock that night, little Vinson died."

The McLean chauffeur was silent for a moment, then he said: "I guess ever since dat day I've believed Vinson was cursed by som'in. It was really scary the way he died like dat."

"What about Mrs. McLean?" Mencken asked. "How do you think she feels about it?"

"Up 'til Vinson's accident, she didn't seem to think much about it. But since then, I've heard her go back and forth."

"Does she really let her dog wear the diamond?"

"Oh yeah. When she's . . . that is, when they're partyin', if you know what I mean?"

Then, rounding Dupont Circle and heading toward 16th Street, still on Massachusetts, Mencken suddenly had an idea: "Why don't we pay a surprise visit to Mr. Gaston B. Means? I think we've got a lot of questions for him about that night Smith died and the diamond. We might have better luck catching him now. Tomorrow, if he doesn't want to talk to us, he'll just refuse our calls and not return them. What do you think?"

"Brilliant, Holmes. You'd make a great detective if you'd just lay off that cocaine."

The chauffeur turned around at that and Mencken said: "We've decided to make one stop before going to the train. You can drop us at Nine-oh-three Sixteenth Street. We'll walk it from there."

"It's a long way to Union Station," the driver replied.

"That's okay. It's a nice day and we need the excercise."

When we pulled up in front of 903 16th, I noticed a big black Cadillac parked in front: "We're in luck, I think. That's Means' car."

Mencken thanked the driver, tipped him and said good-bye. Laughing as he drove away, the McLean chauffeur said: "You take it easy on that powder, boss. 'Tain't no good for you."

Mencken led the way to Means' ground level office door and knocked. Then knocked again. It was a few minutes before Means opened the door, dressed in a loose-fitting cardigan, baggy pants and tennis shoes. He looked dreary-eyed, as if he had been taking a Sunday afternoon nap. We told him there were some things we wanted to talk about. So reluctantly he led us into the large comfortable room next to his office where there was a fireplace in front of which was a leather couch and two chairs. There was only one window in the room and it was shaded. After turning on several lamps, Means motioned us to sit down. Then walking over to a wet bar not too far from a large poker table with a number of chairs around it, he poured himself what looked like a glass of bourbon and said: "Name your poison. I don't think it's too early for a little libation."

"Well, I'm ombibulous," said Mencken, "but if you have some bourbon, that would be fine."

I chose scotch and after we were all comfortably seated, glasses in hand, in front of the fireplace, I was struck with how dark the room seemed, even with the lamps. And it would soon be full of smoke as Mencken pulled out one of his Uncle Willies and Means started the first of his chain-smoked cigarettes. "Mr. Means," I said, deciding to get right to the point, "I was out at the Wardman Park the other night . . ."

"After you saw me at the Washington Hotel?" Means interrupted.

"Yeah. And I located a bellboy who said he saw you out there the night Jesse Smith died. He described you and said he knew you were a private detective, because you had paid some of the other bellboys for information. As he was coming down the stairs, you were coming up, 'huffing and puffing,' he said. And he was pretty sure you left the stairwell at the fifth floor, where the Daugherty apartment is. We'd kinda like to know what you were doing there and if you saw Smith that night."

With a big, dimpled smile, Means replied: "Sure I was there. That was the night you were here, Mencken. I told you I had an assignment. It sure took you guys a long time to find out. Burns' men talked to the bellboy the day after Smith's death. He told them about me—and Roxy. I suppose you know she was there, too. Must have gotten to Jesse's room before I did."

"Who were you working for that night?

"Can't tell you. But I told Burns."

"You were looking for the blue diamond? Right?"

"The McLeans told you about that?"

Without answering, Mencken and I began a rapid fire interrogation, each taking turns with questions, almost as if we had this master crook sitting in a chair at police headquarters, except that there wasn't much light to shine in his face. "Did you see Smith?"

"I saw him all right, but he wasn't in such good shape."

"He was dead?"

"He sure was. Lying on the floor, his head in a metal basket, just like the newspapers said. And the basket had some ashes in it, like something had been burned."

"Did you find the diamond?"

"Nope. It was gone."

"Did you find any papers?"

"Something had been burned in the basket, although there weren't that many ashes. Smith was supposed to have had a good-size package of papers implicating Daugherty."

"Did you know what the papers were?"

"I could guess."

"So?"

"Records Smith had kept of his operation, showing that he was only acting on instructions and orders from 'the general,' as he called his boss."

"Do you think Smith committed suicide or was murdered?"

"I'm positive he was murdered."

"How do you know?"

Means took a puff on the ever-present cigarette and said: "There are two people I know who wanted him dead. And neither of them would hesitate for one moment to have it done."

"And they are?"

"Harry Daugherty, of course, and the bootlegger, George Remus. Daugherty has his fall guy, now. Or Remus has his revenge, take your choice."

"Revenge for what?"

"For Smith not giving Remus protection from, first, indictment, then conviction, then a jail sentence—all of which he thought he had paid for. Then for not returning the money, as Remus demanded."

"Jesse wouldn't return it?"

"That's right. But poor Jesse was caught in the middle. Remus wanted fifty thousand dollars back and Smith wanted to give it to him, but Daugherty refused."

"Why?"

"Daugherty figured Remus would soon be in jail and convicts don't make very good prosecution witnesses. They're always suspected of making deals and testifying to help themselves."

"Burns is investigating the case. Does he think Remus is a suspect?"

"He might."

"Does he think you're a suspect?"

"He knows I didn't do it. He says the most likely suspect is Roxy Stinson. But as far as he's concerned, it was suicide. The case is closed."

"Did you tell him you thought it was murder?"

"Nope."

"Why not?"

"What's the use? That's the way they want it."

"We know that Burns is trying to find the diamond for Mrs. McLean and she paid you a large sum of money to get it back. Who were you were working for that night—Burns or the McLeans?"

"Can't say. I don't like to talk about clients. Why don't you talk to Roxy about this? She was there first. She could have both the diamond and the papers—if there were any."

"Do you think Miss Stinson killed Jesse?"

"Her ex-husband? Not likely. They were very close friends and I happen to know Jesse was giving her lots of money. Why would she want to kill him? But she could have taken the diamond. Why don't you ask her?"

"We can't. She seems to have disappeared."

Means frowned and took a long swallow from his glass. "Damn! I hope I wasn't too late."

"What do you mean?"

Means did not a say anything. He stood up, emptied his glass, walked to the bar and poured another drink. Then he said: "Will you men please excuse me for a moment? There's a phone call I have to make. Help yourself to the whiskey."

Mencken and I both refilled our glasses, and waited for Means to return. When he did, he looked troubled. Then he said: "I've always liked Roxy and she knows it, for all the good it did me. I think she's positively the sexiest woman I have ever known and I've made plenty of passes at her. But she don't give me the time of day." He was shaking his head, but paused to take a drink.

"Anyway, Friday night—remember, Cain? That was the night

we were all following Nan Britton and you and I had our talk in
the Hotel Washington lounge. I called Roxy and warned her that
she ought to get out of town as soon as possible; I was sure her life
was in danger. I told her I thought she should disappear, not even
telling you or Mencken where she was going. I knew you had a
date with her and I was pretty certain you were still with her."

"And how did you know she was in danger?"

"I have to go back a ways to explain that. And this is very
confidential. I'll deny I ever said it, except I won't have to because
nobody would believe me anyway. Mencken, you remember that
night—it was the night Smith was killed—we had nightcaps here
at my house after our dinner at the Washington?"

"Yeah. I remember."

"I got a phone call and while I took it, you waited right here in
this room, all the while, I'm sure, trying to find a phone to listen
in on me. But I was on my confidential phone that no other line in
the house can plug into."

"You can't blame me for trying," Mencken said. "But I see you
don't trust anyone—including your family."

"Right. So I get this call from a voice I recognize—one of my
superiors—giving me an assignment. At eleven P.M., my chauffeur,
my wife and son and I were to be at the corner of Connecticut
Avenue and Wyoming—that's just down the street from the Wardman. My wife and my son and I were to all be in the back seat. A
man would appear and get in the front seat. He would have his coat
collar turned up. He would not want to be seen and we were not to
make any effort to get a good look at him. We were to wait at least
an hour; then leave if he had not appeared. If he did appear, we
were to drive him to Harper's Ferry in West Virginia, where he
would catch a train."

"Did he appear?" asked Mencken.

"He did. At around eleven-fifteen P.M. We drove him to West
Virginia, where he boarded the train for the West."

"Did you recognize him or did anyone get a good look at him?"

"No to both questions. And we didn't want to know who he was.
It might be dangerous."

"Why?

"You haven't figured that out? You guys are really lousy detectives." Then he paused as if deciding whether he was going to

continue. But then he said: This was a government execution."

"What the hell do you mean by that?" Mecken said incredulously.

"To the gang, poor Jesse had become a menace. He had outlived his usefulness. If those papers were made public, an explosion would follow. Many high officials, cabinet members, even the president himself would be blown up. The government must be saved. It was logical! A patriotic duty."

"Come on," was all I could say.

"Hasn't every government on earth," Means rambled on, "since the days of Achan put to death its traitors? Why, in the fifteenth and sixteenth centuries look what happened. When necessary, they slaughtered in wholesale lots. They annihilated nations. Would our little noise of an advanced civilization become weak and futile, when only the execution of one man was necessary to preserve the government? What is one life—in the balance of universal benefit to our millions of citizens? This government had to be saved."

I looked at Mencken, aware that we were hearing a confirmation of what Mencken thought from the beginning—that Means was slightly insane. "So you think the man you drove out to Harper's Ferry worked for someone in the administration?" I asked.

"I don't want to know who he worked for. And if I did know, I wouldn't tell you or anyone else."

"So what did this guy, coming into town on the day Smith was murdered, have to do with Roxy?"

"Very simple. Just before I called her at the Wardman, I received another phone call from the same superior who had called me the night Smith was killed. He told me the same thing: To be at the same place at around eleven P.M.—to pick up a man and take him to Harper's Ferry."

"Same man?" I asked.

"He didn't say and I didn't ask. But remembering what happened to Smith when I got that call, I immediately sensed that someone was in trouble—either Senator Wheeler, who is launching an impeachment charge against Daugherty or, more likely, Roxy, if they decided she had the papers. In fact, I told her that night when I called that her life was in danger if she had those papers."

"I take it you're anxious to find those papers yourself?" I said.

"Sure am. I could put them to good use."

"Why do you continue to work for this administration after Daugherty fired you?" Mencken asked.

"I do what I get paid for. I'm a professional investigator and a good one. And I still do a lot of work for Billy Burns."

"How about Daugherty?" I asked.

"I always admired and respected him, even though I got mad at him when he fired and later insulted me. But he's of much higher quality than the real archenemy of the government—Treasury Secretary Mellon."

"You don't like Mellon."

"I don't believe because a man accumulates millions and millions of dollars and can swing the government and courts that he has got any more intelligence than any other man who is not always vitally concerned in making money. Money is not everything in the world by a long shot. It's no use to worship a liquor-man's boots because he's got money—but that's the way it is in America today."

"Mr. Means," Mencken said, "you sound a lot like a bolshevist."

"Hah! That's a real phony bunch. None of these bombings, including the one intended for former Attorney General Palmer, were real. They were done to stir up things so you could blame anything you want to attack on the Reds. The Reds can't organize anything. I've been to dozens of their meetings. There aren't two hundred and fifty bolshevists in New York; I've been to meetings where they were all in one room. They couldn't start a revolution. Revolutions never start at the bottom. The American people—the masses—are the best people in the world. Coming in contact with the foreigners is not where the Red conditions exist. It exists up with the higher types. Anybody who has read history and studied sociology or anything else knows that. The conditions start from the top. But I never paid any attention to the Red propaganda because the best way to control the Red situation was give the people an opportunity to express their opinions and they will reach, nine times out of ten, correct conclusions."

Hoping to shift the subject, I asked Means: "That 'liquor man,' you referred to; are you talking about—is that Remus?"

"Could be. He's a lawyer and everybody says he's so smart and powerful with all his distilleries and contacts. However, he paid Smith and Daugherty at least two hundred thousand, but was tried and found guilty. He's appealing his case now to the Supreme Court and everybody knows his appeal will be denied and he's going to prison in Atlanta."

"So, doesn't that make Remus the most likely suspect?" I asked. "It's pretty obvious from the slaughter going on in Chicago, that it doesn't pay to double-cross a bootlegger."

"Remus could have done it. But I don't work for him. He was not the person who assigned me to take that killer to Harper's Ferry."

"But he might have killed Smith—before your man got there?"

"Please. He was not my man. And why don't you ask Remus yourself? I hear he's coming into town this week. Probably staying at the Washington. That's where he and Smith used to meet."

"What's Remus coming to town for?

"Probably to make one last effort to see Daugherty and make him deliver on Smith's promises. Fat chance."

"What if he got the papers—maybe from Roxy? Maybe he thinks he can force a presidential pardon, if he has the papers."

"Never thought of that," replied Means. "But if he threatens Daugherty with the missing papers, I'll hear about it pretty fast."

"I hope you'll let let us know, if he does," I said.

"Maybe I will, maybe I won't."

"I'm more concerned about Roxy," I replied, "than I am about Remus. If he did get some papers from her, we may never see Roxy again."

"Sounds like you got it bad for her," said Means.

Ignoring that remark, I said: "Last Friday, when you were supposed to meet the second man at Connecticut and Wyoming and take him to Harpers Ferry, did he show up?"

"No. I waited one hour, as instructed, and then left."

"Did you tell your superior?"

"Yes."

"What did he say?"

"Nothing. He just hung up."

"What do you think happened?"

"I hate to think about it. One possibility—if Roxy was the target—is that he didn't get a chance to fulfill his mission that night because you were with her and he's still stalking her. A worse possibility is that he fulfilled his mission, but had a body to dispose of and didn't want to involve me. Remember, I also had my chauffeur, wife and son in the car, as before."

"That does seem strange. Why do you think they told you to have them along?"

"That's easy. They wanted family and friends waving to him at the station, so it looked like a businessman headed for Columbus or Chicago on a business trip. That looks a lot less sinister than one man, alone at midnight, getting out of a big black Cadillac—or a cab that could be traced—and boarding the train. These people are professionals. That's what ought to worry you about Roxy."

"Aren't you worried about her?"

"Yes. But I have plenty of troubles of my own."

"Means, tell me this . . ." Mencken started to say, but before he could ask his question, we heard a telephone ring in Means' office.

Standing up quickly, Means said: "Excuse me a moment, gentlemen, I will be back in a minute."

When Means had left the room, Mencken stood up and lit another Willie while I wandered around the—by now—really smoke-filled room looking at the photographs, some of them autographed, on the walls. There were a few family photos, but most of them were of Means and, I presumed, various members of the administration. The only ones I recognized were President Harding, Jesse Smith, and Secretaries Hoover and Hughes.

In a few minutes, Means was back but he did not return to his chair. Instead, he stood in the middle of the room and said: "That was Billy Burns. Earlier, when I left the room to use the phone, I called him to suggest that he should talk with you; that you seemed to know a lot about Roxy and Jesse. He said he had heard from the attorney general, who had just talked to Ned McLean. Mr. McLean asked him to grant you two an interview—as a sort of favor for telling them about their missing diamond. The attorney general agreed saying, in fact, that he was most anxious to talk with you. News travels fast in this town and the attorney general had already heard about your meeting with the president. So I suggest you save your questions for Mr. Daugherty. Besides, I promised to take my family for a ride out to Hains Point this evening and it's getting a little late."

Sensing the meeting was over, Mencken and I both rose to our feet as Means continued: "Daugherty said tomorrow at two P.M. will be fine for him and if I don't call Billy Burns back now, he will consider it a date. Can you gentlemen make that?"

I nodded my head and Mencken said, "We'll be there."

"Excellent," Means replied. "You were quite fortunate to get an interview with the president. I assume McLean set that up, too? I'd love to hear what he said, but I'm sure it was confidential."

"It was," Mencken said.

"And I would appreciate it," Means added, as he escorted us through his office and out to the street, "if you would consider everything I have told you as confidential. I have reasons for confiding in you things that I would not tell every reporter."

Deciding to have dinner and catch a late train, we walked to the Ebbitt Grill where we knew we would be comfortable having a drink or two from Mencken's flask. We spent most of the dinner discussing our fast-moving story—speculating on just what the hell Means was up to; what we would ask Daugherty; what Roxy did that night at Smith's apartment and what had happened to her.

On the train back to Baltimore, Mencken indicated he was not in the mood for conversation because he wanted to think about a column idea. I let him take the window seat and as he pulled a Willie out of the supply in his coat, I asked him what it was on.

"Democracy and the presidency—a fitting subject, considering that yesterday we had a conversation with the ideal president for the country—a third-rate political wheelhorse with the intelligence of a respectable agricultural implement dealer and the imagination of a lodge joiner."

I made some notes and then settled down with the Sunday *Post*, which I had bought in the station, trying to stay awake as I read an article about Harding's trip to Alaska. Soon I was drowsily contemplating my footnote in history, having taken part in what was probably the president's last press interview before leaving on what could be a historic trip—considering that he told us that when he returns he was going to shake up his administration and get rid of the crooks! A good story for my grandchildren—if I ever had any. And that started me worrying about Roxy.

Before dozing off completely, I noticed Mencken, an unlit Willie clamped in his lips, staring out the window and occasionally jotting some notes on the back of an envelope. "Henry, you look like Lincoln on the way to Gettysburg."

Taking the Willie out of his mouth, Mencken replied: "Cain, have you ever stopped to think what democracy has done to the presidency? Lincoln, who is a deity now, was an exception, but today no man of sense would think of running for the presidency. When a candidate for public office faces the voters he does not face men of sense; he faces a mob of men whose chief distinguishing mark is the fact that they are quite incapable of weighing ideas, or even comprehending any save the most elemental—men whose whole thinking is done in terms of emotions and whose dominant emotion is dread of what they cannot understand. So confronted, the candidate must either bark with the pack, or count himself lost. In the long run, the odds are on the man who can most adeptly disperse the notion that his mind is a virtual vacuum. As democracy is perfected, the office represents, more and more closely, the inner soul of the people. We move toward a lofty ideal. On some great and glorious day the plain folks of the land will reach their heart's desire at last, and the White House will be adorned by a downright moron.

"In fact, it may have already happened."

CHAPTER NINETEEN

Riding over to Washington on the train the next day, I asked Mencken if he was going to come out in his column and say that, with Harding, we finally had achieved our goal of having a moron in the White House?

"No. I won't mention Gamaliel. That's the trouble when you meet someone you write about. You get soft. But I'll get over it. I wouldn't call him a complete moron. And he is honest. I think I agree with Mary that the president really doesn't know what his Ohio Gang has been up to. But he is close to the ideal—a near-moron who is one of the most popular presidents we have ever had."

This led us into a discussion of the 1920 election in which Mencken almost convinced me that our democracy was, indeed, in dire straits. By the time we finished our conversation with Harry Daugherty, there was no doubt about it.

The office of the attorney general of the United States was on the 7th floor of the Justice Department on 15th Street, not very far from the Ohio Gang's houses on H and K Streets.

When we were ushered into the large office by the woman who sat out in front of it, two men, already in the room, stood up as we approached them. One, stocky with a very dark bushy moustache, I immediately recognized as the man Means had dinner with that night we met him at Harvey's—William Burns, head of the department's Bureau of Investigation. The other man, of average height and build, had cold eyes and a very hard, plain face which was rather drawn.

He was seated at a large desk, centered near the back wall in front of a window, beside which was an American flag in a holder. Several chairs were arranged in a semicircle around the front of the desk. I presumed he was the attorney general. Holding out his hand, he was the first to speak: "Harry Daugherty. And this is Billy Burns, my chief investigator." They looked like models for the chief of police and political boss in any middle-sized Midwestern town.

As we shook what I thought were two very limp hands, considering how much power they held in them, Daugherty said: "Take a seat, gentlemen." Despite his hard face, he looked as if on the right occasion, he could be affable and gregarious, even engaging. This was not one of those occasions. He was transparently grim, calculatingly so, I thought, which was accented by his apparent ill health. "Ned McLean tells me that you requested an interview with me. I also understand that you had a meeting yesterday afternoon with the president. I would be curious to know what transpired at that meeting."

Mencken responded directly and abruptly, indicating at once that he was not going to be intimidated by one of the most powerful officials in the government sitting in his large office, flanked by the American flag and the country's most feared investigator: "You will have to ask the president about our conversation. He requested that it be considered confidential."

"It's rather a coincidence that you asked for an interview with me," Daugherty replied, shifting gears, "because we were about to come looking for you."

"Oh?" Mencken said.

"Yes. We understand that, in connection with a book you are working on, that you have been talking to one of my former employees, Gaston Means, and Jesse Smith's ex-wife, Roxy Stinson."

"That is correct," Mencken replied.

"Well, there are a number of things you ought to know. They no doubt have been feeding you a lot of misinformation, which you may have passed on to the president. First, as everyone knows, Gaston B. Means is the most colossal liar that ever came to this town—our very own Baron Munchausen."

"You mean Gaston is the most colossal liar among non-politicians," Mencken shot back. "Nobody in this town lies more than your average congressman. And if Means is so unreliable, why is it that Mr. Burns here still hires him for an occasional job, even after you fired him? In fact, we saw them having dinner together at Harvey's just last Friday night. Isn't that right, Jim?"

"Yes," I agreed. "And they seemed to be talking serious business."

The attorney general, looking visibly surprised at our revelation, drew himself up in his chair and said to Burns: "Is that right, Billy? Are you still using Means on government business?"

"No," the chief investigator replied in a low voice. "You know what case I was talking with Means about at Harvey's that night. The McLean business."

"You mean finding the Hope Diamond?" Mencken said. "Mrs. McLean told us yesterday that Means is working on that case."

"Yes," Burns replied.

"That's different," Daugherty responded. "That's not really government business. Burns thought that Means, with his connections to the underworld, was the best man we had for that job. And we wanted to keep it out of the papers. I approved Burns using Means on this particular case."

"It wasn't just the Hope Diamond case," Mencken replied. "Means was also used by Smith to check out applicants for a liquor permit—namely, me and my partner, here, Jim Cain."

Daugherty frowned and looked disapprovingly at Burns: "Is that true, Billy?"

Burns hesitated, then said: "Well, I guess so. You know how busy Jesse was just before his death. And with his diabetes, he wasn't feeling very good. He asked Means to do some security checks. He also asked me to keep an eye on Means, which I did. But neither Jesse nor Gaston said anything to me about H. L. Mencken applying for a permit."

"I didn't use my real name," Mencken said. "I don't think Smith ever realized who we were before he died. But Means knew and he didn't tell Smith. I think he decided to deal with us on his own. And I must say he acted confident that he could do whatever he pleased, almost as if he was immune from arrest or prosecution."

"Not now," Daughertey replied. "There was a time when he was trying to blackmail me, threatening to expose some alleged corruption in the Justice Department if I didn't rehire him. I didn't know what he was talking about. I do now, and since Jesse Smith's death, Means has dropped those threats."

I would have asked Daugherty to explain why Means dropped his threats, but Mencken decided to change his line of questioning: "Miss Stinson said that the night before he died, Smith told her, and I quote, 'They put the curse of the blue diamond on me.' He seemed quite worried about that because he apparently believed in the curse."

"I know he did," Daugherty said. "And I don't know what Miss Stinson is talking about. Jesse never told me anything about the Hope Diamond. And if he had it or knew anything about it, he would have mentioned it. He had a nice collection and we talked diamonds all the time. But that's the other thing I wanted to talk with you about."

"What's that?" said Mencken.

"Roxy Stinson. I understand that you two have been seeing quite a bit of her lately and I want to warn you to be careful about what she tells you." Daugherty paused for a moment, expecting one of us to say something, but we remained silent.

"Although I was very close to her ex-husband, I don't think I ever saw Roxy more than couple of times in my whole life and one of those times was at a hospital when I called to see Jesse and she was leaving. But she became my bitter enemy, primarily because I discouraged Jesse from inviting her to Washington."

"It was more than that," Mencken interrupted. "She thinks you drove Jesse to his suicide, by setting him up to take the fall for some of the corruption in your department that's about to pass out of the rumor stage and onto the front pages of the nation's newspapers. I'm sure you know what I'm talking about."

"I've heard the rumors—and in the case of the Veterans' Bureau, some of them are true. But you can ignore everything you might have heard or she told you about Teapot Dome. One of the charges against me is that I failed to take action against Secretary Fall. But those leases to Sinclair Oil and Pan American were perfectly legal and approved by the president. Fall received no money from any oil companies. He did make some expensive renovations on his ranch in New Mexico and purchased a neighboring spread. But, as you heard, yesterday, his old friend, Ned McLean, who is fabulously wealthy, lent him one hundred thousand dollars for that."

"Yes, we did hear about the loan yesterday," Mencken responded. "But McLean says he has no documentation—no note and no canceled checks."

"That's correct. He had a note from Fall, but gave it back to him when the canceled checks came in. Then he eventually lost the canceled checks. And he never makes stubs when he writes checks. That's one of the privileges of being so rich."

"Okay. What about Jesse Smith? They're saying that he sometimes took money to dispense Justice Department favors, like in the Allied Metal settlement. Roxy told us that one time Jesse came back to Washington Courthouse wearing a money belt in which she saw seventy-five one-thousand-dollar bills!"

"Remember, we're still raising money to pay off the 1920 campaign debts." Daugherty replied. "Jesse often carried large amounts of money on him before we put it in one of the Party bank accounts. It used to worry him to death. But just before Jesse died, John Crim, the assistant district attorney, informed me that he had evidence that Jesse might have been mixed up in some questionable liquor permit deals. He confronted him with the truth and told Jesse that I would be made acquainted with the facts. That was just a couple of days before his suicide. And, incidentally, that's why Gaston Means is no longer a threat to me. He knows that if there is any corruption in the Justice Department, it can be laid at Jesse Smith's feet."

When Mencken and I looked at each other skeptically the attorney general reached into his desk drawer and pulled out a piece of paper. "Let me read you an editorial from David Lawrence's *United States Daily*. 'That Jesse Smith received money from various persons who sought to influence government action is unquestioned. That Harry M. Daugherty never knew anything about it until it was too late is also accepted by his friends as absolute truth. Although Jesse Smith worshipped Harry Daugherty,' and I quote, 'he concealed from him what he was really doing in Washington.' "

When he finished, Daugherty tossed the editorial out on the corner of his desk for Mencken to read. "David Lawrence wrote that?" was all Mencken could say.

"He did. It will be published in a couple of days."

"To be brutally frank, Mr. Daugherty," Mencken replied, "Roxy Stinson, who was very close to her ex-husband, disputes Mr. Lawrence. She says you knew everything that Jesse did; that he never made a move without your approval. But you were setting him up to take the fall. Some folks are saying that it was a very convenient suicide for a lot of people."

"And Roxy was one of them," Daugherty replied. "She's free to say that Jesse Smith told her anything. Jesse can't dispute her now."

"And you're free to say Jesse made all the dirty deals behind your back," Mencken replied with that Mephistophelean glint in his eyes that usually appears when he's enjoying a good debate. "Jesse can't dispute you now, either." He paused for a moment, then added: "But maybe Roxy can."

"Just what do you mean by that, Mr. Mencken?"

"We've heard that Jesse had prepared a packet of papers documenting the fact that you authorized most of the deals he was involved in, that he rarely did anything without your approval. We think he had the papers with him the night he died. It's just possible that Miss Stinson has those papers now."

The meeting had been pretty grim and tense from the beginning. Now a frightening chill enveloped the atmosphere dominated by the feeling that anyone who got in Harry Daugherty's way would be justifiably afraid for his life. Leveling a cold stare at Mencken, then at me, he said: "Gentleman, that is another thing I wanted to talk with you about. Our investigation revealed that Roxy Stinson was out at the Wardman twice the night Smith died. In fact, she was registered with a Mr. A. L. Fink, a lawyer acquaintance of mine, as man and wife. Isn't that correct, Mr. Burns?"

As Burns nodded his head affirmatively, I was certain that both of them noticed my sickened reaction to what Daugherty had just said. Daugherty quickly turned the knife a little more: "Fink says that Roxy had a date with him to go over a possible stock deal. That she was going to come into some money soon. And he says that she was definitely in Smith's room for a time that night."

Abruptly, Burns cut into the conversation: "That's right. And to tell the truth, the circumstantial evidence really points to Miss Stinson as the killer."

Then, he looked at Daugherty as if seeking permission to continue. Before he could do so, Daugherty, speaking carefully, said: "We have more than the word of Fink and a bellboy to go on. Because Smith was feeling so despondent that night, I asked my secretary, Warren Martin, to spend the night with Jesse at our apartment in the Wardman. Before he discovered Jesse's body, he had heard him talking in his bedroom. Jesse had spent a lot of time on the phone that night and Warren figured that explained his hearing Jesse. Then he thought he heard a woman's voice."

Daugherty paused for a moment to make sure we were hearing him. "When he heard the shot, he didn't react immediately because he was down the hall from Jesse's room and, as he would later learn, the shot had been muffled in a pillow. But when he heard nothing more, he decided to investigate. As he approached Smith's room, down the hall at the apartment's door he could see someone leaving. Her back was to him, but she was a tall redhead. Martin thought it was Roxy Stinson, but he couldn't be sure. He didn't want to pursue her because he was concerned about Smith. He found Jesse dead—and if that woman was Roxy, she was the last person to see her ex-husband alive."

"I assume you asked Roxy about this," I said.

"Of course," replied Burns. "She admits being in the room that night but she insists that when she left Smith was still alive."

"And I personally think she's lying," said Daugherty. "But we have decided to keep it on the books as a suicide."

"Even if the right-handed Smith was shot through the left temple?" I asked.

"The coroner thinks it was an exit wound. However, if the murder talk continues and someone tries to reopen the case, Roxy would be the number one suspect. Not only did she have the opportunity, she inherited quite a bit of money from Jesse. And we have reason to believe she has a lot of cash stashed away that Jesse had given her to keep."

"Then, there's also the question of the Hope Diamond," Burns said. "If Smith actually had it in his possession at one time, he could have given it to her, or she could have taken it that night."

In an attempt to defend Roxy, I said: "You know Gaston Means was also out there that night. He's a professional crook. He could have killed Jesse, taken the diamond and the papers. With them, he could easily blackmail you into including him in any deal you were involved in."

"We know Means was there that night," Burns replied, "but he didn't kill Smith or come away with anything. If Means had found the diamond, the McLeans would have it back by now and Means would be a lot richer. And if he found the papers, we'd know it by now. But we're not sure about the papers. As you probably read in the press, some papers were burned in the metal trash basket that night, but there may have been more."

"And," Daugherty added, "I suggest you tell Roxy that if she has them, she would be a lot better off returning them to us. If they exist, they are, after all, confidential government documents, which means that, at the very least, she could be facing some time in prison."

I started to say that we did not know where Roxy was, but Mencken intervened: "We heard that the president dropped Jesse from the Alaska trip and said he had to return to Ohio, which, as you know, hurt Jesse very much. But I've read that you were also dropped from the Alaska trip. Doesn't that suggest that the president might think you could be involved in Justice Department corruption, too?"

"I was not dropped from the Alaska trip. The president knows I am not feeling well now and have a lot of work to do. I'm meeting him in San Francisco on his return trip. And I'm going with the president through the canal and around to New York where he's going to give his last big speech of this historic journey."

Before I could ask my question, Daugherty continued: "Getting back to Roxy, she may be in considerable danger. Who knows how many people might be implicated—or think they are—in Smith's alleged package of evidence: bootleggers, gangsters, liquor dealers, speakeasy owners. Any one of them could have panicked and hired a hit man to find them and destroy them at any cost and silence Roxy."

"Agreed," said Mencken. "And that list could include any one of your Ohio Group, or Secretary Fall, or even Mrs. Harding working through someone like Means who will work for anyone. If Smith really did have explosive material in his possession, almost anyone we've mentioned would have a good reason to want Smith silenced. It's quite possible, as you say, that one of these people could have hired someone from out of town to silence Smith? Then, assuming Smith had given her the papers, sent the hit man back to silence Roxy and get the papers?"

Daugherty froze for a moment, then replied: "Mr. Mencken, you have a lively imagination, but you get my point. Please pass it on to Miss Stinson."

"Mr. Daugherty," I said, "you seem to think we know where Roxy is. But as far as we're concerned, she's disappeared. I haven't seen her since Saturday morning."

Daugherty thought for a moment, then nodded to Burns indicating he wanted his chief investigator to reply. "That was also the last time we've seen her. We've been tailing her pretty continually since Smith's death. Saturday morning, she signalled a taxicab at Connecticut and Wyoming, just down from the Wardman, and headed into town. Two agents in a government car followed her to the Shoreham hotel at Fifteenth and H Streets. But by the time one of the agents got into the lobby she had disappeared. Apparently Miss Stinson went in the Fifteenth Street entrance of the Shoreham and then out the H Street entrance. Our agent never found her. Right now we consider Miss Stinson a missing person wanted by the government for questioning. We have alerted the D.C. and Ohio police to be on the lookout for her."

"But you're still not charging her with murder?" I asked.

"No," said the attorney general. "That case is closed. The evidence for suicide is compelling. It's quite possible, even probable, that in a misguided moment Jesse became overzealous in pressing the claims of the American Metal Company, primarily advocated by John King. He had as much legal right to do this as King, but in doing so he deceived me, which was morally wrong. You must remember that poor Jesse was a sick man. His mother died of diabetes, which he also suffered from. And one of his relatives said that Jesse once remarked that if he ever had diabetes, there would be a shorter way out for him. This insidious disease plays sad tricks with the human brain. It has caused loss of memory. It has produced homicidal impulses. It has made suicides. It has broken down the moral fiber of character."

Suddenly, the mood of fear that had permeated the room was smothered by a depressing silence, with all of us looking at one another, not knowing what to say. There was genuine sympathy for Smith. And we had just heard Jesse's boss do explicitly what Roxy said he was going to do—blame her ex-husband, for the crimes which Washington's subterranean rumor mill was attributing to the attorney general.

Finally, Mencken's voice cut through the gloom: "All right, sir, let's say that a few men like Smith and King have been guilty of a little corruption. Nothing new about that. So why this burgeoning Senate attack on you?"

"Mr. Mencken, the answer is easy: Politics and the communist conspiracy. This is no time to get off on my feelings about Soviet Russia except to say that I consider it the enemy of mankind. Soviet agents and our homegrown bolshevists have launched a new religion with which they have set out to conquer not only America but the world. And it so happens that I was the first representative of the present order whom Burton K. Wheeler, the communist leader in the Senate, picked for attack."

"Why did he pick you?" asked Mencken.

"Partly because of my closeness to the president, but mostly because, as attorney general, I have been unrelenting in my war against the bolshevists. But the Red Senatorial gas bags have been pouring poison fumes into the air until an honest man can scarcely breathe within the walls of the capitol. They are out to get me because of my attack against the Reds and supporting Prohibition."

"Prohibition!" said Mencken.

"Yes, the bolshevists are against Prohibition because they want to keep the working man drunk so they can control him. And the communist radicals have given notice on every future attorney general that if he dares enforce the laws of the United States against their organizations he does so under pain and penalty of being haled before the Senate of the United States. The moment we began to elect senators by direct vote, instead by the vote of state legislatures, we destroyed the foundations on which this branch of our government rested."

"Come, come, Mr. Daugherty," said Mencken. "Bad as it is, our federal legislature is a lot less imbecilic and corrupt than our state legislatures." The attorney general was shaking his head, but Mencken did not give him a chance to disagree.

"As for communism, you give its proponents far more credit than they deserve. Considering that Americans are so hospitable to the bizarre and the irrational, you would think they would embrace communism with joy, just as multitudes of them embraced free silver. But they will have none of it. Some say that the reason so few Americans succumb to the blather of communism is that they are too intelligent to believe in such nonsense.

"Others say communism is not taking hold here because Americans are too prosperous, hence, have capitalistic minds. Also nonsense. The Moscow clown show differs very little from the Washington clown show, except that some bolshevists actually be-

lieve in bolshevism. But Americans will resist carrying their democracy that far. And bolshevism will either convert itself into a
sickly imitation of capitalism or blow up with a bang. Probably
both."

"Interesting thesis, Mr. Mencken," the attorney general said, rising to his feet. "Should make a good column. I always thought you
were a liberal."

"Them's fighting words, General. May I call you General?"

"Only my close friends call me that." Then he looked at the large
clock on the wall: "Of course, everything I've said here is off the
record, for background use only. I'll have to wind up this meeting
now. I have an appointment with Mr. Hoover in about two
minutes—that's Edgar, not Herbert."

As we stood up, Mencken surprised me by saying: "Mr. Daugherty, we've heard that a bootlegger named George Remus, whom
you must know because he has been indicted by the Justice Department, is coming in town this week seeking an audience with
you. Is that right? Are you going to see him?"

"I don't know whether Remus is coming to town or not," Daugherty replied coldly, while walking us to the door. "I certainly won't
be seeing him if he does."

Mencken persisted: "Roxy told us about a curious incident that
occurred recently at the shack in Ohio you and Smith shared. She
said that recently a man showed up at the camp demanding to see
you. You were furious at Jesse because it was his job to keep people
like that away from you and you went back into town without seeing
the man. Later that day, Jesse Smith bought the gun that eventually
killed him. Could that man have been George Remus, demanding
that you make good on some promises Jesse Smith had made to
him?"

"Did Roxy say that?"

"No, but she agreed it was possible. That somebody came out
there demanding to see you."

"That man was there on Justice Department business which I
cannot discuss. And Roxy was right to this extent—I was mad at
Jesse for letting a Justice Department employee spoil my brief vacation, especially when I was not feeling well. But you see what I
mean about Roxy. Spreading misinformation about the government
is a dangerous business. What if Remus hears that she's blabbing

off about him trying to bribe a government official? She's asking for trouble. Now, gentlemen, if you will excuse me, I have some business to attend to."

As we left the office, sitting in a chair next to the door of the attorney general was a well-groomed young man in a light gray suit, carrying a manilla folder and visibly preoccupied with the problem which I presumed the material in the manilla folder was devoted to. I happen to have very good eyesight and I noticed that there was a name on the folder—"George Remus." The young man rose quickly and without even looking at us, disappeared into the office, a very model of the young government bureaucrat on the way up.

Out on the corner of 15th and H we just sort of stood around, with Mencken obviously wondering what we should do next, while I was totally preoccupied with Roxy. Not her safety, but like a jealous high school boy, disturbed by the fact that she had registered as man and wife with someone. She had every right to do whatever she damned well pleased, but it still bothered me.

Mencken brought me back to reality: "Cain, what the hell is going on with Roxy? I just can't figure her out. I'm beginning to wonder if she's being straight with us."

"So am I. But we're not going to know until we find her."

"We're not going to find her before they do. We'll just have to hope nothing happens to her. She's not much interested in me, but if she's hot for you, maybe she'll come back."

"I don't know where I stand, but if she still wants us to do that book, we'll probably hear from her. I have her telephone number in Ohio. She lives with her mother. I'm going to call her tomorrow."

"Good idea." Suddenly, Mencken had an idea and he started walking quickly in his mincing step south on 15th Street. "Come, Watson, the game may be afoot! Let's go down to the Washington Hotel and see if George Remus has arrived yet."

Part 4

CHAPTER TWENTY

At the Hotel Washington, we went immediately to the desk and inquired about Remus. "We have a Mr. Remus registered for to-night," the clerk said, "but he hasn't checked in yet."

Deciding to wait awhile hoping to catch him coming in, we were walking toward some seats in the corner of the lobby when Mencken said: "Cain, I'm going to buy some papers; maybe they've got the early edition of the *Evening Sun*. Why don't you call Union Station and see when the train from Ohio is due in. I think Remus' base of operation is Cincinnati."

"Good idea. Get me a paper too, the *Sun* if they have it."

When I rejoined Mencken in the lobby, he was sitting in a chair reading the *Washington Post*. The *Sun* was in a chair next to his. "The Ohio train is already in and unless Remus goes somewhere else first, he ought to be along fairly soon."

After scanning the headlines, I found myself just staring at the page thinking about Roxy. I simply could not get her off my mind. Finally I said to Mencken: "Have you got some change? I'm going to call Roxy's mother in Ohio." Soon I had her on the phone: "Mrs. Stinson, this is Jim Cain, a friend of Roxy's from Baltimore. I'm just calling to see if you know where she might be. I had a date with her Saturday morning in Washington, but she didn't show up and she has checked out of the Wardman Park where she was staying. I'm a little concerned that something might have happened to her."

"Oh, don't worry about Roxy. She often disappears like that without telling anyone where she's going. I have no idea where she is; I haven't heard from her since she left for Washington."

"Mrs. Stinson, have you ever heard her mention a lawyer by the name of A. L. Fink?"

"The name is familiar. She mentioned it once before she left. In fact, I think she was going to see him on this trip. But I don't know anything about him."

"Well, I'm sorry to have bothered you, Mrs. Stinson. If you do hear from her, please tell her to get in touch with me. I'm a little worried."

"Oh, I'm sure you'll hear from her soon, Mr. Cain. I've heard her mention your name. She's very fond of you."

When I returned to the lobby, Mencken was standing near the desk and talking to a stocky, heavy-set gentleman wearing a light summer suit, a Panama hat, white shoes, holding a raincoat draped over one arm and standing next to an expensive gladstone suitcase he appeared to have just set down on the floor beside him. I recognized him immediately as the irritated man we had met in Smith's K Street office—George Remus. Mencken had apparently made a connection with Remus, explaining who we were and what we were doing at Smith's office that day.

"Well, I'll be goddamned," Remus was saying. "I didn't think you two guys looked like cigar makers or bootleggers. But I was too mad then to give you much thought. So you edit *The Smart Set,* eh? My wife, Imogene, loves it. I'll have to tell her I met you."

"Always glad to hear about a happy subscriber," replied Mencken. Then, after introducing me as a journalist who will be writing for his new magazine, he asked Remus to join us in the lounge.

"Good idea. I need something to wake me up; I kept falling asleep on the train. It's a nice day, why don't we go up to the rooftop terrace. Let me check in here. Then I'll join you."

On the roof, we found a table and chairs back against the wall where we could talk with some degree of privacy. "This ought to be instructive," I said. "I wonder how much of what we know we should tell Remus?"

"My instincts are that, except for what the president and the attorney general told us in confidence or off the record, we should level with him. If he thinks we're leveling, he might be more inclined to level with us—at least as much as a man with a case being appealed to the Supreme Court can talk about his situation."

"Which probably won't be much. I read somewhere that he's a former criminal lawyer, which means he'll know exactly how far he can go. He's also a German-born immigrant, so you two ought to hit it off."

"We'll soon see. Here he comes now," and we both stood up to greet the strange looking little man approaching us. He had left his coat and luggage either in his room or at the desk, but was still wearing his hat. When we were all seated, I offered him a drink from my flask.

"No thanks," he said, "I've never had a drop of liquor in my life."

"Well, I won't hold that against you," Mencken said. "But that's hard to believe for someone from the country where they make the finest beer in the world."

"True. My father used to enjoy his stein, but I never could get to like it. I'll just have some coffee now."

"Where's your family from?" Mencken asked after we had given the waiter our order.

"Friedberg."

"I know where that is. Near Berlin. Nice town," Mencken said, taking out one of his Willies and also offering Remus a cigar.

"No thanks, I don't smoke, either."

They exchanged few more observations about the old country, and then Mencken said: "As I told you down in the lobby, we came over here from Baltimore disguised as cigar makers looking for a B permit, hoping that would provide an entry into the inner workings of the Harding administration for a book or an article we might write. And in no time at all we stumbled into one of the most incredible stories either of us has ever encountered."

"I don't doubt that," Remus said. "And you picked one of the best businesses—next to medical—for getting a B permit. I know one cigar maker in Philadelphia who, in eighteen years before Prohibition, had not used more than four hundred and eighty dollars worth of alcohol, but since then has been given enough alcohol B permits to treat the entire tobacco crop of the world."

"Incredible," Mencken said. "I was in the cigar business once— with my father—and I knew they didn't need much alcohol in that business. Anyway, since we met you at that K Street house a few days ago, we have talked to a number of people in one way or another involved with this administration—Jesse Smith; his ex-wife,

Roxy Stinson, Gaston B. Means; the president's close friend, Ned
McLean and his wife; the president himself and Attorney General
Daugherty."

"You talked to the attorney general?" Remus said, visibly picking
up interest. "What did he say about me?"

"Our conversation was off the record," Mencken replied. "But
we have heard from various sources that you are furious at Daugherty—and Jesse Smith—for taking protection money from you then
not delivering what they promised and not returning the money. In
the world of gangsters, of which you may be familiar, that is known
as a double-cross, for which someone usually pays."

"Now let's slow down here, Mr. Mencken. In the first place, I'm
a lawyer and you know I'm not going to sit here and say, 'Yeah I
paid Jesse Smith and Harry Daugherty thousands of dollars for protection from prosecution and a jail sentence and they double-crossed
me, so I had Jesse Smith bumped off.' Am I that stupid?"

"No," Mencken replied. "So what *are* you going to say?"

Before Remus could reply the waiter arrived with the coffee.
When he left, Remus said: "Okay, let's assume, for the sake of this
conversation, that I did pay Jesse Smith a lot of money expecting
him to keep me and my boys out of jail. Just assume it. In fact,
assume that I tried to corner the graft market, but, like some people
who tried to corner the wheat market only to find out that there was
too much wheat in the world, I found that there wasn't enough
money in the world to buy up all the public officials who demand
a share of the graft. But, frankly, it would be no big deal. In the
liquor business you can usually buy off just about anyone you need
to—judges, district attorneys, chiefs of police, cops on the beat,
legislators, whole legislatures in some states. You name 'em, I could
buy 'em."

"I don't doubt a word you're saying," said Mencken.

"Okay. Now Jesse Smith was absolutely my best contact with
the Justice Department. And I've had several meetings with him,
some right here in this hotel, to talk about how my seven distilleries
I once owned—but don't now—could get B permits to legally sell
my liquor. And if I were giving him money, he would obviously
be my best hope of getting the Supreme Court to act on my appeal—which is still before the court—and reverse the lower court

decision. So at that particular moment, no matter how mad I might be at Jesse Smith, wouldn't I be stupid to have him killed?"

"It would seem so," said Mencken.

"And, yes, I've heard the rumors. But that's dumb. Smith would be my only hope, because honestly, I've never had much luck at getting to see Daugherty. That was Smith's job, Harry's bumper, to keep guys like me away from 'the General,' as Smith called him. There was one time at the railroad station in Indianapolis that I ran into both of them and Smith immediately came over to me to keep me away from Daugherty. It was obvious what he was doing, but I didn't make any effort to see the attorney general because I didn't have any bone with him then."

"But you do now." Remus did not respond and then Mencken added: "But Gaston Means says . . ."

Remus interrupted quickly: "I don't want to hear anything Gaston Means says. He's the biggest liar and crook I've ever met. And I've met some in this business and defended some when I was a criminal lawyer."

"Well," Mencken replied, "it was Means who told us you were coming to town this week, that you were staying at this hotel and hoping to get a meeting with the attorney general. Pretty reliable information."

"Yes. I've been acting as my own lawyer—although not in representing me before the Supreme Court. And I admit I'm trying to get a meeting with the attorney general to talk about my case. And I'm not having much success. But let me tell you about Means. Not too long ago, he approached me and said he could fix my case before the Supreme Court—the Supreme Court mind you—for one-hundred and twenty-five thousand dollars. One quarter of the money, he said, would go to him, one quarter to William Burns, head of the department's investigative unit, one quarter to Daugherty, and one quarter to Chief Justice Taft. What a laugh!"

"You saw right through the offer, eh?" Mencken responded, "but you didn't do much better with all the money you gave Smith."

"I don't know what you're talking about."

"Our sources say you gave Smith thousands of dollars which you understood eventually went to Daugherty and although Smith didn't guarantee that you would not be prosecuted, he did say that you

would never be convicted and if you were convicted you would
never serve time. Now, if the Supreme Court does not uphold your
appeal, you are headed for Atlanta."

"I think I know your source for that one—Roxy Stinson. And
let me say right now, that broad can't be trusted any more than
Gaston Means. She's a loose cannon and she hates Harry Daugherty. I don't know why. Maybe because she's jealous of Daugherty
for taking her husband. Everybody assumes that Jesse and Daugherty are pretty close buddies, if you know what I mean."

"Yes they were," Mencken replied. "In fact, Roxy says that one
time when Jesse and Daugherty were alone at the cabin they share
out in Ohio, someone, uninvited, barged in and demanded to see
the attorney general. Daugherty was furious at being disturbed and
refused to see him, even though Jesse was convinced the caller was
very angry and had some serious business to talk about. Was that
intruder you?"

"I'm not saying one way or the other. But what if it was me,
what difference does it make? A guy under prosecution from the
Justice Department has every right to try to gain an audience with
the attorney general."

"According to Roxy, Jesse bought a gun that night," I said,
speaking up for the first time. "The one he was killed with."

"So what! Maybe he was going to use it on Daugherty. I don't
know why that woman doesn't keep her mouth shut."

"One reason," I replied, "is that she hates Daugherty because she
thinks Daugherty set Jesse up to take the fall, which is what's happening. Furthermore, we're quite concerned that something might
have happened to her. I had an appointment with her last Saturday
morning, but she didn't show up. In fact, she seems to have disappeared. Do you know anything about that?"

"I don't know which one of you is screwing her. Maybe both of
you. But I know I'm not. She probably went off with some guy she
met at the Wardman pool. Every hotshot I know in Ohio is after
her. And I don't blame them. The greatest body for a woman of
her age—any age—I've ever seen. And I know several lucky guys
who claim, at least, to have spent a weekend with her. I don't blame
you for being upset that she didn't show up for your date."

"It wasn't a date in that sense." I replied. "Miss Stinson has been
very helpful on our project and impressed us as being very intel-

ligent and, quite frankly, charming. And she's genuinely concerned that Daugherty won't be held accountable for the things Smith might be accused of. Her ex-husband, she says, would never have done anything that the attorney general didn't tell him to do. You must agree. I'm sure that an astute operator like yourself would not have given thousands of dollars to Jesse Smith who is not even on the Justice Department payroll, if you did not think the money was going to the attorney general—if we can go back to that assumption you mentioned a moment few moments ago."

Remus was silent for a few minutes. Then he picked up his coffee cup, which he had been ignoring, took a sip and made a face indicating that it was too cold. Looking around for the waiter, he said: "We're making a lot of assumptions here today and they are just that—assumptions. I *am* trying to get an appointment with the attorney general, but not to get my money back or accuse him of double-crossing me."

He stopped talking while the waiter took our orders for more coffee, then he continued. "What I'm here for is to make a case for myself on the grounds that I never hijacked any alcohol, never cut it with water, never sold any liquor that blinded anybody and have no apologies for selling good liquor since 1919. Even though I've made a lot of money in recent years, I still think the Volstead Act is one of the greatest criminal and legal abortions of all time. Had there been no Prohibition law to fill the coffers of a class that seeks and practices only its venality, I wouldn't have been on trial in the first place. No matter whether I'm found guilty or innocent, I'm going to devote the rest of my life to stifling the insult known as the National Prohibition Act."

"Well, let me know if I can help," Mencken said. "I've already done several newspaper columns agreeing with you and I will be doing many more before this obscene amendment is repealed."

"So why don't you do a column on this business of taking whiskey out of a government warehouse for medicinal purposes? That is a complete farce. While I was in law school at night, I also practiced pharmacy and I don't think there is one scruple of liquor ever prescribed by physicians that is used absolutely for medicinal purposes. That is the greatest comedy, the greatest perversion of justice that I have ever known in any civilized country in the world."

"Well," Mencken replied, "as Will Rogers says, 'Prohibition is better than no liquor at all.' I know you don't drink, Mr. Remus, but for certain things and for prevention, it's the best medicine I've ever taken—and I have, on occasion taken some in considerable quantities."

"Yes. It has some medical properties," said Remus. "Alcohol, which consists of C_2H_5OH, the chemical formula thereof, has stimulating properties, the scientists so hold. But if our forefathers who drafted the Constitution had ever thought that there would be an amendment to the Constitution setting forth that the only way you may have *spiritus fermenti* is along medicinal lines, why they would turn in their graves."

"May I quote you on that, Doctor Remus?" was all Mencken could say.

"Yeah. And I hope you write that next column soon, while the case is still before the Supreme Court."

"Mencken and I both agree with you about the Volstead Act," I said. "It is an abomination and probably unconstitutional. And as he indicated, we agree that it would not be very smart of you to kill Jesse Smith, your only contact with Harry Daugherty."

I paused long enough for that to sink in, then continued: "But Roxy Smith is another matter. She can't help you with Daugherty and she probably knows as much about your deals with Jess Smith—if there were any—as her ex-husband did. You have to admit that it would be to your advantage if she disappeared."

Remus nodded his agreement, but said, "It would also be to Harry Daugherty's advantage—and the president's."

Ignoring that remark, I said: "Frankly, I have become quite fond of her and I think it's fair to say that we're pretty good friends. Since her disappearance, I've heard that she might be in some danger—for obvious reasons. Can you assure me that she has not been harmed or that she is not in your possession?"

"No! I wish she were in my possession. And, in that regard, I want to apologize for my earlier remarks about her. I didn't intend any disrespect. But in Ohio she's known as a pretty high flyer—although she's very smart—which is why Harry Daugherty is scared of her. But she wouldn't be in any danger from me. Unless, of course, we were as close as you two seem to be and she double-crossed me. Then she'd be in trouble. But not now—with me having a case before the Supreme Court. Again, wouldn't it be stupid of

me to risk being suspected of witness tampering—including elimi-
nation? Incidentally, when the word gets out you've been friends
with Roxy Stinson, you're going to be getting congratulatory notes
from half the lotharios in Ohio."

"As one gentleman to another," I said, "I'm going to assume that
you've given me your word that Roxy is in no danger from you. I
feel relieved."

"You shouldn't be—until you get the same gentleman's pledge
from Harry Daugherty, which is highly unlikely."

"Daugherty said just a little while ago," I replied, "that they have
had her under surveillance for some time, but lost her. They now
consider her a missing person wanted for questioning by the government."

Shifting subjects, Mencken asked: "You don't drink, you've been
a practicing lawyer and you probably know the pharmacy business.
Whatever prompted you to get into the liquor business, anyway?"

"I practiced criminal law for eighteen years and after 1920, I
noticed that more and more of my clients were bootleggers. And I
was impressed by how easily these dumbbells were able to make
huge sums of money and avoid going to jail—primarily because
the Bureau of Prohibition—which soon became known as a school
for bootleggers—was so inefficient and corrupt and how it was possible to buy off officials at all levels. It was obvious that someone
with brains could make a real killing. So I bought—eventually—
seven distilleries and began buying B permits, mostly for medicinal
alcohol."

Mencken asked the obvious question: "So, what happened?"

"Eventually, despite what my contacts, from Jesse Smith on
down, could do, I ran into an untouchable agent by the name of
Franklin L. Dodge, Jr. I was indicted at a time when I was preparing
to buy twenty-three additional distilleries and warehouses for five
and a half million dollars."

Mencken and I just looked at each other, not exactly sure how
to respond, as Remus continued: "It's all spelled out in the court
records of the trial and you're probably going to hear more from
me when Senator Wheeler gets his Senate Hearings on the Attorney
General going. The trial verdict—guilty—is being appealed now,
which is why I'm not going to talk about this anymore."

Then, standing up, his coffee not finished and clearly indicating that this conversation was over, he added: "In fact, I've probably said too much already. But if I give you my word that I'm no threat to Roxy, I want your gentlemen's word that this conversation remains confidential, at least until after the Supreme Court decision and Senator Wheeler calls on me to testify. And Mencken, anything you write that will help convince the Supreme Court that the Volstead Act is unconstitutional will be much appreciated."

Abruptly turning and heading for the door, he said: "Thanks for the coffee."

We decided to linger on while we finished our coffee and I excused myself to retreat to the men's room. I was truly disturbed about Roxy. Was she actually the kind of woman Remus painted her to be? Was I blind to the real Roxy because she was so witty and charming and had shown me what it was like to be in bed with a truly passionate woman? I had never known anything like what I experienced with her Friday night and if she disappeared, or at least dropped out of my life for good, I was not sure I would ever experience it again. It was that powerful. But I had to admit, my judgment of her was very much influenced by the passion we had shared.

But not Mencken's. When I returned to the lounge, I found him scribbling some notes on a little pad he usually carried. "I've been using my little gray cells," he said, "and I think I know who killed Jesse Smith. It's elementary, my dear Cain."

That one caught me by surprise and all I could say was: "Well, I know who didn't kill him! Roxy Stinson is no murderer."

"Murderess is the proper word."

CHAPTER TWENTY-ONE

Not believing that he really meant Roxy was the killer, I said: "I presume you are correcting my misuse of the word 'murderer,' not that you really think she shot him?"

"No, by eliminating all other possibilities, I have decided she is the most plausible perpetrator, as they say at headquarters."

"Including Smith?"

"Yes."

"That surprises me. When we first heard he had been shot, you made a very good case for suicide. Remember?"

"I remember. But I've come to agree with that McLean woman. Smith is just too much of a coward to have killed himself— especially with a gun. Guns apparently terrified him. . . ."

"Even though he bought one?" I intervened again.

"He may have had suicide in mind when he bought it, but more likely it was self-protection—for him or Daugherty after that episode with Remus at the shack."

Mencken paused a moment while reaching for his wallet and signaling the waiter. Then he said: "Let's get outta here. We still have time to walk to the station. We can talk about it on the way. I can tell you don't agree with me. But then, you're much more deeply involved with her than I am."

"Yes I am, but that's not the reason I disagree with you," I replied rather frostily. For the first time since we started on this venture I was truly annoyed with Mencken.

He paid the check and we left the penthouse lounge but because there were people waiting at the elevator we could not continue our conversation until we were out on the street. As I walked along in silence, almost seeming to sulk, I had to admit, the more I thought about it, that circumstantial evidence pointing to Roxy was substantial. If Martin's statement was true, any logical and emotionally uninvolved person would have to concede that Roxy was the prime suspect.

We were walking east on F Street when suddenly I was aware that Mencken was speaking to me: "All right, Cain, I can sympathize with your feelings about Roxy, but let me ask you two questions: One, assuming Martin was right, that the woman he saw leaving the apartment was Roxy, how do you explain her actions that night? And, two, who *do* you think killed Jesse Smith?"

"Frankly, I can't explain her actions that night any more than you can. And ever since I talked to that bellboy who said she came back that night—and didn't tell us about it—I've been wondering what she was doing there and why she suddenly disappeared when I was about to talk to the bellboy. She knew he would tell me she was there. Ever since then, I've had this sinking feeling in me that she might have killed her ex-husband. But I have held off judgment, until there was a chance to talk to her again. Maybe she can explain it. Maybe not."

"Fair enough," said Mencken.

"As for who killed Jesse Smith, I haven't the foggiest idea. I'd like to believe that Means' hit man from out of town did it, except that you can't believe what Means says. Who was the hired killer working for? Remus? He says not. Daugherty? Burns? Fall? I don't think any of them would involve Means—even having him help the murderer get away."

"Murderess," said Mencken.

I ignored the remark. "If an out-of-town murderer did the job and what Martin says is true, he must have been the person Martin saw leaving the apartment—perhaps dressed like a woman. But you can't believe anything that Martin says either. As Daugherty's secretary, he's a card-carrying member of the Ohio Gang."

"True," said Mencken.

"Another possibility is that Smith committed suicide while Roxy was still there, though that seems highly unlikely. To tell the truth, I had been coming around more and more to suicide. But Mrs. McLean has a point. Then there's the question of the bullet hole in the left temple."

"We'll have to take the coroner's word on that. An exit wound."

"With Daugherty and Burns running the case," I replied, "how

can we take his word? The coroner's report came through Daugherty."

I waited a moment for Mencken's response, but when there was
none, I said: "So how did you come to your conclusion that it was
Roxy?"

"Simply by weighing all the evidence and stirring in my views
on women. I think Daugherty was genuinely too close to and fond
of Jesse to order his death. I ruled out Forbes and the implied connection between Smith's death and Cramer's because that suggests
a conspiracy in which some mastermind is directing a sophisticated
operation that fakes a suicide to set up a fall guy every time some
scandal is about to be exposed. Also, at his age, I don't see Secretary Fall killing Smith. Besides, if Ned McLean did lend him the
one hundred thousand dollars, we don't know for sure that Fall is
guilty of anything. And he certainly wouldn't have killed Smith or
had him killed to save Daugherty's neck. I think Means is capable
of murder, but I don't think he had any motive for killing Smith—
except, of course, he was a hired gun. But I'm positive Daugherty
or Burns wouldn't have entrusted Means with that kind of job.
Burns might have hired a hit man, but I don't know how anyone
would ever prove it with him handling the investigation."

"But if we can't prove Roxy did it either," I replied, "then I'd
pick Burns over her. Besides, I think she was really fond of Jesse.
And he was giving her lots of money. And what if she was serious
about going into politics? Being a murder suspect is not recommended."

By now we had reached 9th Street and walked south down to E.
As we passed the Gayety Burlesque theater, we stopped to study a
large poster announcing the coming attraction—a very curvacious
blonde dancer whose name I didn't recognize and don't remember.

"You know, Cain, Roxy has a better body than this young lady.
But not as good as one stripper I know, who shall remain nameless.
She does the circuit; I've seen her at the Gayety in Baltimore and
in New York and had drinks with her a couple of times at Sardi's.
One time, she asked me to find a better word than 'stripper' to
describe what she did. I hurled myself into the assignment, assuming that if I were successful, she would accord me special favors or
at least a complimentary ticket to one of her shows. I sent her a
few suggestions and one of them she just loved."

"What was it?"

"Ecdysiast!"

"Meaning?"

"The shedding of an outer layer of skin by a snake or insect. She uses it all the time now. I understand Gamaliel and Ned McLean like to sneak over to the Gayety every now and then and take in a burleycue."

"Really," I said, pointing to the poster we were staring at, "and how do you know that Roxy has a better figure than this young lady?"

Seeming a little startled at my question, Mencken paused and then said: "Did she tell you how our competition went?"

"No," I lied. "You know her ground rules. But she did declare me the winner."

"Oh?" Mencken replied. I hoped he was a little deflated. But if he was, he recovered quickly, Mencken style: "I can see your article in *True Romance* now: 'In Passion Contest, Murderess Picks Cain Over Baltimore Sage.' "

"Henry, I'm not sure I think that's so funny. You have no proof that Roxy killed her ex-husband."

"Certainly, I don't. But the way I see it, women decide the larger questions of life correctly and quickly, not because they are lucky guessers, not because they are divinely inspired, not because they practice a magic inherited from savagery, but simply and solely because they have sense. They see at a glance what most men could not see with searchlights and telescopes; they are at grips with the essentials of a problem before men have finished debating its mere externals. Apparently illogical, they are possessors of a rare and subtle super-logic. Apparently whimsical, they hang to the truth with a tenacity that carries them through every phase of its incessant, jelly-like shifting of form. Apparently unobservant and easily deceived, they see with bright and horrible eyes."

Mencken was silent for a moment while he formed a new paragraph in his head, then continued: "And what Roxy saw that night was that Jesse's time was up. She may have figured she was doing Jesse a favor and in some way paying Daugherty back at the same time, or—and I don't think either of us want to think this—she out-and-out figured Jesse was no longer any use to her and that she didn't want him to admit things before a Senate hearing that might force her to return some of the money he is reported to have given her. There is also the inheritance and the insurance policy."

I said nothing, but had to admit Mencken made a plausible case.

"Then, of course, there's the Hope Diamond. What woman could resist an opportunity to own a gem like that? It's apparently still missing and we can't ignore the possibility that Roxy took it. She has a helluva lot of motives for doing away with Jesse. Using feminine logic and intuition, it's hard not to come to the conclusion that Roxy killed her ex-husband. Remember, as they say at the police station, when they're investigating a murder, look for someone in the family first, especially the spouse."

"I can't argue with you, Henry, but my intuition says that she didn't do it, that she would not willingly kill her ex-husband."

"Well, getting into bed with someone does effect your feelings, maybe even your intuition."

"Which would suggest," I quickly replied, "that you never got Roxy into bed. Or maybe you just fell asleep."

"I won't go into details, but recently my on-again-off-again affair with Marion Bloom came to a climax. She's getting married this month and I was stunned when I heard the news. I felt betrayed. I think I really wanted to marry her, but have been guided by my own propaganda against marriage. I hope you will tell Roxy that I have been poised on the brink of disaster all spring and have hardly known how to act with such a charming woman."

"Charming murderess, you mean."

"Sooner or later, Cain, you're going to come around to agreeing with me."

We had started walking toward the station on E when I said: "Well, you shouldn't be making accusations, until we've had a chance to hear her version of what happened that night. But we may never see her again—even if she's still alive."

That thought seemed to produce a tacit agreement that we would drop the subject of Roxy for awhile. The rest of the conversation on our walk to the station and on the train back to Baltimore centered on what we had learned so far about corruption in the Harding administration and what our next move would be.

Mencken said it was important to have our book out by next summer, before the Republican Convention. The Ohio Gang would try to suppress the scandals as long as possible and if they could, with Harding's popularity and the booming economy, he would probably get the nomination. And with his incumbency and the weakness of his opponents, very likely win the election. William Gibbs McAdoo, President Wilson's son-in-law and former secretary of the Treasury, was the leading Democratic candidate, but Mencken did not give him much of a chance. In addition to his membership in the Satan Wilson clan, McAdoo was also a wet and had the support of the Ku Klux Klan, which he did not court but did not repudiate. Also, some of the *Sun* reporters said (and it was later confirmed) that McAdoo had been a legal advisor to Edward Doheny, whose Pan American Petroleum Company was given a lease for the government's Elk Hill (California) oil reserve. If it were proven that Fall took money from Doheny, then McAdoo's political career would be over.

Mencken was not sure we could count on the *Sun* printing a lot of the stuff we had because of the fear of libel. But, he said: "Maybe we can at least get enough of it into a book or *Mercury* article that would convince the Republicans to dump Harding and send the gang back to Ohio."

We also worked out an approach to jointly write a book. I would do the first draft, making a carbon, which I would pass along to Mencken and on which he would make his contribution and "maybe liven the language a little," as he not so delicately put it. I would do most of the legwork in Washington and he would keep his ear tuned in to the *Sun* newsroom for anything he could pick up about developments that the *Sun* was hesitant to publish.

"One thing we ought to do," I said, "is look a little more closely into the oil leases. That whole business of McLean lending Secretary Fall one hundred thousand dollars without any kind of receipt or cancelled checks to show seems awfully strange to me."

Mencken agreed: "Why don't we try to interview Secretary Fall? We ought to at least be able to say we tried to hear his side of the story. Maybe McLean has put in a good word. We should also call Teddy Roosevelt, Jr., who's trying to follow in his father's footsteps as assistant secretary of the navy. I think he'll talk to us after I tell him I saw his brother, Archie, in New York. Besides, Junior knows I'm a great fan of his father's, which I have said several times in the public print."

"Good idea. Remember that lawyer I talked to, Harry Slattery?

He thought Fall was a dangerous man; maybe even a suspect in Smith's death—although you apparently don't agree with him on that."

"No I don't," Mencken said. In the remaining walk to the station, I refreshed his memory on my interview with Slattery. But by the time we settled down in our club car seats on the train to Baltimore, we both seemed to have temporarily tired of Harding and his cronies. Mencken spent most of the journey reading a copy of *Time* he bought at the station newsstand and savoring one of his Willies, while I skimmed the *Evening Sun* and dozed off in my seat brooding about Roxy.

The next day, I did my best to locate Secretary Fall, only to learn that he was in Russia with Harry Sinclair. Mencken called midmorning to still say that he had no trouble setting up an interview for us with young Roosevelt the next day. That morning it was raining, so we took a taxi from the Washington Union Station to the corner of Pennsylvania Avenue and 17th Street, to the right of the White House, where The State War and Navy Building stood, wet and gloomily resplendent in its immense size and design. "Mark Twain called this pile of granite the 'ugliest building in America,' " Mencken said, "and who is going to argue with the author of the country's greatest novel?"

"You mean *Huckleberry Finn,* no doubt."

"No doubt. But there's been a helluva lot of history take place in this monstrosity, including the signing of the world's worst treaty in 1919."

"The Treaty of Versailles."

"Again, no doubt. Its imbecilities can only be corrected by Bismarckian remedies, blood and iron."

Inside, the building was just as ugly, with its black-and-white checkered marble floors, ornate carvings around the doors and big sweeping staircases. Roosevelt's office was decorated with the prescribed number of stuffed leather chairs, leather couch, two flags in front of a window that looked out on the west wing of the white building he hoped to occupy someday and several walls of photographs—mostly of Teddy Jr. pictured with famous politicians, especially his father.

The interview went rather quickly and it proved Mencken right. The assistant secretary was worried about becoming snarled in the

potential scandal. He admitted that he had approved transferring the
oil leases to the Interior Department, but the president had signed
the transfer and there was nothing illegal about any of it. And he
stressed that there was nothing unusual about Fall's doing it, the
former senator had been on record for years as favoring private oil
companies operating the government oil fields; in fact, it was Republican doctrine.

However, Roosevelt seemed quite concerned about the possibility that Fall had taken some money from the oil companies, which
he admitted "didn't look good," although, until proved otherwise,
he was going to believe that McLean was the source of Fall's new-
found wealth.

"Didn't the conservation lawyer, Harry Slattery, try to argue you
out of transferring the oil leases to Secretary Fall in the Interior
Department?" I asked. "Didn't he predict correctly that the oil companies would eventually be given the right to exploit the government oil reserves and didn't you usher him out of this office when
he did?"

"That's correct. But the real reason I became angry with Slattery
was because he was quite harsh on Albert Fall, my great and good
old friend, who rode with my father in Cuba. I cannot tolerate anything derogatory about a former Rough Rider and even if it is
proven that the secretary accepted money from the head of one of
the oil companies, he looks on it as a loan, not in any way connected
with the oil leases. And I'm absolutely sure that the president has
never benefitted personally from any money given by the oil companies to the Republican Party."

"Do you think these emerging scandals are going to prevent Harding from getting the nomination next year?" Mencken asked.

"The so-called 'scandals' are just rumors now. But if some of
them prove to be true—like what we are hearing about the Veterans'
Bureau—people will understand that Harding had nothing to do
with them, that it was just a case of a couple of rotten apples. . . ."

"His friends," Mencken interrupted.

". . . taking advantage of their positions of trust. Remember, right
now Warren Harding is one of the most popular presidents the country has ever had."

"We shall see," Mencken replied, looking at me as if to say that
this interview was going nowhere. Rising from his leather chair and

extending his hand to Roosevelt, Mencken said: "I can understand your loyalty to the men who were close to the late president. I always liked your father; in fact, I think the year I voted for him was the only time I ever felt any exhilaration about a presidential election."

Roosevelt also stood up and shook Mencken's hand. "I hope you reserve your judgment on Secretary Fall—and the president, for that matter—until all these rumors are put to rest. And just watch. Some heads are going to roll when the president comes back from Alaska."

The interview was over and when we were out in the eerie halls of this cavernous building and heading for the stairs, he said: "There's a man who is ready at the appropriate time to abandon ship with the rest of the rats, but right now he doesn't think the ship is even listing."

CHAPTER TWENTY-TWO

Back in Baltimore, Mencken said he had to put our project aside for now and devote a little more time to his column and the new magazine. He thought I should settle down to some serious writing, which was fine with me. For one thing, when—or if—I heard from Roxy, I wanted to be able to say that the book was coming along fine, hoping that would encourage her to keep in touch. Frankly, I was so anxious to see her again that I was ready to do anything to maintain some kind of relationship. Mary had not consented to a divorce yet, but I think I had convinced Roxy that we were really separated and would eventually be divorced. I phoned Roxy's mother in Ohio again to see if she had heard anything and she said she had not. But she still seemed unconcerned.

I was also anxious to make some sort of assessment as to whether we had enough material for a book, or just a magazine article, or maybe, after eliminating all the unverifiable rumors, anything at all. The only way to find out was to start putting words on paper, which has a way of riveting your thoughts.

So I started writing and after the first few days became very discouraged. For example, how do we treat Secretary Fall and Teapot Dome? If McLean really lent Fall the money or gave it to him, which he could easily afford, there is no story. It was simply a case of Secretary Fall carrying out a Republican campaign pledge.

And how do we deal with Smith's death? No matter what Mencken says, I refuse to even mention Roxy as a potential suspect. But we have to question the suicide story, considering all the rumors going around about murder. But who? With Burns, who will do anything Daugherty wants, in charge of the case, it may go down as one of the most suspicious deaths in political history with no one ever being charged and no one believing it was suicide.

And the Hope Diamond? I think we have more or less given our word to the McLeans that we will not reveal that it has been stolen; in fact, do we really know that it is missing? Who knows what the McLeans might be up to? Maybe the Great Dane ran off with it and the McLean woman faked a theft to keep from looking so stupid.

Finally, there is Gaston B. Means, one of our best sources. Almost everything we print emanating from him has to be accompanied with an asterisk which says, in effect: "The source for this story is an outrageous liar!"

It was beginning to look like it was going to be a long summer. Then my job was not made any easier by the arrival of the hot weather and the departure of the president's huge party on June 20, which virtually emptied Washington. Not only do politicians always flee the heat of the capital come summer, but no top Republican wanted to be seen as not being included in the president's entourage. The best thing all around was to just get out of town. And with them went some of my best sources. There were not too many journalists left either; and few of them wanted to talk with me about the Harding scandals. They were planning their own books.

But those of us left behind were able to follow the president through the newspapers and the radio. Harding's train had ten cars, the last one of which was named the *Superb*. And from its rear platform the president made a speech at virtually every stop. In Kansas, he toured the city in a motorcade and entertained at dinner in the Muehlbach Hotel, before giving a speech at Convention Hall that night. Reporters made much of the fact that Secretary Fall's wife, Emma, "an elderly woman, veiled and furtive," as one reporter put it, was a dinner guest and emerged from a meeting with the president looking scared and shaken.

The next day William Allen White rode in the president's car across Kansas to Hutchinson. Then he returned to Emporia where Mencken, thinking White might tell us something about the president's present state of mind and whether there was any significance in Harding's meeting with Emma Fall, finally reached him by phone.

The Kansas editor said that although he did not attend the dinner, the reporter Raymond Clapper, who did, told White that he saw Harding immediately after his meeting with Mrs. Fall and that he looked perturbed and obviously shaken as if she "had told Harding something that was a wallop on the jaw." Another curious thing: White said that the next day, while he was traveling with the presidential party, Harding mentioned three times that he wanted to have a long talk about something H. L. Mencken told him just before he left for Washington, "but we never had the chance." So what did you tell the president? White asked.

"I just told him that Attorney General Daugherty was a crook and he couldn't trust former Secretary Fall. That's all," Mencken replied with mock surprise.

White said that reminded him of what Nicholas Butler told him recently. Just before Harding left on his Alaska trip, the president called Butler in New York and asked him to come to Washington. He wanted to talk about something he could not mention over the phone. He spent most of a weekend in Washington visiting with the president and several times he seemed to be on the point of "unbosoming himself," as Butler put it, but he never did.

The presidential party proceeded on to Denver, where Harding told an audience of twelve thousand that the Eighteenth Amendment would never be repealed. In Salt Lake City, he spoke in the Mormon Tabernacle, where he said he wanted "America to have something of a spiritual ideal" and play her part in "helping to abolish war" by supporting an international court of justice. From there, they took an excursion down to Cedar City and then on to Zion National Park in a one hundred–automobile motorcade to dedicate a new thirty-five-mile section of Union Pacific track.

When they reached Tacoma, they embarked on the troop ship *Henderson* for a four-day trip to Alaska. Despite the slow erosion of the president's standing in Washington, he still remained immensely popular across the country and would be a formidable candidate next year if the emerging scandals could be stifled.

Mencken followed the president's party with more than passing interest because he was, by now, an official presidential candidate himself. A year ahead of the convention, the Seven Arts Club of Chicago had proposed a Mencken-Nathan ticket again, pledging twenty thousand dollars for the campaign. They argued that Mencken had liberated American letters and Nathan had liberated American drama—so why couldn't they do the same for American politics?

The following month, a host of young intellectuals in New York

added their support holding their own conventions in the form of
house parties where they argued about cabinet posts.

Mencken accepted the nomination in June at about the time
Harding left for Alaska. And in the spirit of the occasion he promised to:

- liquidate all homely women politicians and all members in
  good standing of the New York Stock Exchange;
- bring the kaiser to America and make him Governor of West
  Virginia;
- give the Liberty Bell to the Turks; and
- make a replica of the *Mayflower* at the Norfolk Navy Yard,
  load it with all the living descendants of the Pilgrim Fathers
  and use it as a target practice for the North Atlantic Fleet

Mencken had fun with his presidential candidacy, but I didn't
share this brief era of good feelings, primarily because of my concern about Roxy. I called her mother two or three times, but she
insisted she still had not heard from her and professed to be unconcerned. I finally decided she did know something about her daughter
but had been told, or elected on her own, not to say anything about
it to me.

I worked on the book, but put it aside every now and then to
interview a union or corporate official for my article on the labor
leader scheduled for the first issue of the new *American Mercury,*
to appear on the newsstands at the end of December.

I also went with Mencken to New York once in July. We each
brought our copy of the book manuscript with us and the four-hour
train trip provided an excellent opportunity to discuss the project.
We agreed that it would not be much of a book until we could turn
all the rumors into facts; you should never talk about rumors in a
book, in the interval between writing and publication the rumors
may turn out to be false, which opens you to libel or, if proven
correct and discussed in detail in the press, will be treated as "old
news" and greeted with a "so what?"

The long trip and the partying I did with Mencken and his friends
in New York and New Jersey helped cement my growing friendship
with him. He also took me by the offices of *The Smart Set* on 4th
Avenue, where I finally met Nathan, an extremely handsome, well-

dressed, debonair gentleman who presided over a couple of rooms that looked more like the headquarters of a college humor magazine than one of the most sophisticated publications in the country. The walls were adorned with new Mencken and Nathan campaign signs, temperance posters Edna Ferber had sent them from Paris and photographs of Czar Nicholas, Archbishop Manning and Lillian Russell (in tights). There was also a gilt chair guaranteed to collapse if a fat lady poet sat in it.

Mencken always stayed at the Algonquin Hotel, between 5th and 6th Avenues on 44th Street (where I also took a room), and usually brought with him a suitcase containing enough bottles of whiskey to last him while he was in New York. Before lunch or dinner, he would have drinks with his friends in his suite because he did not want to go into the lounge or dining room and get involved with the "hollow frauds," as he called the New York editors, writers, critics and cartoonists who were usually at the big round table.

He especially disliked one of their ringleaders, Alexander Woolcott, the drama critic for the *New York Herald* (and Willie Woolcott's brother). In her current bestselling novel, *The Black Oxen*, Gertrude Atherton said these "sophisticates" who gathered at the Algonquin roundtable "were so excitedly sure of their cleverness that for the moment they convinced others as well as themselves." But not Mencken. He thought most of them were "literati of the third, fourth and fifth rate."

Mencken's own clique consisted primarily of Alfred Knopf, his publisher and founder of the soon-to-be-launched *American Mercury,* the three-hundred-pound Levantine Jew, Phil Goodman, who dabbled in book publishing and Broadway show productions (his most successful one being the *Old Soak* which launched the career of Bill—W. C.—Fields), and Sinclair Lewis, a born mimic who was amusing when sober and hilarious when drunk.

Mencken invited me to go along one night with Lewis, Goodman and two other occasional drinking buddies, the biologist Raymond Pearl and anthropologist, George A. Dorsey. Mencken said that "in deference to the Constitution, I always make the journey blindfolded, led by one of the official guides." Actually, it is easy to find; any cop in the neighborhood would point the way for you. The Rathskeller had been discovered by Goodman, and Mencken labelled it the "most comfortable I have ever encountered on this earth. Its beers were perfect, its victuals cheap and nourishing, its chairs designed by osteological engineers specializing in the structure of the human pelvis and its waiters were experts at their science."

Well, great wits have to have someone to respond to them and I was picked that night. The conversation was literary and against almost every aspect of American life: Goodman looked down on the human race with humor and pity and Lewis thought he was the wittiest man he had ever known. Lewis himself was especially against small town boosters, and the ministry. When I got into the conversation it was usually to comment negatively on rubes, politicians and academics. And anything we three critics overlooked, Mencken, who was acknowledged to be "ag'in everything," especially any or all organized religions and their apostles and the Deep South, also known as the Bible Belt.

Lewis hardly noticed me until we arrived at the pub and he greeted Tommy, the owner, with a mock introduction in which he said we were all doctors who had formed a company called Doctors, Inc., to deal in Florida real estate. He introduced me as "Dr. Cain, our dentist. Of course, in a development as extensive as ours, we have to consider our prospect's teeth, and I'm glad to say that Dr. Cain has just about as advanced ideas in that line as any dentist you are likely to find."

Tommy looked skeptically at the author of *Babbitt* for a moment, then ripped out his uppers and handing them to Lewis said: "If he's all that good, maybe the doc'll be kind enough to say what these cost me."

"What do you think, Doctor?" Lewis said to me.

"This denture you didn't get for one cent less that fifteen hundred dollars," I replied quickly.

"Three thousand smackers they cost me," said Tommy with an air of a man who has just unmasked a fraud.

"Upper and lower?" I asked.

"Why sure," answered Tommy.

"Well, goddamnit, you just gave me the upper," and the looks Lewis and Mencken gave me confirmed that I was now a full-fledged member of Mencken's gang, which also included, on other nights, in addition to Knopf and Nathan, Ernest Boyd and Joseph Hergesheimer. The composition of this "roundtable," as with the

Algonquin group, was constantly rotating and occasionally a woman
was admitted—Hollywood writer Anita Loos.

The pub looked like a scene out of an old fairy tale. It was
patronized by a colony of midgets who lived in the neighborhood
and the giant steins they hoisted, fed by what Mencken claimed was
a direct pipeline to a brewery in Munich, made them look unusually
grotesque. As the evening wore on and we also emptied one big
stein after another, all of us sophisticated intellectuals from across
the Hudson looked the same.

When Mencken's business at *The Smart Set* was finished the next
day, we took the train back to Baltimore. Before settling down in
our seats (which he insisted should face toward Baltimore) to continue the discussion of our project, we obtained from the club car
a bottle of soda water and two cups, which we fortified with shots
of whiskey from my flask. Mencken also lit up one of his Willies
and the first swallow of whiskey and soda and first long inhalation
of cigar smoke seemed to inspire philosophical speculation.

"You know, Cain, behind us lies the greatest city in the modern
world, with more money than all Europe and more clowns and
harlots than all Asia, and yet it has no more charm than a circus lot
or a second-rate hotel. For despairing men like ourselves, escaping
from it to so ancient and solid a town as Baltimore is like coming
out of a football crowd into quiet communion with a fair one. For
more than twenty years I have resisted a constant temptation to
move to New York, and I resist it more easily today than I did when
it began. I am perhaps the most arduous commuter ever heard of,
even in that Babylon of commuters. Four hours! But when I leave
there I am comforted by the fact that behind me lies a place fit only
for the gross business of making money; ahead is a place made for
enjoying it."

With that, Mencken paused and held out his cup for a refill, still
puffing on his first Willie. I thought maybe he was ready to talk
about the book, but, instead he continued.

"I've mentioned this to you before, but what makes New York
so dreadful is mainly the fact that the vast majority of its people
have been forced to rid themselves of one of the oldest, most powerful of human instincts—the instinct to make a permanent home,
which enables you to follow the tradition of sound and comfortable
living, impossible in New York. A Baltimorean is not merely John

Doe, an isolated individual of *Homo sapiens,* exactly like every other John Doe. He is John Doe *of* a certain place—Baltimore, of a definite house in Baltimore. It is not by accident that all the peoples of Europe, very early in their history, distinguished their best men by adding *of* this or that place to their names."

"When I mention you in forthcoming books or articles, it will always be as 'H. L. Mencken of Baltimore.' "

"You won't have to. Everyone knows that there's only one place H. L. Mencken will ever be of. But how about yourself? Where shall I say you're of?"

"Good question. Right now, you'd have to say Chestertown. I've only lived in Baltimore about three years; and I'm about to move to Annapolis. And if I ever go back into journalism, I'll probably end up in New York. That's where the jobs are. Right now I kinda like the place. It's exciting."

"A nice place to visit, as they say," Mencken responded. "Let's talk again after you've lived there for awhile."

The rest of the trip was devoted to our book, with the discussion ending on the first discordant note of our otherwise pleasant excursion to Babylon—disagreement, again, over Mencken's theory that Roxy was the most logical suspect in the "murder" of Jesse Smith.

I knew that there was something unusual and significant about her disappearance. But with the head of the Bureau of Investigation—whose only interest in her was to get back Jesse Smith's papers he assumed she had—in charge of the case, there was not a damned thing I could do about it. The Wardman Park bellboy had convinced me that the Washington police didn't trust Burns any more than we did. So who else was there to turn to?

Back in Baltimore, I phoned Roxy's mother again, but no one answered the telephone, despite repeated calls. Maybe she was travelling; perhaps even meeting Roxy somewhere. That thought cheered me somewhat.

July dragged on, getting hotter and duller by the day. Mencken was very busy and didn't seem to have much time for me or the project. Most people remaining in Washington appeared dedicated to a moratorium on Harding administration gossip. Like Baltimore, it was too damned hot, even to spread rumors. Every time I went there to have lunch with a reporter or interview a government official, it was apparent why some foreign governments considered our capital a hardship post and gave their diplomatic corps extra pay.

Then, it suddenly became apparent why life in Washington is so uncertain and politics such an unpredictable game. People stopped talking about the weather and started reading the newspapers and gossiping again about the president. He had become alarmingly sick returning from his Alaska trip. There were reports that several members of his entourage had eaten some giant crabs. Many became ill, including Mrs. Herbert Hoover, George Christian and the president. Harding recovered temporarily, but then became sick again, some people calling it ptomaine poisoning and others a heart condition.

I called Mencken at the *Sun* to see what they had heard there. He confirmed that the president was quite ill and confined to room 8064 of San Francisco's Palace Hotel, his condition grave. I decided to go over to the *Sun* building to meet with Mencken and follow the news from California on the Associated Press wire. At 7:32 P.M., August 2, San Francisco time, President Harding died.

CHAPTER TWENTY-THREE

The suddenness with which my life was turned upside down by the death of Harding made me realize how glad I was not to have chosen a career in politics. One day I was totally preoccupied with a project that revolved almost exclusively around what we could learn about the emerging scandals that threatened the president of the United States. The next day, the president was gone and suddenly the rumored corruption in his administration seemed little more than the misdeeds of a handful of corrupt politicians trying to line their own pockets while they had the opportunity. So, what else is new?

But one thing in this moment of national turmoil was certain: No one thought that Calvin Coolidge, who was on vacation at his parent's farmhouse in Plymouth, Massachusetts, and sworn in as president late that night by his father, reading the oath of office with the help of a kerosene light, had anything whatsoever to do with the rumored corruption in the Harding administration. At the same time, although the martyred and probably betrayed President Harding [whose body was borne slowly across the country while thousands of Americans mourned his death alongside the train tracks] may have picked some rotten apples to serve in his administration, in the wake of this tragedy, no one had an unkind word for him.

No one, of course, but H. L. Mencken of Baltimore. In the period immediately after Harding's death, I saw a lot of Mencken, at lunch, at the *Sun* and occasionally at his house on Hollins Street. He was very busy, developing ideas and calling potential writers for the new magazine, trying to ease his way out of *The Smart Set,* which no longer interested him, and writing his column. We had a lot to discuss in assessing the impact on our project of Harding's death. I dropped by his house to bring him some carbons and he was dressed in his undershirt and pajama bottoms and typing furiously. Baltimore can get just as hot as Washington and it was miserable in his upstairs office. I set my envelope on a little table and was about to leave when he said: "Wait a minute, Cain. I want you to read this, then we can palaver."

The time had come, he said, to give his own assessment of Harding and he apparently wanted my reaction. He handed me a few pages from on his desk, indicating I should start reading the piece before he had finished. It began:

> The funeral orgies over the most amiable of presidents being over at last and the members of his entourage having vanished into the folk whence they came, it becomes possible, perhaps, to consider his career realistically without violating decorum, and even to speculate discretely upon the view that posterity will take of him. Certainly no man ever passed into the eternal vacuum to the tune of more astonishing rhetoric. The Associated Press dispatches, printed in the *Sun* papers during the ghastly progress of the funeral train, were not merely eloquent, they were downright maudlin. They gurgled; they snuffled; they moaned. Who wrote them I don't know: If I did, I'd be glad to print his name and pay obeisance to him as a supreme master of bilge. A very gifted journalist, as journalists go in the Republic.

Pretty strong lead at a time of national mourning. But that was just the beginning. Mencken said he could see no evidence for the AP writer's

> doctrine that Mr. Harding was a great and consecrated man, loved this side of idolatry by the plain people and destined to go down into history in a purple halo . . .
>
> He leaves behind [*Mencken wrote*] a career so bare of achievement and so bare of intelligible effort, that the historians will have to labor, indeed, to make him more than a name. What did he accomplish in his life? He became president. What else? I can think of absolutely nothing, save the one thing that he gave current English, a new barbarism.

Before I had finished the first sheets he had handed me, he stopped typing, pulled the last sheet out of his typewriter with a flourish, said "Good-bye Gamaliel" to no one in particular, handed me the last portion of his piece and disappeared into the bathroom to wash his hands as I finished reading his critique.

He quickly summarized the president's lack of accomplishments in the Senate and the White House and said that his devotees had to fall

> back upon lavish praise of his honesty, as if honesty were rare in Presidents.

Conceding that Harding might have been personally honest, Mencken challenged his political honesty—citing the president's announcement that he would make his chief campaign plank for reelection the preservation of the Eighteenth Amendment.

> Is it maintained by anyone that Mr. Harding, personally, was a prohibitionist? If so, then it is maintained only by the sort of half-wits who still believe that the kaiser . . . planned to conquer the United States.

As I was reading, Mencken came back in the room shaved and fully dressed for the office, except for his coat. Seeing me still concentrated on his article, he opened my package and started reading some of the carbons of my work in progress. Curiously, I remember this moment quite well because, for some reason, I started a fit of coughing, which I had not done for a week or so.

After a few minutes, I continued reading Mencken's article. He took issue with the AP journalist's contention that the president had been done to death by overwork, a martyr to the complex and cruel demands of his high office. This was not true, Mencken said. Harding died while on an arduous and summer-long campaign trip for reelection. But he concluded, charitably I thought, that historians would eventually rank Harding with the reigns of Millard Fillmore, Franklin Pierce and Benjamin Harrison,

> a transition between the old traditions that blew up in 1917, and the new ways that no one of us, today, knows the direction of.

This last remark, I thought, was exceptionally perceptive. The country was, in fact, experiencing a post-war intellectual, social and economic turmoil without any idea of where it was going. But even with the moderated conclusion, I thought his piece was too strong and too soon for a mainstream newspaper and I told him so. "Maybe in one of the magazines," I said. "In fact, why not *The Smart Set?*"

Mencken seemed to agree with me about the *Sun* and the piece did not appear.

He had only read a couple of the pages I had brought him when I finished his piece and now he threw my efforts on his desk and said: "Good stuff, Cain, but I can't put much time on it now. I have to go up to New York for a few days on *Smart Set* business and to talk with Knopf about the *Mercury*. I'm running into trouble on the new magazine. A lot of potential writers are getting nervous about writing for me right now. I think they're afraid I'm going to suggest in the first issue that someone ought to assassinate Cal. God! Dumb as Coolidge is, he's better than Harding. And I think he'll eventually send Harding's gang back to Ohio, although I must say he seems to be resisting getting rid of Daugherty. And he's still defending Secretary Fall.

"But by the time we can get a book out, most of the people involved in the scandal rumors will be gone with Harding—not dead, but on their way to jail or impeachment."

"Sound's like you're having second thoughts."

"You know, Cain, I am. Having to do *The Smart Set* while developing the new magazine, writing my column and my daily correspondence [Mencken says that he sometimes writes sixty letters a day] is really putting the pressure on me.

"Then there's my book on democracy," he added. "I started it long before we decided to see what we could find out about the Harding administration, which doesn't exist anymore. And can you imagine anything duller than a book about the Coolidge administration? Remember, we thought our book on Harding would have an impact on the 1924 Republican presidential race. I doubt now if the Harding gang's corruption—even if proven true—will have any effect on the election next year. I don't have an advance on the democracy book—you know I don't believe in 'em—but I have promised it to Knopf and he's now asking me about it."

Mencken paused to put on his coat and then said: "Tell you what.

Why don't you put Harding aside for awhile and get to work on your labor piece for the *Mercury*. With that and Boyd's article on the Village intellectuals, that'll give me two solid pieces for sure in the first issue. As for Harding's gang, I know I can get a couple of columns out of them. You can keep digging, if you want, after you finish your *Mercury* piece and maybe do something on Harding for me too. We can wait until the last minute—sometime in late November or early December—to see how the rumors play out. Maybe we'll learn more about Jesse Smith's death—and the diamond-almost-as-big-as-the-Ritz, which has gotten entangled in our tale."

"Don't you think we have any obligation to Roxy? She gave us a lot of help getting our investigation underway."

"Look. I know how you feel, but I don't think we owe Roxy a damn thing—at least until we hear from her again. We don't know what the hell she's up to. She could turn out to be just as devious as Means—and being a woman, she's a helluva lot smarter. When Roxy surfaces, listen to her story and then we'll talk. And, incidentally, I think when you find Roxy you're going to learn what happened to the diamond. Maybe she's already returned it to the McLeans."

"So you think she copped the diamond as well as knocked off her ex-husband?"

"Apparently Smith had it when he died, and Roxy might have figured it was rightfully hers. She hadn't seen Jesse's will yet, so she could plausibly think, then, that she was Smith's sole heiress. And I have another hunch. You ought to stay near your phone in the next week or so."

"Why do you say that? You think she's going to call me?"

"If she's still alive. There's a fifty-fifty chance that she's either keeping out of sight or being forcefully held captive because of what she knows, through Smith, about Daugherty's corruption—and maybe others. But now that Harding's dead, I don't think Roxy's life is in danger."

"I'm not sure I follow you on that."

"Okay. There's never been any evidence whatsoever that Daugherty has been skimming money off their operation for himself. Maybe Smith, but not the general. He appears to have been motivated solely by a desire to protect and help the president, primarily by paying off campaign debts, Harding's girlfriends and especially

Nan Britton. But Daugherty has personally never been a high-liver."

"Well, Roxy said that Smith and Daugherty's expenses at the Wardman ran to fifty thousand dollars a year. That ain't peanuts."

"It is compared to the money they must have taken in. And Daughertry could have figured that was just part of doing business for the Republican National Committee. Roxy was not a direct threat to him. Whatever she could say Jesse told her would be just hearsay and could not convict Daugherty. But if Roxy had linked Smith's and Daugherty's corruption to Harding, that would be different. Being hearsay, it probably would not have impeached the president. But it would have forced his resignation or, at the very least, denied him the nomination next year."

Mencken stood up abruptly, looked at his big pocket watch. "Roxy is no longer a threat to Daugherty because sooner or late he's going to have to resign—or Coolidge will be forced to fire him. Daugherty knows this. But mark my words, Roxy's hearsay testimony will never send Daugherty to jail. In fact, they may have already blackmailed Roxy into silence by threatening to charge her with Smith's murder."

Mencken's sudden revelation of his conclusions took me by surprise. Even if he had given me a chance to reply, I frankly am not sure what I would have said. I had to concede that he had logic on his side, not only about Roxy but also Daugherty. His decision to abandon, at least temporarily, our project had also caught me off balance.

I hoped that Roxy would soon appear and explain everything. But I was very worried, and her mother was beginning to sound as worried as I was. However, I finally decided that the most important thing in my life right now was my friendship and professional relationship with Mencken. And if he wanted me to put the Harding project aside and get to work on my article for the *Mercury,* that is what I would do. My time was running out. I would soon have to be apartment hunting in Annapolis.

Naturally, I followed the Harding story closely in the newspapers and on the radio. And I could tell Mencken was doing the same. A couple of days after our meeting, he called me to report on another conversation he had with William Allen White in Kansas. White said Commerce Secretary Hoover, who had joined the party in Tacoma, told him that Harding had asked him what he should do if he knew a scandal was brewing in his administration. He said the president never told him what it was, but that Hoover said, by all means, reveal it and dismiss and punish the guilty party or parties. "And just before he died," Mencken continued, "Daugherty had a brief meeting with the president but no one knows what was discussed.

"That same evening, Mrs. Harding was reading the president an article about him in the *Saturday Evening Post*. It was by Samuel Blythe and entitled 'A Calm Man.' At one point, Harding said, 'That's good,' then slumped over and died. Can you imagine! Reading the *Saturday Evening Post* on your deathbed? No wonder he croaked."

The papers also reported that Evalyn Walsh McLean had come rushing back from Maine, where she was on vacation, to be with her friend, Mrs. Harding—which reminded me that I had planned to call Mrs. McLean and inquire about the Hope Diamond. When I finally reached her on the phone, she said the diamond was still missing but that Gaston Means insists that he will retrieve it.

I was aware that Ned McLean knew Roxy quite well, so I also asked Mrs. McLean if she or her husband knew the whereabouts of Miss Stinson right now, that "she appears to have disappeared."

She had no idea where Roxy was and did not consider her disappearance as particularly significant. "Roxy's been known to run off with some man to places like the Caribbean or Maine, depending on the weather," she said—which annoyed me. I have been thinking about trying to persuade Roxy to go off with me someplace for a week. And, assuming that she still liked me, I knew she would not hesitate for a moment to ignore propriety and take off. I liked that about her.

I also asked Mrs. McLean how Mrs. Harding was holding up. "After the initial shock, she's been doing just fine. She told me that she finally decided his death was 'for the best.' She didn't want Warren to have to go back to the strain of that job. I guess you've read in the newspapers that she refused an autopsy because she didn't want to damage her Warren's body. She also wouldn't permit a death mask to be made. And, of course, she's been burning a lot of his papers: 'We must be loyal to Warren,' is the way she puts it. 'I'm burning these things because some of it would be misconstrued and harm his memory.'

"Then there are the rumors," she added. "I guess you've heard them?"

"No," I replied. Actually, I was aware of the wild speculation that had started immediately after Harding's death but I let her recount what she had heard. The rumors ran in two main currents: First, that his death was "strange" and "mysterious," that the doctors were incompetent and didn't seem to know exactly what caused it, and there was a certain amount of "covering up" going on. Even the *Baltimore Sun* said the final bulletins pointed to an "obscure and puzzling malady." A cerebral hemorrhage was the original diagnosis, but some doctors thought the heart attack was caused by a cardiac arrest. Some thought he died of a "sudden epileptic seizure," others that it was the ptomaine poisoning, others that it was a coronary occlusion, others apoplexy, and still others, pneumonia.

But one doctor, Ray Lyman Wilbur, who was present at Harding's death, said that, "We shall never know exactly the immediate cause of President Harding's death, since every effort that was made to secure an autopsy met with complete and final refusal."

The confusion over what actually killed the president naturally led to the second current of rumors—that the president was poisoned. One scenario supposed a conspiracy involving a love affair between the Harding's personal physician, Doc Sawyer, and Mrs. Harding, another had Mrs. Harding poisoning her husband because Daugherty told her that the president faced an impeachment because of the corruption in his administration, another that she poisoned him out of jealousy over one or more of his lovers, or that she killed him to spare him the agony—due to his health and the scandals—of his final years in office. Take your choice.

I called Means, but he said he had no idea where Roxy was although he had been looking for her continually. Before hanging up, Means also said that the reason he was still looking for her was not just for the papers Smith was presumed to have, but for the diamond.

Then, the next day, I received a letter in the mail—and Mencken was right. My name and address were typed on a small hotel-sized envelope. But the return information on the back flap, which I presumed to be the name and address of a hotel, was blacked out with ink. I quickly opened it and drew out a sheet of paper, which had heavy ink marks at the top of the page, which indicated something else had been blacked out: It began:

Dear Jamie,

I miss you so much. And I want to see you again as soon as possible. I have a couple of things for you that can't be sent through the mail. I know I have a lot of explaining to do and I had planned to write you a long letter, which you could also use to grade my writing ability. Remember? But that will have to wait because some of the things I have to tell you, I did not want to send through the mail either, even to someone I trust.

So here's the plan: After noon on August 14, I will be in room 502 at the Hotel Rennert in Baltimore. I have already made reservations. I hope you can come to the Rennert. Don't tell anyone you are meeting me and don't bring Henry. We can call him later after we have had a chance to be alone for awhile. Knock three times quickly, then three times again. I will know it is you. If you can't come that day, leave a message for me at the desk suggesting another date. My reservation is under the name "Carol Robinson."

Wasn't that terrible about the president? I cried for two days.

Love,

(it was signed "Roxy")

CHAPTER TWENTY-FOUR

I arrived at the Rennert on the 14th shortly after noon. The ornate hotel, on Saratoga Street at Liberty, was one of Baltimore's favorite meeting places for politicians and socialites. And its high-ceilinged restaurant, according to Mencken, was the "undisputed capital of gastronomy in the terrapin and oyster country." My heart was pounding like a high school boy's on his first date.

I went straight to the elevator and up to the fifth floor, where I found 502 and knocked quickly, three times, then again. I would absolutely *not* make love to her until she had a chance to explain her abrupt disappearance, which still offended me. Furthermore, if Mencken was right, did I really want to be a "murderess's lover?" I had alerted him that I might have something important to report that afternoon. He had said he was having lunch at Marconi's with Sara Haardt, who was in town from Montgomery. "She's promised to bring me some genuine corn liquor, but I'll be back at the *Sun* in the afternoon."

I am not sure what—or maybe even who—I expected to see on the other side of the door, but I can assure you I was not prepared for what it was about to reveal. The door to 502 opened rather quickly and before me stood a tall, middle-aged woman with long, graying hair wrapped in a bun. But she wore only a robe, which was open, permitting me to see large, firm breasts that were part of a well-rounded and definitely not middle-aged figure, at least in appearance. And I noted that the little triangle of hair that my eyes were immediately drawn to was red. Just for a moment I thought to myself: "Could this be Roxy's mother?"

She dropped her robe to the floor (fully revealing a body that was gloriously familiar), stepped forward, put her left arm over my right shoulder to pull me to her and her right hand down between

my legs: "Oh Jamie," she breathed more than spoke, "I've missed
you so much."

Then she kissed me, opening wide and inviting my tongue to
explore a mouth I recognized at once. I knew it was Roxy and my
firm resolve to abstain from making love melted in seconds.

Here was a lady who appeared not to have made love for some
time and I know that I had not been in bed with a woman since
that night we spent together at the Wardman. It was passion meets
passion.

I undressed while she let her long hair down and we were in
bed. I cannot honestly say how long we kissed, clutched and ex-
plored each other, but I do know that we shared a climax to the
occasion and I am certain that I have never been so enraptured at
high noon at any time in my life.

She excused herself afterwards and by the time she came out of
the bathroom, I had come to my senses: "We've got to talk," I said.

"Shouldn't we ask Henry to join us? I think he'll want to hear
what I have to say. There's lots of it and I don't want to have to
go over it all again."

"He won't be back at his office until this afternoon," I said,
looking at my wristwatch, the only thing I was wearing. "I'll call
him then."

"All right," she replied, closing and belting her robe. "Put some
clothes on or I won't be able to concentrate."

While I put on my shorts, shirt and pants, she sat on the bed,
with both pillows behind her. Then, I pulled up a chair and sat near
the bed.

"First," she said, "let's start with how I met you at the door. I
wasn't naked just to seduce you, but the clothes I have been wearing
make me look dowdy and old. That's all part of my disguise. I have
been talking to Senator Burton Wheeler—a wonderful man—who
is going to be on the committee looking into the impeachment of
Harry Daugherty. He thought it was a good idea if I went out of
sight until the hearings start and he's been helping me keep a low
profile. I also got a job, which I'll tell you about later, that calls for
me to dress and look like a nanny, which is a wonderful way for
me to change identity."

"Well, until you dropped your robe, I hardly recognized you.

Then I knew it couldn't be anyone else." She leaned forward enough
to rub my leg and kiss me on the cheek. "You said in your letter
that you had a couple of things for me that you could not send
through the mail. What are they?"

"One of them, I just gave you and I'm going to give it to you
again after you've heard my story—if you'll still let me. And here's
the other."

She rose quickly from the bed, walked over to the table where
she had put her large pocketbook and took out a parcel. It was an
object wrapped in a small hand-towel. Climbing back into bed, she
put the wrapped object on the sheet in front of her, but did not
unwrap the hand-towel. I could see that it was monogrammed with
the red letters "W. P."

"Who's your friend, W. P., with the monogrammed bathroom
hand-towels?" I asked.

"Why, you're jealous. This is not from a bathroom I share with
an intimate friend; I stole it from a hotel called the Wardman Park.
Remember?"

"Did you also steal what you have wrapped in it?"

"No. Jesse gave it to me. You can probably guess what it is,"
she said as she began slowly and theatrically to unwrap the object,
being careful not come in contact with it. "It's not as big as the
Ritz—or the Wardman. You can look, but don't touch."

What she finally laid out on the bed, but still resting on the hand-
towel, almost as if she did not want the stone to touch the bedspread,
was an incredibly blue, captivating gem. It was about the size of
four or five fifty-cent pieces glued together, but with their edges
rounded. It was not mounted in a circle of small diamonds, as was
the stone we saw Mrs. McLean wearing at Friendship. Nor was it
attached to a necklace. It was just a big, mesmerizing, blue jewel
sitting there on the bed with "millions of sardonic winks," as a
French ambassador to the U.S. put it, looking as eerily unearthly as
it did the night it was stolen from a Hindu totem pole three hundred
years ago. Or, at least, that's the way I saw it.

Transfixed, I instinctively reached over to pick it up. But Roxy
quickly pushed my hand away: "Don't touch, unless you're absolutely certain there is no validity to all the voodoo tales associated
with this thing. You know it's the Hope Diamond. I don't believe

in any of that curse business and I don't think you do either, but I haven't touched it since that night Jesse gave it to me. Jesse said he handled it several times before he realized what it was. And that's why he said 'they passed the curse of the blue diamond on to me.'"

"So Jesse gave it to you that night he died?"

"Yes. I went back to the Wardman that night. Jesse had phoned me in a terrible state and begged me to come out to his apartment again. I said I was tired but would think about it. I hung up and waited for a few minutes expecting you to call one more time. Frankly, I was hoping you would and I was ready to let you come back."

As she was telling me this she carefully rewrapped the diamond in the hand-towel, which she set on the table beside the bed.

"But you didn't call and then I got a really strange call from someone else who also asked me to come out to the Wardman. I'll tell you about that in a minute. So with two reasons to go back, I cut off my phone (because I didn't want you to know I went out) and returned to the Wardman."

"Where did Jesse get the diamond?"

"He said he got it from Gaston, who didn't tell him it was the Hope; just that it was an 'unusual' diamond that Jesse could have for a good price because it was 'hot.' He let Jesse keep it for awhile to see how he liked it.

"Jesse was terribly upset when he said: 'I didn't figure out at first how it could be the Hope, but then remebering what we heard about it being stolen, I got to thinking it might be her big diamond. And you know what? I think Gaston gave it to me hoping I'd believe it and feel the curse would be passed on to me. He was working for Burns, you know, and I think it was Burns' idea.'"

"I can't believe that Burns—or even Means—really thought the Hope's curse would get rid of Jesse permanently."

"I'm not so sure," Roxy replied. "They're pretty smart. But in lots of ways they're kinda dumb, superstitious, that sorta thing. Gaston less so. But I think he would have gone along with the idea because he saw a way to make some money with a diamond heist which would never be investigated—for the same reason Jesse's death was never really investigated. Because Burns and Daugherty could quash it."

"Incredible!" was all I could say. It didn't make sense.

"Well, that's what Jesse figured. He said he planned to give it back to the McLeans the next day in Leesburg, but he had decided not to go. He wanted me to return it, making sure they understood that he didn't steal it."

"Sounds like he really was thinking about suicide."

Roxy nodded, as she continued. "Jesse said: 'Roxy, I know you don't believe in this voodoo stuff, but as a favor to me, please don't touch it. Evalyn says that she never lets any of her friends touch it; that she thinks there may be something to the curse. I've touched it and look at all the trouble I'm in.'

"By this time, I was crying like a baby, but then I realized this was no time for me to lose control."

"Let's go into that in a minute. I'd like to hear about this lawyer A. L. Fink, whom Burns and Daugherty say you saw that night at the Wardman; in fact, you were registered as man and wife."

"What? That bastard! I was never in his room and had no idea he registered me. But it helps explain what happened. Remember, I got another call that night I kicked you outta my room? It was from Fink, a lawyer I had met once through Jesse. He said he had heard that Jesse and I did some speculating in the market—which was true enough. In fact, I often went along with Jesse to New York when he bought some stock for the president with money the president or Harry gave him. But that's another story."

Roxy was shifting around trying to get comfortable on the bed and she let her robe come open, purposely, I thought, exposing most of one breast.

"Anyway, he said he had a great stock deal that I might be interested in. I thought it was strange he didn't mention Jesse, and if Jesse had been in better shape I simply would have told Fink to call Jesse in his apartment and talk to him. I knew that Jesse was in no condition to think about stock investments, but I agreed to go out to the Wardman to see Fink and Jesse. That was the worst mistake I ever made."

Roxy shifted again in the bed, tightening her robe and recovering her breast, convinced I guess, that I was not going to try to swallow the bait.

"I met Fink in the lobby of the Wardman and immediately

walked over to one end of the big room and sat down on a sofa ready to talk about the stock deal. But Fink just stood there saying we ought to go to his room, that it wasn't a good idea to be seen together too much, considering that what he wanted to talk about might be construed as an insider deal. He continued to persist that we best talk in his room, and that made me suspicious. So I stood up and said: 'Mr. Fink, I'm going up to Jesse Smith's apartment now. If you want to come with me, we can discuss the stock there.'

"He jumped back, as if I had pushed him. 'I'm sorry, Miss Stinson, I thought this was a deal that might interest you. I don't think it would be appropriate for me to discuss it with Jesse. Good evening,' he said, touching his hat. And he walked quickly to an open elevator door and disappeared."

"Weird! What do you think he was up to?"

"My first reaction, of course, was that he was just trying to get me to his room with an elaborate seduction ploy. But by the time I reached Jesse's apartment, I had decided that he was trying to set me up for something, although I didn't know then that he had registered us as man and wife. But that's one of the things Senator Wheeler says I have to watch out for. They're trying to discredit me as a witness. I remembered that Fink was really a good friend of Daugherty's and I finally decided Harry, that jerk, was behind the whole thing. I can understand how you felt when you heard about it."

"I was hurt."

"Oh, Jamie," she said, quickly getting off the bed, sliding down on her knees on the floor in front of me and clasping her hands behind my waist, "although I know a young man like you wouldn't be much interested in an old nanny." Then she buried her head in my lap with an intimate display of affection. The surge I always felt with her started up again, which she could not help but know. But I pulled her back, putting my hand under her chin to lift her head.

"Henry thinks you are the logical murder suspect."

She rose quickly. Looking me directly in the eye, she said: "I did not murder Jesse! I loved him. And I'm not going to discuss that night any more unless Henry is here."

I rose from the chair and walked to the phone. "I'll call him."
When I had him on the line, we had a brief conversation:

JMC: This is Cain. I'm here at the Rennert with our friend. We'd
both like you to join us.

HLM: I trust you have engaged in an appropriate reunion. I don't
want to be in the way.

JMC: You won't. And we have.

HLM: Has she confessed yet?

JMC: No, because you're wrong.

HLM: Oh.

JMC: The room number is five-oh-two.

HLM: I've got some copy I must edit, so it'll be about an hour.
But I'll be there.

JMC: Good.

I hung up and returned to the bed. "He won't be here for about
an hour. What'll we do now?"

Before I could resume my seat in the chair, she grabbed my
arm and pulled me into bed: "I have a suggestion" and with her
tongue leading the attack, she kissed me hard on the mouth. We
continued that sort of thing for a few minutes and while we did I
suggested: "You know, there's a way the French make love,
which I learned when I was in the war. Would you like to learn
how it goes?"

"Try anything once, as they say. What do I do?"

"You don't have to move. I'll do it. It's an upside-down sort of
thing."

"Oh, how exciting."

I didn't really have to do much explaining to Roxy. When we
were finished she said: "That was lovely, Jamie. But we must have
a lot of French blood in Washington Courthouse because I did that
in high school."

There was a knock on the door. "That couldn't be Mencken," I
said, looking at my watch. "Way too soon."

"Quick, get dressed," Roxy said. And she disappeared into the
bathroom.

I put my shorts, pants, shirt and shoes back on, but before I could
tie my tie and put on my coat, there was another knock on the door
and I could hear a key turning in the lock. Slowly the door started

to open and into the room stepped a tall, heavy-set man wearing a tan trenchcoat and brown felt hat.

It was unmistakably Gaston B. Means. And I started coughing uncontrollably.

CHAPTER TWENTY-FIVE

With Means was a short, swarthy gentleman, not wearing a coat and holding the hotel room key in his hand. I began to move toward the phone, but Means quickly spoke: "No need to call the house detective, Mr. Cain. He's right here. I would like to introduce Sergeant Scarpetti, formerly of the Baltimore City Police Force, now chief security officer for the Hotel Rennert."

Behind Sgt. Scarpetti was another short, unruly little man who closed the door after him. "This other gentleman shall remain nameless," said Means. "He works for me." Then looking around the room, he said: "Where's Miss Stinson? In the bathroom, I assume."

"Yes. I'm here, Gaston," Roxy said entering the room. She was still wearing her bathrobe and had left her hair long, rather than putting it back into a bun. I assumed she did not want Means to see her in her nanny clothes and new hairdo.

"Good to see you again, Miss Stinson. Looks like you've done something to your hair. I must say I like the old Roxy better, but then that grayish-blonde color is much more suitable for a redhead in hiding. Is it a wig or did you dye it?"

"How 'bout your hair, Gaston? Is it yours, or do *you* wear a toupee?" she said, as she slowly, and awkwardly I thought, walked over to one of the two chairs in the room and sat down.

"Only my barber knows."

"All right, Means," I said. "Let's cut this little vaudeville act. What are you doing in our room?" Then I did some more coughing, which annoyed me.

"I'm here to search it, with full authorization granted to me by the Rennert Security force. I'm seeking certain items which I have every reason to believe are in Miss Stinson's possession. A packet of government documents and a jewel."

God, I thought. I had forgotten all about the diamond.

"What makes you think . . ." she asked Means.

(And as Roxy started to reply I stole a quick glance at the little table by the bed and noticed that the wrapped gem was gone; Roxy must have taken it into the bathroom).

". . . I have these items? And if I did, what makes you think I'd bring them along for this little assignation with my friend, Mr. Cain?"

"Maybe you wanted to give them to him. But we'll soon find out," and he nodded to his two henchmen, who immediately started a search of the room. Means himself went slowly through Roxy's pocketbook and personally frisked both of us. "Careful, big boy," Roxy said, standing up to permit him to feel her. After running his hands up and down her robe, he then tried to look inside it to see if she had anything strapped to her body. "Sure you're not just trying to get a free look?"

"Just doing my job, ma'am. But I'll say, for a gray-haired old woman, you're beautifully preserved."

"And you're forgiven," said Roxy, sitting down again.

"The hell you are," I chimed in. "You can back away from that robe, Means, or we're going to have a fight."

"Oh, wouldn't that be nice," said Roxy.

"Don't be stupid," Means said, patting his right hand coat pocket.

Then turning to Scarpetti, he said: "You stay with these two while I look in the bathroom. Yell if they try anything dumb."

Roxy was sitting in one of the room's two chairs and I took a seat in the other. The intruders kept an eye on us while they searched for the papers and diamond in places they had already looked. In the closet, Sgt. Scarpetti found a long, gray dress, which I assumed was the nanny attire that she did not want to put on. I could see why. But after going through it twice, the sergeant put the drab dress back on its hanger, while looking in the direction of Means' man and shaking his head.

Finally, Means emerged from the bathroom carrying the Wardman Park hand-towel in his hand: "Very interesting, Roxy. You're in the Rennert Hotel, but you're using a Wardman Park hand-towel. Now how do you explain that?"

"I collect hotel souvenir towels—and sometimes ashtrays. Don't you? I'm sure Sgt. Scarpetti must know all about that; it's probably one of the hotel's biggest problems."

"That's right," said the sergeant.

"Well, I promise you I won't walk off with any of those lovely, thick Rennert towels—if you will leave us alone now. And Gaston, before you say good-bye I want to thank you for advising me to disappear for awhile. As you probably figured out, I took your advice, even to the point of not contacting Henry and Jim, which I might mention, made my friend here pretty mad." And she looked at me, while I wondered what in the hell she was talking about.

"Don't mention it, Roxy. And if you'd followed my advice not to contact Cain, I wouldn't be here now. I've had a tail on him for some time. And I still think you ought to lay low. I know for a fact that Jesse was killed, probably by that man I told you about. But look here," Means continued, holding up the Wardman towel, "could it possibly have been used to conceal something that Jesse gave you that night and you wanted to give to Cain?"

"If it did, don't you think you would have found it by now? It's not that small, you know."

"We haven't found it, but that doesn't mean it isn't here. . . ." Means obviously intended to pursue the whereabouts of the diamond when there were a couple of loud firm knocks on the door.

"Ahhhh," I said, looking at Sgt. Scarpetti. "That will be Mr. H. L. Mencken of the *Baltimore Sun* papers. If you have a public relations hand at the Rennert, I think you better call him."

The three men seemed frozen, although Means, with the towel still in his right hand, slowly put it in his pocket. "Means," I said, "if you do have a gun in that pocket, I would advise you not to bring it out. That would make a column irresistible for Mencken, assuming he survived your threat to shoot Baltimore's most famous citizen and two of his friends. I don't think that would be very good for business, do you?"

Means quickly held up his right hand holding the towel, indicating that he was just putting it in his pocket. There was another knock and I opened the door. It was Mencken, beaming as he stepped into the room looking directly at Roxy still in her chair. "Ahhhhh. Miss Stinson, what have you done to your hair?"

Then he stopped, abruptly, when he saw the rest of them. "I haven't seen this many men waiting around in a room since my youth when I played piano in one of Baltimore's finest whorehouses. Must be a convention of Methodist ministers in town. I think I'll join my mother and brother August at our summer place in Mount Washington."

Never missing a beat, Roxy said: "Well Mr. Mencken, it is sort of crowded tonight. But if you'll be patient, I think I can put you with a lovely young girl—although you'll have to wait until Sergeant Scarpetti, here, is through. He's taken a fancy to Mary, haven't you, Sergeant? The sergeant is employed by the Rennert Hotel security police. This other gentleman works for Mr. Means, whom you know."

Turning quickly to the sergeant and taking out a small notebook and a pencil, Mencken said: "How do you spell that: S-C-A-R-P-E-T-T-I? Good. Now if your group is not out of this room in thirty seconds, I promise you that within the hour there'll be a *Baltimore Sun* reporter up here wanting to talk to your manager. And here's a twenty for relinquishing your place in line for Mary."

Ignoring the proffered twenty-dollar bill, a very confused former police sergeant brushed by Mencken and headed for the hall, followed by Means' henchman, who did not wait for his boss. Means himself moved slowly toward the hall, as if he was about to leave. But then he slowly closed the door in front of him, turned around and as he started moving his right hand toward his coat pocket, said: "One more thing, Roxy."

I was standing directly behind him and before he could put his hand into his coat pocket, I stepped forward quickly and reached in before he could to see if he really had a gun. He did and I pulled it out. A small automatic.

Means, ignoring me as if I had just relieved him of a toy, pulled the towel out of his pocket and held it so we could all see the initials on it: "Your little souvenir, with its telltale 'W. P.' intrigues me. And it started me to thinking. Do you remember that dinner at the Washington Hotel a few weeks ago, when I first met Mr. Mencken and Mr. Cain?"

Roxy, still sitting in the chair, silently nodded yes. I was beginning to wonder if she was feeling all right.

"Well, do you also recall that night telling us that you had read *Candide* in high school?"

Roxy was silent. I almost said "Voltaire isn't all she learned in high school," but thought better of it.

"It occurs to me that perhaps you recalled the passage in Vol-

taire's novel about the old lady who was travelling on a galley when
it was overtaken by some knights of Malta. Remember? They
stripped everyone on board 'naked as monkeys,' and searched in
the travellers' most intimate parts—looking for diamonds. Con-
cealing jewels like that is a very old trick in the smuggling business."

"That's true," said Mencken. "One of the biggest problems facing
the DeBeers company in South Africa was retrieving diamonds stolen by their workers. At the end of every day, they insisted on
inspecting the orifices of suspected workers. The blackamoors didn't
object, but the whites did, protesting that they would not be searched
like common servants or slaves. It caused DeBeer labor problems
for many years. Voltaire was right. Searching women like that had
been common practice among civilized nations since time imme-
morial. Incidentally, those knights of Malta were religious gentlemen and they especially relished their search for diamonds."

"Well, Miss Stinson," said Means. "Did you remember your Voltaire well enough while you were in the bathroom for him to inspire
a hiding place for a large diamond, which you had in that Wardman
Park towel that you used to wrap something when you left Smith's
apartment that night?"

"Gaston," Roxy replied. "You ought to be a detective."

"I am."

"Do detectives have large diamonds? That's where Jesse told me
he got it. From you."

"You'll have a hard time proving that one, Miss Stinson."

Slowly moving toward the door as if to leave, Means asked me
if he could have his gun back. "No, I think I'll keep it. If I can ever
find an honest policeman in Washington I'll have it matched with
the bullet that killed Smith."

"Look, I told you who shot Smith that Sunday afternoon when
you came by my house on Sixteenth Street."

"You mean the hired killer from out of town?"

"Yeah. And be careful with that gun. It's loaded."

"Don't worry. I was in the war, I know how to use it. I wouldn't
have killed you, of course, but I could have shot you in the leg,
claiming it was an accident when you were handling the gun.
You're outnumbered three-to-one, Means—three honest citizens
testifying against the biggest liar in the nation's capital."

"Excepting a congressman or two." Mencken said, then he added: "By the way, Means, how do you feel about Harding's death? Do you believe the rumors that he was murdered?"

"Certainly. And I know who killed him!"

"Who?" Mencken and I both asked at once.

"The last person to see him. Mrs. Harding. She poisoned him."

"What about Daugherty?" Mencken said. "He was one of the last persons to see the president."

"Daugherty didn't have to. He knew the Duchess was going to do it. But he's the one spreading the word that Mrs. Harding killed her husband. And he's right. Mrs. Harding virtually confessed to me."

"Why the hell would she tell you?"

"We were a lot closer than most people think. Mainly because I did so much investigative work for her, getting information about the president's lovers—especially Nan Britton. She had to have somebody to talk to and she trusted me because I knew all about Nan and had kept that secret. But jealousy wasn't the main reason, although it played a part."

"What was the main reason?" I asked.

"Well, she told me how the gang's hold on the president had been getting tighter and tighter and even more merciless; how he was being compelled to sign more and more papers that were put in front of him for his signature, how she was finding it more and more difficult to check up on her husband's official activities; how the president seemed to be losing his jovial, confident demeanor, and was looking and acting more and more like a hounded animal, tracked and with his back against the wall; how she became more and more convinced that disaster was inevitable, and that only she could frustrate the infernal machinations of the gang. It'll all be in the book I'm writing."

"Well, you've got the imagination to do a novel," Mencken said. "And you'll have plenty of time when you retire to Atlanta."

"Yeah, and Henry's right," said Roxy. "You oughta do a novel because that's all fiction about Nan. Mrs. Harding knew her husband had lovers, even that he entertained one of them in the White House coat closet. But she didn't know it was Nan. You weren't tailing her for the Duchess, but to blackmail Daugherty and the president to keep from being indicted."

"So how do you know so much?" Means replied.

"I may have been underground, but not out of touch," Roxy said, shifting in her chair, obviously uncomfortable. "Gaston, I'm going to have to ask you to leave now. Good day."

Means tipped his hat and opened the door slowly: "Cain, you ought to see a doctor about that cough. I have a friend who developed one just like it and he's in the lung house now. But they say he's going to be all right."

"One last thing, Gaston," Roxy said holding out her hand. "My little towel. It really is a souvenir."

Means tossed her the towel and then left. When he was gone and the door was closed, Roxy rose and just stood by the bed for a moment as if she was waiting for something to happen. "I've got to do something about this diamond quick, its beginning to hurt."

"I don't doubt it," said Mencken, "My Hollywood friend, Anita Loos, was right when she said it looks 'like a piece of pale green glass cut from a beer bottle.' "

"That's what it feels like," said Roxy. She slowly and carefully took a sitting position on the bed, leaning back on her elbows and spreading her legs. She still had her robe on: "Jim, I'm going to need some help. How about it, Henry? You two want to assist at the birth of a diamond?"

Mencken reacted almost as if a vision of the Virgin Mary had suddenly appeared in the room, stark naked. His face blushed crimson. But he instinctively responded with a good line: "No thanks, Miss Stinson. You're in good hands, if I may say so, with Doctor Cain and I'm sure he knows his way around the mine a lot better than I do," and he disappeared into the bathroom: "Yell, when the extraction's over."

It was over in a minute, but I did have to touch the diamond. Whatever happens to me now I can blame on the curse. I yelled to Mencken and when he came out of the bathroom I showed him the stone, holding it in the towel Roxy had given me. "Now remember the curse. Don't touch."

"Why not?" said Mencken "If I don't believe in the Holy Grail, I certainly don't believe in a cursed stone, whose beauty, as Anita says, 'is as nonexistent as the Emperor's new clothes.' " Picking the big gem up and examining it disapprovingly with an imagined jeweler's glass, he said, "Besides, Roxy's concealment has purged it of all its voodoo and turned it into a holy object we can all worship now. In fact, I'm already beginning to see angels dancing on it." Then he tossed the diamond to me. I caught it and instinctively tossed it to Roxy, who was still sitting on the bed.

Roxy squealed and caught it. "Ohhhh. Now we've all touched it," she said, tossing it to me.

"The Holy Trinity of the new religion," said Mencken. "Now Apostle Cain, if you will wrap up that sacred stone, we can palaver. I know Roxy has a lot to tell us; maybe she's already told you, Jim."

"No. She was waiting for you. But, believe it or not, we haven't had lunch yet. I'm starved." And then I started to cough again.

Mencken said: "I wouldn't delay, Jim, seeing a doctor about that cough."

Before I could respond, he added: "I've eaten, but we can go down to their great dining room and I'll join you with a coffee and dessert."

"No," I said, "we'd better have something sent to the room."

With that, Roxy took the gray dress out of the closet and went into the bathroom to put it on. I explained to Henry that she was in hiding, that her dyed hair and the dress she was wearing were part of the disguise and she didn't want to be seen in public dressed that way. Mencken understood immediately, so I called room service and ordered Roxy and me a sandwich and iced tea. Mencken had coffee and pound cake.

As I hung up the phone, Roxy came back into the room and the change was startling. She had put her long, grayish, blonde hair back into a bun and removed all traces of lipstick and rouge. And with the long, drab dress, she looked like a fifty-year-old governess or mistress of a small girl's school. "This is not only a good disguise," she said, "it makes me look perfect for my new job. I'll tell you about that in a minute."

"I don't know why you need a disguise or what kind of job you have," Mencken said to Roxy, "but if I'd passed you on the street this morning I'd never have recognized you. To tell the truth, I hardly recognize you now."

"Maybe this is the real me and the Roxy you had dinner with that night was an imposter."

Apparently not wanting to get into a discussion of the real Roxy, Mencken replied: "Okay, we know you went back to Smith's apart-

ment that night he was killed, although you didn't tell us. Why did
you return?"

"Well, as I told Jim, Jesse phoned after Jim went back to his
room and said he had to see me. I said I'd think about it. Then a
lawyer, Fink, called and asked me to come to the Wardman. So I
went back, talked with Fink briefly, which I've explained to Jim,
and then went up to Jesse's apartment. I'm pretty sure that Buddy
didn't know—at least then—I was at the apartment a second time
that night. Meanwhile, Jesse was having a nervous breakdown right
then and there. He always was a physical coward, a sissy, as they
say, almost effeminate. You probably noticed. The first thing he
said was: 'Oh Roxy, I'm so scared! I don't want Harry to send me
away and I don't want to go to jail. And now they've put the curse
of the blue diamond on me and I just want to die. That's why I
bought the gun in Washington Courthouse. But I'm afraid. You've
got to help me.' "

Roxy paused and sat down in the chair near the bed.

"Jesse was scared of more than a voodoo spell. He said that
George Remus had threatened to have him killed if he didn't return
the money he had taken to keep Remus from having to go on trial—
and more to keep him out of jail. He said they only had fifty thousand of it left, but the General had it stashed away somewhere and
refused to return it."

"Did you find Jesse's money belt?"

"No. Jesse also said that even his beloved friend Harry had hinted
that Jesse would be in great danger if he decided to tell anyone in the
Congress or with the press that some money they had used to pay off
campaign debts and Harding women was raised by crooked means.
Jesse was being set up to take the rap and he knew it."

"Didn't we all," said Mencken.

"Even if Daugherty acknowledged his part in their operation,
Jesse would end up in jail, no matter what—and that seemed to
frighten him more than anything. 'Roxy, you know what happens
to gentlemen like me in prison,' he said, almost blubbering. 'They
attack them and make them do very ugly things. I'm not a well
man and I know I'd never come out alive. I'll never see Harry and
you again—the two people I love most in the whole world.' And
then he broke down into uncontrollable crying, so that I had to tell
him to get hold of himself or someone would hear us. Jesse was

definitely a coward and he had been dying a thousand deaths for a couple of months. He wanted to put an end to it but couldn't.

"I knew something had to be done. I was convinced that Jesse was beyond salvation and truly preferred to be dead: 'Get hold of yourself, Jesse,' I said, shaking his shoulder. 'What can I do?' "

There was a knock on the door and as I reached for Means' gun in my back pocket, Roxy quickly went into the bathroom and Mencken moved slowly to the door. After a moment he said: "Who's there?"

"Room service, with your food."

After Roxy signed the check, we spread the sandwiches and drinks out on the one little table in the room. Then she continued: "Well, when I started shaking Jesse's shoulders, that seemed to calm him down a little, and then he whispered: 'In my top drawer there's a large blue diamond wrapped in a hand-towel. I'm now sure it's the Hope Diamond, but I touched it several times before I realized that. Now they've passed the curse along to me.' He had pointed to a large chest of drawers against the wall and under a window. And for the first time, I noticed a metal trash basket in which there were some ashes—some papers had just been burned.

"Then I asked Jesse: 'What about that envelope of papers you were going to give the Duchess today? Is that what you burned in that trash basket over there?'

"He hesitated a moment before he replied: 'No. Those are some more intimate things—letters between Harry and me. There are no other papers, although everyone thinks there are.'

"I lied to you about the papers, which I'll explain in a minute. However, Jesse did give me his little green notebook that he always carried around. He said to guard it with my life, because it would prove that whatever he did was authorized by Harry. I've read it now and have it hidden away. I don't know what I'm going to do with it. The trouble is, it tells too much about everybody, including the president. He wasn't innocent, but now he's dead too. I think it's just going to get lost."

Roxy paused for a moment, carefully picking the exact words for what she wanted to say next: "Next was the hard part: How to help Jesse with his suicide because I knew he was serious. I had to help him. But the more I thought about it, the more worried I became. He was quite calm now, almost peaceful, like a man on his

deathbed resigned to the inevitable. Hating guns almost as much as
Jesse, I said: 'What about lots of sleeping pills or some kind of
poison? Do you have any?'

" 'No, it's got to be the gun—in the head, so it'll be fast.' "

"That figures," Mencken said. "Remember that scene in *Hedda
Gabler* by Henrik Ibsen, when Dr. Brack comes in with the news
of Lovborg's suicide? Hedda immediately thinks of him putting the
pistol to his head and dying instantly and magnificently. The picture
fills her with romantic delight."

Roxy looked puzzled for a moment, then went on, ignoring
Mencken's remark.

"And then I had a crazy idea. I knew Jesse was right-handed, so
I said we were going to try to do this on his left side so that it
might look like murder. People would probably look on suicide as
an admission of guilt, like they're doing with the Cramer suicide.
If they decide it was murder, then several people who thought he
knew things that might point to them would be under suspicion.
That would take the heat off Jesse. And that also explains why I
lied to you about the papers. Jesse said there were no papers. But
I wanted people to think there were so that it would appear as a
motive for killing Jesse—to get the papers as well as silencing him."

"I'm not so sure that was smart," I said.

"Well, that's what we did. It was the most horrible thing I've
ever been involved in. I prepared for a quick getaway: I put the
notebook in my large pocketbook into which I had also dropped
the diamond wrapped in a small towel. I used a pillow to muffle
the sound of the shot. I had positioned the metal trash basket so
that his head would fall into it—which it did, just as reported in
the newspapers. But Jim is right . . . Later, I decided that was pretty
dumb, making it look like a murder—and me the murderer."

"Murderess," Mencken interrupted, looking at me.

"Do you think I'm a . . . murderess?" Roxy asked, visibly upset
and fully aware of the spot she was in. "They decided to call it
suicide. Maybe they'll never reopen the case."

"Maybe," said Mencken. "Let's talk about that later. What happened next?"

"I grabbed my pocketbook and the notebook and got out of there
fast, crying all the way. Rather than take the elevator, I went down
the back stairs to the lobby, where I saw the bellboy—the same

one, I'm sure, you talked to that Sunday morning when we were last together. And here come the reasons I ran out on you, Jamie. I hope you will believe me; it was nothing personal.

"When you went down that morning to talk to the bellboy, I knew he'd tell you he'd seen me the second time that night. I also knew that you would want to know what I was doing there and either I would have to lie or stonewall it because, at that moment, I didn't want to tell you—or anyone—what had happened.

"Also, I had not decided what to do with the diamond. It was beautiful, now in my possession and maybe I could get away with keeping it. And you would probably continue to believe me if I insisted that I hadn't seen it there that night. Gaston would end up getting the blame for the missing diamond, which delighted me.

"But I'm not a good liar and you'd eventually get it out of me, which meant that if I decided to keep the diamond, I could never see you again. That, I didn't like. But there was more to my disappearance than that.

"I had a meeting with Harry Daugherty that Friday afternoon before our dinner at Harvey's. Among the things we discussed that day was Jesse's death. Daugherty said he and Burns had decided it was suicide and I said if it was, he had driven Jesse to it. Of course, I didn't tell him what really happened that night. But when he saw that I might be giving him some trouble, he let me know that Billy Burns, in his investigation of Jesse's death, had located a bellboy who saw me at the Wardman twice that night—once when I brought Jesse home from dinner and later, after Jesse and Fink had asked me to come back. He also asked me if I had seen a large, unusual diamond in the box in which Jess kept his jewels and whether I might have seen an envelope full of papers he was sure Jesse had with him.

"I said I hadn't seen a diamond and that Jesse told me there weren't any papers. But Daugherty didn't believe me. I didn't mention my meeting with Fink, and he knew about it. I said that Jesse had asked me to come back more or less just to hold his hand; that he was terrified that George Remus was going to have him killed because he, Daugherty, would not return any of the money Remus had given them. I also said I thought it was a terrible thing the way Daugherty and the president had turned on Jesse.

"Daugherty seemed genuinely upset at this, but said Jesse had done some things that might prove embarrassing to the president. Then he really scared me: 'You know, Roxy, if people start calling Jesse's death murder and not suicide, you're going to be a prime suspect. You inherited quite a bit of money and may know where there's more.'

"Then he added: 'I also suggest that if you know where those papers are, you'd better let me know. You'll be a lot safer with them out of your possession.'

"So, now I had Daugherty threatening me. Then, that last night I saw you, Jim, I had a call from Gaston. Remember? I said it was a friend from Ohio? He said I had better stay completely out of sight for several days. He seemed to know that you were still with me, but the best thing for me would be to disappear immediately and not tell anyone—including you two—where I was. He said a gangster hit man was in town, just like the night Jesse was killed, and that he suspected I was the target this time. He hung up before I could ask him anything.

"I knew that Jesse wasn't killed by a gangster. Still, a killer might have been in town to take care of Jesse, but I beat him to it. And Gaston usually tells just enough of the truth so you can't completely ignore him. I was already scared enough with Daugherty threatening me. Either Remus or Daugherty could have a killer out looking for me and with good reason. So I spent the rest of the night, after we made love, jumping whenever I heard a noise in the hall and thinking I had better get out of there fast in the morning."

She paused and finished her coffee, before she concluded: "I hope you will both forgive me for disappearing, especially you, Jamie. Mother told me how concerned you were, but I told her not to say anything."

Then she stood up, walked to the bedside table where she had put the Hope Diamond, rewrapped in the towel, picked it up and handed it to me: "And I have a confession to make about this. For awhile, I was, frankly, tempted to keep it. In the first place, it amounted pure and simple to the theft of one of the most famous jewels in the world, which nobody could hope to get away with forever. Sooner or later, I would be caught. Second, it provided even more of a motive for my helping Jesse if the question of, God forbid, assisted suicide slash murder ever becomes an issue. I hope you will return the diamond to the McLeans. I'm sure they'll want to keep its theft quiet and the whole silly incident will just fade away without Jesse Smith's name—or mine—being added to the legend."

"Miss Stinson," Mencken said, "you're very smart to return the diamond; it would just cause you a world of trouble, even without the curse. But I'm afraid you still have problems—serious ones."

"You mean, by helping Jesse kill himself?"

"I'm afraid so. Although some people might call it 'justifiable homicide'—and I certainly would—most people would call it 'mercy killing,' which is still viewed as a crime in most courts, although you might find a jury that would be sympathetic. But most religions now consider any form of suicide a crime against God, who is the only one empowered to make such decisions. Despite the general belief, the Bible does not condemn suicide. But by the fifth century, St. Augustine had come out against it and in the twelfth century St. Thomas Aquinas was calling suicide a mortal sin. So you're not likely to find a jury that would condone what you did, even if you were a doctor. There are some countries in Europe—Holland, for example—that tolerate what they call 'euthanasia,' but I can tell you, it's going to be many years before the laws in this country will permit someone to assist in a suicide. So pray to an understanding and a tolerant God—if you know one— that Daugherty and Burns stick to their suicide verdict. And don't do anything to try to convince them otherwise."

"I had pretty much decided on that by the next morning," Roxy replied. "But I'm going to continue insisting that it was Daugherty who drove him to suicide."

"That might be risky," I said. "All they would have to do is get Daugherty's man, Buddy Martin, to decide that that woman he saw leaving the apartment right after the shot was you, and that would be that. With the financial motives they can attribute to you, you'd be on your way to prison."

"Jim's right," Mencken added. "So cross your fingers. What happens next?"

"I'm not sure where we go from here. I have talked to Senator Wheeler, who's going to be running the forthcoming investigation of the attorney general, and he agrees that I ought to stay completely out of sight until the hearings begin some time early next year. He says that already somebody—probably Gaston Means working for

Burns—has ransacked several senators' offices and homes looking for things that might be used in blackmailing the senators. And he knows George Remus is furious and desperate because he's heading for jail. Senator Wheeler has worked out some kind of witness protection program for me—not run by the Justice Department, but a Congressional agency. And I trust the senator completely.

"And once I get on the stand for Senator Wheeler, I'm going to be able to tell him—and the world—that, no matter what Jesse did, it was for his friend and boss, Harry Daugherty."

"So, you plan to go through with it, to keep blaming Daugherty?" I asked.

"Yes. And, incidentally, Wheeler says that Gaston is going to be a witness for the investigation also. That should be quite a show."

Then, before either Mencken or I could react to this long confession, Roxy walked quickly to the door, turned around and said: "I want to you to meet my new employer's sister. I'll be right back."

CHAPTER TWENTY-SIX

Mencken and I just stood in the middle of the room looking at each other in disbelief, until I said: "One thing about Roxy, you never know what she's going to do next."

"You're right. And I sure can't get over how she's aged, or made herself age," Mencken responded.

"She's not that old. I wonder who she's working for?"

"I think I have a hunch."

"Shhhhhhhhhhhhh. Here she comes."

As the door opened, Roxy ushered a young lady into the room. She was probably in her twenties, had brown ruffled hair and a pale, roundish little-girl face. Certainly not beautiful, but attractive in a small-town sort of way, and enhanced, overall, by a very nice figure. She was wearing a white lace blouse and a long white skirt. With her was a little girl who looked to be about three or four; she had dark, blonde hair, trimmed in bangs, and looked very much like the young woman she was with.

"Henry, Jim, this is Nan Britton. I know you've met her, Henry."

Then she held up the little girl's hand: "And this is her daughter, Elizabeth Ann. I've been serving as her nanny for a few weeks. Nan has some business things she wants to talk with you about, so Elizabeth Ann and I will leave you all for a little while. We'll be next door. Call us when you're through."

When Roxy and the child had left, Britton said: "Gentlemen, I want to thank you both for taking the time to talk with me. Mr. Mencken, I remember our conversation that evening in the Hotel Washington and I was impressed by your general concern for my situation. And I especially appreciated your saying that you were not interested in the fact that the president was meeting a young woman, not his wife, in private. Not all newspapermen would have respected our privacy and I was dreadfully worried about what the awful Mr. Means was going to do. I still am. Anyway, Miss Stinson said you might be able to help me."

"How's that?" asked Mencken, offering her a chair.

"Well, first off, Elizabeth Ann is the president's daughter!"

She paused a moment to let that sink in. When it did, Mencken said: "Harding's, of course, not Cal's. Did the president know about her?"

"He never saw his daughter. But he knew about her and contributed to her support when he was alive. And that's the problem."

"How's that?" I said.

"My sweetie never told anyone except Jesse Smith and Harry Daugherty about Elizabeth Ann. In fact, we tried to keep the whole affair a secret. After Mrs. Harding died, we planned to get married and move out into the country somewhere. But the executors of his estate do not believe me and refuse to even acknowledge that Ann exists. Jesse is dead and Harry Daugherty refuses to confirm our romance. The president's sister, Daisy, has been friendly and sympathetic, but she seems more interested in protecting her brother's reputation than helping her niece—and, believe me, we need help. My debts are growing huge and neither my sister nor I have any money."

"Does Elizabeth Ann know who her father is?" I asked.

"Not yet."

"Who's raising Ann, now?" said Mencken.

"My sister, Elizabeth. Miss Stinson is acting as a nanny, which is a great help because she doesn't charge very much. She says it's a good way to go into hiding for awhile. I don't know exactly why. Something to do with her late husband, Jesse Smith. He was a wonderful man. He often gave me money for support, especially after Elizabeth Ann was born."

"So how do you think I might help you?" Mencken asked.

"Well, I thought I might write a book and I wanted to talk with you about that. Miss Stinson says you know all about books."

"Do you plan to write this book yourself, or bring in a ghost writer?"

"No. I'm going to do it myself. I always wanted to write," and Mencken had that Oh-God-another-nice-lady-who-would-just-love-to-write-an-article-for-your-magazine look.

"Funny thing," Britton continued, "when I worked at the Town

Hall Club, in New York, I met Rachel Crothers, who was vice president of the club. I delivered proofs of some club dinner invitations to her apartment. Do you know her?"

"She writes plays; in fact, she's got a play on Broadway now. I know her, but I'm not a big play man. Crothers writes mostly about the problems—mostly moral—of young women."

"That's right and when I told her how much I admired her writing, and said: 'It's the work I want someday to be doing,' she replied: 'Have you ever written anything?'

"I said, 'No, not much.' And you know what she said? 'Well, what you need to do is have a child and some experience, *then* you can write.' I wondered if she has ever experienced drama such as mine—and she's written so many successful plays."

"You have had the experience," Mencken said.

"The problem's not the writing. I've done a couple of chapters and they go along pretty well. The trouble is finding a publisher. Richard Wightman, who runs the Bible Corporation of America, where I'm working now as a secretary, is helping me try to find one. But he's been turned down several places. One publisher said: 'Take back your ball of fire. We're passing up one hundred thousand dollars and we know it.' The editor of *Cosmopolitan* read the first two chapters and said it was the 'most astounding' document he had ever read, but rejected it."

"I don't doubt it," said Mencken, "I know my publisher, Alfred A. Knopf, wouldn't touch it. His wife, Blanche, would probably get it first and reject it before Alfred ever saw it. It's far too early for something like that. Here's what I'd do. I'd go ahead and finish the book. But take your time. You may have to wait a couple of years. It would be a lot better if Mrs. Harding had died. In fact, the book will probably be ignored as long as she's alive. But her health's not good, you know."

"I know," said Britton, visibly disappointed.

"Then, when the time is right, you and Wightman should publish it yourselves. But you can't let it look like you're just trying to make money, even if you desperately need it to support the president's child. Work up some kind of organization and say you're trying to spotlight the problem of unwed mothers and illegitimate children."

" 'Love children'—that's a subject I'm really interested in," Britton said. "If love is the only right warrant for bringing children into the world, then many children born in wedlock are illegitimate and many born out of wedlock are legitimate, like my little Ann."

"You're absolutely right," Mencken replied, "and I'd put that in the lead of your introduction."

Then he stood up, looked at his watch and said: "I've got to be on my way, but let me know if there's anything I can do to help. Be sure to send me a review copy at the *Sun*. Now, could you tell Miss Stinson we're ready to go?"

When Roxy returned and thanked us for seeing Miss Britton, Mencken said: "Nice girl. She's in one helluva mess. But I'll certainly give her book a push if it ever comes out."

"It will," said Roxy, "she's a very determined young lady."

After hugging Roxy good-bye and telling her, "Keep in touch with us now," Mencken turned to me and said: "I'll meet you in the lobby. I hope they have some good cigars. I've run out and I need one."

When Mencken had gone I said to Roxy: "I agree, please don't disappear again."

"I have to for now. Senator Wheeler still thinks I might be in danger, even with President Harding dead. Daugherty is doing everything he can to protect the president's reputation—and save his own neck. The senator would have fits if he knew I was seeing you now. But if you absolutely have to contact me, you can go through Nan, at the Bible Corporation in New York. But be careful and use another name, like, say Tom Richmond, I'll tell her." And she put her arms around me.

Although Roxy may have looked like a fifty-year-old nanny, she didn't feel like one, pressing her body against mine. "We better not get started again. Henry's waiting for me in the lobby. And I don't think I should kiss you again, until I find out what's causing this cough."

She took her arms off me and reached in my coat pocket where she knew I had put the Hope Diamond still wrapped in the Wardman Park towel. Walking to the bathroom with the wrapped diamond in her hand, she said: "Just a minute. I'll be right back."

When she returned, the re-wrapped diamond was in a Rennert towel which she put back in my pocket. "Be sure to return this." Then holding up the Wardman Park towel, she said: "This is my souvenir. It will always remind me of you—and Jesse." She tried to kiss me. But I pushed her away.

"Silly, we've been kissing each other all afternoon," she said. "What difference will one more make?"

"I don't know. It just makes me feel safer. It might be contagious."

It probably was. But I should have kissed her. At that moment I was very much in love with this fifty-year-old-looking nanny.

Mencken and I were not very far from Marconi's on Saratoga Street. It was beginning to cool off a little, so we decided to walk over, have a couple of beers and maybe dinner. I didn't pay much attention to him at the time, but when we were leaving the Rennert, I noticed an odd looking little man in a seersucker suit leave the hotel after we did and walk about half a block behind us as we went west on Saratoga.

"You know, Cain," Mencken said, "I'll be a lot more comfortable when we return that damned diamond to the McLeans. Means is still after it and I think he'd do anything to get it back. It would put him back in good with Daugherty and probably enable him to get more money out of Mrs. McLean. I think we ought to call them from Marconi's and let them know that we have their jewel and want to return it as soon as possible."

I was tired by the time we reach Marconi's and started another fit of coughing before Mencken went to the pay phone to call Mrs. McLean. While looking at the menu, I happened to notice that the strange little man in the seersucker suit had come into the restaurant and seated himself near the street door entrance.

When Mencken returned to our table, he said that when he told Mrs. McLean we had the diamond and how anxious we were to unload it, she said she and her husband were dining that night at their I Street house, so why didn't we come right over to Washington and have dinner with them. She would have her car meet us at Union Station. "They've already started their cocktails," said Mencken, "so they'll be pretty well soused by the time we get there."

We could catch the six o'clock train to Washington. We took a cab from Marconi's and when we were pulling away from the curb, I looked back and noticed the little man in the seersucker come out and try to hail a taxi. We turned off Saratoga at the next street, so

I could not see whether he was able to find a cab. "You know, Henry, we've been followed by a little man in a seersucker suit ever since we left the Rennert. But I think we lost him when we took the cab."

"Well, I'll be damned. Must be one of Means' thugs. We've got to be careful. Do you think he was going to stick us up and try to retrieve the diamond?"

"I can't think of any other reason he'd be following us. Means really wants that jewel."

"Can you blame him? He's got more than money riding on this job. His reputation."

When the train was pulling out of the station, I saw the little man watching it from the door that led onto the platform. "Look Henry, there he is. But he's making no effort to get on board."

"That's odd. What do you think he's doing?"

"Maybe he's going to call Means in Washington and tell him we're on our way. He should be back from Baltimore by now."

"We better watch for him at the station. I'll be glad when we get rid of this damn diamond!"

On the train, Mencken was uncharacteristically silent, spending most of the time staring out the window, savoring his soda water, which he had reinforced from his flask, and smoking a Willie. Then, about halfway through the trip, he said: "You know, Cain, Roxy could be in serious trouble. She nursed Smith through one of the most difficult, but at the same time, sensible acts—departing this vale of tears when you know the jig is up.

"As I mentioned to you earlier, it's difficult, if not impossible, to discover any evidence or logical reason for remaining alive. The universal wisdom of the world long ago concluded that life is mainly a curse. Disappointment is the lot of man. We are born in pain and die in sorrow. The lucky man died last Wednesday. Turn to the works of that other bard—of Avon. They drip of pessimism. If there is any general idea in them it is the idea that human existence is a painful futility, 'Out, out, brief candle.' 'Life's a tale, told by an idiot, signifying nothing.' "

He paused for a swallow and puff, then continued, just warming up: "Yet, we cling to it in a muddled, pathological way, even trying to fill it with gaudy hocus-pocus, often striving mightily for distinction and power, for the respect and envy of our fellow men."

"So, why?" I intervened.

"If I knew, as much as I love to work, I'd certainly not be doing it in this infernal American climate; I'd be sitting in state in a hall of crystal and gold; and the yokels would be paying ten dollars a head to gape at me through peepholes."

I tried again. "So why do *you* work?"

"That remains a mystery to me to this day. But here's my hypothesis, which I arrived at after much thought and I think it applies to me: Men work simply in order to escape the depressing agony of contemplating life—that their work, like their play, is a mumbo-jumbo that permits them to escape from reality. Both work and play are illusions, but life, stripped of such illusions, instantly becomes unbearable. But don't take too much stock in my talk of agonies and tragicomedies. The basic fact about human existence is not that it is a tragedy, but that it is a bore."

"So you think Jesse Smith was tired of erecting this gaudy structure and Roxy did the right thing by relieving him of his agony."

"Right! Jesse had lost what I call the secret of contentment—i.e., the capacity to postpone suicide for at least another day. Roxy knew it and did the humane thing. But there isn't a jury in the land that would see it that way."

"I don't know. Roxy's not a doctor, but Jesse was certifiably ill, both mentally and physically. And he knew he'd been caught in corruption and was as terrified of going to jail as he was of guns. She might find a good defense lawyer that could convince a jury that it was an assisted suicide if there is such a thing in the law."

"I doubt it. And then there's the distinct possibility that she was *not* telling us the truth. Her story is something of a stretch. Have you thought of that?"

"No I haven't, probably because I don't want to. I have to admit, she has a powerful effect on me."

"Now we're getting to the nub of it, my boy. You're thirty-one now. In ten years, Roxy *really* will be in her fifties and you'll be my age—in your forties, the prime of life, as you can see from my energy and creativity. That I have escaped marriage is not my fault, nor is it to my credit; it's due to a mere act of God. I am no more responsible for it than I am for my remarkable talent as a pianist, my linguistic abilities or my dark, romantic, somewhat voluptuous beauty."

"Well, I wasn't so lucky. And if I did marry Roxy after my divorce from Mary, it probably wouldn't work out. . . ."

"Especially if she's serving time in Atlanta with Means."

"You really think she didn't assist Jesse in suicide, but out-and-out murdered him, don't you?"

"Don't you?"

"Certainly not!"

I don't really know," Mencken said, "and I'm willing to take her word that she didn't. But even if I thought she did murder Smith, I'm not going to tell the cops. Practically all so-called crimes are justifiable on occasion and nine-tenths of them, to certain kinds of people, are unavoidable on occasion."

"Okay, case closed," I said.

"Case closed," he replied, holding up his cup as if in a salute. "In whatever we write about Smith's death, we officially accept the conventional wisdom that it was a suicide."

Then all we had to do was close the book on the Hope Diamond caper. At the station in Washington, we could see no evidence of Means or any of his men and no indication that we were followed in the McLean car. The chauffeur took about fifteen minutes to reach the McLean I Street mansion, which, except for all the windows, looked like a prison. Inside it looked like a potentate's palace. Mrs. McLean met us in the large entrance hall to the house and Mencken's prediction was confirmed. She obviously had been imbibing for some time and continued to do so as we joined them for cocktails in a large parlor off the entrance hall. She was wearing the fake Hope Diamond necklace.

In the parlor, Ned McLean was slumped down in the corner of a big, overstuffed couch, drink in hand and seeming unable to rise. "Howdy, gentleman, good to see you again," he greeted us, raising his glass, but continuing to remain seated. Their Great Dane was sprawled out on an oriental rug over by the empty fireplace.

When we were all seated and drinks had been served, I said to Mrs. McLean: "Well, as Henry told you over the phone, your diamond has been retrieved. We don't know all the details, but Jesse Smith had somehow come into possession of it and planned to return it to you. Instead, he gave it to Roxy Stinson, telling her to give it to you. She gave it to us to pass along to you. Here it is," I said, walking over to her chair and handing Mrs. McLean the diamond still wrapped in the Rennert Hotel towel.

"I see you're taking no chances on the curse," Mrs. McLean said, looking at the towel. "I assume Miss Stinson didn't touch it either. But I must say, she kept it some time."

"She's been staying out of sight at the suggestion of a senator." I said. "But she finally decided to surface long enough to give us the diamond to return to you."

Mrs. McLean looked skeptical as she said: "I think I can guess why."

Her reply puzzled me, but I ignored it and said: "I'm afraid we've all disregarded the curse and touched it. In fact, Henry thinks it's become a holy relic."

"Interesting," Mrs. McLean said, unwrapping the stone and holding it up to the light. "Very pretty. Good job. Holy relic, eh?" And then she hurled the jewel across the room in the general direction of her dog.

"Get the relic, Mike," Ned shouted, laughing like a little boy. That was the last thing he said all evening.

As the Great Dane chased after the jewel and brought it back to Mrs. McLean, Mencken and I looked at each other, stunned. Then I realized what was happening. What Jesse had given Roxy was not the Hope, but the fake and Mrs. McLean knew it. She must be wearing the real jewel. And Mencken must have realized it at about the same time, because he stood up with an extremely annoyed look on his face.

But before he could say anything, Mrs. McLean said: "Well, no need to worry about the curse, because you and Roxy—and Jesse, too, for that matter—have all been handling the imitation Hope. I'm wearing the real one, as I was on the day of that party."

"Mrs. McLean," said a seemingly, at least, irritated H. L. Mencken, "I think you owe us an explanation."

"I do indeed, Mr. Mencken. And I apologize if we have offended you. Here's how it all came about." She took a swallow from her glass, put it down on the table beside her, stood up and slowly walked to the large empty fireplace, then turned her back to it while holding her hands in front of her, not unlike a defense attorney getting ready for his final summation.

"When you were kind enough to call us with the information that someone might have substituted a fake diamond for the Hope—and let me assure you, we appreciated that very much—I immediately had the diamond assessed by a prominent gem expert and he determined that it was real. No substitution had been made. At the same time, he said he thought he knew how the rumors had started, that there had been a theft. A professional colleague told him he had heard that someone in New York had ordered a glass duplicate of the original Hope be made.

"Now this is the kind of rumor that goes around all the time. But I decided to keep quiet about it for awhile, just to see what would happen—and maybe find out who had ordered the fake. So I put the diamond away in the safe, wearing it only on special occasions and playing my little game of not saying whether it was real or fake—as I did at the party at Friendship for the press. But I insisted to the authorities and my jewelers that the diamond was safe and sound."

"Why didn't you tell us?" Mencken interrupted.

"Ahhhhhhhh. I'm coming to that. I told Billy Burns, of course, because I didn't want Department of Justice investigators running around looking for a diamond counterfeiter under the false pretenses that a famous gem had been stolen. You can imagine what a stink that would cause if it ever came out. But I told Burns not to tell Gaston B. Means because, with his underworld connections, there would be an excellent chance of finding out who might have ordered the fake diamond made. So I agreed to pay Means to search for the Hope and the counterfeiter and offered a special reward if he found the diamond.

"He apparently did—and decided to let Jesse have it for awhile, thinking he was laying the curse on him. Then Roxy got it before Means could get it back."

"You sure fooled Means," Mencken said. "He's still looking for it."

"In fact," I added, "when we went to Baltimore this afternoon to meet with Roxy Stinson and get the diamond, Means showed up at Roxy's room with a gun, the hotel detective and one of his hoods, and searched everybody."

"How come he didn't find it?" Mrs. McLean asked. "Means is a professional investigator."

"Because," said Mencken, "Miss Stinson had found an ingenious place to hide it."

"I always thought Miss Stinson was a clever woman. Where did she hide it?"

"You might say, in the plumbing," I answered.

"Oh?"

Then, something flashed through my mind. Turning to Mencken, I said: "Henry, do you remember in Roxy's room when she gave you the diamond and, after looking at it carefully in the light, you tossed it to Roxy? Did you know then that it was a fake?"

With that sometimes insufferable, know-it-all-look that he reserves for comments about the Comstocks and Methodist ministers, he said: "To answer that, Watson, I would have to reveal secrets of the detective trade. But I will say this: One, it didn't make any difference to me if it was real or counterfeit. I don't have much use for baubles, under any circumstances. Two, if it was a fake, it wouldn't make much difference if it hit the floor or not. And if it was real, I could have dropped it out the window and it wouldn't hurt it. Real diamonds are pretty tough."

I just shook my head and smiled, as I said to Mrs. McLean: "So, as it stands right now, Means thinks we have the real diamond. In fact, we think he had someone following us all the way to the Baltimore train station, and if that was his man, then Means knows that we are in Washington now."

"Frankly," Mrs. McLean replied, "we don't know what Means has been up to or how Jesse ended up with the fake diamond. After he had been on his wild goose chase for awhile, Means came back to me and said he'd need another ten thousand dollars to get the real stone back from the jewel thief he knew. I had offered him a ten thousand dollars reward to begin with—if he found the real diamond, although I was ready to give him something if he came back with the fake. What happened next, I don't know. Maybe he found the original fake that started it all, or maybe he had one of his own made."

Then, she paused and very deliberately said: "And maybe Roxy Stinson had the fake appraised and only decided to return it to me after learning that it was not the real Hope Diamond, but a piece of glass. Have you ever thought of that?"

"But if she had done that," Mencken replied, "then wouldn't the jeweler have alerted you that someone was showing the Hope around for appraisal?"

Mrs. McLean seemed unsure how to repond, but then she said: "Possibly. But she might have persuaded the appraiser not to say anything, perhaps using her feminine charm to win his silence, if you know what I mean?"

Mencken, who had visbly cooled down, said, "Smith told Roxy he got the diamond from Means. He didn't tell him it was the Hope, just an interesting, big diamond Jesse could have for a good price. But Jesse decided that it must be the Hope and that Means, or more likely Burns, was trying to put the curse on him."

"I can't believe that," said Mrs. McLean. "But then, who am I to question this damned thing's curse," she added, lifting the diamond necklace off her chest.

Then, she walked over to the table by her chair and took another drink from her nearly empty glass before continuing her story. "As I said, gentlemen, I apologize for letting you get involved in my little game. But I hope you understand what was behind it and why I couldn't tell you. I didn't know you personally and Ned even suggested you might have planted the idea of a fake diamond yourself, hoping to develop a story out of it for the *Sun*. Didn't you, Ned?" she said, looking at her husband on the couch.

But Ned was fast asleep.

"And we also knew from Harry Daugherty," she continued, "that you had become friends with Miss Stinson and we couldn't trust her to keep quiet about it. So, I just didn't say anything, figuring you probably weren't spending much time worrying about my loss of a diamond anyway. And I'll certainly pay you any reasonable reward you ask for returning, in good faith, what you thought was the missing Hope Diamond. Let's go into dinner now. I think I'll just let Ned sleep here for awhile. He can join us later." He never did.

"One thing before we eat," I said, when we were in the hall, heading for the dining room, "could you call Means and tell him you have the diamond? No need to go into any detail; he'll know who returned it. But I just want to stop him from stalking us with a gun. Who knows what he will do."

"Good idea," Mencken seconded.

Mrs. McLean agreed and went into what looked like a study,

which also opened onto the large hall. She was back in a couple of minutes: "Means wasn't home. A woman said he was out of town. So, I asked her to have him call me immediately, that I have something important to tell him. He'll probably figure out what I was calling about."

"Odd, he must have stayed in Baltimore," I said. "He's had plenty of time to come home."

"He probably decided to have dinner there," Mencken replied. "He knows that Washington has no decent restaurants and Baltimore has dozens of great ones, especially if you like seafood."

"I hope you do," Mrs McLean said. "Guess what we're having tonight—lobster thermidor."

"Delicious. One of my favorites," said Mencken.

The lobster was delicious. Dinner went rather quickly and Mrs. McLean kept on drinking. But it did not seem to impair her ability to carry on a conversation, most of which was devoted to the late president and assessments of his administration. We also discussed the rumors that Mrs. Harding might have poisoned her husband. McLean insisted absolutely not. "You have no idea how much she loved her 'Wurr'n.' I spent one evening with Florence in the White House while the president's body was still in the casket. It was open and she just sat there on a chair talking to him as if he was still alive. 'The trip has not hurt you a bit,' she said. 'No one can hurt you now, Wurr'n.' "

"I've also heard that Mrs. Harding has been burning her husband's papers," Mencken said.

"That's true," McLean replied. "I can testify to that. She's burned a lot of them out at Friendship. And she's going to burn some more in the next few days."

Knowing how little Mencken thought of Harding and his administration, I was surprised that he was so gentle on the president during the dinner conversation. He even agreed with Mrs. McLean that the president was honest and probably knew nothing about the corruption going on under his nose—at least until just recently.

As the dinner came to an end, I learned why Mencken had remained so uncritical of the late president. "And now, gentlemen," McLean said, "about the reward for retrieving that diamond? And who knows? It might have been the real Hope. But I think Mr. Mencken knew all along which was which."

"Elementary, my dear Mrs. McLean," Mencken said, "Elementary. We, of course, don't want any money. But there are two things I would like: One, we have a gloomy, forty-minute train trip back to Baltimore and we would appreciate it if you would refill our flask with the best brandy you have in the house. That would make the trip much more bearable. Two, I'm very much indebted to you for arranging the interview with President Harding that Sunday afternoon. And if you could, I'd like you to try to arrange a similar interview with Mrs. Harding, you seem every close to her; maybe a good word from you is all it would take."

"The first request is no problem. I'll be right back." And she disappeared into the hall.

"Cain, empty your flask and give it to me," Mencken said quickly, as he passed me a glass with a couple of swallows of wine left in it. I poured what was left of my bourbon into the wine glass and passed the flask to him.

Soon McLean was back with a bottle of brandy, which she proudly showed to Mencken. I could not see the bottle well enough to identify it, but Mencken said: "Ahhhhhhh," as he filled the flask. "Thank you very much. Fair exchange! A silly bauble, whether authentic or not, for a flask of Napoleon brandy."

"Now," McLean said: "I've been thinking about the second request. And I just might be able to arrange something. Florence said the president spoke highly of you after that interview. He thought that if a journalist of your caliber was giving credence to rumors he had better investigate. The president said that your comments really alerted him to what might be going on with Secretary Fall."

Suddenly, Mrs. McLean froze, as if she realized that the alcohol had loosened her tongue too much.

"What about Fall?" asked Mencken.

"Oh, that business about him suddenly having a lot of money to spend on his ranch. He knew that Albert Fall was not a wealthy man. The president told Florence that you were one of the first to alert him that something might be wrong."

"But you told us," Mencken stepped in rapidly, "that your husband had loaned Secretary Fall one hundred thousand dollars."

Mrs. McLean thought for a moment and then surprised us with her answer. She would regret it in the morning if she remembered. "No, I've convinced him that he shouldn't insist on that. That's going too far for a friend, Ned could end up in prison."

"That's right," said Mencken.

"I tell you this in strictest confidence: Secretary Fall got the money from Edward Doheny, head of the Pan American Petroleum Company and an old friend. It was a loan. Fall's friendship with Doheny goes back a lot longer than with Ned. And Doheny has way much more money than Ned does. It'll all come out in the Senate Hearings."

Mencken and I could only react to that incredible statement with silence, which McLean finally broke by saying: "Excuse me, there's something I want to check on upstairs. I'll be back in a minute."

While we were waiting for her return, we discussed what she had just let slip—we presumed it was a slip—that the head of a major oil company, which stood to make millions of dollars from the lease of government oil reserves, had made a loan of one hundred thousand dollars or more, to the Interior Department secretary who had engineered that lease! Even if none of that money had ever reached the White House, this would be one of history's greatest scandals.

"No wonder," said Mencken, "Mrs. McLean convinced her husband that he doesn't want to have anything to do with Teapot Dome. And I'll bet she gets us that interview. Mrs. Harding will be anxious to assure any credible journalist that her Wurr'n didn't have anything to do with Teapot Dome, either."

Mencken was right. When Mrs. McLean returned, she said: "You probably aren't aware of it, because there's only been a couple of mentions of it in the papers, but Mrs. Harding has been with us while she continues to go through her husband's papers. She's spent most of the time at Friendship, but we did come into Washington this afternoon so she could pick up some more documents at the White House, which is why you happened to catch us in town. She's upstairs now. She didn't have dinner with us for obvious reasons. But she's agreed to have an informal conversation with you, not an on-the-record interview. She'll be down in a minute and join us in the parlor."

We went back to the parlor where I noted that Ned McLean was no longer passed out on the couch; his body had been removed. I thought she might comment on this but she didn't, and Mencken said: "Mrs. McLean, one more reward. Would you mind letting me have that fake diamond you threw at your dog? It would be a nice souvenir from our Washington caper—and I'd know for sure that Roxy didn't have the real diamond."

"No, Mr. Mencken, you'll have to trust me."

We heard a sound at the door, and the butler was ushering into the room a statuesque, elderly woman, attired in a long black dress and wearing a black lightweight shawl over her shoulders, despite the excessive heat. She did not appear well. I knew immediately that it was Mrs. Harding and she did indeed look like a duchess. But she looked a dozen years older than the photographs I had last seen of her in the newspapers.

After Mrs. McLean made the introductions and seated Mrs. Harding at the other end of the couch that Ned McLean no longer occupied, Mrs. Harding spoke in what can only be described as a regal manner. There is little doubt that this woman was a power behind the presidential office: "Mr. Mencken, I know you have heard all the rumors about me poisoning my husband, but such a suggestion is absurd, absolutely absurd—and monstrous! For anyone to experience the tragic loss of a beloved spouse and then in your grief to hear people suggesting that you might have killed him is the height of cruelty. I hope you will remind your fellow journalists of that. And maybe you could write something about it."

"Mrs. Harding," Mencken replied softly, "I sympathize with you fully, but you are familiar enough with the newspaper business to know that you can't stop the rumors, especially when a lot of people think it was very strange that you would not permit an autopsy. It was not simply a question of whether he was killed by someone— and, as you know, there are other suspects—but that there is a great mystery about exactly what he did die of. I have one friend, a doctor at Johns Hopkins, who says that 'because there was no autopsy, we will never know what the president died of.' "

"He died of a heart attack, just as the doctors said. And I would never permit them to cut up my Wurr'n. You don't mutilate the body of a dead president who has to lie in state for several days."

"There's also the question," Mencken said, "of your burning lots of his papers, which suggests to the public that there is something to hide, which, in turn, would provide a motive for at least assisting in his suicide."

"Not at all. There was nothing to hide, because the president knew about the corruption, knew he had been betrayed by his friends. And believe me, this upset him. I remember when that Destroyer hit the *Henderson* and everybody was rushing topside in case they had to abandon ship, he just lay in his bunk with a pillow over his eyes, saying, 'I hope the ship sinks.' He fully intended, as he told me on that trip many times, to return to Washington and 'clean house'—his very words."

"So, why burn the papers?" Mencken insisted.

"Because, I must be loyal to my husband. Many of the papers would be misconstrued and would harm his memory. I have to say, in hindsight, that I may have destroyed too many papers, because I plan to write an intimate biography of my husband. I'm going through the papers more carefully now and save some."

"Everybody seems to be writing books," Mencken replied.

"Wurr'n thought you were," Mrs. Harding asked. "Is that correct?"

"We've gathered a lot of material and started the first draft, but it's turning into a much bigger job than we bargained for."

"I don't doubt that. And I hope you will ignore the rumors about the president having a lot of girlfriends."

"Mrs. Harding, that doesn't interest me, one way or the other. Anyone who has been working for newspapers as long as I have knows that men of the highest eminence sometimes have love affairs. In fact, they are more likely to have them than more obscure men because women pursue them with greater intensity."

"Especially true when the man is as handsome as my Wurr'n."

Mrs. McLean and I remained silent in this conversation; it was apparent that Mrs. Harding was primarily intent on talking only to the illustrious H. L. Mencken.

"You said your husband intended to 'clean house' when he returned from Alaska," Mencken said. "Who, exactly, did he have in mind?"

The Duchess hesitated. Then she said: "I'd rather not get into that now. I've talked with President Coolidge about the things Wurr'n told me, and what happens to some of his friends will eventually be made public."

"Secretary Fall has already left the Cabinet. Did your husband think his old friend from the Senate might have accepted money for leasing the oil reserves at Teapot Dome to an oil company?"

"Absolutely not! Wurr'n went to his grave convinced that Albert Fall was an honest man—that however he obtained the money to fix up his ranch had nothing to do with oil leases."

"What about Jesse Smith? Do you think his death was a suicide—or murder?"

"Suicide. Although, I must say if Jesse had gotten involved with some bootleggers and was about to confess to Harry Daugherty, I can see why the gangsters might want him out of the way."

"Daugherty might have wanted him out of the way, too."

"I don't like Harry Daugherty. Never have. But he didn't kill Jesse; he was too fond of him."

"He might have thought he was doing Jesse a favor, just as some people are saying that you might have decided to do your husband a favor, by saving him from the scandals that would surely greet him when he got home?"

Mencken had gone too far. Mrs. Harding virtually bristled, and Mrs. McLean said: "Henry, I think you better leave. Duchess has not been sleeping well and she's very tired. It's time she went to bed."

Mencken rose quickly to his feet and offered Mrs. Harding a hand as she tried to rise from her seat. He too knew his last remark had been a mistake. Mrs. Harding said that Mrs. McLean was correct, that she was getting very tired. Mrs. McLean walked her to the hall door and signaled the butler to escort Mrs. Harding to her room.

We thanked Mrs. McLean for dinner and for arranging the conversation with Mrs. Harding. Soon we were in her car on the way to the station.

On the train, fortified by cups of powerful but unbelievably smooth brandy, we went over everything: Roxy's return; her new persona; the diamond—real or fake; Nan Britton; her book and the president's daughter; Means' appearance and the man who followed us to the station; the drunken McLeans; did Roxy return the diamond only after learning it was a fake? Mrs. McLean convincing her husband to change his story about the loan to Fall; the secretary of the Interior; Doheny and Teapot Dome and the conversation with Mrs. Harding.

We also talked about Jesse's death, Roxy's involvement, Gaston Means and the diamond. "Can you imagine," Mencken said, "poor

Jesse going to his grave because they put a curse on him with a diamond—that turned out to be fake! Incredible."

"Henry, did you really know that the diamond Roxy gave us at the Rennert was fake?"

He turned, looked out the window and thought for a moment before he said: "I thought there was a good chance. Elementary, Watson. If it was real, Roxy would not have returned it. She didn't really have to. The only person who knew Smith had it was Means and who would believe him? What woman could pass up such an opportunity?"

I was shaking my head as I said: "Well, I believe she thought it was real and was doing the right thing."

"We'll never know," said Mencken.

Then we began to slide into a conclusion finally expressed by Mencken: "You know Cain, we've bitten off more than we can chew—at least, more than I can. It's simply too big a project and will take more time and digging to authenticate than I can devote to it. I've got a column going, another book and two magazines to think about. Let's have some more of that brandy."

I poured him more and as he took a long swallow, I knew what was coming next: "Ahhhhhhhhh. Cain, I'm going to have to pull out of this story. With Harding dead, it doesn't have the same bite for me. But I think you ought to go on with it. You've got a lot of it in your manuscript now and you have the time to keep digging. I have an idea: Why don't I speak to the *Sun* people about rehiring you to take on a special assignment digging into the Harding corruption, with the understanding that you can do a book on it later? I know you know more about what's been going on in Washington than anyone on the paper, including Kent."

I thought about this, while Mencken looked out the window at the trees rushing by in the lingering twilight. It was August and the days were still long. I did not know how to respond. I had given a pretty firm commitment to St. John's. And I thought the *Sun* bringing me back to work on a Washington story would be kind of a slap in the face to Frank Kent, whom I considered a friend. And this infernal cough had me concerned.

"Let me think about it for a day or two," I finally said, "while I try to digest all the stuff we've just learned and get it down on paper. It's been some day."

It was dark by the time I arrived home at my apartment, which was something of a mess because I had started packing for my move to Annapolis. I had hardly turned on some fans and poured myself a shot of McLean's brandy, when the telephone rang. It was Mencken.

"Cain, don't you think it's a little hot for a fire?"

"If your house is as miserable as my apartment, I do."

"Well, when I came home, there were ashes still smoldering in the fireplace. I knew my mother or August didn't burn anything because they're up at our summer place in Mount Washington and have been for a couple of days. I couldn't figure out what it was, and then I had a flash. I checked my office upstairs and, believe it or not, the carbons of the manuscript you gave me are missing! And the back door definitely showed signs of a break-in. I checked the fireplace again and the black mess definitely looked like the remains of some manuscript pages. Considering that there were still red sparks in the ashes, whoever did it had not been gone too long when I arrived home."

"Just as well you didn't get home while they were there, or you might have got yourself shot."

"Except you still have Means' gun. Of course, one of his men could have had a heater, as they say in Chicago."

"So you think Means did it?"

"Who else? It all fits together. First, he knew my mother and August were not here. And that explains why the little man who followed us to the station didn't get on the train. He was just keeping an eye on us, with instructions to call Means at my house—or your apartment—and warn him when we headed home."

"Jesus! Yes! Or my apartment!" We both had the same idea at the same moment: "Hang on, I'll check."

I had made no effort to hide my copy of the manuscript, which I kept in a large manila envelope in the bigger, right-hand, lower drawer of my desk.

When I returned to the phone, I said: "Damn it! Henry, I think we've underestimated this Means. My manuscript's gone, too."

CHAPTER TWENTY–SEVEN

Means had, indeed, outsmarted us. He could now score points with Daugherty by telling him that he had destroyed both copies of the manuscript we were working on. Meanwhile, he, no doubt, kept my copy of our work for use in developing his own book.

The loss of both copies of the manuscript really finished it for Mencken and it was clearly my project now. There was no question about his withdrawal. But I was undecided about continuing the investigation alone, even though I still had my notes (which were in a box in another drawer of the desk). The truth is, politics and politicians are not my favorite subjects and I did not consider myself much of an investigator. I had gone along on this adventure primarily as a way to solidify a friendship with Mencken. And, frankly, I was more interested in writing for his new magazine than going back to work, even temporarily, as a reporter for the *Sun*.

That was my thinking when I went to the doctor to see if it was tuberculosis causing my cough. "You've got it all right," he said. "Now let's let an X-ray tell us how much."

What the X-ray told us was that I had an active lesion about the size of a quarter in my right lung. He said that I could probably teach the first term at St. John's but I would eventually have to go into a sanatorium. He also said my symptoms would get worse— loss of weight and appetite, pains in my chest and increased coughing that would eventually be accompanied by hemorrhaging.

As soon as I had the doctor's verdict, I wrote Roxy through Nan Britton, about the bad news and told her that we probably would not be seeing each other until I was completely cured; for one thing, I said, "I have been advised not to engage in strenuous exercise."

This was one of the most difficult decisions I ever made. My feeling for Roxy had reached the stage of passion, which is the secret word I use to describe my feeling about a woman and which signals to me that I could be moving toward love. When the desire becomes incandescent enough, which doesn't happen very often, you have passion. And that I had.

However, as we exchanged letters for awhile, gradually the passion—on both sides—began to wane. I'm sure she had second thoughts about being in love with a lunger, who as everyone knows, must have limited ambitions. She did not show much enthusiasm when I told her that after my cure, I was heading for New York in search of a writing job Mencken had promised to help me find. But she had no interest in New York; her main desire seemed to be to return to Ohio, get married ("I'm getting along in years, you know") and "never again go any further east than Pittsburgh."

I would never ever *really* know whether she was telling us the truth about that night. Was she just a little too eager to assist Jesse in his suicide? Did she find Jesse's money belt and keep the cash? And did she decide to return the diamond only *after* she learned, somehow, that it was the fake? I was willing to give her the benefit of the doubt and had. But I knew it would always be in the back of my mind. Mencken, on the other hand, didn't care one way or the other.

When I called him to tell him about the diagnosis, we agreed the project was dead, except, perhaps, as an article for the *Mercury*. We decided to give our notes to Senators Burton K. Wheeler and Thomas Walsh, the two Montana senators leading the investigations of the Justice Department and Teapot Dome.

On the train to Washington, we got to talking about Roxy, Nan Britton and President Harding. We agreed we would not tell the senators about Roxy's assisting Jesse with his suicide or what we knew about the late president's affair. "They probably know about it anyway," Mencken said "and if they're gentlemen, they won't be interested except as gossip in the Senate speakeasy."

"Maybe they've had a couple of affairs themselves," I said.

Probably not, we decided after meeting them. Walsh was short, with a manner that was both alert and severe. He had cold, blue eyes, a determined jaw, light gray hair, but black, bushy eyebrows and moustache. With his jacket, bow tie and white slacks he gave the appearance of a college professor. Wheeler looked as plain and undistingished as Calvin Coolidge, maybe because he was also born in Massachusetts, although he represented Montana in the Senate.

Mencken had made the appointment, which did not last very long. They thanked us for the notes and when it became evident that most of what we knew came from Roxy Stinson and Gaston Means, they assured us that they would be among their first witnesses. When we mentioned that Roxy might be in some danger, Wheeler agreed, but said nothing about having her in hiding. He did say he was aware that the "Ohio Gang," as Wheeler persistently called them, would do anything to prevent the hearings, that both his and Walsh's office had been ransacked; and that Walsh's daughter had been stopped on the street while wheeling Walsh's granddaughter and threatened if he did not cancel the hearings. "Naturally, I've ignored them," Walsh said, "but I have sent my daughter away for awhile."

When we were leaving, Mencken said, loud enough so that it echoed up and down the cavernous halls: "Jeeeeeeeesus Christ, Cain, a couple of really tough, honest politicians! I like the way they breed 'em in Montana."

I did not see Mencken for a few days after that, but we had agreed to have one last lunch at Marconi's before I started teaching, to talk about other ideas for the magazine. I told him my work on the labor leader was progressing, and he said: "Great. Bring what you have along and we'll talk about it."

Our luncheon date was for noon and, as usual, I arrived a little early at Marconi's. It was a hot, sunny day in late August, a sharp contrast to that chilly, drizzly day in spring when we began our Washington caper. Ah August, certainly not one of those months of which the poets sing. I checked my *Bartlett's* and was unable to find a single reference to it, although May has twenty-three and even December has six. And if April (or is it November?) is the cruelest month, surely August is the dullest. But if anyone could liven up a dog day and make you feel good, it was H. L. Mencken.

Brookes escorted me to Mencken's table and I took a seat with my back to the door. I had ordered my pilsner and was deep in a curious little story in the women's section of the morning *Sun* about A. Conan Doyle trying to communicate with the dead President Harding, when heads started to turn and comments could be heard. I didn't have to look at the clock on the wall to know that its two hands pointed straight to noon and that I was about to be greeted by that slave to punctuality. I knew exactly what he was going to say: "Christ, Cain, I'm thirstier than a Pizbyterian minister!"

After taking his usual seat, waving ceremoniously to a couple of *Sun* reporters across the room, and signalling Brookes for his two pilsners, he said: "Jim. I hope you're feeling better now and following doctor's orders. Did you bring what you have of your article? I'd like to take a look at it."

I thought he had planned to take it home or to the office and read it later. "Yeah, I got it," I said, pulling it out of my coat pocket and handing it to him. "It's about half done."

While he was reading quickly through it, Brookes brought the pilsners and Mencken gulped one down. Then, flipping my article back to the first page, he said: "Good stuff. Let's see how this sounds." Then he started reading the lead, loud enough so that the couple at the next table, whom he apparently did not know, could hear him:

> He is recruited from people of the sort that nice ladies call common. Such people are mostly out of sight in the cities. The streets they inhabit are remote from the boulevards; their doings are too sordid and trivial for newspapers to notice, save when the police are called in. In the small towns they are more openly on view, to the horror of old families. Big city or small town, they are all alike.

"Very nice, Jim, very nice." After taking a gulp from his second cup, he continued:

> They are the sort that mop up the plate with bread. That have six-by-eight porches on their homes, and wash flapping on the clotheslines. That take a bath every Saturday night and slosh blue, soapy water down the gutters. That own a twenty-five-dollar phonograph and these four records: 'In the Shade of the Old Apple Tree,' 'Barney Google,' 'Walking with Jesus' (Orpheus Quartet), and 'Cohen on the Telephone.' That join the Heptasophs, the Junior Order, and (if getting up in the world) the Odd Fellows. Whose women-folk grow fat and rock on the porches wearing blue check dresses. Whose men-folk are laid up with elusive ailments related to the stummock. . . .

Then he folded the pages and tossed the unfinished manuscript back to me: "First rate, Jim. This is just what I want for the new magazine. I see a couple of places where I might put the pencil to it. But you finish it, mail it back and then we can palaver. It'll be a good excuse for another lunch. Get it to me by the end of October. I'm definitely scheduling this for the first issue. Let's talk about some more pieces just like it."

More than the weather had changed since that day in the spring. There was also my relationship with Mencken. He was still my idol and I was the aspiring young writer looking up to an author and editor who had already achieved far more that I ever would. But now I felt that we were good friends and that he had seen enough of my writing to consider me a serious writer with real potential. That was a great lift to my professional morale at a time when personal morale, because of my health, was very low.

After we ordered, Mencken began probing me for article ideas and we came to a tentative agreement about three I would be developing for the future—one on editorial writers; another on the pedagogues in the universities; and a third on female politicians.

"Of course," I said, "I don't know how much I'll be able to work on these. The doctor said that as my condition gets worse, I'm going to get weaker and probably by the end of the first semester I'll have to go into a sanatorium for awhile."

"Well, if you can get your research done before you go, you'll have time to write in the sanatorium. You may even do your best work there. I've always been convinced that tuberculosis is very stimulating to the mind. The consumptive may be weak physically, but he's very alert mentally. I think Somerset Maugham started *The Moon and Sixpence* in a sanatorium. He was working in British Intelligence in Russia during the war, when his doctors diagnosed his coughing and fever as TB. 'A sanatorium is the place for you, my boy,' one of them cheerily told him. So he went for a stay at a sanatorium in Northern Scotland. Not only did he start a novel there, but later he got a short story out of it—'The Sanatorium.' It's about two patients who decide to marry, although they know it will shorten their lives. You might think about that, Jim."

Passing that up, I asked: "Do you know Maugham?"

Brookes arrived with our food and when he had gone, Mencken said: "Yeah, we published one of his stories—'Rain'—in *The Smart*

Set after several magazines turned it down. I met him a couple of times—once in New York, where we talked until two A.M.; another in Baltimore, where we talked for a couple of hours. This was a few years after his time in the sanatorium."

"How did he look? I mean his health?"

"Oh, he looked well enough; a little drawn and pale."

"That's good news about writing in the lung house," I said just before Brookes brought our coffee and Mencken lit up a Willie.

Reflecting for a moment as he stared at his cigar smoke, he said: "Jim, has anyone worse than Harding ever been the head of a great state?"

Not waiting for the answer, he continued: "Certainly, not in modern history. One must go back to the mad princes of the Middle Ages to find his match. As a fool he was almost unparalleled. No other such complete and dreadful nitwit is to be found in the pages of American history. Compared to him, even a Millard Fillmore begins to take on the stature of a Barbarossa. His reign lasted only two years and five months, but into that short space was packed more tin-pot melodrama and slapstick farce than you will find in the whole four years of any other president, a saturnalia in the grand manner. But with all that, Gamaliel still replaces Grover Cleveland as my favorite president. He does Grover one better; not only did he father an illegitimate child, he needed upwards of one thousand dollars a month of graft to pay for his extra-marital gambolling. And he's the only president who ever did anything sensible in the White House—making love to his mistress in a coat closet. I'm sure ol' Grover never did that."

"What do you think is going to happen to the crooks in his administration?"

"That depends primarily on what Roxy, Means, McLean and Remus tell the Senate investigating committees. I think we're going to see some people go to jail. I'm not sure about Fall, Doheny and Sinclair. The plain truth is that corruption in public office is no longer a criminal offense. During the two war years, the business of looting the Treasury was developed to such a colossal magnitude and engaged in by so many citizens that all efforts to punish it or even challenge it broke down. Many men were jailed for protesting against the pillage but not one was jailed for taking part in it."

"Do you think they'll ever implicate Harding?"

"No. But, of course, he's every bit as guilty as Fall. Remember, De Tocqueville said corruption is inseparable from democracy. This is because public office under a democracy is not conferred by a power that thinks only of the public interest, but by powers that think only of private interest. To argue that there is a difference between Fall accepting private loans from Sinclair and Doheny and Harding accepting campaign contributions before the act is to argue the difference between Tweedledum and Tweedledee."

"How 'bout Coolidge? Will he survive the scandals?"

"Certainly, By the time of the Republican Convention in Cleveland next year, Teapot Dome and the crooks in Washington will be so stale that even vaudeville comedians will have forgotten them. Add to the fact, which I'm sure you've seen in the press, that Cal's only serious Democratic opponent, William Gibbs McAdoo, will certainly be eliminated by the revelation that he was once on Doheny's payroll as a legal consultant—and you can be assured that on the first Tuesday after the second Monday in November next year, cool Cal will be elected president in his own right."

"What if Miss Britton gets her book out, won't that have an impact?"

"Not much. She's going to have a tough time publishing it under any circumstances; she can't possibly get it out by next fall, and when she does it will probably be discredited and ignored because Americans do not want to hear about the private lives of their high dignitaries. And here is one area where the responsible press shows some sensitivity and discretion, because it's aware that when people hear you talking about personal hanky panky, they know that somebody's privacy has been invaded. And if there's one thing Americans value as much as liberty, it's their privacy."

"Incidentally," I said, "did you see that item in the paper this morning about the Duchess getting all excited by A. Conan Doyle claiming he has spoken frequently with the late president?"

"No!" Mencken responded incredulously.

"Yep. So now she's trying to reach her husband through a medium. According to a *Washington Post* story, for which we know the source, Mrs. McLean went to see Doyle when he was in Washington on a lecture tour, and told him, 'You better go back to writing detective stories.' "

"That's right. When Doyle steps out of his persona as Sherlock

Holmes, he reveals himself to be a colossal moron, which makes you wonder about the vaunted brilliance of his creation. Speaking of Doyle, you remember we started out last spring pretending like we would pull a Holmes-and-Watson-go-to-Washington caper to expose the corruption in the Harding administration?"

"I do, indeed. And I think we did a pretty good job although we didn't end up solving the case."

"Ah Cain, but we had fine investigation and a good time. Why don't you forget an article or a non-fiction book and write a Washington novel? The novelists who write about Washington are mostly recruited from the ranks of Washington newspaper correspondents, perhaps the most naive and unreflective body of literary men in Christendom. They see the essential Washington drama as a struggle between a powerful and corrupt senator and a sterling young uplifter. The senator is about to sell out the republic to the steel trust or the Russians. The uplifter detects him, drives him from public life and inherits his job."

"And the love interest?"

"Usually it's supplied by a fair stenographer who steals the damning papers—just like Smith's presumed papers—from the senator's safe or by an ambassador's wife, who goes to the White House at three A.M., at the imminent peril of her virtue, arouses the president and tells him what's afoot. All this is poppycock. There are no sterling uplifters anymore. The last one was chased out after the Mexican War. Today there are only men looking for jobs."

Mencken was not joking. He was serious.

"But you have a perfect love interest, Jim—Roxy! I almost fell in love with her myself, especially after it became clear that she'd be willing to assist me in leaving this vale of tears in case He botches the job."

"I don't know about a novel," I said. "I proved down in West Virginia that I couldn't write one. Besides, when you write a novel, you need something stronger than political graft. I want to write about the juicy stuff—incest, whores, adultery and murder you get away with but haunts you for the rest of your life."

"All right. What about a good mystery? We know Samuel Hopkins Adams is writing a conventional novel. But we have a couple of possible murders over there that may well go unsolved."

"I know one possible murder—Jesse Smith. But Cramer is pretty well established as a suicide. Who's the other murder victim?"

"Gamaliel, of course. I'll bet you right now that for the next fifty years they're going to be speculating on who killed Harding, with the Duchess being the primary suspect."

"And Jesse?"

"Take your choice. It's fiction; you can do anything you want. Just start telling the story we dug up. You can change the names later."

And I well remember Henry's last comments, as we headed for the door and Saratoga Street: "The main thing on your book, Jim, is: Keep it interesting. In that you don't compose symphonies, your best bet for immortality is not prayer, but a good novel. Writing is our religion. You know I'm a pious man who devoutly believes that Jonah swallowed the whale—or was it the other way around? And I'm going to pray for you every night, giving thanks to the Almighty."

"Why's that?"

"Well, we know the cosmos is a gigantic fly-wheel making ten thousand revolutions a minute and man is a sick fly taking a dizzy ride in it. And religion is the theory that the wheel was designed and sent spinning just to give us the ride. He gave us a good ride for the last three months and, with His help, you ought to get a pretty good book out of it."

So that's how it ended—and began. I decided not to change the names.

APPENDIX

Much of what the main characters in the preceeding pages did in this story is in the realm of fiction and fantasy. However, what is reported below actually happened to these people in the months and years following the fall of 1923. (See page 381 for sources which suppport the factual outcome of this fanciful tale.)

James M. Cain. Cain finished and was paid $60 for his article on "The Labor Leader," but when he received his advance copy of the January, 1924, *Mercury,* he was horrified to find that his piece was not included in this future collector's item. The union printers hired to print the magazine would not typeset the article because his portrait of the labor leader was not 100 percent flattering, although Cain was a supporter of the union cause. Mencken found another printer, but explained to Cain that "in case we had to sue them, we had to show some tangible injury the brawl had caused us and so we held the article out. It'll appear next month." It did and Cain went on to write more than a dozen major pieces for the *Mercury.* Mencken said Cain was "the most competent writer the country ever produced; he never wrote a bad article."

When Cain came out of the sanatorium at Sabillasville, Maryland, Mencken gave him a letter of recommendation to Arthur Krock, who was then an assistant to the publisher of the *New York World.* This led to a job as editorial writer for Walter Lippmann at the *World* in New York, where he met and married his second wife, Elina Tyszecka. Cain went on to a sucessful career as journalist, Hollywood screenwriter and novelist—and two more wives.

H. L. Mencken. As the Senate investigations of Attorney General Daugherty and Teapot Dome began in 1924, Mencken wrote several columns on the corruption in the Harding administration. After his coverage of the Scopes "Monkey Trial" in Tennessee in 1925, he emerged as the most powerful voice in American public affairs, the leader of a second American Revolution—this one in morals and literature. However, his power and influence gradually began to diminish in the late 1920s and completely waned after he was forced to resign as editor of the *Mercury* in the early 1930s. In 1930, at the age of fifty, Mencken, the most confirmed bachelor in the country, married Sara Haardt. When Prohibition ended in 1933, he was photographed at the Rennert Hotel bar, where everyone wanted to hear the country's most vocal wet's comment on—at last—being served a legal brew. "Ahhhhhhhh," Mencken said, downing a large glass of water, "my first in thirteen years." He and Cain remained friends until Mencken's death in 1956.

Roxy Stinson. Roxy was the first witness called in March of 1924 by Senator Burton K. Wheeler's committee investigating Attorney General Daugherty. She created a sensation. The newspapers commented on her good looks, striking red hair and "chorus girl figure" and the *Washington Times* said the hearings "had all the atmosphere of a murder trial combined with the bated breath of the opening of King Tut's tomb, King Tut . . . being poor Jesse Smith" (the reference was to the opening of King Tutankhamen's tomb in Egypt two years earlier).

Roxy told of the little houses on H and K Streets where deals were made, poker was played, whiskey permits were sold, liquor was consumed and women were entertained. She said Smith (and Daugherty) made $180,000 on the showings of the Dempsey-Carpentier fight film; that Jesse came back to Ohio with a money belt carrying seventy-five thousand-dollar bills; and that Jesse told her that five of his friends made thirty-three million dollars in a Sinclair oil deal, in which Jesse and Daugherty were not involved and "that is what we are sore about." She told about the incident in Ohio at the shack, after which Jesse bought the gun. She said that Jesse was right-handed but that he was shot through the left temple. She thought it was suicide, but told the committee: "I consider Harry Daugherty as morally responsible for the death of Jesse Smith."

Roxy Stinson was on the stand five days, and James M. Cain, the *World* editorial writer and future novelist, must have followed her testimony closely while working in New York. He later recalled that her manner of speech "burst on the country like a Fourth of July rocket," and that she became something of a cult literary figure. "She could come popping out with some bromide," Cain said, "a cornball expression that should have been pure hushpuppy, and somehow transform it, the way Dvorak transformed folk music."

After Cain became famous as a novelist, people started saying that his style had been influenced by Hemingway. Cain said not so, that it was Roxy Stinson who had influenced his style the most. And he must have assumed that Hemingway followed the Hearings from the Paris edition of the *Herald Tribune,* because he thought Roxy Stinson influenced them both. And he was even more convinced of this theory when he finally read Hemingway's short story *Fifty Grand,* which had an incident in its plot similar to one described by Roxy Stinson in her Senate testimony.

But Cain never met Roxy, who returned to Ohio, eventually remarried and lived out a happily married life in Oklahoma. Just before she died, at the age of eighty-two, she told a *Columbus Dispatch* reporter: "I've had so many writers here. I'm sorry I can't help you. I'm a rock-ribbed Republican, but I can't stand politics. It's so dirty. I drew a lot of notoriety once, and if I were to say anything it would start all over again."

Gaston B. Means. Means was the next to appear at the Hearings. Senator Wheeler called him "one of the most incredible figures in the annals of cloak-and-dagger work in this country" and Means' biographer, Edwin P. Hoyt, aptly titled his book: *Spectacular Rogue.* Just before he was to appear, Means notified Attorney General Daugherty that there was still time to call off his prosecution of him before he went before Wheeler's committee, where he promised to blow the lid off the Harding administration. "Daugherty told Gaston to go to the devil," wrote Harding biographer Francis Russell.

Means, if anything, created more of a sensation than Roxy. He appeared before the committee carrying two accordion cases containing, he said, all of the diaries of his government years. And after being introduced by William Burns (in charge of the Justice Department's investigative division) as one of the ablest investigators he had ever known, Means started off by proclaiming dramatically:

"I waive immunity. I ask no quarter and my intention is to give no quarter. I have been advised by counsel and urged not to appear here." And he put on quite a show, giving a dimpled smile to all the senators, occasionally and mysteriously producing a piece of paper from one of his boxes to quote from and responding quickly, cooperatively and often wittily to all questions. When asked if he had ever been convicted of a felony, he replied: "I have been accused of every crime in the catalogue, but not convicted, so far." And when asked what his current business was, he said: "Answering indictments." By the time he finished, the whole country was reciting:

> *Who spilled the beans?*
> *"I," said Gaston B. Means.*
> *"I was behind the scenes.*
> *I spilled the beans."*

Means said he had worked with Jesse Smith, giving him at least a quarter of a million dollars in graft and payoffs over the years. He remembered one payoff of $100,000 in connection with the settlement of the Standard Aircraft case. He told of investigating Daugherty for the president, of investigating bootleggers in an effort to have the enforcement of Prohibition laws transferred to the Justice Department; and investigating several senators, always looking for something that might discredit them. Nothing wrong with that; "Bradstreet and Dun makes the most minute credit investigations; banks do it; everybody is investigated some way," including, he would like them to believe, Means himself. Virtually all of his bizarre testimony depended on the documentation in his accordion cases, which he continually refused to produce. Finally one morning, Means told the committee that all his files had been stolen by two men claiming to be assistant sergeants-at-arms of the Senate.

His testimony failed to kill his own indictment and he was put on trial, during which he implicated Harding, Daugherty and Secretary of the Treasury Mellon—before he was found guilty and sentenced to two years in prison. During his appeal, he repudiated Roxy Stinson's testimony and signed a statement repudiating his charges against Daugherty, claiming that Sen. Wheeler had prompted him to lie. He still went to jail, but that was not the last the country would hear of the incredible rogue (see below).

The Death of Jesse Smith. Jesse Smith's death was never completely resolved, especially in the eyes of Evalyn Walsh McLean, who hired two detectives to find out what really happened. They reported that Gaston B. Means was most likely involved, based on an interview with a bellboy who passed a large man with dimples that night on the back stairs of the Wardman. When McLean confronted Means, he admitted that he was in Smith's apartment, but that Smith was already dead. Soon after Smith's death, the records of the D.C. police were destroyed. There was no inquest and no autopsy. The only remaining police document said: "Wound of entry on the left side of head shows powder burns, considerable damage to right side of head at hole of exit. . . ." As late as 1957, a D.C. policeman said that "it don't hardly happen" that a right-handed man shoots himself in the left side of the head.

Attorney General Daugherty. Because Daugherty still had powerful support in the Republican Party, President Coolidge was reluctant to fire him. But after Daugherty was found to have burned key papers involving bank transactions with his brother's bank in Ohio and refused to appear before the Wheeler Committee, Coolidge forced his resignation. Then, he was indicted with Colonel Miller, the Alien Property Custodian, for conspiracy in the American Metal Company case in a manner that implicated Harding in the scandals. Daugherty's lawyer added credence to this thought when he said that his client feared that the prosecutors would "cross-examine him about matters of politics that would not involve Mr. Daugherty, concerning which he knew, and to which he would never make disclosure . . . If the jury knew the real reason for destroying the ledger sheets, they would commend rather than condemn him." Was there a woman involved? At least one chronicler of this era decided that this ploy probably saved Daugherty.

Although Miller was convicted for his part in the crime, the jury, after sixty-five hours of deliberation, was hung about Daugherty. He was re-tried and the jury was hung again. And Daugherty went to his grave boasting as he did in his whitewashing book, *The Inside Story of the Harding Tragedy,* that "no charge against me was ever proven in any court."

Florence Harding. The Duchess died of chronic nephritis in November of 1924. Because she had refused to permit an autopsy of her husband, rumors persist to this day that she played a role in the death of her husband. A recent biography by Carl Anthony maintains the president's death was caused by one too many purgatives given the patient by his personal physician (and Mrs. Harding's), "Doc" Sawyer. The last was administered while Mrs. Harding was in the room and she was said to have assisted in the ensuing cover-up of just what did happen in those last minutes of the president's life. She apparently never knew about Nan Britton and the president's daughter.

William J. Burns. Burns was forced to resign from the Justice Department after he failed to tell the Senate that Daugherty had sent Justice Department agents to Montana to investigate Senator Burton K. Wheeler when the senator was investigating the Teapot Dome affair. Burns was found guilty of contempt and sentenced to fifteen days in jail. His reputation was ruined and his son replaced him as head of his world-famous detective agency. J. Edgar Hoover replaced Burns as head of the Justice Department's Investigative Division.

Nan Britton. Virtually non-existent in the eyes of Harding's family and executors, Britton finished her book, *The President's Daughter,* in 1927. Publishers and magazine editors refused to consider it and when she brought it out herself, under the imprint of Elizabeth Ann Guild and assisted by her boss, Richard Wightman, head of the Bible Corporation of America, bookstores and reviewers ignored it until H. L. Mencken wrote a long review in the July 18, 1927 *Sun.* After Mencken's article, Brentano's ordered ten copies, then fifty copies, etc., and by September the book was a bestseller.

It was dedicated "with understanding and love to all unwedded mothers and to their innocent children whose fathers are usually not known to the world." Mencken said he was not concerned about Miss Britton's "highly romantic account" of "Warren's mushy love-making" but rather the unsuccessful efforts of the Comstocks (who raided the printing plants and seized the plates) to keep the book from being published, which he thought would, as usual, give the book a wide circulation (he was right).

But what really intrigued him was Nan's portrait of Harding as the worst statesman in modern times. He concluded with the suggestion that the Carnegie Institution put a young researcher to work immediately, writing a complete history of the Harding administration. "It will throw more light upon the inner workings of the American system of government than even the secret archives of the Anti-Saloon League or the Ku Klux Klan."

As for the primary subject matter of Britton's book, Mencken said it was "intimate and confidential." The fact that "men of the highest eminence," he said, sometimes have cladestine love affairs is "surely not a secret to anyone who has been working for newspapers as long as I have. They are more apt to have them, in fact, than more obscure men, for women pursue them with greater assiduity and they themselves stand in greater need of sentimental relaxation."

The president's daughter, Elizabeth Ann, grew up carrying the name of Harding through high school, then married and had three sons who did not know their name was Harding until they graduated from high school. Nan lived to be almost one hundred, maintaining her concern for unwed mothers until the end of her life.

George Remus. After Jesse Smith's death in 1923, Remus had no way of stopping the indictment, trial and guilty verdict that he had paid Smith so much to prevent. He started his two-year jail sentence in 1924, but was let out long enough to return to Washington as a witness in the Senate Hearings on the attorney general. While he was in jail, his wife, who he said had used up at least two million dollars of his fortune, met and fell in love with Franklin L. Dodge, the handsome Justice Department agent who helped put Remus in jail. Remus was naturally furious and, one day, after he was released, followed his wife and daughter who were in a cab. When it stopped at a light, he pulled his wife out of the taxi and shot her, confirming that you don't double-cross George Remus. He turned himself in to the police and at the trial defended himself and the "sanctity of the home." He was found not guilty because of insanity and served six months in a state mental institution, before three judges, for whatever reasons, agreed that he had regained his sanity.

Secretary Albert Fall. The Teapot Dome and Elk Hill oil leases were investigated by a Senate committee under the general direction of Senator Thomas Walsh of Montana. The hearings began in October of 1923, during which Walsh's office was ransacked, his phones tapped, government agents looked into his past and his daughter was even stopped on the street and warned that her father should stop the investigation. After witnesses testified to Fall spending up to $175,000 improving his ranch, Fall insisted that he had never received any money from either Harry Sinclair or Edward Doheny. At the hearings, Doheny denied giving Fall money and Sinclair said he had only given him some cows and a bull. But when Walsh persisted in his inquiries into Fall's new-found wealth, Fall asked Ned McLean to say that he had lent Fall one hundred thousand dollars. McLean said he would, and Fall, now in seclusion in an Atlantic City hotel and drinking a lot, wrote Senator Walsh that his good friend, McLean, had lent him the money. McLean wired Walsh from Palm Beach a confirmation—whereupon Walsh wired McLean that he was coming to Palm Beach to get his testimony under oath.

With this, McLean panicked. When Walsh arrived, McLean told him that he had never really loaned Fall any money. By now, Fall was also in Palm Beach, holed up in a suite at the Breakers and refusing to see Walsh, who wanted to tell Fall what he had just learned from McLean. When McLean went to Fall's room to tell him that he could not lie about the loan to a Senate committee, he learned for the first time that Doheny had lent Fall the one hundred thousand dollars. "That day at Palm Beach," wrote Harding's biographer Francis Russell, "was the turning point in the investigation, the day that would eventually make Teapot Dome a household phrase and begin the erosion of Harding's reputation."

But the hearings really made the headlines when it was revealed that the one hundred thousand dollars in cash was delivered in a black suitcase to Secretary Fall at the Wardman Park Hotel by Doheny's son (who was later shot by his secretary). The money was no big deal, said Doheny: one hundred thousand dollars to him was "no more than twenty-five or fifty dollars perhaps to the ordinary individual." He admitted that he expected to make one hundred million dollars out of his Elk Hill oil lease.

Although Fall continued to be uncooperative, it was revealed that he had also received several thousand dollars from Harry Sinclair (who said he had expected to make one hundred million dollars out of his Teapot Dome lease). After the hearings, Fall was indicted in criminal court for contempt of the Senate. The government cancelled the oil leases and the cases against Fall, Sinclair and Doheny dragged on in the courts for several years before Fall was convicted of bribery in accepting the black satchel of cash and eventually went to jail.

Edward Doheny and Harry Sinclair. In *The Incredible Era,* the first account of the Harding administration corruption, Samuel Hopkins Adams called the seven years of trials following the Teapot Dome hearings an "opera bouffe." In summary, he wrote: "Fall was guilty of receiving a bribe from Doheny, but Doheny was innocent of giving a bribe to Fall. Sinclair and Fall were innocent of defrauding the government through the Teapot Dome oil leases, but those same leases were secured by collusion and conspiracy on the part of Sinclair and Fall. Fall and Doheny were innocent in the deal for Elk Hill oil, but that deal was adjudged by the highest court of the land to be the product of fraud and corruption."

Fall was sentenced to a year in jail and fined one hundred thousand dollars; Doheny was acquitted of all charges and was given a hero's welcome when he returned to Los Angeles after the trial; Sinclair served three months in jail for contempt of the Senate.

Charles Forbes. The Director of the Veterans' Bureau was found guilty of bribery and conspiracy, fined ten thousand dollars and sentenced to three years at Leavenworth.

Calvin Coolidge. With his chief Democratic rival, William Gibbs McAdoo, out of the race because of his involvement with Edward Doheny, and apparently untainted by all the scandals that emerged in 1924, Coolidge was easily the victor in the presidential election of that year.

Gaston B. Means (continued): After he was released from prison, he teamed up with a writer for *True Confessions,* May Dixon Thacker, to write a book, *The Strange Death of President Harding.* It created even more of a sensation than Nan Britton's book. It was published in 1930 and with the Hardings, Jesse Smith and Doc Sawyer dead and Daugherty no longer in power, Means was free to say almost anything he wanted without fear of contradiction, not that that bothered him. Here are some of his "revelations":

- Florence Harding, as a "Child of Destiny," murdered her husband to break the hold the "Gang" had on him and because of her jealousy of Nan Britton, who Means said he had spied on for the Duchess.
- Jesse Smith had been murdered because he was a traitor to "the Gang" and had papers which he was going to turn over to Mrs. Harding which would bring down the government. The killer, Means implied, was someone he had never seen before and who, on the night of Smith's death, the gang instructed him to meet on a Washington street corner and drive to Harper's Ferry, West Virginia, where the man boarded a train for the West.
- Charles Cramer, the Veterans' Bureau lawyer, was also murdered.

Summarizing Justice Department crimes, he said Daugherty:

- modified decrees of federal judges;
- dismissed civil and criminal cases;
- forced collection of tribute in ongoing cases;
- altered prison sentences;
- sold paroles;
- sold federal judgeships;
- sold U.S. District Attorney offices;
- removed whiskey from bonded warehouses;
- violated federal laws in disposing of seized property;
- showed the Dempsey-Carpentier film, netting several million dollars.

He said that "everything in Washington was for sale—except the dome of the Capitol" and they planned to "throw high dice" for that.

A year later Thacker repudiated the book saying Means never produced the documentation he promised. And Means admitted that as he was writing the first draft of the book he and his wife would sit around in the evening and laugh at the tall tales he had invented that day. But, as always, with Means, there was just enough truth in his claims so that they cannot be ignored, and his statement that Florence Harding was involved in her husband's demise helped establish the mystery of his "strange" death as part of the historical record of the Harding administration. Frederick Lewis Allen, Oswald Garrison Villard and James Truslow Adams all thought it quite plausible that the president did not die a natural death.

At least one person must have believed that Means knew what was going on in the underworld—Mrs. Evalyn Walsh McLean, who became involved with Means in a real fraud even more bizarrre than my fictional caper involving the Hope Diamond (see below).

The McLeans, the Lindbergh baby and the Hope Diamond. The revelation that Ned McLean had not lent Secretary Fall the one hundred thousand dollars was not only the turning point in the Teapot Dome scandal, but the beginning of the end of the McLeans' good life. By the early 1930s, Ned was in a mental institution in Towson, Maryland, denying to all visitors that he was Ned McLean. And their fortunes were slipping away, a situation not helped any by Mrs. McLean's experience with Gaston B. Means during the national agony brought on by the kidnapping of the Lindbergh baby. When the whole country was nervously hoping the baby could be found and returned, Mrs. McLean contacted Gaston B. Means and asked him if he knew where the Lindbergh baby was. Means said he did and that he could guarantee the little boy's return for one hundred thousand dollars—plus four thousand dollars to cover his expenses. Later, when he failed to produce the baby, saying that the kidnappers were demanding another thirty-five thousand dollars, Mrs. McLean realized she was being swindled and her attorney called J. Edgar Hoover. Means was found guilty of fraud and sentenced to Leavenworth, where he died of a heart attack after serving six years of a fifteen-year term.

Mrs. McLean's alcoholism increased as her fortune decreased. She lost the *Washington Post* and her Friendship estate but she hung onto her famous, if "cursed," diamond, often wearing it during World War II to Walter Reed Hospital where she worked as a volunteer with wounded veterans, who she would let play catch with the necklace. Although she insisted that she did not believe in the curse, it seemed to persist in her life. In addition to her son's death and her husband's mental breakdown, her daughter committed suicide at the age of twenty-six, a tragedy from which Mrs. McLean never really recovered.

After she died, the Hope Diamond had to be sold to pay the estate taxes. It was bought by the New York jeweler Harry Winston, who later gave it to the Smithsonian, where it is today. Winston had mailed the diamond to Washington and the postman, James Todd, who delivered it to the Smithsonian, seemed to have come under the curse. Within a year, he had one of his legs crushed by a truck, his head injured in a car crash, lost his wife and dog and his house burned down. But when asked if he felt his troubles were the result of the diamond's curse, Todd said: "I don't believe any of that stuff."

Sources

Cain, by Roy Hoopes, Holt, Rinehart and Winston, 1982.

The Impossible Mr. Mencken, ed. by Marion Rodgers, Doubleday, 1991.

Mencken, by Fred Hobson, Random House, 1994.

Ardent Spirits, by John Kobler, Putnam, 1973.

Investigation of the Attorney General, United States Senate, 1924.

Yankee from the West, by Sen. Burton K. Wheeler, Doubleday, 1962.

Spectacular Rogue, by Edwin P. Hoyt, Bobbs Merrill, 1963.

Shadow of Blooming Grove, by Francis S. Russell, McGraw-Hill, 1968.

The Inside Story of the Harding Tragedy, by Harry M. Daugherty, Churchill Co., 1982.

The Incredible Era, by Samuel Hopkins Adams, Houghton Mifflin, 1939.

Florence Harding, by Carl Sferrazza Anthony, Morrow, 1998.

The President's Daughter, by Nan Britton, Elizabeth Ann Guild, 1927.

Prohibition, by Edward Behr, Arcade, 1996.

Teapot Dome, by M. R. Werner and John Starr, Viking, 1959.

Teapot Dome, by Burl Noggle, Louisiana State University Press, 1962.

The Strange Death of President Harding, by Gaston B. Means, Guild Publishing Co., 1930.

Father Struck It Rich, by Evalyn Walsh McLean, First Light Publishing Co., 1996.

Maunscript of *Father Struck It Rich* in the Library of Congress, which contains portions of ms. not used in book.

Blue Mystery: The Story of the Hope Diamond, by Susanne Steinem, Smithsonian Institution, 1976.

Lindbergh, by A. Scott Berg, G. P. Putnam's Sons, 1998.